CONSIDER MY SERVANT

1020-BERM

CONSIDER MY SERVANT

Leonard H. Berman

To order additional copies of this book, contact:
Xlibris Corporation
1-888-7-XLIBRIS
www.Xlibris.com
Orders@Xlibris.com

With the exception of historical figures, all characters in this novel are fictitious, and any resemblance to living persons, past or present, is coincidental.

1020-BERM

For Toby Epstein Berman
who makes my life beautiful.

and

Estelle and Milton Berman
who gave me a vision of what life might be.

ACKNOWLEDGMENTS

I am fortunate to have family, friends, acquaintances and teachers who, over the years, have been supportive of my efforts to write this novel. At this time I wish to express my sincere thanks to them for being part of this effort, and for their teaching skills, their typing skills, their editing skills, their critiques and their over all comments. My gratitude and affection go out to Valborg Anderson, Connie Coplein, Ann Rosenberg, Sandy Loewe, Trudy Dubitsky, Estelle Berman, Stacey Krantz, Penny Postal, Arthur Lewis Berman, Steve Silverman, Edmund Weiss, and my wife, Toby.

The woodcut image of the family depicted on the cover was created by Stanley Kaplan.

CHAPTER 1

St. Petersburg, Russia
December 12, 1882

A diffused and jaundiced light, flecked with particles of luminous dust, filtered down between the bars of the high window and the straw mattress where Zeena Bendak lay in her pain and sweat.

Jonah's mouth opened when he saw her. She no longer looked like his sister. The months of dark internment, of brutality and indignation, had drained the beauty from her face, and save for the extended stomach that held her child, she looked gaunt enough to have been starved.

She looked at him through a veil of agony and wet hair that partially covered her face. Her eyes burned from the salt in her sweat, but she hadn't the energy to wipe them dry. An old woman, squat and rotund, was standing next to the cot, casually sipping a cup of hot tea. He glanced at the woman and silently poured his hatred over her, but neither his face nor voice revealed his anger.

"You are the brother?" the old woman asked flatly.

Jonah did not reply. Zeena lifted her head and peered at him as he moved closer.

"Jonah?" she said weakly. "Jonah?" And her body began to quiver. "Jonah!" she screamed, "Jonah!" and she reached up and encompassed him in her arms and held him with all her strength, crying his name over and over again.

"I am here, Zeena, I am here," he said softly. "Sha, sha, I am here."

Another sudden wave of pain tore through her. Jonah's thoughts raced to Leah, his own wife who had also held on to him for strength in just such a moment. Again, he felt the profound helplessness of one trying to ease the pain of a loved one, when such pain could not be eased. He longed to hold Leah and the daughter he had never seen.

"How did you find me?" she whispered, daring not to hope that she might be saved by him.

"They let me come to take the baby," he said in a low voice, knowing that his words would murder her hope. "I've been talking about your innocence all over Europe. There is enormous pressure to save you." He paused again. "Every paper outside Russia writes something about you every day and about the injustice of your captivity."

His hands were wet from the sweat on her back and he felt her tremble violently, and groan as another contraction tore through her body. He eased her back gently.

The midwife moved to her bed. "Her time has come. Get out of my way."

Jonah stood quickly and menaced the crone with a stool. "You touch her and I'll open your skull with this," he spat through his teeth.

The woman froze. "I have been paid to deliver the child."

"You have been paid to murder the child. Now get away from us or I will make sure you never touch another human being again." His eyes blazed with such intensity that the woman stepped back, her fists clenched in frustration.

"I was ordered to deliver this child," she insisted fearfully.

"And I am ordering you out of here," he screamed, "before I tear you to pieces with my bare hands. If the child dies, it dies, but it will not be murdered, and if I die, I die, but I will first choke the life out of your body."

The woman knew the look of such final desperation; a look that spoke of hope lost, a time when one could only turn with one's back to the wall and face, with bared teeth, their enemy. Jonah had that look and she knew her life was in danger. She backed over to the door and cried out to the guard. The door opened and Jonah could see Alexi Malinovitch waiting there.

"I will take all responsibility and speak to Karpov for you," Malinovitch said pushing several bills into the woman's palm. "This brother is an arrogant fool who knows nothing of such things. If the child dies, you will not be to blame and I will charge the brother with murder."

The woman smiled, bowed and fled the corridor.

Jonah felt that he had at last done something good for Zeena, and he turned back to her with a strange feeling of well being. She was between pains and he wished his mother were here. He knew nothing of child birth. He put the bundle on the table and unwrapped it. In it he found a sharp knife and a fine silk cord among the clean linen. A paper fell out and floated to the floor. He lifted it and held it up to the light of the stove.

'After the child is born, tie the silk cord close to the child's navel and cut it.'

"Tell me of home," Zeena said weakly. "How is Papa?"

Jonah froze for a moment and sadness overwhelmed him. "Everyone is well," he lied, forcing a smile, "except Papa's foot is bothering him because it's so damp, but beyond that, he's fine. I'm a father, Zeena." He sat down and took her hand. She clasped it tightly.

"Leah gave birth to a fine little girl with a wonderful head of reddish hair, just like her mother's. Mama absolutely dotes on her and says that she's the brightest child she has ever seen. Her name is ..." Jonah stopped mid sentence because he was about to weep. "She's a wonderful little girl. And I have another wonderful piece of news. Dora and Jonathan are married and Dora is pregnant. Isn't that wonderful news?"

The news of Dora and Jonathan poured over Zeena at the precise moment of another contraction and the scream that engulfed her spoke of her anguish, her rage, and her ultimate defeat. She screamed again and panted for breath. Her face contorted and her eyes glazed. She clutched at her stomach and then raised her hand and tore at the small silver ring she wore on her finger.

Jonah pulled the blanket across her neck to warm her.

Zeena cried out again. Jonah reached for the bundle and tore a piece of cloth. "Here, Zeena, bite down on this, and lift your legs. I can see the baby's head. It has dark hair."

He placed his hands on the baby's head and felt the warm new life pulsating under his fingers. Zeena gasped and dug her fingers into the straw mattress.

"Push, harder," he said, "bear down." Jonah saw Leah writhing in the pain of birthing their own child and the horror of that night pulled at him like an evil undertow. In helping Zeena, even if he were to die doing it, he would feel redeemed in a small way. He was making something right. Perhaps his wife would never forgive him, but at the very least he was making something right by helping his sister.

Zeena sucked in breath after breath without exhaling. The baby's head moved slowly out of her and its shoulders spasmodically inched into the cold air of the cell. Jonah hooked his fingers under the tiny arms to support it.

"Push down again, Zeena. The baby is almost out."

There was a slurping noise as the infant's arms became free, and floundered in the strange world. With another tug, the child was born. For a moment, Jonah forgot where he was and a wave of elation swept over him as never before. He had helped life to be born and he would protect it with his own. He felt, for a brief moment, clean and whole.

The child screamed into the damp cell as her tiny lungs gulped in their first breath of frosted air. Jonah held the infant in his trembling hands and laughed triumphantly with joy and wonder. Zeena breathed heavily, her eyes closed. He unwound the bluish-white cord from around the little girl's leg and placed her on her mother's stomach so he could tie the cord and separate them.

"Zeena," he whispered softly. "Open your eyes and see your daughter. She is beautiful and healthy. Look."

"Take her away, and let me die now," she said faintly.

"No," Jonah said, offering her the same intense joy he felt. "Listen to her cry. She is strong and perfect."

"Take her out of here Jonah and let me die."

"Oh, please take hold of her Zeena. Don't let her go without knowing you for at least a moment."

"Oh, God, please Jonah, take her. Am I to love her only to lose her? Am I to touch her, never to touch her again? Take her, take her," she gasped for another breath. "To love her and lose her would make the dying unbearable for wanting her."

Jonah severed the cord as directed and watched it fall away. Zeena and the daughter she would never know were separated and the joy that had enveloped him fell away as if it had never been. He could not understand, and in some ways he could. The water near the stove was warm and he dipped a cloth in and gently washed his niece. He could not help smiling at her. His mind hummed the song his mother sang when she washed him as a little child and he wondered if she sang it as she washed his daughter. As he gently patted the baby dry, tears blurred his vision. Then he wrapped her in a warm, soft blanket and put her on the table.

Zeena breathed deeply. He watched her and he felt as if his heart would break. Why did this have to be her end? Neither of them had acted well, but their punishment surely was not in proportion to the deeds. Yes, they had created pain for others, but they had not created the evil in which they found themselves. Evil people had created this and he and his sister were not evil.

"Zeena," he said softly. She did not open her eyes. "Zeena," he continued, "I need to ask you something." He paused and waited. "Zeena, what shall I name your child?" Again, she did not respond.

"Zeena?"

"Name her after me."

Jonah lowered his head and reached for her hand, wanting to assure her that she would live and all would be well. But they both knew better. He hated to ask the next question.

"And what of your husband?" he said softly. "He wants his child. Dora wrote me and told me so. She wrote about meeting me in Paris and then going to America and your husband has agreed to pay for everything. As much as I hate him, Zeena, Ezra is entitled to his child." Jonah could say no more for fear of telling her everything.

Zeena's eyes opened suddenly and a hysterical laugh tore from her throat. "The baby is not his, Jonah. Isn't that worth laughing about, Jonah? I married him to protect the family and to give the child I carried a name. She is not his, Jonah, so he has no right to my baby!" She continued to laugh and her eyes blazed with resolve. "We never know what tomorrow brings, do we Jonah? I married Ezra to save the family, my baby is born in a prison, and tomorrow I hang for murdering the Tzar. We are all fools, Jonah. What clever, fools we are."

Her words stunned him and froze him where he stood.

"Tell him his wife came to him as a pregnant whore, and make sure you laugh in his face when you tell him. He will not believe you," she continued. "That makes the joke even better." She fell back and closed her eyes.

Jonah lifted the crying child. He was relieved that this infant, whom he immediately loved, was not the issue of the one man in the world whom he so completely hated. It made the child even purer, but he knew that Ezra would never believe the story and that there would be a battle for her. Jonah decided at that moment that he would hide this knowledge until his entire family was out of Paris and safely in America at Ezra's expense. That would also be part of the joke. Then he would see how he would proceed and how Ezra would be punished.

"Who is the father, Zeena?" he said, moving his eyes from his sister's haggard face to the black haired infant. A hundred feelings crowded in on him as he waited for her response, but she said nothing.

"Zeena, a father has the right to know his child. At least tell me the name so I can contact him."

"It's all over, Jonah. Let Ezra have her. Let her at least have the benefits of his money. Let him raise the child believing it's his, but always with that doubt. That will be his torment." Zeena turned her face into the mattress and began to weep.

Jonah rocked his niece back and forth in his arms to ease her stress. He knew Zeena would not reveal the name of the father. He and Ezra shared no blood and he would feel no obligation to him. The child was comforted and slept. Jonah wrapped her in another blanket and placed her back on the table.

He sat on the edge of the bed again and began to wash his sister's face and body. The warm water eased her and he placed the bloody sheets and afterbirth in the bucket and slid it under the bed. He put a clean sheet next to her and rolled it out.

"Sha, sha," he said to her sobs. Again he felt the words, "everything will be all right," forming on his lips, but he stopped himself from saying them. Those same words uttered once before, a lifetime ago, had proven themselves to be lies over and over again. Everything was not all right and it could never be made right. There was no comfort to be uttered, and perhaps the warm soothing water on her brow, his loving touch, his silent presence in the face of her anguish, was all the balm left him to give. I will never be whole again when you are gone, he thought, and I will always be alone. She was going to die and he felt partially to blame. The realization left him naked, vulnerable, and inadequate to a depth never felt before. He was at the edge, overcome by a need to flee from himself and his inability to save her or comfort her with anything of meaning beyond his silent presence and some warm water.

"Zeena," he said softly, desperate to reassure her. "I do not know tomorrow. I only know yesterday. But I've learned from these past months that as long as there is a tomorrow, there is hope that good may yet come our way."

Zeena caught her breath and turned her face to him and opened her eyes.

"Am I not tormented enough without your empty promises of hope? Don't lie to me Jonah! Jonah!" she screamed at him with incredulous anguish. "Save me, damn you! I don't want to die!, Do something!"

Jonah's rage overwhelmed him.

"Zeena, hope is all I have to give you," he shouted into the cold cell and it was as if they were children again. "Hope is all that is left!"

The cell echoed with their fear and she threw herself into his arms and they held each other and wept because tears and love were the only things each could guarantee the other. Jonah wished he could absorb her life and hold it for her and return it to her at another time. But for this brief moment, they were whole again, weeping softly on each other's shoulders.

"Why, Jonah, why did this happening to us? What was it Jonah? Tell me so I can at least understand."

CHAPTER 2

Russia
June 18, 1881

Sarah Chernov hurled a fistful of salt into the bubbling pot and then raised her hand in a gesture towards the door and the figure beyond whom she imagined stood laughing at her somewhere in the twilight.

"You heard how she talked to me?" she said in a voice that strained her throat. "Like I was dirt!" She picked up another log, opened the iron oven door, threw it in, and slammed it shut. "A daughter speaks to a mother like that, slams a door and leaves?"

She briskly scraped the skin of a large carrot with a knife, her voice and stroke never out of cadence. "She wants thanks for breaking dishes? She wants applause for letting cakes burn?"

"Sarah, Sarah," her husband repeated trying to find the words that would calm her and return his home to some semblance of peace. Reuben Chernov thought for a brief moment and then smiled broadly. "Sarah," he began, again holding up his hand to emphasize his point. "Do you remember last year when those gypsies came to town with that dancing bear?"

Sarah looked to the ceiling with exasperated disbelief and moved to the table.

"Wait, wait," he said. "I'm making a point," and his eyes laughed.

Sarah pursed her lips and began formulating a counter argument before he began his daughter's defense.

"The bear danced," he said, "and you applauded." He paused for her understanding, but only saw her eyes narrow.

"Don't you remember why you applauded?" He did not wait for a reply. "You applauded the bear not because it danced well, but because it was a bear that could dance at all! See?" Again he waited for comprehension, but she swept past him with an apron full of carrots and a broad gesture for him to get out of her path.

"Dancing bears he gives me. His son gets married the day after tomorrow, his daughter is God knows where, the Sabbath is almost here, a thousand things need to be done, and he talks about dancing bears."

"Sarah, I'm only saying that Zeena, like the bear, at least is trying. Applaud her effort if not her performance."

"Let me tell you something my dear Reuben," she said turning on him, her fingers pulling the skin off an onion. "The only similarity between your daughter and the bear is that they both need to be muzzled. And furthermore, I'd applaud a bear in my kitchen sooner than your daughter because a bear you can teach and a bear would show some respect." She paused, put down the bowl of onions and turned to the thin figure before her.

"Zeena doesn't do well, where Zeena decides Zeena doesn't want to do well. I know her better than you know her. I carried her and I raised her. I try to teach her what a wife and mother are supposed to know, and she throws it all back in my face like it's garbage." Reuben shifted uncomfortably near the table and gestured to her to lower her voice. Jonah, Zeena's twin brother, looked up from his work and was about to speak when his father motioned that he remain silent. Sarah Chernov would not be silenced.

"She is selfish and willful," she continued as if no request of her had been made, "and I'd marry her off to anybody foolish enough to have such a witch. She'll bring us to ruin with her self-centered spitefulness. You mark my words, Reuben. As God is my witness, she'll bring us to ruin."

The cast iron cover clanged down on the boiling pot of carrots and the room was silent except for the overtones left by the reverberating pot.

"There! That's it! I've said what I had to say. Where's Dora? She has to set the table. Did you hear how she slammed that door? The house shook. They could probably hear her mouth in Kiev." She paused to breathe. She did not pause for a response. "I was already married when I was her age. Responsibility of a husband, a house and children are the only things that will make her see what life is about. She's almost twenty, and no one will come near her. The whole world knows the mouth on her."

"Doors get slammed around here all the time," interrupted Jonah, unable to listen to his sister being maligned without coming to her defense, "and she yells because she feels you always pick on her."

Sarah's eyes focused on her son sitting by the window. He did not look up from the garment he carefully stitched.

"Another somebody with an opinion," she said. "You sit there and do what you have to do my dear son or I'll show you what it is to be picked on. And stay out of what doesn't concern you. Don't think that because you're getting married you have anything more to say about what goes on around here than you did before. When you're in your own house, you'll have something to say. Here, you do what you're told."

Sarah's eyes drank in the darkening, white washed walls of the single room in which she had spent more than half of her life, and she looked past the pale young man who sat etched against the dying light to the table, still not set, for the Sabbath meal. Always so much to be done and never enough time. She felt suddenly old. She was thirty-eight and her son was to be married. She turned quickly, as if to flee from the thought, but caught her image in the mirror above the painted sideboard. She peered at herself briefly. She saw a woman whose husband still called her beautiful in the few private moments they had. Her skin was still unblemished and tightly drawn across her high cheek bones. But her deeply set black eyes, eyes that more often than not spoke of her rage and frustration, had long ago lost the excitement and expectation of life. She was too young to have a married son, she thought, and she was too young to have wisps of gray hair peep out from the shawl she wore tightly drawn over her black hair. The hard years of scrimping and paying and going without, so her children might have, weighed like the memory of a bad dream. Around her, also reflected in the glass, was the evidence of a twenty-one year marriage to a man who should have been an honored scholar, but was only allowed to be a tailor. A coarse wooden table and six wooden chairs, a green painted cupboard, a pine sideboard, a worn, velvet-cushioned settee that belonged to her mother, a matching chair, a hanging oil lamp. Her life surrounded her in one room. A few things. Some nice. All old. And now another person, Jonah's wife Leah, to question her and doubt her word. She heaved a sigh. She was so very tired, but she had to make the Sabbath and she had to make a wedding.

"Dora?" and her voice rose so it could be heard behind the bedroom door. "I told you to set the table. I bet she's playing with that clock," she muttered. "Put down that clock, and set that table now!" she bellowed again.

The door opened slowly, and a tall, slender girl just turning seventeen, with long, soft, brown hair and hazel eyes, entered. Jonah laughed, at the thought that his mother could see beyond the closed door. Dora glided silently to the cupboard without confronting her mother's stern gaze, and took out the dishes from the shelf.

"Did I tell you, Reuben? Do I know your children?"

"Why are they always my children when you're angry with them?" He caught a slight smile at the corner of her mouth which meant that the most immediate crisis was over.

"Sarah," he said taking both her hands and leading her to a chair.

"I have a thousand things to do," she protested avoiding his eyes, "and I can't talk now."

"Sarah," he persisted. "Look what's happening. Look what you're doing to yourself. How will you be able to make the Sabbath beautiful, let alone a wedding, if you let yourself get upset over a broken dish?"

"All right, Reuben, it wasn't the dish. But Reuben, I can feel my blood boiling in my veins when she's with me. I can never say anything right. What did I say? It's a crime for a mother to tell a clumsy child she's clumsy? How will she learn not to be clumsy if I don't tell her?"

"Sarah, Sarah, you've been telling her for years to be careful, but she still drops plates and she still mixes meat dishes with milk dishes. Maybe you should not be such a good mother. Maybe you should not tell her so much."

Sarah took a deep breath and expelled it slowly. She studied her husband's face. His pale blue eyes twinkled their invitation for her to give up her anger, and his pepper and salt mustache widened as his lips formed an impish grin. She saw his hand reach out and she felt the tender stroking of his finger in the hollow of her cheek. Look how his beard is graying. Such a handsome man has to get old. The thought that they should have had more time to be alone intruded, and she dismissed it immediately. She had no time for old dreams.

"You're a good father, Reuben," she said. "You're a learned man, and a kind man, and you are right many times. But you're not right this time!" She turned from him and tore at an onion so he would not see the tears forming in her eyes. He followed her. "I know our children better than you do, Reuben."

Reuben could never fathom the war that raged between his wife and eldest daughter, nor why the struggle even existed. To him, they were so alike, they should have been friends.

"Look at him over there," she began, wiping her eyes. "Hours of work left, the sun almost set, and he sits looking out of the window dreaming. I ask you," and she gestured broadly at the young man, "is that someone who lives in a real world? He'd sooner talk to God or to himself than to people, and that's your fault, Reuben. You made him into a dreamer when all he needed to know was how to be a tailor."

"Schools are opening to us. This Tzar is different," he countered.

"You're dreaming if you think things will get better. Things don't get better for Jews in Russia, and the dreams you gave him are luxuries he can't afford. He doesn't need to know languages. Of what use is German or French or English here? Where is he going? Who comes into the shop who speaks anything other than Yiddish or Russian? Did you give Zeena the same knowledge you gave him so she could curse me in more than one language? Yiddish wasn't good enough? You see the books she brings in? You see the political trash she reads? You made her too smart for her own good, and that's another reason none of the young men will come near her?"

Reuben looked over at his son. In this, his wife was wrong. Both Jonah and Zeena were quick and bright, and Jonah had a gift for language that surpassed his own.

"You let him think he could be a something in the world when the world will only let him be a tailor. With all your languages, Reuben, did our beloved Tsar, he should burn in hell, let you become more than a tailor? Jonah's a child wearing a man's suit. And Zeena can't wait to run into her fantasies. He sits inside himself and she runs. If they were one person, maybe that one person would be normal. The way they are now, I don't know how they'll survive. This is your fault, Reuben."

Jonah closed his eyes and withdrew into himself where he could filter out his mother's voice.

Reuben looked at her and shook his head. "I leave prophecy to prophets and what becomes of him will be God's doing. Your reality is your reality, Zeena's reality is hers, and Jonah's reality is his. When his time comes to make his choices among all the realities, he will choose wisely. I'm sure of that."

Jonah stood suddenly. Enough of his mother's words had torn open the thin, protective wall behind which he hid.

"I have to go out for a minute," he said, brushing his hand nervously through his hair. "I have something I forgot to do." His eyes implored his father for support because he knew what his mother's response would be.

"It's almost Shabbos," Sarah exclaimed incredulously, throwing up her hands in a gesture of helplessness. "There are clothes still to be altered for the wedding, and a hundred little things to do, and he's off to someplace? Reuben, that's what I mean. He has no idea of what's real or what's needed. Reuben, say something to him!"

"Jonah, Mama is right. There are things to be done and we need you here."

"I know Papa, but I have this very important thing to do, and I've been sewing all day, and I really need a little time just for myself."

The corners of his mouth turned up slightly, and he smiled a warm, pleading smile that belied his inner turmoil. He approached his mother as he buttoned his jacket.

"Everything will get done on time and the wedding will be perfect." He kissed her quickly, a kiss that was more an offering of appeasement than one of affection, and picked up a slice of freshly baked cake. "Oh, this is really wonderful cake, Mama," he mouthed his words barely and backed towards the door.

Sarah's look berated her husband for not standing firm, but Reuben returned a half smile and shrugged shoulders.

Jonah opened the door. Zeena stood there like a rock.

"I'm back," she announced flatly as she swept past him. The bedroom door slammed after her. The old wooden house shook again. Jonah fought back any expression of relief because he knew his mother's focus would move back to his sister. He did not like himself when he felt that way, but he had learned long ago that any respite from his mother's attention was welcome even if it were at another's expense.

He lifted the wooden gate from the leather hinge and immediately dismissed the loud voices coming from the house. The distant town was already dotted with Sabbath lamps glowing through shutters. His need was to do something that would take him beyond the overwhelming fear of his forthcoming marriage. He balanced himself, arms extended, along the rim of a rut, grinning whenever the caked earth gave way. It was a childish thing to do, and it helped. It always helped.

Twilight enveloped him. The sun slowly eased itself down

through horizontal pink clouds like an old man easing himself onto a bed, while tinges of azure and green clung to the horizon. A single star heralded the day of rest. He knew he should not be out walking when so many things needed to be done at home. But he had had enough of shoulds and shouldn'ts this past week to last him a lifetime, and he needed a moment to think and breathe. In a moment he would be at the top of his hill, his sacred, secret place, where he prayed his deepest prayers and where he listened to the whisperings of the universe. He would bring Leah here. She would understand this place.

He sat down facing the town. Another star peered through a blackening sky urging him to return home. But he pulled his coat tighter around his thin frame and retied it against the evening chill. He took a deep breath and felt the cool night in his nostrils. He held it, savoring both the sweet, sticky smell of late spring, and that very special moment where endings and beginnings are caught in time and linger in the senses. He sensed the earth gathering its strength and its resources; restless and vague new energies. He, too, trembled with the potential of a new life and new beginning. Both he and the earth were alive and trembling.

Jonah took a small volume out of his pocket and opened it to where he had left off. The words of Solomon reached out from ancient days.

> 'Rise my love, my beauty, come away. For, lo, the winter is over, the rain is past and gone; the flowers appear on the earth, the time of song has come and the call of the turtle dove is heard in our land, the fig tree is ripening its early figs, and the vines in blossom give forth their fragrance. Rise, my love, my beauty, come away.'

There was so much he needed to know about love and he knew nothing. He did not have such words and he wondered where words came from and, if they came at all, when were they to be uttered. Perhaps all the words were there, waiting in his brain to be uttered at the right moment. Jonah read that passage over and over again trying to make the words his own.

Ever since the betrothal a year ago, such questions and thoughts followed him and cluttered his waking hours. How did one love? How did one speak to a wife when alone? What did they talk about when everyone was asleep? Mama and Papa talked about the children and the house and the business and the town and the money, but he never knew what they talked about when they were alone. Did they speak of love? Love. The word stepped prodigiously before him as if in confrontation. Love. In two days he would be tied forever to a girl he barely knew. Love. That was what would bind them. Would he come to love Leah Shanagrotsky?

He closed the book and put it to his lips. He did not love Leah. That was his horrible secret. How could he love her? He did not know her. He could not love without knowing. Still, he would be married to her whether he loved her or not. That was the way of things, and that's what he would do to preserve that way. His parents did not meet before they were married. They could not have loved like the young man and young woman in the little book, and yet they were married and had lived together for twenty-one years. They cared for each other. Of that he was sure. They worked together and they looked at each other tenderly at times. They even seemed to know each other's thoughts. No matter, he thought. What did it matter? His life was set and love was . . .well, love. He stood. The sad, reflective haze before him melted, and his eyes slowly refocused themselves on the little wooden town.

Once, about two years ago, a stranger, traveling from Kiev, came into the shop and pointed out, on his small map, a little dot at the northern tip of an oddly shaped lake. The words read Krivy Ossero. That was what the stranger and peasants called it. But to Jonah and all the generations who lived and died there, it was Krivozer, a town pieced together out of nothing, generations ago. In this place he would live out his life with Leah. Here, God willing, they would have children and bring them to the marriage canopy. Here they would see grandchildren born and grow, and perhaps even a great grandchild. Jonah felt a sense of comfort knowing what life would hold, a comfort derived from a sense that what had always been, would be there for him too.

"If this is how it must be, Lord of the Universe, I will be content." he whispered to the night. "Blessed be the name of the Lord, forever."

"Jonah, Papa wants you now."

Jonah felt a tug at his coat, and looked down at Ruth, his ten year old sister, with reddish curls and bright, blue eyes like his own.

"Mama is telling Papa how inconsiderate you are."

Jonah smiled to himself, reflected, and scooped her up in his arms. He took long strides down the knoll and Ruth laughed and tightened her arms around his neck.

They were almost to the fence. He swung Ruth from his back gently and took her by the hand. She broke away and climbed on the rim of a dried rut in the road and turned to look at her brother. Jonah recognized the challenge and laughed at himself. She extended her arms and moved deftly across the rim. Jonah followed, but the earth gave way under his weight and he lost his balance. Ruth glanced over her shoulder and taunted him with laughter each time he lost his footing. Suddenly, he raced towards her, buried his mouth in the side of her neck and exploded his lips. She squealed with delight as he swung her around. "That will teach you to tease your big brother."

As they approached the house, they met Zeena pulling the goat through the gate.

"You left the gate open again, you little dope, and the goat got out."

Ruth moved cautiously now and stuck out her tongue as she passed her sister who was tying the goat to the post.

"I saw that!" snapped Zeena.

Ruth took refuge behind Jonah as Zeena lunged for her. At that, Jonah pulled Ruth out of her path, and Zeena fell forward. Jonah laughed and immediately extended his hand to her. Zeena scowled, and muttered, and pulled herself up without his help.

She glared at him with contempt and ran into the house, slamming the front door and then the one to the back room.

Reuben turned from the window, looked at his pocket watch again, and frowned the moment he surmised that Jonah and Ruth had caused another disturbance.

"Your children are home," said Sarah, looking at the door to the bedroom with renewed resolve.

"What a pain the two of you are," he said as he approached the laughing pair. "A pair of tight shoes. My big one and my little one! You torment her. You do it on purpose."

Ruth giggled again at the thought of her triumph over her older sister, but Jonah did not smile because he did not feel that he was an instrument of Zeena's torture. Zeena was Zeena. You watched her and marveled at her anger, and you just let it run its course. You did not say anything because she could not be comforted, and you could not yell back because that increased her rage. Jonah found that just watching her was the best way to handle her, and that's what he did. Of course, he realized some time ago that just watching her and saying nothing also caused her to rage.

"Zeena, come out. I'm lighting the candles." Sarah stood at the door. She did not touch it, fully confident that her voice was enough to call forth her recalcitrant daughter from the room. The door did not open.

There was a stirring behind the door, a rustling of bed sheets and the creaking of a bed frame.

"Zeena," Sarah said emphatically, "I shall not make the same error Moses made by striking the rock, but if I have to touch this door, I can assure you that I shall touch you the moment the sun sets tomorrow. Now your father, Jonah, Dora, Ruth and I are waiting, and I will not light these candles until all my children stand with me."

The door opened slowly. Zeena stood there, her hair tousled like a hank of raven flax, her head tossed back with a childlike defiance that said, I do what you want and I do as you say, but I do not do it graciously. Sarah knew this look and chose no response at that moment. She merely threw a penetrating glance towards her daughter, a glance Zeena also understood, and Zeena knew to proceed no further. It was late. The sun had set.

Sarah discounted the lateness of the hour and knew God would wink at her transgression. Does God not forgive? Besides, God gave her these children, and had to take some responsibility for their behavior. God also knew what it was like to run a house, especially just before a wedding.

Reuben stood at the head of the table now covered with the white linen cloth that his wife had painstakingly embroidered. Sarah's table was a field of honor, and the cloth her flag, the symbol of being the woman of valor in her home; the respected and honored wife and mother.

She stood opposite him in front of the twin brass candlesticks her mother had given her on her own wedding day. Upon her head she placed the lace shawl her grandmother had stitched for her when she married Reuben. It was the shawl Reuben lifted to help her begin and fulfill her life and purpose, and it had covered her head each Sabbath for all years of their lives together.

She lit each candle and uttered the words, "observe and remember." Her fingers came together above the flames, strong fingers that baked bread daily, that milked and churned, that mended and cleaned, that cooked and counted and saved, that stroked her children, that patted and encouraged and also rebuked. Her hands gathered in the light, and she placed her hands over her face.

When she lowered her hands from her silent prayer, the glow from the candles sprang to erase the shadows on her face. She radiated in her husband's eyes as only one who stands before Sabbath candles and blesses her family from the goodness of her heart can radiate. Reuben saw her as only he could see her. In the glow, time melted and the lace he had lifted from her face so long ago, still framed the beauty that was his Sarah. Her dark, intelligent eyes looked at him briefly, and in that look, all tensions, frustrations, and disappointments melted from her life. A blush rose to her cheek. They smiled the secret, knowing smile of old lovers

whose love renews itself in candlelight. Jonah saw the look also.
Next week, next Sabbath, he will face Leah. Please, God, he prayed,
let me look at her that way.

Jonah and Reuben walked slowly to the synagogue for evening
prayers.

"Papa," Jonah began. "Papa," and he broke off not knowing
how to ask his father what he needed to know. Why didn't his
father sense the urgency in his voice and in some way miraculously
hear and answer the question his lips could not frame?

"Papa," he began again. "I'm getting married."

Reuben smiled and nodded his head in agreement. Jonah felt
foolish. Of course his father knew he was getting married.

"Papa, there are questions I have, and answers I need, but I
don't know where to start and I don't know if you or anyone else
can help me."

"That may be true," said Reuben, "but a man does learn something living with your mother for twenty-one years. Ask me, maybe
I can help."

"Papa, how do you make it good? I mean marriage. How do
you make a good marriage? How do you live day by day with one
person and make it a good life?"

Reuben smiled. He was proud that he had a son who would
be concerned about making life good for himself and his wife, a
son who cared about family.

"I think," he said reflecting on his life, "if you remember that
everything you say becomes a memory, you may build a happy
life, a good life. Nothing, my son, is ever forgotten on earth, or in
heaven, and sometimes things are said and done that need forgiveness." He paused to give Jonah a moment to digest the thought.
"You will also learn, Jonah, that it will be easier to get forgiveness
from God, than it will be from your wife." He saw his son smile.

"So I tell you to always think before you speak, and if you're smart, say nothing at all if what you intend to say will hurt."

Jonah was silent for a moment and Reuben slowed his pace.

"Jonah, there is much to learn about life with a woman and some of it you will learn slowly and painfully. What I'm saying is that there are no guarantees. You can't control what happens outside your house, but you can try to make what happens on the inside, good. No one's life is all good or all bad, and if you think the rich don't have trouble at home, you're wrong. What I say is keep God's holy law before your eyes, honor your wife as that law demands of you and you'll stand a better chance at making a good life. But remember, there is nothing in the law that promises that life is going to be good even if you are blameless."

"But what about love?" Jonah interrupted. I don't know if I love Leah, Papa." He said it. Now, another human being also knew. Would his father be angry or ashamed?

"Jonah, I'll tell you a secret," said Reuben beckoning him closer. "I didn't love your mother when I married her. We had just met. Yes, I knew my duty to honor her and my responsibility to perform my obligations to her as her husband, but I did not love her. How can you love someone you don't even know?"

Jonah felt less alone and less fearful at his father's confession. He was relieved and less ashamed.

"But you love Mama now, don't you?"

"Certainly, I love her now," Reuben responded. "About eighty-nine percent of the time," and he winked and they laughed together.

"But when does it happen, Papa?" Jonah continued, not willing to let the moment go.

"Jonah," said his father pulling the belt on his coat tighter as if the flimsy belt were added support for his spine. "Let me tell you something about loving a woman." He looked at his son, but his son looked away to the night, too embarrassed to meet his father's eyes.

At last. Finally, his father had heard him and would talk about touching a woman. Jonah felt his face flush and he glanced furtively at the man at his side. Sometimes he had heard his parents when the house was very still and all supposed to be asleep. He had tried not to listen to the creaking of the ropes under their mattress, but he had heard this many times and was ashamed of his knowledge. For years he had felt the tensions and the desires of his body that he had satisfied secretly, and the thought of being touched or held by someone other than his parents, sent a shudder of excitement through him.

"Jonah," he continued, "loving is a chance and sometimes a match is made where the two people love from the moment they first see each other. But sometimes a match is made where love never grows. And sometimes a match is made where love learns to find a place like it did for me and your mother and sometimes a match is made where love comes and then, dies."

The child in Jonah noticed a high rut in the road and he wondered if one might walk and balance for a lifetime or was one destined to feel the ground give way and shatter under the weight of daily living?

"We are promised nothing when it comes to life and loving," he heard his father say after something about the Jacob of the Bible. "Try to love Leah because she is God's handiwork and because loving another person and having another person love you back makes living in this world a little easier."

"Papa," he stammered suddenly. "I've never been alone with a woman." He felt his voice tighten, and heard it fade into an embarrassed whisper. "Papa, when you touch a woman . . . when you . . .how do you? I mean, at first when a man . . ." Reuben stopped, faced Jonah and patted his son gently on the cheek.

"You will know, my son. You will know. I can only tell you to be tender and considerate of her and move slowly. She will be as afraid as you."

The Sabbath table was prepared. Two twisted challahs and the knife rested under a blue embroidered cloth. The water in the laver shimmered and the rich, purple wine was warm and inviting. "Peace be with you, ministering angels," they sang. "May your coming be in peace. May you stay in peace and depart in peace."

Each child, in turn, stood before Reuben for the blessing. Sarah stood silently, watching, imagining and longing for the little ones who had been born, and lost to them after Dora. First Jonah stood before his father, his head reverently lowered. Reuben wondered at the number times had he placed his hands on his son's head and poured blessing after blessing upon him. A thousand hours of teaching him and laughing with him flooded his memory in the few seconds it took to bless him as a child for the last time. Sarah knew what her husband was thinking.

Zeena was next. Her ebony eyes softened and her body relaxed at just the thought of his hands on her head. His was a love that had no conditions. His was the gentle voice that soothed the harsh world she saw daily. For a brief moment, she did not have to share him with anyone. She, too, lowered her head reverently. For while she laughed at this man's traditions, and at his God, she did not laugh at him. Only Jonah knew her thoughts.

Dora was next. Dora, the obedient one who was reliable and straight and whose hazel eyes offered unbounded kindness to whomever she met. At sixteen, she was a head taller than Zeena and took silent pleasure in having something more than her beautiful sister, even if it was only in height. She knew she was not as quick with books as Jonah and Zeena, not as beautiful as Zeena, nor as endearing as Ruth. But she knew in some way that her patience and devotion were needed, and she was therefore needed.

Ruth thrust herself in front of her father. Sarah's prayer was answered, and the pain of having two stillborn children in succession, eased when Ruth was born. Ruth became her comfort and her joy. The little girl threw her arms around her father and squeezed his waist. There were no solemn moments for her but only gaiety and laughter and the love of the tall man whose hands firmly straightened her head in a proper attitude towards God.

"May the Lord bless you and protect you," he said. "May the Lord cause his countenance to shine upon you. May the Lord favor you and give you peace."

After the meal Jonah excused himself from the table and went outside. Zeena and Dora cleared the dishes and placed them in the dish pan under the careful supervision of their mother. The candles glowed warmly.

"Dora," Sarah began, "bring more water. Zeena, you don't go anywhere because I want you and your father to hear something I have to say."

Zeena rolled back her eyes as she faced the window, wondering which lecture she was about to get and for what offense. Sarah sat herself at the table and began to brush crumbs of bread out of the delicate threads. Reuben glanced up over his glasses at his wife and muttered some words that he was attentive but went on reading. Sarah cleared her throat as prologue. The muscle in Zeena's jaw twitched.

"Zeena is almost twenty and when I was her age I already had her and her brother." Sarah paused for a response but there was none. "Reuben, are you listening to me?"

Zeena hands clutched the counter rim as if letting go would cause her to spin off into space.

Reuben took his glasses from his face and bought time by pretending to clean them.

"I believe I heard you say that you wanted to find Zeena a husband. I thought that that was not going to be a topic of conversation for at least a day." He could not contain his sarcasm or anger. "Must there be drama also on God's Sabbath? If I am not to have peace, can't you at least let God have some?"

Sarah continued to busy herself with the crumbs and discounted her husband's plea to let the subject go.

"Whether you like it or not, it's time to think about Zeena's future."

Reuben held his spectacles up to the lamp to examine them for spots. He glanced towards Zeena in time to see her turn to her mother. Zeena's face was flushed and her mouth quivered. Sarah did not look up, preferring not to see her daughter's anger and preferring not to see her husband's distress at the potential eruption of recriminations. She merely continued to pick minute slivers of bread out of the cloth.

Reuben stood and walked slowly to his wife. He concealed his anger with her because he knew that three angry people in one room would serve no one's needs.

"Sarah, my dearest Sarah, listen to me. Why do you overwhelm yourself with talk of more weddings? Let's take one wedding at a time."

Sarah's fingers curled on the cloth and flattened in acquiescence to her husband. She knew his way, and she knew when to let him have it. She knew it could wait because she had established with him that it would not wait very long. She would have her way.

Reuben looked at his daughter and put his fingers to his lips to quiet her. Tears were on her cheeks.

Sarah took a deep breath, held it briefly, and let out a deep sigh as epilogue.

Reuben retreated back to the comfort of his chair, fully cognizant that Sarah's determination was as formidable as heaven itself. Zeena knew this too. She knew her mother because she knew herself, and as much as she hated to admit it, they were alike in their need to exert control over their lives. And, alike in their genuine fear of tomorrow.

Sarah let the cloth billow into the air and settle on the table like a great balloon deflating. A crease here, a wrinkle there, she thought, but all would be made smooth in time. Reuben heaved a slight sigh and resumed turning the pages of his book.

Zeena turned back to the window. She looked at her shaking hands and took hold of the counter to steady them and herself. The pain in her stomach was severe. She turned slowly, and with measured steps moved towards the door. She could feel her body shake, and a rush of heat surge through her. The familiar pain fed and grew on her mother's words and her own fear of the future. The anguish churned round and round and she could feel herself heave. To marry was to stay forever, to become like everyone else who washed and mended and starved and grew old and died. To marry in this place was to die without having lived.

"Where are you going?" snapped Sarah as Zeena eased past her. "The dishes are not finished."

Zeena curled her lower lip into her mouth and bit down. The pain gave her control. She did not look at her mother. She spoke to the floor.

"I'm going to the toilet."

She heard her voice and knew she could not control it if the sham continued for another exchange. She was at the point of flailing her arms wildly and throwing herself against the wall. She made no response. She moved past her father and saw him raise his finger to his lips in that old familiar gesture that told her that he understood her agony and that the moment would pass. She wanted to take his look and dissolve in it, to cover herself with it, and hide forever in its comfort. But she knew that in this world it would be her mother who would prevail, and though her father would protest on her behalf, a higher law held him bound.

"Put on your shawl," Sarah called after her. "Reuben, stop her. We don't need anyone sick for the wedding."

Reuben nodded to Zeena, and for his sake only, she reached for the peg on the wall and put the shawl over her shoulders. She continued to the door with the same deliberate motion as before. She knew she would have to reach the open yard before her voice and body could give way to the shaking and uncontrollable sobbing that was at the bottom of her despair. She saw her hand on the latch. She saw the door open. She felt the night air envelop her. She closed the door behind her and ran into the yard. She ran along the path by the cornfield choosing to be oblivious to the dangers of that road at night. When she was far enough away, she turned, first towards the town she despised, and then towards the little wooden house in which her mother sat. She saw the woman as some gigantic, watchful bird looming over her life. Her body heaved. Bursts of air exploded out the anger and the frustration of being caught in a place where her life was not her own. She clenched her fists at her sides and finally, a prolonged, mindless demonic scream ripped out of her throat into the night. She screamed at the house until she could scream no more and then fell to her knees sobbing and sank back.

Suddenly, boots confronted her. She screamed and tore away, but two hands held her shoulders.

"What are you doing out here, Zeena?" Jonah said incredulously, looking at her and then over her shoulder into the darkness of the field. "You know the danger. I saw you running." Jonah stepped back so he could see her more clearly. "What if peasants were out here and found you? You know they come into the fields at night to drink." Again, his eyes searched the black, furrowed earth. "Come, now!"

"Let them come. I don't care what happens to me. Just let me alone. Let me die."

"You're talking foolishness," he said holding her and supporting her along the path. She was limp and spent from crying, but she held him around his waist as if he were the only anchor she had in the world.

"Jonah, please don't get married," she suddenly blurted. "We could run away together. It would be like when we were little. It would be just the two of us again and we could take care of each other. We'd never be afraid again. Please, Jonah, please take me away from here. I can't do it by myself. But I could do it with you. We could do it together."

The fear poured out of her and he felt himself drowning in it.

"Mama will force me into a marriage. She can do it, and Papa will be helpless to stop her. I won't be able to stop her. Jonah, don't let her do this to me!"

Jonah knew the depth of her anxiety and vulnerability and he also knew that for all her ranting and apparent strength, at her core, there was a helplessness that was as great as his own. With all his life, he wanted to make her world secure and happy, but he knew he could not, and in shame, he constricted behind his impenetrable wall where he felt safe.

Both of them were tightly cradled in the unseen arms of tradition and the limitations imposed upon them by the world in which they lived. Marriage with Leah was his chance to make a life with someone who would not hurt him or make him feel the way his mother made him feel. Marriage was the tradition's way of letting him become a man. He would not lose that chance. He could never become the man he dreamed of being with his sister. Only a wife could help him do that! And running away was unthinkable. As much as he loved his sister, he would not sacrifice his dream of what his life might be.

"I'll talk to Mama," he said softly, needing to say something of comfort. "Everything will be fine."

Zeena tore her arm from his hand and looked at him contemptuously.

"You don't understand, Jonah," she screamed, her black eyes flashing rage. "Everything will not be fine." She turned and quickly moved away.

He ran up to her and his touch was an apology. They walked together in silence. The clouds passed from in front of the moon and they and the field suddenly were enveloped in silver.

"Zeena," he said softly. "What else is there to do if not marry?"

"Else to do?" she replied in a tone that rang of disbelief. "What else is there to do? How can you say that? There's a world out there. Krivoser isn't the world. Am I the only person in this place who has an idea that there's a better life out there someplace? Jonah, when we were young we pretended that we would sail away on the lake and into the pictures in the books. The pictures and the words gave us dreams. We tasted the words and they danced in the air before our eyes. We made a pact that we would always be together. Don't you remember? Whenever we were afraid we would hold each other and pretend we were in a magic circle where we were safe. Remember that wonderful light that seemed to shine on everything when we held each other? In that circle, we were whole again like it must have been before we were born. We were complete. We needed no one else. We still need no one else, Jonah. What happened to the promises we made each other in that circle? We're still one. It wasn't make believe. Why can't you still feel it as I feel it?"

"I remember, Zeena," he said and he felt a shudder run down his spine. "But we were children playing make believe and it's not right that we do that anymore. It was not a good thing to do. It was a thing children did."

Jonah could feel the tears right behind his eyes and knew he would not be able to contain them if he continued. The feelings being conjured at the thought of the circle brought back the memory of old childhood fears and made him realize that these fears were still very much part of his life. With Leah, he could once again hold another being and feel complete and safe, but it would not be pretend, and what he would feel for his wife would not be forbidden.

Zeena began to sob with such pathos that he was beyond refusing her anything. He took her in his arm. He would have given her whatever strength he had so she might not feel such despair if he could. The wall crumbled as he took her into his arms to comfort her. Her pain and fear flowed into him like a sudden chill, and they became his. "You're strong, Zeena," he said, trying to reassure her. "You're stronger than most people."

Zeena lifted her head and looked him squarely in the face. "Oh, why can't you hear me and understand me," she wept. "Jonah, I'm not strong and I don't want to be strong. I don't want to fight the world. I want to feel young. I want to laugh and dance and enjoy life. But here in Krivoser, and in that house, I can't be young and how can I laugh facing a life that was planned for me centuries ago?"

Anguished by the morbid specter of the future, she sank to her knees before him. "Please, Jonah, please help me." she whimpered.

"I'm begging you, Jonah. This place and Mama are killing me. Don't let this happen to me, Jonah. Don't let this happen to us. Please see what is happening. Please, Jonah, only you can help me."

She continued to pour her desperation into him and it was unbearable.

"Please, Zeena, please stop it! If you love me, stop!"

He pulled her to her feet and she encircled his body with her arms. He tried to pull away, but she would not free him.

"Please, Zeena, stop," he begged.

"Swear that you won't let Mama force me into a marriage. Swear it to me here in the circle," she cried desperately.

"Please, Zeena, don't do this to me."

"Swear it to me in the circle and then I'll believe you!"

"Zeena," he cried, as if he were being torn apart. "I swear it," he said, gasping for breath. "Now, please, let me go."

Zeena kept her eyes riveted on him though tears blinded her. She had extracted his promise and she knew how compelling and binding an oath made in that circle was. She released him and they stood facing each other like the frightened, angry children they were.

"You shouldn't have made me swear, Zeena, he gasped, "that's not what the circle was for. I hate you for doing that to me. I hate you for doing that."

They were at the door of the house.

"I am afraid, Jonah. I am more frightened than I have ever been in my life." She felt her jaw tighten as she placed her hand on the latch. "I am in a life and death struggle, Jonah," she said with intense resolve in her voice, "and I will not martyr myself so Mama can have her way. There is nothing I will not do to save my life. I will cause pain beyond belief if it means my survival. You would too, if you really understood."

"Then run away by yourself, Zeena. Run away."

Jonah watched the door close behind her, and his body shuddered as if he had been touched on the neck by something cold. This moment with her was the darker side of their oneness and it was not as it was when they pretended as children. Something powerful and frightening within Zeena had reached into him, grabbed at his soul and extracted the oath. He was bound to her and the circle had to be broken if he were to be happy with Leah. He believed this completely. A marriage for Zeena would save him and he would belong to Leah only. This is what he understood, and Zeena would have to be complete with someone else.

He climbed the ladder as if in a trance. At the base of his fear was his breaking this oath before God, and Zeena's threat to act if he did. Zeena's actions could bring repercussions that might come to lay at his feet. Such things had happened before. The future was overwhelming him, and he forced himself not to think of it. He would think of Leah. He would wonder what it would be like to share the tiny room and his bed. He would cancel Zeena out. His thoughts raced to that evening when his father had come home and announced that he had decided on a wonderful girl for Jonah, one from a fine family.

"Aha," Sarah had responded. "From a fine family means she's pretty and a pauper. Who? Who?" she had continued, interested and very annoyed that he had taken the father's prerogative and found a spouse for their son without involving her.

"I remind you my dear wife," he hastened to add in his attempt to soothe her, "that you were also pretty, not from a wealthy family, and we did make beautiful children. Did we not? In any case, she is not rich, but in times like these my son needs someone who will work along with him, not someone who'd sit and demand like she might, had she been brought up in a rich man's house."

"So who is this hard working wonderful girl?" Sarah asked, preparing herself for the worst.

"Isaac Mitvoy's youngest niece, Leah Shanagrotsky."

"Isaac Mitvoy's niece!" Sarah bellowed throwing her hands into the air. "The little dark one who looks like a foreigner? Malka Mitvoy is crazy." Jonah saw her covering her face with her hands and collapsing onto the chair. He laughed again at the memory.

"I'll not have you speak of that family that way again," he heard his father shout, slamming a book on the table in a rare display of anger. "Where is your charity? They were old people who took on responsibilities of orphaned children. They made good marriages for Leah's older sisters and they are making a good marriage with our son. You know the sadness of their story as well as I. Have a little pity on them!"

"And it's pity you're having on my son by throwing him in with such an unlucky group?"

"The matter is closed!" Reuben stormed. "Isaac Mitvoy and I have an agreement that Jonah and Leah will meet. If they like each other, we'll make an arrangement."

He turned to Jonah, and his voice softened. "Jonah, tomorrow I want you to go the bakery and look at her. She goes at night to make extra money. During the day she works in Isaac's store. Jonah, such a girl will work beside you and be a help. Believe me, Jonah, she's a real catch. And may I remind you that your mother also made matzah at night to earn extra money, and I don't mind telling you that she was also a catch." He hoped that his praise would soften the tightness in his wife's jaw, but it did not. "Isn't that right, Sarah?"

The memory carried him to another place, and Jonah saw himself standing at the bakers waiting for it to get dark. His father had told him she was small and olive skinned, a girl with long red hair and large dark eyes. From the moment his father had described her, Jonah had fantasized her as the Shulamite shepherdess of whom King Solomon wrote. He had pictured her a thousand times in the pages of the little book. He had seen her a thousand times, the dark, yet comely one, whose teeth were pearls and whose lips were the color of a pomegranate. He had seen her a thousand times in the dark shadows of his room as he waited for sleep. His father had misled him. Leah Shanagrotsky was not just a pretty girl. Leah was strangely beautiful and indeed, had she lived in the days of Solomon, she surely would have been taken to the palace as a priceless treasure. He stood, transfixed by her black, almond shaped eyes and the sounds of the bakery faded. He did not know how long he stood staring at her, but he was rudely shaken from that moment by an explosion of laughter when all there realized that Leah had captured the fancy of the shy and awkward tailor whose eyes became riveted on her the moment she turned her head.

Tomorrow, in this very bed, she would be at his side and he had no idea what to do or to expect. Then, something occurred to him.

He bolted out of bed to the small book case and ran his fingers over the worn leather bindings until they rested on the Code of Law. Why had he not thought of this before? The Code contained all. Surely it would have an answer or give some direction.

"Yes, yes," he said with relish, "Laws Appertaining to Marriages." He scanned the yellowing pages in the flickering light. 'A man is duty bound to take a wife.' "Yes, I'm doing that," he said. His finger moved quickly over the phrases. 'Marry a woman who is modest, merciful and charitable.' He did not know if Leah was those things. How could he? 'Those who marry for money will produce evil offspring.' "Nothing to worry about there," he laughed. "We both have nothing."

Jonah's eyes raced over page after page of prohibitions all the while looking for some words that would give him some idea of what to do on his wedding night. He was becoming annoyed. Finally, his eyes rested on the word, 'intercourse.' His pulse quickened.

'It is forbidden to have intercourse during the day unless the room is darkened and it is forbidden to look upon the wife's nakedness.' "What?" he exclaimed. "If this is forbidden, than what is allowed?" 'One who marries a maiden should perform the marriage duty that is mandatory upon him and although there is an issue of virginal blood, he may conclude the conjugal intercourse and not have any apprehension.' Jonah leaped on the positive suggestion with renewed interest and turned the pages to the last paragraph in the hope that there would be a more detailed description on how a man should proceed.

'The learned physicians said that one out of a thousand die

from other diseases, while one thousand die from excessive cohabitation; therefore, a man should be very careful about it.'

Jonah sat back on his bed and shook his head in disbelief. What he looked for he hadn't found. What was found was better not found. He put the book back on the shelf. He sat on the edge of his bed and looked down at the floor trying to impose reason between the law and his heart. If having children was a blessing, he reasoned, then the way of making children had to be a blessing, also. Blessings are good! So if blessings are good, then the law must be wrong!

Jonah stopped himself. What was he thinking? The world was held together by people agreeing to follow the law. It was all part of the balance. If he dared challenge it, what would happen to that balance? It was Zeena who upset the balances, not he. But this Code was written by an old man who had never seen Leah Shanagrotsy. Again, he caught himself. How do you take a piece of the Code you like and leave the rest because you don't like it?

He fell back on his bed. Something new to worry about. I think you are a fool, Jonah Chernov, he said to himself, looking through the open shutter. He closed his eyes and thought of Leah. Soon he would be able to look at her as often as he wished. A shattered glass was the only thing that separated them. A shattered glass! What if I don't break the glass? Did that ever happen? There was always a first time. He sat up suddenly. He would have to practice. But when? How? He could not. It was the Sabbath and he could not break anything.

"Lord of the Universe," he said. "A good Sabbath to you. I know I must not pray for something unnatural to happen for my benefit, but when you look down on my wedding, I was wondering if, perhaps, you might just strengthen my foot.".

He smiled at the stars and fell asleep. That night, he slept fitfully and dreamt of his sister.

CHAPTER 3

As was the tradition in Krivoser, all weddings, when weather permitted, were held before the great wooden door of the synagogue and Jonah's wedding would be no exception. Sarah had decreed it and asked God for a bright sunny day, and a starry night, and that is exactly what she got. Jonah had asked his cousins Saul and Ralph to hold two of the poles of the marriage canopy. Leah's brothers had returned from Kiev to hold the other two.

Down the aisle separating the men and women were two cords Dora and Ruth had entwined with field flowers. All was in place. The guests started to move in, finding seats on the borrowed benches, some vying with others for seats close to the canopy. All were chattering about the bride and how lovely she was, how sad for Rebecca, and how tragic for Malka Mitvoy who couldn't even enjoy the wedding. How wonderful it would have been if her son had lived . . .on and on and on.

Zalman Yavna surveyed the tables again to see if enough wine had been brought from his tavern and then took his seat.

"You know, Yavna, I practically introduced them," said Mr. Koslofsky, the baker. "Sure. Last Passover in my store. Am I a matchmaker or am I a matchmaker?"

"Look," said another, "is that Putinsky? He dares come uninvited?"

"Sha, lower your voice. You never know who's listening."

"Putinsky would dare the Angel of Death for a free meal. You think he cares? You think he worries that someone won't like him? Everyone hates him. So he must figure he can only get better. Right? I ask you Yavna. Am I right?"

Mr. Koslofsky looked for some agreement among the others and decided to change the subject.

"Yavna," he continued, "What happened in St. Petersburg? I hear a Jewish boy is being held for killing a prince. Can such a thing be true?"

"Who knows what's true? From newspapers that are owned by the government you want truth? I know only what I read. A young revolutionary. A crazy person. You ever listen to them in the market? They should all be put in jail. Just what we need. More trouble."

A large man on the bench behind them lightly tapped Mr. Koslofsky on the shoulder and pointed to the synagogue. The Rabbi stood silently before a small table under the canopy on which rested a silver goblet of wine and the marriage contract. Mr. Koslofsky looked around into the stranger's eyes and turned to his companions for identification, but they shrugged their shoulders.

Jonah and Leah stood before them. The Rabbi's voice rose.

"He who is supremely mighty; He who is supremely blessed; He who is supremely sublime, may He bless the groom and the bride."

Jonah shifted from one foot to the other. I'm going to be married, he thought. I'm really going to be married. I'm doing what I must do. Forgive me, Zeena. Forgive me for not being able to take you away and keep you safe. It will be all right. I'll talk to Mama soon. Let me think of Leah. He sipped from the first cup of wine. Leah sipped also.

Leah's eyes remained fixed on the little table before her. Mama, Papa in heaven, she thought, I don't know anything. I'm afraid. I'm not ready. Maybe next year. Oh, Mama, Papa. Oh, Rebecca, help me.

Jonah was speaking. "With this ring you are wedded to me in accordance with the Law of Moses and Israel."

Leah saw her forefinger reach out and felt the band of gold slide onto it. This is my ring, she thought, this is my husband. I am a wife for all times. It's too soon. It's too soon!

Leah circled Jonah seven times as was the tradition, with Sarah following her.

"I betroth you to myself forever; I betroth you to myself in righteousness and in justice, in love and in mercy; I betroth you to myself in faithfulness." Leah stood again at his side.

Yes, thought Jonah. I will be all of this to you. Oh let us love one another as Jacob loved Rachel. Oh, please God, let us love each other. Oh, please God, let Zeena forgive me.

"Blessed art thou Oh Lord our God, King of the Universe, who brings forth the fruit of the vine."

"Raise Leah's veil," the Rabbi said. "Jonah?"

Leah looked up at her husband and modestly lowered her head again, but not enough to hide the bright sparkle of joy in her dark, topaz eyes.

You are beautiful my love, he thought. Your eyes are dove-like behind your veil . . .your lips are like a thread of scarlet, your mouth is comely . . .you are altogether beautiful, my love, there is no blemish in you.

"Sip the wine," reminded the Rabbi. Jonah sipped the wine. The moist stain of his lips on the silver goblet met hers. I kiss you in this cup, he thought. We have kissed, my bride, my beautiful wife. We are one in the wine and the kiss. We are one in the circle of the goblet.

Jonah moved imperceptibly closer to Leah. She glanced at him and smiled. A tear rolled down her cheek. Somewhere beside her, or near the groom, there were muffled sobs. Reuben put his arm around Sarah's shoulder and patted her. Zeena stood looking at the ground.

The Rabbi nodded to cousin David. David took a glass and wrapped it in a cloth, placing it between groom and bride on the earth. Jonah looked at her and her eyes nodded the confidence that he sought. He knew he would do it well. He raised his foot slowly, deliberately, over the cloth. It hovered briefly.

Please God, please, he thought, and then, because there was nothing else to do, he smashed down on the fragile glass with the might of Samson. The cloth flattened instantly under the bridegroom's heel and guests, right to the very last row of benches, heard and applauded.

I did it. I did it, Leah, he thought, and a wave of relief ran through his body. Blessings erupted on all sides, hurled at them with kisses and heart felt warmth.

"Mazel tov."

"May you live under a good star."

"May God bless you and give you long life."

"May only God judge you."

"May you be blessed with wonderful children."

Old men, young men, friends and acquaintances, leaped to their feet and joined hands in front of the bride and groom, dancing backward up the aisle, parting the sea of well wishers crowding in on them.

"You should both live for a hundred and twenty years."

"Love each other."

The guests moved around them and ushered them to the side door of the synagogue. The room where the marriage contract had been read and signed was now set for a private meal, their first together as husband and wife. The candles on the white cloth welcomed them to their red orange warmth.

The door closed behind them and cousin David stood sentinel, insuring their complete privacy. The clamor of voices faded and they were alone. They stood there for a moment looking at each other, awkward like children in awkward silence.

"Are you hungry, Leah?"

"Not really," she replied, her eyes avoiding his. "I think I'm too excited to care about eating. But if you're hungry, you can eat."

He stood there.

"No," he said, and at that very moment his stomach growled audibly. He flushed with embarrassment. Leah forced back a smile but could not hold it. She put her lace handkerchief to her lips to muffle the laugh, but it was no use. She looked at her new husband through her laughter hoping that her laughter did not hurt him. He was laughing too.

"Do you know," he said, "that this is our first laugh together as husband and wife?"

She stepped slightly closer. "Everything will be a first for us, Jonah."

They were very close now. He focused on her eyes and she on his. His hands moved from his sides hesitantly and lightly held the tips of her fingers. She responded and stepped closer again, her hands moving into his.

She raised her face and closed her eyes, waiting. Time briefly faded. He studied the soft clear skin and the natural blush of her cheek. His eyes caressed the waves of hair, parted in the center, discreetly peering from the white veil. Her silent black lashes fluttered. Her lips poised, waiting for his. Again the words came to him. You are beautiful, my love. You are beautiful.

Jonah felt dryness on his lips and moved his tongue quickly over them. Slowly, in hesitant degrees, he lowered his mouth and ever so softly let his lips caress hers. They were warm and moist and his lips lingered, hovered just to fully experience this new sensation, this new beginning, this new wonder called woman. He was Adam and she was his Eve and all was new and good and innocent in their own Garden. And then, because they were man and wife or perhaps just because he was a man, he brazenly took her in his arms and pressed her close, losing himself more and more to her touch; dissolving into her lips and wanting more and more. There was a stirring in his groin, a new feeling, strange and wonderful and exciting. It was as it must be, but he loosened his hold on her. His hands moved slowly across her back to her shoulders. Their lips parted yet clung and he placed his cheek on hers just to feel it, to prolong the new sensation.

He stepped away, slightly flushed and embarrassed by his response to her body. Leah stood there, her eyes still closed, swaying slightly. He had kissed her tenderly, passionately. He could do that and he felt wonderful. But how to end the moment? What must he say? How would he glide into the next moment of time with her and keep the wonderful moment just passed fresh and vibrant?

She opened her eyes and smiled. I have done well, he thought. She is pleased.

He took the chair opposite Leah's and sat. His stomach ached from the fast. He took a sweet roll from the plate and made the blessing over it. He divided it and gave her half. He picked up his fork and helped himself to the corner of the noodle pudding Sarah had made the night before, but Leah did not move. She merely watched him.

Jonah looked up and hesitated, fork in midair, balancing some carrots. "Is something wrong Leah," he said. "Why don't you eat?" "No, nothing is wrong. I want to watch you eat. I want to see how you eat and what you like and don't like. Everything is happening so fast. I really haven't had time to even look at you."

"So what do you see?"

"I see my husband and he has hair the color of wheat, soft hair on his upper lip, blue eyes like the river in early morning, and a big appetite."

"You're playing with me," he said. "Now what do you really see?"

Jonah was curious to know. No one had ever looked at him or watched him with such expectation and newness. He urged her further.

"I see a young man whose eyes laugh and whose eyes are tender. I see a young man who sometimes is not so sure of himself. I see a young man with a big appetite who had better eat before everything gets cold." She paused briefly.

"Leah," he said. "Do you feel any different? I mean we are married and I thought that surely I'd be different in some way. But I don't feel any different. I don't even feel married."

Leah smiled. "I thought about the same thing. Now I don't feel as silly. Sometimes Rebecca tells me I'm silly for what I think and how I feel. But I don't think a person is silly for thinking something or feeling something. It's just that people are different."

"Leah," he said, "when you say different do you . . ." David knocked softly on the door.

"Have you finished? Everyone wants you out. Jonah, Leah? When will you be out?"

Jonah pushed back on his chair and moved to the door, opening it a crack.

"We're talking, David," he whispered with some urgency.

"You have a lifetime to talk. Everyone wants you out here."

He closed the door and turned. Leah was already standing.

"Wait," he said, taking a spoon full of honey and pouring it over half a roll.

"Here Leah. Mama thought it would be nice if our first meal together was sweet."

"That was very thoughtful of her," Leah said softly, biting off a corner rich with the thick amber liquid. He ate from the same roll, and with honey still on his lips, bent down and kissed her again.

"Jonah, I want you to know that even if we had no honey, this has been the sweetest meal of my life." She smiled tenderly, and touched his cheek.

"I am sorry we have to leave," he said as he opened the door. Strains of the violin and rich base fiddle blended with the high pitch of the flute and clarinet. The music coaxed them out of the room, inviting them to the gaiety. The men and women had already formed separate circles and were dancing around. When the bride and groom appeared at the door of the synagogue, the circle opened and friends took them by the hands and led them to the center of each circle pressing each on to a chair. The circles closed again and the bride and groom were caught up in the vortex of swirling skirts and shawls and black coats and fur hats. The dance went on. Four laughing friends broke from the circle and, with arms held high, danced and twirled around Leah and then danced back in place. Sarah gasped when she saw Myer Putinsky daring to eat her food and enjoy her son's wedding. She left the woman's circle.

"Reuben, do you see who's here? Do you see that animal? That filth! Get him out! I don't want him soiling our joy."

Reuben dropped his brother's hand and left the circle around his son. Together they walked to the table where the old man sat alone.

"Let me talk to him, Sarah," Reuben cautioned. "He is a very dangerous man."

"You can't come here to bleed us for more money, Putinsky," Sarah began. "It's over. For seven years, seven years mind you, you've stolen the food from my children's mouths."

"Sarah, please don't get upset. He is leaving," Reuben responded. The old man continued chewing on a roll and swallowed before looking up.

"Mrs. Chernov, why not just say you bought the peace of mind I was in a position to sell," he said as he stood and steadied himself against the table. "You wanted your son not to go into the army and I arranged it for you. So why can't we be civil to each other?"

"Civil? You . . ." she hissed. "For seven years we lived in poverty!"

"What can I do?" protested Putinsky half heartedly. "The Tsar wants children to go into the army and the Tsar wants children to convert. If I didn't do this, one of the government agents would. At least we keep it in the family and with me at least some people have a choice. You might even say that if it wasn't for me, all these fine young men might be serving the Tsar right now. Bribing officials to turn their eyes is expensive. If not for me, Chernov, you would not be witnessing your son's marriage today."

Putinsky stood up and put a boney hand on Reuben's shoulder. Reuben pulled away.

"Chernov, I thank you for your food and I wish the bride and groom happiness. You had good food and a lot of it so I know you have money."

"If you want to know, Isaac Mitvoy paid for everything," interrupted Sarah, "I just cooked. You want to thank someone, thank Isaac. Or better yet, stop and see Malka."

"That happened a long time ago," Putinsky said slowly and deliberately. "I had nothing to do with it."

"You forget that I was there," Reuben countered, "I was seven years old and I saw. You had dealings with the man who kidnaped Alta Mitvoy. I had seen him with you a dozen times in the market. I would have been taken too had my foot not been crushed by the stone. Alta could have escaped, but he tried to help me. No, Putinsky, you're not clean in that one. You destroyed them when you sent their only child to God knows what horror and his death. They buried eight children, and the only one who lived, you helped kidnap!"

"You shouldn't talk to me that way. I can break you like a twig," he scowled.

"We all know what you can do to us Mr. Putinsky, and I am remembering that there is not a man that has not his hour, and there is not a thing that has not its place.' You are capable of great evil. You were born one of us, but you are not one of us, and you may still have your hour, and I fear what your hour may bring us."

"Get out, scum," fumed Sarah.

"Tell her to be quiet, Chernov," the old man croaked.

"Sarah, please go join the others."

Putinsky took a last mouthful of fish and wiped his mouth.

"You are not a hospitable man, Chernov," Putinsky said. "Perhaps I have been a little too generous with you and your family."

"You are a man without generosity and without mercy," Reuben continued, swallowing his fear. "We can expect bitterness from the outside, but when one of our own causes such anguish, how can it be explained? You are a reminder of the evil each of us carries within, but only you have let the evil out and made your living from it. Go, Mr. Putinsky, before I forget how much I fear you."

Reuben turned and walked away. He felt his body shaking. Strains of the violin caught him and drew him into the circle. He pulled a handkerchief out of his pocket and waved it over his head. Mr. Putinsky was forgotten for the moment.

Simon and Jacob parted the line of women as they danced in towards Leah. They danced around her, arm on arm, and then took the legs of the chair and lifted Leah high in the air. Leah let out a squeal of delight tinged with fright and grabbed the sides of the chair until she was sure that she was safe, and her brothers were strong enough to sustain her. They danced around in a circle, the women waving their handkerchiefs at her and wishing her well.

"Dance me over to Leah," cried Jonah. "Papa, your handkerchief. Here, Leah, don't be afraid. Take hold of it and dance with me."

Leah's hand bravely let go of the side of her chair and reached out. She laughed as she caught the cloth and they laughed to each other and to the dancing people below them.

The stranger who had quieted Mr. Koslofsky before the ceremony silently observed the abrupt movements of Sarah and Reuben and listened carefully to the confrontation. His sudden awareness of this old man would have overwhelmed him like death overwhelms, had his attention not been turned to the distraught face of Malka Mitvoy, his mother.

CHAPTER 4

The line of broken shutters and dimly lit, silent houses became a barrier that absorbed and muted the sprightly tunes of the wedding band. The lingering melody Putinsky carried from the gaiety played in his memory and conjured up blurts of youthful images; images of a time that lived prior to his decision to become what he had chosen to become. He smiled to himself at the faded pictures and his shuffling footsteps moved to the inner beat of his reverie until even that small thread of his link to his people trailed off in the silence. Again, he was alone with the darkness and the bolted shutters.

Alta Mitvoy, who was now called Alexi Malinovitch by his subordinates in the Tsar's secret police, followed Myer Putinsky. Malinovitch wrapped himself in the silent shadows and moved in timed cadence with the old man's steps. Slowly, careful of creaking boards and rocks that could sound an alarm and send the old man banging on doors for help and mercy, the tall man stepped lightly and with controlled rage.

He had never met this old man and yet, in a few moments, he would take the knife he had concealed in his coat and plunge it through the dry wrinkled skin of Putinsky's gut. In another life, Alexi Malinovitch might have passed this man on some street and nodded a greeting to him. But today, because he now knew who he was, he would insert a knife in such a way as to maximize the pain while prolonging the agony of death. He knew how to do such things.

Putinsky, knowing how to survive hatred, turned periodically to inquire of the darkness. When he was sure that someone indeed did dare to follow him, he quickened his pace, planning the revenge he would take upon that person so stupid as to think that he, Meyer Putinsky, could not outwit all the fools among whom he lived. He knew them all. He would turn and confront the fool by name. His assailant would shrink from recognition and beg for forgiveness. The steps behind him quickened. A barrel fell. Somewhere behind him a shutter banged against a wall. The old man turned the corner into an alley and caught on to a post to catch his breath. He could go no further. He would confront his pursuer.

Suddenly, Malinovitch was there. Putinsky peered at him through his gray, clouded eyes and, at the moment when he recognized that he did not know this man and therefore could not threaten him, he felt a searing, white hot pain rip between his stomach and chest, and stagger him backwards into a pile of crates and empty barrels. A short, high pitched staccato shriek, like that of a wounded animal caught in a trap, strained in his throat. He struggled and pulled himself up against the wall behind him, but his legs gave way and he slowly sank to the dirt, his hand pulling at the knife trying to dislodge it. His arms went limp and his palms fell open at his sides. He sat there gasping in pain.

"Open your eyes, Mr. Putinsky," said the murderer very slowly. "You are not dead yet. Besides, why hurry to your hell?"

Alexi Malinovitch righted one of the barrels and, placing it in front of the limp body, sat down as if to play a game of chess.

"You should be pleased with yourself, Mr. Putinsky. After all, were it not for you, I would never have had the opportunity to learn to kill without the slightest remorse. I will tell you a little secret, but you must promise never to tell a soul."

He leaned closer to the dying man's ear.

"You never really get used to it. Killing is not a thing a man should ever get used to."

The old man grunted a plea as tears ran down the corners of his eyes.

"You kill in a different way, Putinsky," he said. "You kill memories. You wipe out lives and the hopes that parents have to see their children grow and marry and become part of something of value.

You, too, do this without remorse so I think we understand each other."

Putinsky slowly opened his eyes. A trickle of blood mixed with spittle formed at the corner of the old man's mouth and ran slowly down the gray stubble on his cheek. His jaw moved and dropped open, but only an agonized expulsion of breath disturbed the silence.

"Don't try to speak, Mr. Putinsky," said Malinovitch. "I want to tell you a story and you don't have very much time. It's a story about a little boy who tried to release his friend's foot from under a boulder that had fallen on it. He saw the man approaching and he knew the man to be a thief of children. He thought to run but he would not leave his friend. But he could not free his bleeding friend and the friend was left to die in the darkness. I'll tell you Putinsky, that for years the little boy was haunted by the vision of his friend dying and blamed himself for not being strong enough or brave enough to lift that rock. But after a long while, like so many things, that too didn't make a difference either."

Alexi Malinovitch put his finger under the old man's chin and lifted his head upward.

"Keep your head up old man so I can tell by your eyes how much more time I have. I wouldn't want you to miss any part of my odyssey by dying too quickly. Oh, did I tell you that I was that little boy? Did I tell you that my name was Alta Mitvoy then? Did I tell you that I was taken to a strange town and thrown into a cold cellar with other little boys? It was cold in that room and the frozen dirt floor stuck daggers into our bodies where we lay. Did I tell you they took our coats? Did I tell you how we huddled together for warmth and cried for our mothers until we had no tears left? Let me tell you of the sour milk and stale bread and how your friends made us relieve ourselves where we ate and slept because they told us we were animals and deserved no better. And then, after three days of torment and fear, when we were weak from being starved and sick with fever, a soldier came in and told us how we little Jews were going to be part of the glorious Russian army. We were taken from our parents because we were cursed by God. Did you know that they told us how our father, the Tsar, would save us from the useless lives we would otherwise live? And then he said that one day, if we did exactly as we were told, we would be able to see our mothers and fathers. And do you know what he wanted us to do first, Putinsky? He wanted us to kiss a picture of the Holy Mother and her Child. Yes, that's what we were to do. And then, as if by magic, there appeared in the doorway, like some massive black tower, a priest holding this wondrous jeweled picture in his hand. I remember the contempt in his dark eyes for us as he pushed the gilt picture in our dirty faces. I remember how the jeweled cross he wore swung from side to side as he lurched through the frightened children who were caught between the commandment forbidding them to worship idols and the promise of seeing their parents again. None of us kissed that picture that day, but I sometimes wonder that if we had abandoned the God that had abandoned us, some might still be alive. Of course, none of us knew then just how silent God could be."

The man, who would have been known in Krivoser as Isaac and Malka's only child, Alta Mitvoy, moved close to the dying man's face.

"Eventually, I did kiss that picture and became the model convert and best soldier they ever had. I became crueler than any-one else, and for that I was greatly rewarded. But that was much later. That is also an interesting tale and it is a pity you will not hear it. But I will tell you that when I decided to kiss that picture, that was the very first time in my life that I actually knew what hatred was. An officer spit on me that day even after I took his God. I can still feel his hatred on my cheek and I also remember how I hated that mother and her child on the picture because they allowed other mothers to suffer so. You, Mr. Putinsky, put me into the hands of those who taught me how to hate everyone and how to hate myself.

A sudden gust of wind blew down the alley and Malinovitch wrapped his coat tighter. The old man's head dropped again and Malinovitch's finger raised it up.

"I'm not finished, my dear benefactor. I haven't told you of the wooden cart into which we were thrown, and how the mothers and fathers of that nameless town pressed their lips against their children's faces through the slats. Let me tell you quickly how they pressed into their son's hands prayer shawls and phylacteries with the exhortation to remember their people and their God. Let me tell you of the mothers who sank on the earth with their hands extended to this God to send fire onto the heads of the soldiers so their children might escape. That's when I began to learn that there was no God. One last story, Mr. Putinsky. You are very close to death. It's a short story about a little blond boy about seven or eight who clung to my arm and to a yellowing talis. He was sick and feverish and dazed, and do you know Mr. Putinsky what your friends did when they saw that he was sick? They picked him up and threw him out onto the road. I watched him through the slats as he staggered and fell calling for us to stop. I started to cry also because that was all I could do for him. And I'll tell you another little secret no one knows. Sometimes, when I think of that little blond boy, and it's very quiet except for the wind, I still cry. Can you believe that someone as indifferent as I can still cry for a child whose name I never knew? But why should I trouble you with the death of another little boy. Now I will tell you what I learned. I learned that there are those in this world who hate so completely that they cannot be pacified or swayed. And do you know how to live and survive with such hatred, Mr. Putinsky? Do you hate back? No, Mr. Putinsky. You become numb. You cease to care or feel, and that's how a child survives their hatred. That's why I can sit here today, the child grown to manhood, and watch your life flow out of you and feel nothing. But I'll tell you another secret, old man. Sometimes I comprehend what I am and I cannot be numb to myself when I see what I've become and what I've lost. For myself, at those times, I feel only hatred, but I wish I could be numb."

Somewhere on another street, a door opened to laughter and closed.

"I'm leaving you now, old man, because I want you to die

alone and frightened like the little blond boy. I am sorry there are no wolves to howl for your final entertainment. The little boy heard wolves."

He stood.

"Chance is a funny thing. Had I not come to investigate nihilist activity in the region, I would not have happened upon my cousin's wedding and I would not have learned of you. I imagined that those involved in the theft of my life had died years ago. I'm glad you didn't."

Putinsky fell over, his face in the dirt.

"Die with no human voice to comfort you, old man. Die as I and my little friend died so long ago. There are ghosts here, Putinsky. There are ghosts watching you and waiting for you. They are the ghosts of children and parents who were torn apart so you and your family might prosper. What if there is an afterlife? My torment of you was brief. They will torment you for eternity."

Alexi Malinovitch turned away and moved towards the center of town and the lilting strains of a violin. Guests moved past him and offered greeting. He smiled at them. The music ended and did not begin again so he stopped mid-stride. The wedding was over. He turned and walked slowly among the departing guests and listened to their chatter about how nice Jonah looked and how beautiful Leah was, and how outstanding was Sarah Chernov's chopped goose liver.

CHAPTER 5

Jonah lay next to Leah without speaking. From the moment their thighs touched, he could feel the heat from her body radiate over his leg and groin like warm, slowly moving oil. First, he concentrated on the new sensation but then, aware of the passing time, the silence, and his own inner mandate and expectation to act, he rose from her warmth and moved across the room to the shutters to close out the night. He felt her eyes on him and felt uncomfortable standing there in his night shirt. Quickly, he returned to their cot and blew out the candle. Again, he lay next to her in silence. Slowly, the rays of the moon eased their way through the shutters and bathed the far wall, the floor, and the bedclothes with silver, striated light.

"Why did you dampen the candle?" Leah inquired softly. "I wanted to look at you."

Jonah tightened, remembering the text he had read about the modesty of darkness, and suddenly felt caught between the natural curiosity of his new wife and the mandate of the Code of Law. But he did not want to appear foolish or old fashioned.

"I like the shapes the moonlight makes through the shutters," he said quickly. This was also a truth, and he hoped his response would satisfy her question while covering both his need to address the law and his need to hide his fear of not knowing how to proceed. He tensed and felt inept and prayed that she did not sense or see how frightened he was.

He tried to concentrate on her warmth, searching for the feeling that would ease the anxiety he felt creeping between them. He breathed deeply and exhaled slowly. He earnestly tried to go limp and dissolve into their new, soft, down mattress. He tried to dissolve into the warmth that was again creeping over him.

Soon their breathing became syncopated. Each hoped the other would speak first and say something so the fears and doubts and questions each had could be eased.

"Do you have enough room?" Jonah asked, and he laughed because he knew that the bed was barely large enough to hold him.

"Do you have a larger bed in here?" and Leah laughed also as she had laughed when his stomach growled earlier.

Jonah turned to her, resting his cheek upon his arm. The white pillow framed her moonlit face and she appeared to him as if an angel.

"I like how you laugh," he said. "I will always want us to laugh together. I like laughing with you."

The laughter and her understanding helped to ease his anxiety. He was now turned fully towards her and he felt the total warmth of her entire body beneath her nightgown. Every inch where her body touched his seemed to caress him. Perhaps his body was radiating too, and inside, Jonah felt a steadily growing urgency rapidly overcoming the cautions planted by his father's admonition to move slowly and tenderly. He wanted Leah to think of him as knowing and capable, not the unsure youth she had seen at dinner. But how would he convey this to her when he did not know what to do or how to do it? Certainly she was his wife and duty bound to accept him, but would she also see that he was, in fact, the fumbling fool he believed himself to be? That thought injected itself between them and the pleasure of the moment. So he thought of a way to begin.

"Perhaps we might start by kissing," she said softly, turning her face towards him, then brushing the hair away from his forehead. "We did that very well, I think."

He was thankful she had spoken first and he moved his face closer to hers, her sweet breath already caressing his face even before their lips met. He moistened his lips and lightly touched them against Leah's.

The sensation was much different from before and yet the same. He did not press down, but lightly, and deliberately, moved over them, and filled his memory with their newness. Her lips were small and moist and warm and Jonah closed his eyes to feel them completely. The warmth of their bodies grew, and in the warmth, Jonah felt what he thought were feelings of love. His arm slowly slid under the small of her back to bring her warmth closer. He could feel the heat rise to his face and felt his nostrils grow hot. How wonderful this thing called touching was. How wonderful to speak so lovingly without words.

With the same steady deliberate motion, Jonah allowed his other hand to move slowly, cautiously from her shoulder down the bodice of her night dress to where the rise of her small breasts began. Shy in his assertion, measuring his boldness against her response by taking her sighs as approval, his fingers slowly eased over her and rested on the small mound no larger than his palm. Through the cloth he could feel the softness, a strange and wonderful softness. He lightly pressed and squeezed her and sought her lips with a newer, bolder urgency. He felt his own body begin its natural response beneath his nightshirt. He opened his eyes to look at her, to know more than just his own body's response. Her eyes were closed and her lips slightly parted. In the slivers of moonlight that slatted the bed, she appeared like a delicately carved cameo, her perfect profile etched by moonbeams. She was indeed his Shulamite, and he was the shepherd youth. His hand reached for the bow of her nightgown and it opened at his touch. He eased his hand onto the soft warm breast. It was wonderfully smooth and round and he cupped it gently, aware, so very aware, that this small warm breast was as delicate and fragile as the woman whose heart pulsated beneath his palm. He, too, pulsated at the direct touch of her flesh, and he let his finger tips explore the hardening nipple and circle of protrusions surrounding it. Under his lips, she sighed and laughed slightly and he moved his lips from hers to explore the softness of her cheek and the moist crevice of her neck and shoulder. He closed his eyes, allowing his lips and the tip of his tongue to feel their way over her skin, knowing, perhaps instinctively, that sightless touch heightened the sensations and intensified the moment. He could feel himself very hard now and he pushed down his own embarrassment by concentrating on the softness of her body beneath his lips. She turned to him and pressed against him and he knew that this slow, moving encounter was a natural prelude to their act of love.

The heat in her own body seemed more intense, something he had not felt before. Again, he pressed his mouth over hers and let his hand inch its way down the front of her gown towards the soft mound between her legs. Her inviting sighs and movement enticed his hand to move further over her lower body. He was doing this. He was actually doing this to a woman, his woman, his wife. Then he reached the softness he sought and she moaned at his touch. He explored her through the gown and he felt her push up against his hand.

"Oh Jonah, my Jonah," she said tenderly. "Touch me there. Touch me there."

He moved his hand to the hem of her nightgown and raised it over her stomach. His fingers, unsure, hovering, touched her knee and eased over her soft thigh. He felt her shudder as his hand moved closer and closer to the source of her heat. And then he touched her again and she sighed as his finger tips slowly explored the yielding, moist rim. His fingers moved over it slowly, carefully remembering what his father cautioned and wondered at the ease in which his finger opened and parted her. She responded to his hand by pushing towards it as if she, too, meant to explore and experience this new sensation. He felt a moistness that was also different, a thick honey like moistness that covered his fingers as he carefully penetrated the inner lining of her body.

A new sensation in his loins took hold of him and he gave himself up to it. He was suddenly someone else and this someone else was pulling up his own nightshirt and raising himself on top of Jonah Chernov's new wife. This other Jonah was not cautious or steady, and would not be stopped. This other Jonah pressed his lips passionately to Leah's and the hardness between his legs sought its own pleasure oblivious to holiness codes or parental admonitions. He pressed against her, the tip of his penis blindly probing for the entrance he knew was there. The slick moisture his hand had found enveloped him and he felt the pent-up energy surge through his body, building momentum. He had never known such desire or that there even could be such desire. He had never known that in him there was something so primitive and so frightening. Then this primitive thing in him wanted her immediately and it wanted to be one with her, to be completed by her as he had never been completed before. He wanted to be engulfed by her, to possess her, to become one flesh and one body. And suddenly, in the intensity of his passion she screamed and the moment froze. He had hurt her. Her scream returned him to himself. How could he have been so selfish so as to release his evil within and to hurt her so? How could he have abandoned himself so completely to his own passion?

Leah opened her eyes questioningly.

"No, Jonah, you must not stop. It's supposed to hurt but for only for a moment. You must break what is in there and then it will never hurt again."

She looked at him lovingly and reassuringly through liquescent eyes. He looked down at her, the beads of sweat glistening on her forehead like a diadem. He did not understand anything of her body, but he knew that she understood something which he could not yet fathom.

"Please, Jonah, please," and she closed her eyes again and pressed up against him with a short staccato motion that invited him again to the barrier. She met each of his renewed thrusts with her own and he moved back into the moist channel despite his knowing the pain he would inevitably cause her. He pressed down. He could feel her body tense with the determination that she would fulfill her duty as a wife despite what pain may come. She suddenly cried out, and then, wonderfully, he felt himself penetrate her body until he could go no further. She let out a small laugh and

Jonah laughed also and kissed her tenderly. They became suspended in time and motionless love. He was surrounded by her and she held him with throbbing pulsations. She felt herself filled up and complete as never before and flooded with the most amazing warmth she had ever known. Jonah withdrew and entered her gently again. He continued, savoring every movement, every moment, every place where their bodies touched. Now he felt something building in him, a something that demanded a faster more abandoned movement. There was a tension in his groin and a kind of electric rippling across the muscles of his thighs. A dull, pulsating ache, a secret ache, began to gestate deep within his loins and began to pound in rhythm with his heartbeat. But this time it was different. This time the inevitable tension building would find free release inside the body of his wife with no fearsome afterthoughts for his soul. All his being and all his strength gathered like storm clouds in him. The cadenced undulations of his body into Leah's increased as the urgency increased. More and more, faster and faster, his need to pour himself out and create life became the fulcrum of his mindless action. Then Jonah felt his mouth open and his teeth involuntarily clench. His breath tore from his chest in rapid bursts till he reached that moment when the ecstasy and pain were indistinguishable. He arched his back so he was pressed into her with all his might. His body shook and his throat emitted a wonderful triumphant groan of a man in the act of creating life for the first time.

"Leah, my beloved Leah," he whispered, and he fell exhausted on her. The words of Solomon again reached out to him. 'Open to me, my love, my innocent one; for my head is drenched with dew, my locks with drops of the night.' Now he understood the words with both his body and his soul.

They lay there, side by side listening to each other breathe, each delighting in the sound and lingering sensation. Their hands met.

"I'm sorry if there was pain for you," Jonah said apologetically. "I didn't know there would be pain. I didn't want to hurt you."

"It was nothing," she said softly. "I knew. My sister told me."

Jonah was surprised that girls would speak of such things and said nothing further about it. He was wondering about something else. He was wondering if she took as much pleasure from his body as he took from hers. He needed reassurance of his love making, but he did not know how to ask without appearing foolish. Leah moved closer to him and kissed his cheek and ear. She playfully bounced the damp curl in the middle of his forehead and traced the silver silhouette of his profile with her finger.

"Leah," he whispered, mustering some gravity to his voice. "Do you think that what we did is something you would want to do again?"

Her finger poised between the indentation of his nostril and lip and he heard a throaty chuckle that gave way to uncontrolled laughter. Immediately he realized how foolishly stated his question was and that it had nothing to do with what he needed to know.

"You mean did I also take pleasure?" she said, laughter in her voice.

He looked at her wondering how she could possibly conclude what he meant from his foolish question.

"Yes, my dearest Jonah. Oh, yes," she said softly.

CHAPTER 6

Leah opened her eyes. If there was the slightest hint of confusion as to this place in time and space, no conscious recognition of it was made. She looked up at the eaves as if she had looked at them a hundred times before. She was where she wanted to be.

Leah turned her head towards the young man who slept peacefully beside her. She lay still, and quietly studied his face, tracing with her eyes the outline of his forehead and the forest of curls. Her eyes moved down the straight nose to the full pouting lips and she giggled to herself at the small bubble appearing in the center of his lips that popped with each outward breath. She reached up and straightened one of the curls and watched it spring back. The pupils under his closed lids fluttered briefly. The short bristles on his upper lip stood like little black, blonde and red pins and she remembered how they had stuck and tickled at the same time. This was Jonah, her husband. She would love this man and spend her life with him.

In his sleep, he pressed closer to her and smiled. His arm moved over her and collapsed on her chest. His face rested on her shoulder.

Now she was a married woman and it was up to her to take her portion and make life good for both of them. But how? Might a person choose to make it good by choosing not to make it bad? Could choices make things in a person's life change? She tried to divine the future from the lines and crevices in his face and she paused to smile at her own foolishness, for all she could tell from his face was that he slept soundly and blew little bubbles at her.

The sleeping figure stirred. He was kind and gentle, unsure

and as innocent as she. She liked him. Yes, she liked this stranger whom she married. She was comfortable and unafraid.

Leah moved her face closer to his and lightly kissed him. Jonah pressed closer to her again in his sleep, undulating against her thigh, while entering that vague twilight consciousness between dream and reality. He smiled, his eyes still closed. She felt the stiffness against her leg and wondered how it came to be there when they had not even kissed. The thought of the past evening brought heat to her cheeks.

Sure he was asleep, she moved her hand slowly down her own body to her thigh and let the tip of her fingers inch their way towards him. She watched his face for any sign that he might awaken. The thought of touching him as he slept both excited and unnerved her, for she knew her desire to know more of his body was brazen and immodest. She allowed the tip of one finger to touch his manhood. It was warm and hard as she remembered it, and she traced its shape to the place where it flared out and rounded. He moved again. She pulled her hand away and forced back her laughter.

Slowly he opened his eyes and smiled. The sensation that had entered his dream was real. The room danced with the bright morning sun. He looked at her dreamily, still half asleep, and moved his body as close to her as he could. When he realized he was pushing his penis against her thigh, he suddenly tensed and pulled back.

For as long as he could remember, he had been admonished by his teachers and his parents to thank God upon awakening for a new day and the gift of life. Now he awoke undulating against his wife's body, delighting in the sensation and not thinking of God at all. But the sudden thought of God withdrawing His blessings because of his discount, his shame regarding his immodest movement against her body, and the sheer surprise of waking up with another person in his bed, all conjoined at the same moment and he constricted.

Leah responded also, but her response came from the thought that she had done something wrong and he had been repelled by her immodest advance.

He read the confusion and pain on her face and the questions in her eyes. Immediately, he regretted his response and he became ashamed of that, too. Jonah did not know what to say to her. How could she understand that he had discounted God and what he had been taught all his life? He would sound old fashioned if he spoke of it. "I was startled," he said quickly, hoping his weak explanation would soothe her and explain his response. "I'm not used to getting up with someone looking at me," he stammered. "I was startled. That is all. The sun was so bright. It was the sunlight, also." Excuses raced through his brain but each seemed weak and meaningless as he spoke them.

She turned away from him to the wall, confused at his response and feeling ashamed at her immodest advances.

"Leah, don't turn away from me," he said softly coaxing her to turn to him again. His hand hovered above her shoulder, but he did not lower it for fear of it being pushed away. He saw a tear slide down the side of her cheek and it felt like a wound on his own.

"Please, Leah, please don't cry. I didn't pull back because of you. Please believe me." His mind raced again for the words that would explain. "Things go on in me that I don't fully understand. And there are things I've been taught about, and things I've read in religious books, that sometimes put me in conflict with things I feel." He took a breath. "Leah, this is the truth. I pulled away because I realized that my first thought in the morning was not of gratitude towards God for life, but thoughts of making love to you. I was ashamed of what my body was doing and I was ashamed of my thoughts. I did not pull away because of you. That you must believe."

Jonah sat up in bed. "Leah, I am very new to being married and I don't know how I can make you understand how I feel. I'm sorry! What else do you want me to say?" He was beginning to feel angry.

He would have to be on his guard not to say or do anything that would cause another moment such as this. He would have to be more careful of his reactions. He did not want to hurt her. He did not want any conflicts.

She turned and looked at him sadly. Their first difficult moment was passing, and Jonah studied her tear streaked face as if seeing her for the first time. He thought her just as pretty.

Jonah knew he could make it better. The Code of Jewish Law had told him things about love and marriage that did not seem to apply or feel right. What did an old man writing centuries ago know of love? He would make love to his wife at that very moment. He would challenge the Code and make love to her in the daylight to prove to her that nothing was wrong.

The door downstairs rattled and burst open.

"Can you imagine," said Sarah over her shoulder. "Right here in Krivoser! A murder! Now I'm not ashamed to say that he deserved it. Dead, buried, and off the market! But who would do such a thing on the same night of our son's wedding? I ask you Reuben, who would do such a thing?"

"Sarah," Reuben continued protesting. "We have no right to be here. We promised Jonah and Leah they could have the house for a few days by themselves. I can't see where Putinsky's death means we can't continue to stay with your father."

"Oh, so you don't see? Open your eyes and see! Every time somebody important breaks a nail, there's a search. You wait, Reuben. They'll search every Jewish house. You mark my words, and I don't want anyone going through my things and seeing what I have and then stealing it. We have little enough and I'm going to make sure we keep it. What do Jonah and Leah know about searches? He'll sit and read a book and they'll carry out the stove. You don't remember the last search? Jonah? Leah? Are you up? A terrible thing happened last night." She swept to the stove oblivious as to whether or not her words were reaching the lovers above her head.

Jonah's eyes blazed with anger at the intrusion. His fingers curled into two fists and he banged them simultaneously on the mattress. Leah watched his jaw tighten. She moved to her knees and rested her head lightly, reassuringly, on his shoulder, but he did not feel it.

"I didn't want it to be this way," he said, forcing down the rage he felt building towards the woman who moved below them.

"You didn't make it this way," Leah replied, trying to calm him and herself.

They looked at each other, each knowing that the moment for working out their first problem together had passed, and the wonder of discovering a solution so naturally and spontaneously had passed also.

"We're up, Mama," he droned.

Leah sat up and back on her heels.

"Jonah," she said brightly, "I'm going to get up and fix you the best breakfast you've ever had. I'll make you eggs and I'll beat in the honey left from last night. Or maybe I'll dip the sweet rolls in the eggs and fry them in butter." Her face became as bright as her voice at the expectation of their first breakfast together. For a moment she had forgotten that they were no longer alone.

"I didn't want to get up at all today. I wanted to stay in bed with you and just feel you near me and talk and look at you. I wanted to learn about you . . ."

She put out her fingers to his lips to quiet him and he took them and kissed them.

"Look at me then," she said, arranging her nightgown around herself. Her voice rang with playful seduction. "You look at me and I'll look at you just as if we were alone."

Jonah smiled a half smile and stood up to take off his nightshirt, but suddenly realized that she would be looking at him. He turned quickly so she could not read his face. Maybe if Mama and Papa were not downstairs, he thought. Maybe if it wasn't so bright. He reached for his trousers, sat down, and pulled them on.

Leah giggled and he turned knowing why she laughed.

"You're embarrassed," she teased. "You're embarrassed to let me look at you naked."

Jonah was surprised at her forwardness and wondered if all new wives were as open and outspoken as his was.

"All right," he rejoined in a whisper. "Go ahead and take off your nightgown right now. Go ahead."

Leah looked at him, half amused, half surprised by his challenge and started to laugh.

"I can't," she said.

"See, you're embarrassed too."

He had the fantasy of counting to three and each tearing off their night clothes at the same moment. It would be like jumping into a cold lake in springtime and it would be done and over. Then each could feel what had to be felt. Now was not the time. He wanted to see her body in his own time and in his own way. Why had they come back? This was his time. Their time. Why had his mother intruded? Leah saw his face sadden and his eyes narrow at his thoughts. She knew another moment had been lost.

He walked silently to the dresser and poured water into the laver. Leah watched. She saw his anger and she did not want to put herself between it and his parents. It was all so new.

"They might have a good reason," she said, going back to the earlier conversation.

"They promised, and a promise is a promise. We were promised time by ourselves." He gargled and spit out.

Leah would have liked to have taken the time to watch her husband wash and dress and note what he did first and second and why a man does this or that. But she, too, was pressed for time.

"I will get up and make my husband the best breakfast of his life. Now do you like your tea with sugar or without? Do you like . . ." and again the voice from below called for them to get up.

Jonah had already placed the phylacteries on his arm and head and was oblivious to anything but his prayers. She watched his body bend forward and back in quick movements and from side to side. She watched him and thought of the morning and how many different things and feelings could abound in such a short span of time. She thought of how important moments can be lost and she thought of embarrassment. She wondered at all the loose ends there were in day to day living and how many unexpected interruptions can end good beginnings. She looked at Jonah in prayer and wondered how he would respond to his parents, and how he would respond to his own feelings.

She slipped off her night gown and washed her legs and inner thighs and then she opened the window to empty the laver. The sun flooded the room and she looked around at the loft and at her husband. Jonah became aware of her as she moved to the dresser. He continued his prayer and watched her out of the corner of his eye. Jonah thanked God for having made her as she was, and for having brought her to him. He took three steps backward from God's presence, bowed and kissed the book.

"Now I know why men and women do not sit together in the synagogue," he said playfully.

"And why is that?" she laughed.

"Because if they have beautiful women around them, they would not concentrate on prayer." He touched the tip of her nose for emphasis.

"Then it would seem that their devotion to God is less intense than their animal urges," she responded touching the tip of his nose also.

He looked at her and smiled. The thought of clever banter with her was exciting although the thought of bantering about prayer and synagogue with a woman made him uneasy. He didn't know why.

He moved behind her and fumbled with his buttons in the mirror.

"Passion is more basic than prayer," he said in his best scholarly voice. "God created both; the former naturally, the latter through divine inspiration." He tucked in his shirt. "The former is for the bed chamber and the latter is for the synagogue. And that is why we are separate." He stressed the word that to reinforce his meaning. "God created both and both are, therefore, good. But because both are good, that doesn't mean they both have to be together." He was satisfied with his logic and explanation.

"Are you saying that lovemaking or passion is only for the bed chamber and praying is only for the synagogue?"

He immediately knew where she was going with her reasoning and was delighted and surprised by her acuity. He also immediately saw the mistake in his own argument. She turned towards him.

"Then why do you combine both here in our bed chamber?" she said moving him playfully backward and pushing him down on the bed.

"It sounds as if your next question might be why don't we make love in the synagogue?" He felt himself fall backward onto the bed with her falling on top of him. The bed groaned and they laughed. "That borders on profound disrespect and immodesty!"

"But I didn't ask that," she said kissing his nose. "You did."

She had caught him again. They would never want for something to talk about. She was clever and interesting and he would have to be clever and interesting, too. His mother only talked about things like eggs or business or the children or money or general gossip. But Leah was different. Thank God she was different. She was clever like Zeena. He would never be bored with a woman like her. No, he would never be bored.

Her body on his, though fully clothed, was also a new sensation and he felt himself respond, but he was reminded, by a clattering of dishes, that his family was downstairs. He felt himself tighten and Leah saw his eyes change from laughing tenderness.

"Up, my dearest wife."

"You're suddenly different, Jonah. It wasn't what I said about making love and praying, was it?"

"Oh, no Leah," he sighed. "It's not anything you said. It's nothing. It's everything. Oh, damn! Why did they have to come back?"

"Button me up," she said turning her back and dropping the conversation as if it had never happened.

Jonah fumbled with the buttons and when he finished, he kissed the nape of her neck. She shuddered and moved away.

"None of that. Not with your family downstairs. Besides, I have to make my husband breakfast." She moved to the ladder.

"Wait! I'll go down first so I can make sure you don't fall." Jonah swung onto the ladder and started down. "Now hold onto the side and put your foot on the rung. Now are you holding on tightly?"

"Yes."

"Good," he continued. "Now I'm going to run my hand up and down your leg," he said in a whisper, "and look up your dress!"

"Don't you dare, Jonah Chernov. Don't you dare!"

"I'm sorry we're back," said Sarah ingeniously as she tossed another log into the stove and slammed the door. "Police are searching houses and I don't want anyone going through my things without me being there."

"Leah and I are here," he protested, "and we'd make sure nothing was taken."

"Will you listen to your son, Reuben? He'd make sure nothing was taken. A lot you'd be able to do," and she dumped a mountain of spoons and forks on the table. "Leah dear, set the table."

Jonah's face flushed from embarrassment. How could she speak like that to him and in front of his wife. He looked at Leah whose face spoke both of her annoyance at the family's return and of her resentment at being ordered to set the table as if she were a nobody. Jonah also read the silent expectation there for him to say something. He felt like a juggler who was suddenly made to juggle his own feelings, Leah's expectations, his mother's manner and his own fears all at the same time and do it in such a way that he would not brand himself inept. He knew immediately he could not win and he would have to choose whose feelings and whose expectations would be satisfied. In any case, he would lose.

"Mama," he said finally forcing himself to speak before the demand in Leah's eyes burned through him. "You said Leah and I could be alone. Besides, Leah was going to make me breakfast." He looked over to Leah in the hope that her face would speak approval, but her eyes spoke only of her exasperation. He did not know that what he was doing was displeasing her.

Sarah attacked him with a barrage of information.

"Myer Putinsky was murdered last night during your wedding and your father and I were the last ones to talk to him.

Mark my words that someone will tell the police that we argued with him and threw him out. You mark my words. Leah, the milk dishes are over the sink and remember that I took the spoons and forks for milk from that drawer. You'll be good enough not to mix them."

Sarah took a cast iron pan and put it on the stove and called for Dora to break the eggs. Leah stood near the table, her fingers resting on it. She did not move. Jonah felt his jaw tighten.

"But, Mama. You're not letting us have our time together as you promised." He looked again at Leah, who remained solid. What was he doing wrong? He looked helplessly at Reuben.

"Sarah," Reuben interjected. "Jonah has a nice idea. What would be bad if Leah made breakfast? Be a guest in your own kitchen."

Sarah was not convinced, as she was never convinced when Reuben tried to dissuade her from her chosen course, but she stopped breaking the eggs and took off her apron.

"Now make sure there is no blood in the yolks."

Leah moved to the sink and stopped.

"I'm going to the toilet." Her voice shook. Jonah crossed the room and opened the rear door. The goat stuck its face in as Leah swept past. Jonah followed and took her by the arm. She pulled angrily away.

"Leah, I'm sorry. I didn't know they'd be back."

"Being back is only a small part of this, Jonah. The smallest part!" She looked at him. "You don't even know what's bothering me do you? You don't see anything except that they're back!" She paused again and studied the confusion on his face. She put her hand on the outhouse door.

Jonah stood in the center of the yard and looked at the shed and then back to the house. Things were different and they were not really different. To act for Leah was to offend his mother, and not to offend his mother was to be judged by Leah. He was caught no matter what. Things had changed, and things had remained the same.

He had only one choice. He would tell his mother that if she and the rest of the family did not leave, he and Leah would. Yes, that is what he would say. He stood facing the back door of the house and felt his stomach lurch into his throat. He swallowed hard and opened the door. His mother had resumed cracking the eggs.

"Mama, you said Leah could make breakfast."

"Your father said that. What should I do? Should I let broken eggs stand? Leah can make breakfast another day. I'm nervous. Leave me alone."

Jonah swallowed again and paused.

"Mama, I want you and everyone to go back to Zedde's house. You promised that Leah and I could be alone."

"So this is what your new wife puts you up to? Another enemy I have in my house?"

"Leah didn't say anything to me. She didn't tell me what to say. Why can't you imagine that I can think for myself?"

"I know you better than you know yourself, my dear son," she retorted sarcastically, "so don't you compound your disrespect with a lie and don't think I'll forget this either."

The vision of Sarah confronting Leah frightened him and he became overwhelmed by it.

"Please believe me," he pleaded. "Leah didn't say anything and please don't accuse her of doing something she didn't do."

"See, that proves it. She put you up to it. I know you well enough to know that you would never tell your mother or father to get out of their own house."

"I didn't say it that way. Why don't you understand the situation? Leah and I just want to be alone. That's all I'm saying."

"Go see where your father is, and then have your eggs."

"I don't want any eggs. I don't want anything except a little understanding."

"Understanding you want? Understanding? Then understand this. Putinsky was murdered on his way home from your wedding. Things like murder upset the balance in the town. Everyone is being questioned. Everyone is being searched. Everyone is a suspect and you worry about not having your privacy?" She ran to the table and stood there weeping into her apron. Reuben came through the door, paused, and rushed to her.

"Sarah, Sarah, don't cry and don't be afraid," he said softly. Jonah sat next to her and put a hand on her shoulder.

"Don't be afraid, Mama. Nothing will happen. We don't have anything to do with Putinsky. So he came to the wedding. No one can suspect us for that."

"People saw me and your father fighting with him. They'll find someone who will accuse us. For money or a favor, some would sell their children."

Leah came into the room and was startled at the sight. How was it possible for two men to be comforting this woman when it was she who had had her wedding morning interrupted, and it was she who had been treated as if she were a servant? She drew her conclusions from the scene and moved to the stove. Jonah felt cold and uneasy with her silence. Normally, he welcomed silence but this silence was not a good silence. Still, he sat there holding his mother's hand all the while looking at his hurt and angry bride.

"Let me help you Leah," he said when the silence became unbearable. He took the plates. She avoided his eyes, and again he felt as if he had done something wrong. Should he have gone to her immediately? Should he not have comforted his mother? His father was there to do that.

Sarah wiped her eyes with the apron and waved Reuben away.

"I'm all right now. I'll be all right. Zeena, go help Leah. Tell her where things are and don't think your responsibilities end because there are two more hands."

Jonah saw Leah tighten. Seconds passed.

"I am fully aware of how to move around a kitchen, Mrs. Chernov," said Leah, filling the silence that she felt should have been taken up by Jonah's response to his mother. "I, too, come from a kosher home, and all you have to do is tell me once where something is and you will never have a problem from me." She was very careful of her voice, monitoring her tone and inflection so as to give no hint of the underlying feelings at work within her.

"I know where you come from Leah, but I also know that young girls sometimes do not give the greatest of care to the old ways."

"Don't worry, Mama," said Zeena who knew exactly for whom her mother's words were meant. "I won't pollute Leah," she said sarcastically.

"Mama," interrupted Jonah who sensed the potential for a new conflict.

The door burst open. Ruth ran in with the news that the constable and two of his officers were coming up the road.

"Oh, my God," she exclaimed standing suddenly. "Quick the candle sticks and the spice box. Quickly Dora."

Sarah opened the cold side of the stove and thrust the treasures inside. She took off her earrings and bracelet and held out her hand for Reuben's watch. She poured these into her bosom. Then she thrust wood in front of the silver already in the stove and moved the boiling pot of water to the cold side so that side appeared to be hot. How often this ritual had been undertaken. Each time the tax man came it happened. Each time Putinsky came it happened, and for each search it happened. Each time they were helpless to do anything but to try to protect their few belongings.

"Now sit down everyone as if nothing was doing. Ruth come away from the window. They'll be here soon enough. Jonah, make sure the goat and chickens are in the barn and tie the goat behind the hay. They don't need to know we have a goat."

"Let Dora tie up the goat. I'm not leaving."

"Dora, go tie up the goat and come back immediately."

As the back door closed the front door shook. Reuben motioned for them to be quiet and limped over to the door and opened it. The constable and two young men stood there, each with a truncheon dangling from his belt.

"Mr.Chernov," the constable began. "I regret to disturb you, but I'm sure you've heard that Mr. Putinsky was murdered." His voice was routine and his apology insincere.

Reuben stepped back as the constable stepped over the sill into the front room followed by the two others. The constable surveyed the room and fingered the back of one of the chairs.

"You live better than most," he said dryly.

"Not better than Putinsky," retorted Sarah and immediately regretted her words.

"Ah, yes Putinsky. It would seem that you did not like the man."

Sarah was still recovering from her misjudgment and thought better of her next response.

"What do you want with us?" she asked nervously.

"We're doing a routine check of the district in the hope that perhaps someone who attended your son's wedding might have seen something." He looked around the room. "You knew Putinsky. You were seen talking to him."

"Everyone knew Putinsky," Sarah affirmed. "So what does that matter?"

Reuben hushed her, not because of her assertion, but because her tone might trigger in the constable some reckless response. The constable continued to scan the household goods and scrutinize the faces of the family.

"You have a lot of books," he said as he ran his finger over the worn bindings. You even have books in Russian. That's good. Good Russian people should have good Russian books. All of you Jews have books, but few have books in Russian. Things would be better for you Jews if you tried to be more Russian and did not keep only your own ways." He looked at the family for a response.

"Do you ask the peasants if they have copies of Jewish books also, or are they above suspicion and not searched."

The constable looked at Zeena and smiled briefly.

"The peasants were born Russian."

"I was born Russian and I am as Russian as they!"

"That may be true, young lady, but you are not really Russian."

"Maybe if I were illiterate and got drunk more often you'd think me more Russian?"

"Zeena be silent!" Reuben shouted.

The constable laughed. "No, no Mr. Chernov. It is interesting that your women are clever and can argue. I must admit our peasant women can argue, but they are not clever. He fingered more volumes. Who taught you to read Polish and German, Mr. Chernov?" he continued in a voice more inquisitive than hostile.

The constable had been taught that these people were parasites living off the backbreaking work of the peasants. Yet in his day to day movement through the town, he had seen their efforts to make a living from almost nothing. He had seen their struggle to survive and he had seen most deal honesty with the peasants. But he had been taught to hate them for their history, for their faith, and for their clannishness. Even as he saw the daily reality of these people, he did not choose to, or could not choose to, overcome the teachings of his own people or church. They remained a curiosity for him, especially for clinging to a way of life that kept them in constant danger and subjugation. He continued moving around the room, but avoided looking at any one of them directly, lest he establish their humanity and challenge his education.

"My father taught me to read and I was a student until the laws were passed that excluded me. Then I taught myself," Reuben replied.

"And I suppose this is your son and you taught him to read too?"

"Yes, and I also taught my daughters to read."

The constable raised an eyebrow and looked past Reuben to the loft and motioned one of the men to climb it. He motioned the other to the two back bedrooms. Dora returned and moved silently to the protective arm of her mother.

"What are you looking for?" asked Reuben.

"A match to a knife that we took out of Putinsky. Is this the bride?" He looked deeply at Leah. "I had a daughter with such hair color. My daughter was about your age when I lost her."

He reached out to touch Leah's face, but his hand hovered in the air near her cheek.

Jonah felt a flush rise to his face and he stepped slightly in front of her in a gesture of protection.

"Ah," said the constable, "the young bridegroom moves to defend his woman. That's good. That's very good." He laughed.

The constable's laugh fell on Jonah like an anvil and added to the trembling and weakness he felt. He was frightened and filled with shame at his fear.

"Your son was not in the army," he said suddenly as he turned to Reuben. "You were paying Putinsky, weren't you?"

"What does he mean, Mama?" whispered Jonah.

"Nothing, I'll tell you later." Sarah looked at the constable. "A lot of people pay Putinsky and a lot wanted him dead."

"Were you among those people?"

"We do not wish any man dead," said Reuben. "We finished paying Putinsky. We had nothing to gain from his death."

"You know it's illegal to buy off conscription," he said.

"Tell Putinsky and the town council. The council winks when there is money to be made. If we are guilty, so are they," Sarah shot back.

"You have a point," he said again, moving around them into the kitchen area. "I see you were about to have breakfast. These little rolls . . ." he said picking one up and breaking it in half. "You don't mind if I . . ." and he filled his mouth. "You use eggs to get them yellow don't you? Very expensive rolls." His eyes scanned the table and rested on the crock. "Is this honey?" he exclaimed with the excitement of a child, and his whole manner changed.

Sarah moved forward slightly to rescue the treasure, but Reuben caught her skirt quickly and motioned for her to say nothing. The constable opened the small crock, scrutinized the contents and dipped the broken roll into the meager remains. He exclaimed his satisfaction as he chewed and licked his lips. Then he poked the other half of the roll around until it absorbed the last bit of golden liquid. He closed his eyes and placed it on his tongue. The family watched in silent resentment as the constable slowly ran his tongue over his lips again.

"You must be doing well in the tailor business, Mr. Chernov. Honey is not found in poor homes."

"It was a wedding gift from a relative in Odessa. They sent it for the bride and groom's pleasure."

"A very nice gift," he said ignoring her subtle attack. "Where do you keep your knives?"

Sarah moved to the counter and pulled open one drawer and then the other. "There are my knives."

The constable took out one of the knives and turned it around in his hand.

"Putinsky was killed with a knife very like this one."

"There are a thousand knives like that one in Krivoser," said Sarah, "and besides, if Putinsky was murdered with a knife like that one, you eliminate all Jews as suspects because that type of knife is used for dairy products only. No Jew would use it to cut into meat."

Sarah had not intended that to be a joke, but Zeena laughed. Reuben lowered his eyes and sighed.

"Most people here have knives like that," she continued. "They are all over the market place. Is every one who owns a knife like that a suspect?"

"Oh, no, Mrs. Chernov. Only the owner of the one we took out of Putinsky's stomach. Sooner or later we will find the owner of the knife and when we do, we shall perhaps find our killer. You're a nice family," he continued in a more hospitable tone. "You work hard and you don't cause trouble. I'm sure that if you hear of anything that will help us, you will tell us. Murder is such an ugly business."

One of the men approached him as the other descended the ladder and whispered something in the constable's ear. They laughed hoarsely together and Jonah felt the blood rise to his face.

"I bid you a good day," he said touching his finger to his cap. Then he moved to Leah. "I called my little girl Natasha after her

mother. You look like her. She was also little. What is your name?"
he asked softly.

"Leah," she said lowering her eyes.

"You're a lucky man to have such a one as she," he said looking
at Jonah, as he turned and left, followed by the two others.

The family stood silently for a moment, each feeling the tension in his own way. They watched the door close. Each sighed
relief, but the sigh did not ease the moment.

"Why did you say that about the knife?" Reuben said in a
tone that was close to anger.

"I said it because when I counted the knives last night, one
like that was missing. Is that a good reason?"

"I'm going to the shop," said Reuben. "They won't be back
here." Sarah could feel his body shake as he kissed her good-by.

Breakfast was eaten in silence. At one point Jonah questioned
his mother about Putinsky, but she waved him off and told him
she was too upset to talk. The dishes were cleared while Sarah
prepared the midday meals for her husband and father and instructed Zeena and Dora to deliver them. Then she went into the
back room, closed the door, and cried into the pillow so she could
not be heard.

Leah climbed the ladder to the loft. Jonah followed. The room
had been thoroughly searched. Books lay here and there and drawers
remained partially opened. The wedding sheet lay crumpled on
the floor. Leah picked it up and turned to Jonah. Tears sat on the
rims of her eye lids.

"Look, this is what they laughed at!" and she threw the sheet
into the corner as if it had been defiled. Jonah took her in his arms
and patted her back.

"No, no," he said. "They didn't laugh at that. It must have
been something else."

"I know what they laughed at so don't try to make me think it
was something else." Her voice suddenly changed. "Jonah," she
said flatly, "I don't want to live here. I want to go back to Uncle
Issac or I want a place of our own."

The demand burned like sparks on his skin and he searched for some response that would satisfy her and not force a confrontation with his parents.

"But why? Today isn't a normal day. Murders don't happen every day and the police don't search every day. My mother isn't this upset every day. Please Leah, don't ask me. Let things quiet down a little."

"Please do this for me, Jonah!" She sat down on the bed and started to cry. "I know that if we stay, we will not be happy."

Jonah found himself suddenly watching the scene but not being part of it. His hand reached out in comfort, but he watched it being rejected. With Leah he had hoped he would never have to feel vulnerable and inadequate again, yet that was what he was feeling now. Things were different and things were not different. It was wrong for her to make this demand on him and he resented it. "Leah, let me think. Everything is happening so fast. Please don't cry. I'll talk to Mama about how she speaks to you."

"It's not only how she speaks to me. This is her house. What's mine? It's not going to be good here. I feel it. I know it. Jonah, if you want me to be happy, please tell them we'll be going to my uncle. Your father will understand. He'll help us."

"This isn't the way I wanted it, Leah," he said in a voice close to tears. "It's not the way it's supposed to be." His stomach was in a knot. He had nothing else to say to her other than he would tell them that they would leave, but he knew even as he heard himself promise, he did not know how he would do it. But one thing he did know was that his mother would blame his wife and accuse him of not having a backbone. And he knew that he would have to speak in Leah's defense and that there would be no way to convince his mother that he had also made the decision to go. Now he had to think and figure out how to maintain his balance.

"Leah, I'm going to the shop," he said suddenly. "I need to think and I need to talk to Papa. Come later so we can have lunch together and we can talk."

He did not look at her. He sighed deeply and kissed her cheek.

She sat impassively on the bed and did not respond with a kiss.

"We were supposed to be alone for a few days Jonah, and you're going to the shop and leaving me here with her?"

"Leah, if I am going to do as you ask, I need time to think about how I can do it without hurting my parents. I have to talk to Papa. He'll help us."

"I don't know why you just can't go downstairs and tell her we're leaving. What are you afraid of Jonah? Just what are you afraid of?"

He heard the challenge fly at him and shatter against the wall. She could not possibly understand the balances in his life and how he maintained them.

CHAPTER 7

Leah worked in the kitchen that morning in silence, and when she had finished with the tasks that were set for her by Sarah, she went back up to the loft. Jonah was right. Nothing was as it was supposed to be. She counted off the hours until she could be with him again and talk, because she did not understand his behavior and she did not understand his family. She might come to understand all in time, but she would not come to it in Sarah Chernov's house.

It was near midmorning when Zeena called to her to help bring the lunch baskets to town. Leah was pleased to have a reason to leave and was eager to be with someone who might be sympathetic to her feelings.

They walked without speaking at first. The unseasonable warmth delighted Leah and she turned her face to the sun. It had rained sometime during the night and the road, scarred into little valleys and hills from the endless train of cart wheels moving to the market, held pools of standing water that soiled and weighed down the hems of their skirts.

"Watch where you're walking," cautioned Zeena, "or you'll step in a pile of dung."

Leah stopped herself abruptly from taking another step and looked down. She laughed her relief.

"You'll always have to watch your step around here," said Zeena, with a tone in her caution that spoke of moments beyond the present.

Leah heard the caution clearly and took it as an invitation from Zeena to join her as an ally in the perpetual war she waged against her mother. Leah was weary of the tensions and wished them over. She declined the invitation and changed the subject.

"It's a pretty day," she said, realizing that she would have to say something, "and the sun feels good."

"It's never a pretty day here," retorted Zeena, somewhat annoyed that Leah chose to remain aloof from the fray.

Leah continued in silence.

"I'm sorry," said Zeena after a moment. "You've had enough unpleasantness for one day."

Leah welcomed Zeena's apology.

"You can dislike something and still recognize good in it," Leah said softly. "A thing can have different faces."

"Leah, you will have to understand that I do not like this place and I don't want to see any good in it," Zeena continued. "For me, this place has only one face, and it's a forlorn, dried out old hag who'll damn you for having an idea different from what has always been, and will curse you for wanting to be more than what its tradition has set out for you. This place sucks out your life and takes and takes and takes until there's nothing left to take. Then it kills you, and after you're dead, praises you for becoming nothing. This place is a coffin for anyone who has a dream."

Leah had never heard such talk, and she felt an unseen wedge come between them. Certainly she had not sensed anything of this in Jonah. Jonah also spoke of dreams and she wondered if they were the same.

"What do you dream of Zeena?" she asked simply.

"I don't dream any more," Zeena said quickly, as if she knew the question that would follow, and was prepared. "Children dream. I plan."

"Then what do you plan?" Leah asked slightly annoyed.

Zeena did not speak immediately, but smiled slightly. "I plan how to get out of this place. We're going . . ." Zeena caught herself and began again. "I'm going to find a place where I won't have the burdens of this broken down hell. I'm going to find a place where I can move into the world and become someone and never again be told who or what I can be or where I might go or what I can say."

Zeena's step slowed and she hesitated a moment as if making a decision about the safety of her new sister. Zeena had no confidants except Jonah, and even he did not know of the young man whom she secretly loved.

They moved to the bridge. The wooden planks groaned under the ox cart ahead. An old man sat fishing with his grandson, their legs dangling over the side. Mothers and daughters stood or kneeled on the bank of the rushing stream beating nightshirts and undergarments with wooden paddles while others waded deeper to rinse and wring and rinse again. The rivulet swept under them, turned and widened and deepened where they could not see, and fed the lakes that took barges of produce to the train bound for Kiev.

The two slowed their pace, falling in behind a cart loaded with vats of milk and sacks of cheese dangling on ropes. The planks rose and fell to the step of the lumbering ox, and that rhythm became their own until the cart rolled off the rickety bridge. At that point, the road widened and moved between rows of wooden houses that huddled together like gossips. Great tree trunks, perhaps a century ago, had been floated to Krivozer from somewhere far away and had been shaped and stood up to hold overhanging roofs that rested heavily and precariously on cross beams. Shutters, pieced together from scraps, hung loosely on horizontal planked walls wanting pitch and lime. Boulders, too great to move, sat solidly in contrast to the houses that stood behind them, and bed clothes were laid across these rocks to dry in the morning sun. Tormented by little children in tattered clothing, chickens scurried in and out of dark doorways. The housewives on their makeshift balconies called to one another as they hung clothes to dry while men in carts below, exhorted them to buy their fresh vegetables or housewares at bargain prices. More and more people moved from the side streets into the thoroughfare that led from the bridge to the market. The slowly moving line came to a halt. A cart up ahead had thrown a wheel.

"Why don't they move?" complained Zeena. "This street sickens me. Look at these filthy brats and those fat old hags hanging their gray wash. I tell you Leah, I'm getting out of here, and if you are smart, you'll make Jonah get you out of here, too."

Zeena pulled her shawl tighter around her shoulders as if shielding herself from the presence of those near her who were haggard, old and illiterate. It was, to her, as if their very existence could in some way imprint itself on her being and become part of her.

"What's going on up there? Why can't we move?" Zeena called to a man standing on top of his wagon. Her voice choked with fear as more and more people wedged their way into the narrow street.

Leah saw the strange transformation in Zeena's face. It was more than a reflection of the disdain for her surroundings. It was a genuine horror caused by the mob and the overwhelming stench of their unwashed bodies mixing with the animal dung that lay in the road. Leah took her hand and pulled her off to the side.

"Zeena, you look sick. Are you all right?"

"I'll be all right. I get like this in crowds sometimes. My chest tightens up and I just can't breathe when they get this close. I'll be better as soon as they start to move. It's like I'm being invaded and I lose myself." She was flushed and beads of perspiration stood on her brow and upper lip.

Leah maneuvered her to a bench and called to a woman on a balcony.

"What's going on? Why can't we move?"

"The police are searching and asking questions," she called back.

Leah touched Zeena's cheek. It was cool and the color was returning to her face. She stood, and together they moved a few steps and waited again.

A woman, not much older than Sarah, stood near them in silence, her face broad and lined. She looked straight ahead at nothing, oblivious to the mud in which she stood, and oblivious to the young girls who were suddenly seized by her utter despondency. The woman's gray skirt hung mid ankle under a soiled, patched, threadbare apron. The sweater covering her large frame had, perhaps, once been green, but appeared brown. Around her shoulders limply hung a tattered, fringed shawl. She was weather worn and gray herself and the cracked skin of her jowls pressed down upon the sides of her mouth forming a perpetual frown. She must have sensed at some point the girls staring at her for she slowly, like a heavy statue being moved by unseen hands, turned and looked at them through empty eyes. The six eyes met briefly. Leah shuttered and understood Zeena's fear. The woman turned away slowly and pulled the frayed shawl up against her face in a protective gesture as if whatever dignity she still retained would not permit such an intrusion.

The specter of what life might be, reared up from the uncertain future like a snake and shook them both. In that silent space of understanding and resolve, they formed a bond and sealed it with the anxious laughter young girls laugh to break tension and move into other moments. But Zeena would not let the moment pass, not when someone had finally understood what she had known and lived with for so long.

"That woman," Zeena said. "You saw her. You felt it. I saw you feel it. Now you see what this place can do to a person. All she ever got from this place was starvation and misery and somewhere in there is some man who cared more about his tradition and his God than he did about his wife. You're looking at what a woman trapped in this place becomes."

While Leah understood Zeena's fear and vision, she did not feel herself trapped, even after considering the events of the morning. She was married to a good man, a man who would never let life turn his wife into such a person as the one they saw.

"Your mother doesn't look like that and neither do any of the women I know," she replied. "A woman doesn't have to become that. Not every life leads to becoming like that. You're frightening yourself by what might be and you're frightening me also. If that woman wasn't here she'd be somewhere else and that's all you can really say.

Her life has been hard. Maybe somewhere else it would have been different and maybe not."

"If I ever saw that happening to me I'd kill myself."

"Don't say such things like that, Zeena. You deny God's will when you talk of killing yourself."

"Oh you are a perfect match for my brother," she said turning on her scornfully. "The two of you pretend the reality you live in doesn't exist, and when you finally see through your fog and don't like what you see, you conjure up a nonsense called 'God's will' as an explanation. I don't believe that any God has anything to do with what goes on here. I ask you Leah, does God actually take pains to create dirty, starving people?" Zeena's question was rhetorical. "That woman wasn't created by any God. She was created by her husband and tradition. This town helped also and so does the hatred dear Mother Russia lavishes on us for refusing to give up this gracious God of yours."

"Now you sound like one of those anarchists who yell their own brand of hatred," Leah said. She was overwhelmed by Zeena's open blasphemy and anger.

"My hatred?" Zeena said incredulously. "Leah, the world is filled with hatred. I'm only pointing it out." Zeena felt a familiar rush of heat throughout her body. "The world thrives on hatred and we are packed into these dirty towns by the haters so we will be available whenever they need someone to blame for the destruction they cause. We are like pieces of fruit waiting to be plucked by politicians for their own ends. But the real horror is that when we are blamed, and we are hurt and bleeding, no one in the world cares or lifts a finger to help us. Destruction can fall upon us at any moment and the hypocrites of the world just yawn and close their eyes. No one should know that better than you."

Leah walked along in silence. She was absorbed in the vague, painful memory that Zeena's words had conjured up of when her own parents were murdered, and she was also trying to understand a very ugly reality that Zeena seemed to live with daily.

The line of carts twisted in and out and finally the cart in front of them was stopped. A young officer in a short, belted jacket with epaulets, jumped onto the cart. Another ordered the driver off and searched him. The cart rolled into the market square. The two policeman swaggered to the two girls slowly. Leah moved a step backward.

"And what do we have here?" said one to the other, both fingers locked around his belt. "Perhaps they are part of the conspiracy. What do you think?" His eyes laughed as he picked up the cloth covering Leah's basket and inspected the lunch she had prepared for Jonah. She looked away, trembling. He gave a hoarse laugh and put his finger under her chin and turned her face towards his. She feared to resist and did not open her eyes.

"Ah, this is a pretty one," he said. "With this one . . ."

"I am a married woman," Leah said softly, as if all the shame she felt at being touched by this stranger was expressed in that simple statement.

"Leave her alone," interrupted Zeena, sensing her sister- in-law's embarrassment. "What do we know of conspiracy and murder and knives? Do you think we'd kill someone and then go out shopping?"

Her ploy had worked. The officer moved from Leah and faced her.

"Ah, this one has spirit and is beautiful, also. She also knows something because we didn't say anything about murder or knives. Maybe we should take them in for further questioning."

"How about Yavna's tavern?" laughed the other.

"How about leaving these young ladies alone," said the constable who had come up behind them. He looked at Zeena briefly and then at Leah. The two policemen laughed again and moved on. The constable touched his finger to his hat and smiled at Leah before disappearing into the crowd.

"See," said Zeena, jumping on the moment to underscore the earlier conversation. "That's exactly what I mean. At any moment anyone can be stopped, and searched and who knows what. No one is safe here!"

They moved into the market square, relieved to be out of the press of people. On all sides, vendors and shop keepers, street urchins and beggars exhorted them to tarry a moment here, inspect a garment there, or see the wonderful produce in this carton or that basket. Everywhere, pools of muddy water lay caught in crevices and depressions that had been etched by the wear of ox carts and centuries of burden. The market was like a giant wheel, with each vendor setting out his wares on the line of the imaginary spokes that were established long ago by some ancient plan.

It was a place where the disenfranchised of both peasant and Jewish cultures mixed freely and where their invisible outer electrons bonded briefly, forming unlikely structures. Everywhere, the heat of transactions moved the atoms faster and faster, so the frenetic moment to moment encounters were too quick and too fleeting to make anything but temporary and uneasy bonds.

The peasants looked upon the Jews with a mixture of awe and suspicion and these feelings gave birth to envy and hatred. The Jews could read and compute and had facility with learning and inventiveness. These omnipresent strangers, these people who spoke one language to each other, prayed in a second and negotiated in the market in a third, maintained unseen bonds that reached out to one another and back into the shadows of centuries long past. The peasants could not understand the Jew's unwillingness to give up their strange ways, their unseen God and their ancient law and languages. The Jews stood apart, and their very separateness as a people was interpreted as a condemnation that all other ways but their ways were meaningless and futile. Beyond these very real disturbances lay the very practical realities of daily living. The Jews were middlemen and tradesmen and in a position to cheat the peasants out of what little the great absentee landholders allowed them to keep for their back breaking work.

The peasants were also viewed with awe and suspicion and out of both, fear. They were powerful in their numbers, intense and overt in their passions, and robust from work in the fields. They could wrest sustenance from the land as if by magic. Yet they were illiterate and easily led by the clergy and government agents who whipped them into a frenzy when the economic or political climate needed a scapegoat.

Through the uneasy truce, a balance was maintained.

Dora had gone to town earlier and by the time Leah and Zeena arrived at Reuben's shop, she and Zedde had been working for hours in the shop across the street.

"Zeena just came with Leah," she said looking up.

Zedde continued the careful winding of a customer's watch.

"Doraleh, please get me the box with the eye glasses. These aren't working so good."

He removed the glasses from his grey eyes and wiped tears from their corners. Dora watched him. Wisps of straight white hair fell upon his wrinkled brow like strands of corn silk, and she thought of the many times she sat on his lap when she was little and twisted and curled them to his mild protests. They were silver then. Now they were white. So, too, the full beard that lay softly upon his chest. It was not right that such a man had to grow old and feeble and bent. His eyes still had the laughter of a rascal youth though these same eyes were quickly losing their ability to see.

Dora carefully placed the fly wheel she held in a tweezer into the watch casing and reached for the box of glasses. Zedde tried one pair and then another.

"My eyes are getting worse. Soon only you will be able to fix the watches."

"I'm not good enough yet," she said simply.

Zedde looked at his granddaughter, smiled, and scratched his beard. "I'll tell you something about yourself. You only think you're not good enough. But I see you work and I see you. You know something my little Dora, you're smarter than the whole family put together. You have a good head for business and you learn quickly. You believe me. You're good enough. You'll break plenty watches, but you learn plenty too. You'll also be a good catch. Not many girls have a trade."

Dora accepted his praise modestly, as she did all things.

"Doraleh," he said standing up slowly for what seemed to her no apparent reason. "Close the shutters. I want to show you something. Pull the shade on the door and lock it." He shuffled to the rear of the shop and locked that door also. He motioned her to follow. Dora smiled a small smile at his secrecy, and moved to the back counter.

"I'm getting old, my little Dora," he said taking her face in his hands gently, "and when I die, I want you to have the shop and the tools and the stock. It will make you a living. And as long as you have skills and tools, you can live. You're a good girl. You listen and you don't talk too much. You do what you're told. You're the best from all of them."

Dora started to speak, but he put his hand over her lips. "Now you listen to me. You always come to the shop after I open it. You've never seen where I keep the tools or the stock of good watches. The watches that hang here all day are just samples. They're made of tin and only coated so they look like gold and silver. They are worth nothing. These others are just old and broken and are not worth even fixing. I let them hang so people think I have a lot of work. That gives them the idea that I'm a good watchmaker," and he chuckled to himself. "Always remember people need to think other people trust you. That lets them trust you, too."

Dora watched him wondering why he had taken her over to the rear wall.

"Now Doraleh, come over here behind the counter and reach under. Feel for a little lever. You feel it? Good. Now give a pull." His eyes danced like a child's might in sharing a secret with a friend. "Even your mother doesn't know about this. I'll tell you, Doraleh, your mother talks too much and she can't keep a secret either." He put his hands to his own lips which meant she was not to tell her mother what he said about her.

Dora gave a tug on the lever and heard a click. She turned quickly and her eyes widened. Her grandfather giggled again like a mischievous spirit. She scanned the wall where the broken watches hung. They were swaying slightly. Something had moved them.

Zedde took her hand and placed it on the edge of the wall and pulled it back. A piece of the wall gave way and opened like a door. She was startled. A small closet, wide enough for both of them, was hidden behind the wall, and beautiful silver and gold watches hung silently on all sides. Dora stared wide eyed as Zedde continued.

"Now this is where I keep the tools. A person can't work without tools so never leave them out at night. You must always put them in here. Now when somebody comes to the shop for a new watch, you show them the sample ones on the wall. You tell them the prices, and tell them it will take a couple of days for the watch to come from the city. They like it when they think the watch has to be special ordered for them. It makes them feel special too. Then, on the morning they come for the watch, you lock the door behind you, and before you pull up the shades, you take out the watch. Remember, never open the closet when anyone is in the shop. Good Doraleh? You understand?"

Dora nodded. He took both her hands and looked hard at her. "Tell no one what I've told you. Secrecy is the only way you'll keep what you have. The only secret kept is the one that only one person knows. Now you close the door and show me how to open it."

Dora did as she was asked and Zedde reopened the shutters. She looked at him as he moved slowly to his seat by the window and sat down. She came up behind him and kissed him on his head.

Alexi Malinovitch stood on the corner of the market square watching people go in and out of Reuben Chernov's tailor shop. He had not as yet accomplished what he had come to do. The murder of Putinsky was a spontaneous act.

He had come to the Ukraine to ferret out rebellion, never imagining that his return to his old home would conjure up the dead specters of his aborted life. What he thought was dead, was in truth, only dormant, and what he believed he had hardened himself to, did, in fact, reach out over the dark years of his life to touch his being with searing memories and anguished longings.

He saw himself reflected in the store front glass, magically superimposed on the scene within, and he imagined himself as he might have been. His image stood between the father and his son, a transparency of a yearning ghost. He, too, would have had a son. He, too, would have brought him to the marriage canopy. He, too, would have had his name continue. All the might have beens crowded around and mocked him and he saw himself again being dragged, bleeding to the baptismal font. Again, the tormenting thought that had he not succumbed to the beatings and starvation, he might have returned here after his ordeal to also become a father and husband. He, too, might have given something of value to the world instead of the pain and death that accompanied his footsteps. Again, as in the past, he considered what he had thrown away for a guarantee of warmth and food. Again, as in the past, he tormented himself by weighing his loss against his gain. He had to survive, and survival came to him with a dash of water and his lips on a painted picture. He would not be killed. Yet now, some thirty five years later, that unhappy child that yet lived in him and still yearned, continued to quietly push its tears up behind the grown man's eyes and overcome him with such shame that he still could not bring himself to stand before his parents though he ached to do so. They would see the blood on his hands and they would see in his eyes how he had violated the Commandments and blasphemed the word of God by ignoring the anguished pleas of those he condemned to torture and death. In dreams he still heard their pleas, and his own parents would also hear their voices and curse him and the day they gave him life. Others had been assaulted and brutalized, beaten, exposed and ridiculed. They did not break. And how could he explain away the years that he had allowed them to live in tortured silence and grief? How could he explain why he had not returned before there was blood on his hands? Better he remain dead.

He watched his image hover between the father and the son and he saw it beckon. Something deep within his being stirred, reached out and became one with the reflection in the glass. He felt himself move. Something secret, something within him with an intent and will of its own, a secret self that drew sustenance from the air and earth he breathed here long ago, willed him involuntarily towards the shop and recalled him to this life.

"Jonah, why don't you just come out and say what you have to say." Reuben put down the bolt of cloth and looked at his son over his spectacles. "Why you came in this morning, I don't know. And as far as doing any work, you haven't done a thing. So say what you have to say and either get on with your work or go back to your bride."

Reuben's voice was gentle, but firm. Jonah knew he could not put off the problem any longer.

"Papa," he began slowly. "Leah, is not happy. I mean Leah and I are not happy living in the loft." He waited.

"So what are you saying, Jonah? Are you just telling me you and Leah are not happy, or are you telling me that you want to leave?"

Jonah hesitated. He did not want to leave. It was Leah who wanted to leave, but he did not want to give his father the impression that he was not in control.

"I do not want to leave, but Leah does and I don't know how to balance her need and my feelings."

Reuben put his hand to his mouth and moved his fingers across his lips.

"Your Mama will not be happy," he said.

"I know, Papa, so what am I to do? If I say we go, I hurt and anger Mama, and if I say we stay, I hurt and anger Leah. So what am I to do?"

Reuben looked at his son as he had when Jonah spoke of his fears of being married. It saddened him that such conflict had slithered into his life so soon.

"The answer is simple. You are a husband now and your task is to protect your wife and do your best to make her happy. A man must always honor his parents, but he must always choose his

wife. Mama will not be happy, but Mama has been unhappy before. Maybe it's for the best. With the trouble she has with Zeena,
she doesn't need more trouble from you and Leah."

Reuben read his face.

"I see you don't like what I just said to you, Jonah. Well, I will
teach you a new lesson. As you try to protect your wife from the
pain and trouble of the outside world, you also attempt to protect
her from the pain and trouble her children knowingly or unknow-
ingly cause her. Though you may not see yourself as causing your
mother pain now, you do."

"I don't want to cause her or anyone pain."

"I know that, Jonah, but you are going to cause her pain and I
will have to deal with it. You must do what a husband must do,
and I must do what a husband must do."

"How will I tell Mama?" he asked.

"How you tell her is something that you will have to come up
with yourself." Reuben re-rolled the bolt of cloth and placed it
back on the shelf, put some pins into his mouth and took them
out again. He looked at his son. Perhaps Sarah was right. Perhaps
he had given Jonah too many dreams. Jonah did not see reality.

"Jonah," he began. "The world is not an easy place. There are
things we do not control. So much of what we find in life is chance
and so much is often caused by people and events over which we have
no control. Things change so quickly and everything can be taken
away for no reason." He took a breath, hoping his son was understanding his words. "This is Krivoser. This is Russia. This is the Tsar's
world. People like us are pawns and we are acted on because we do not
have power or friends in power. You think I taught myself to read and
write Russian and German because I have an international trade? You
don't think I would have liked to be a scholar? You don't think I
would have liked to sit all day in the House of Study and argue the
points of law? You don't think . . ." and he cut himself off mid-
sentence because nothing was being accomplished.

"Jonah, like Moses, we, too, are strangers in a strange land. We
have lived and died on this land for generations and we are still

kept strangers. Wherever we go, it is like this, and even when we rise above what we are allowed to be, we are pulled back down by some evil law. Jonah, you see our people standing idle because we are not permitted to work, and then we are called lazy by those who won't let us work. When women, like your mother, are forced to haggle for kopeks because all we have to live on are kopeks, we are called misers. We are forced to stay within certain towns and then we are hated for our clannishness. Those who keep us destitute, turn on us and hate us for what they have forced us to become."

Jonah sat silently.

"We are running low on black and gray wool," Reuben said. He closed the topic because the truth of his lesson was still as harsh and unchanging as when he learned it. He had not been able to make the world better for his son as his father could not make it better for him. "We'll have to go to the city."

Jonah retreated into himself, trying to understand what had just happened, when the small bell above the door announced a customer. Jonah stood and excused himself. He did not want to deal with a customer at that moment and moved to the back door.

Alexi Malinovitch stood solidly in the doorway.

"Good morning," Reuben said, looking at him over his glasses. "How might I be of help to you?"

The stranger peered deeply into his old friend's eyes for the slightest hint of recognition, but could discern none. There was a brief silence. The back door closed.

"Is there something I can do for you sir?" he repeated, taking a step closer to the man.

Malinovitch looked around the small shop, remembering how he and Reuben would dash under the table fleeing from the yard stick in old Mr. Chernov's hand.

"When did your father die?" he said suddenly. The question was as much a surprise to him as it was to Reuben.

"Do I know you?" Reuben asked, stepping around the corner of the table. His eyes narrowing as he scanned the lined face,

Reuben searched his memory for a friend who had moved. The image of Alta Mitvoy being carried away briefly imposed itself, but was quickly dismissed. Again, he squinted into his memory as one does to sharpen focus, and again to the stranger's face. But still the image of his long dead friend persisted. It was impossible, yet his eyes went wide with disbelief.

"Your eyes tell me you do not believe what you see my old friend."

Reuben slowly extended his finger and let it wave limply in the air as if waving it would help him formulate the words.

"Alta Mitvoy?" and his voice choked with tears. "Alta, Alta, is it you?"

He took Reuben's hand from the air and caressed it between his palms saying nothing. For the first time in so many years he was touching someone he had loved.

Reuben could not speak. He studied and searched the face through a tearful blur trying to read the answers to questions of a life that had disappeared so long ago.

"Do not ask," said Malinovitch. "I cannot stay. I should not have come. I should not be here."

"Where else should you be?" laughed Reuben with joy. "It's a miracle. It's a miracle God let your parents live to see you. Have you seen them?"

"This is not my world, my old friend. I do not know its people or its ways. I do not even know why I decided to let you know that I am still alive." He paused and took a breath. "I must remain dead to all," he said, "and you must promise me you will say nothing." He covered Reuben's hand with his own and held it there until Reuben's eyes acquiesced. Reuben heard the urgency and command in the man's voice and the pain and passion in his dark eyes frightened him.

"But surely your parents must know," he pleaded. "Let them at least know," and he sank to the bench under the burden of Alta Mitvoy's mandate of silence. Such a silence was impossible.

"Papa, are you all right?" said Jonah closing the door behind

him. Reuben had turned pale at the request and Jonah, not knowing what had transpired between the two men, was apprehensive.

"It is nothing. It is nothing. This is my son, Jonah," he said
staring into the past. "This is . . ." and he paused and looked at
Mitvoy for some response.

"I am Alexi Malinovitch," he said interrupting and extending
his hand. Jonah took it forcing a half smile, and the powerful figure, whose eyes seemed intense enough to pierce his soul, cradled
his hand as gently as if it were a small bird.

"Jonah, do me a favor," Reuben continued. "Put up some water for tea. I'd like a glass of tea."

Again, the fantasy enveloped Malinovitch like a mist, and he
saw himself as if he were Reuben, and this his own son; living
happily with a wife and family. Perhaps if he did stay. Perhaps if he
did reveal himself and come home. Could he? What would he be if
he did?

The door opened. The bell jingled impatiently.

"It's disgusting the way they treat you like you're something
less than human," Zeena said. "Papa, we were stopped and searched
as if we were the murderers."

Reuben got to his feet and moved toward the two girls.

"Zeena, Leah, I'd like you meet Mr. Malinovitch. This is my
daughter Zeena and my new daughter-in-law Leah. Mr.
Malinovitch is . . ."

"An old business acquaintance," Malinovitch added.

"You should have been there. They looked us over like we were
cattle," she continued, smiling an obligatory smile at the guest. "If
I were a man I would have hit them!"

"And what would you have done after that?" said Malinovitch,
laughing at her bravado.

"I don't know," she said after a short pause. "Run probably,"
and she laughed at her own foolishness. "But we have to do something, and you believe me that day is coming."

"Hush, Zeena. Mr. Malinovitch does not need a lesson in anarchy. Excuse her please," he said. "She picks up pamphlets in the streets. She listens to maniacs on street corners."

"She's a bright and pretty girl, this daughter of yours. How old are you child?"

Zeena looked at her father and wondered at the stranger's familiarity and ease.

"I am almost twenty," she said proudly. "Who are you?" she said in her abrupt way that most took as rudeness.

"I said I was an old business friend now living in St. Petersburg."

"St. Petersburg," she repeated. The words rang like a bell. "I saw a book with pictures once," and her eyes widened. "But Jews aren't allowed to live in St. Petersburg."

"Some are permitted, but I am not a Jew," he said flatly. Reuben froze.

"That's enough Zeena," cautioned her father.

"No, Reuben, she is pretty and quick as well." For a brief moment, the secret Alexi Malinovitch saw himself as he might have been years ago standing in this shop with his friend Reuben and flirting with two pretty girls who had come in by chance.

The silence became awkward. Zeena felt his eyes on her and felt the rush of heat flow from her cheeks down her face. She averted her own eyes, uncomfortable with the feeling and fascinated by the new sensation.

"Let me help you with Papa's tea," she said quickly, and moved towards the stove. Jonah looked up surprised as she brushed past him. Zeena never offered to help. He saw the disquiet in her face and the furtive glances she passed at the stranger.

Leah also looked at the stranger's face. There was a strange familiarity about him behind the well trimmed beard and mustache. The slant of the eye, the high forehead; perhaps the mouth. She, too, avoided his direct gaze, sensing an almost hypnotic power in this man's intensity and an awful emptiness in his black eyes.

"I must be going, Reuben," he said after a moment of having memorized them. "Jonah, Leah. I wish you both well and many good years." And, as he said this, he pressed into Leah's hand a fold of bank notes. "I was at your wedding last night. I believe it is appropriate to give a gift to the bride and groom. Use it for something important. And you," he said turning to Zeena. "Your father is correct. It is not healthy for a person in these times to publicly denounce the police or the government; Jew and non-Jew alike." He reached out and patted her cheek. "You're a beautiful, young woman. You're a very smart girl. Don't get in trouble with your talk."

The door opened suddenly. The constable and the two young officers who had stopped Zeena and Leah earlier, entered. The same helplessness took them as they looked at each other and waited. Jonah moved slowly towards Leah and stood in front of her.

"Ah," said the constable in his steady voice. "Again the bride-groom moves to defend his bride from the wicked policeman. That is good. That is very good."

The two younger men moved towards Reuben.

"Mr. Chernov," the constable continued. "It seems that you were the last person seen speaking to Mr. Putinsky before he was murdered."

"That's wrong," interrupted Zeena. "The last person to talk to Putinsky was the murderer, and my father is no murderer."

One of the soldiers lifted his hand to strike her, but Malinovitch grabbed it mid air, exerting enough pain to force the hand to go limp. The constable looked past Zeena and moved slowly towards the stranger.

"Do you know what I could do to you for touching one of my men?" he said, his eyes blazing with anger and his teeth clenched.

"Mr. Chernov did not kill your murdered man," he said dispassionately, his eyes forcing the constable to halt in his tracks.

"And who is this who will put himself against one of my witnesses?"

"Please do not get in trouble because of me," Reuben pleaded. "I'm sure there is nothing to worry about. Many people know I did not leave the wedding."

"Ah, yes, Chernov. But perhaps Putinsky was killed after the wedding."

"I was with my wife and children and father-in-law all night."

"And what if I can produce witnesses to swear you were not? But we will have to decide that truth at another time, won't we, Mr. Chernov. You must come with me."

Something in Jonah surged and he was caught between his fear of their power and his compulsion to do something to protect his father. Zeena had jumped to his defense while he stood by Leah. Now he had to act. His heart pounded and his perspiration went cold on his brow as he moved in front of Reuben.

"My father is innocent," he said, visibly shaking as he forced himself to look at the constable.

"Ah, now the bridegroom moves to defend his father. You are starting to weary me, bridegroom." He motioned to his men.

"May I speak with you constable?" interjected Malinovitch. The two policemen froze and looked at the constable for direction. The constable saw their response.

"I will take care of you later. I have not forgotten your arrogance."

"I don't think I made myself clear, constable," Malinovitch reiterated, barely moving his mouth.

"You must be a Zhid who doesn't care much for living." The anger rose in his face. The two young officers waited like guard dogs for their master's signal to attack, their hands moving to their truncheons. Zeena felt her knees shake and moved to the protection of Reuben's arms. Leah moved closer and took Jonah's cold hand. The room vibrated with tension, as their terrified glances shot like sparks.

"I am not in the habit of being challenged," said the constable, hoarsely.

"I do not wish to challenge you," replied the antagonist still moving slowly and drawing the police away from the Chernov family. "I merely want to make you aware that none of the Chernov family could possibly have been involved since none were out of my sight for the entire evening. I even watched them take the old grandfather to his house."

"One Zhid lies to protect another Zhid," scowled the constable. "Why should your word stand against trusted informers?"

Malinovitch reached into his coat and withdrew a leather folder and passed it to the constable.

The constable's back was to the small group so they could only see him straighten his back, rigidly salute in deference, and step backward.

"I'm sure you see the error," continued Malinovitch. "Reuben Chernov and his family were never out of my sight. I would interrogate your sources once again if I were you."

"Certainly, certainly, Alexi Malinovitch, certainly," he repeated obsequiously. "Our people were misinformed. We regret to have caused you this inconvenience."

"It was not I who was inconvenienced, constable," he replied. "Your regrets should be extended to Mr. Chernov and his children."

Reuben noticed the constable stiffen under the thought of an apology to a Jew, and sensed the repercussions of such an action.

"No, no," he interrupted before his old friend compelled the constable to speak. "It was all a mistake. No apologies are needed here."

An awkward moment of silence followed, each party to the silence wondering if that statement would stand in place of any further comment. Malinovitch pursed his lips and nodded agreement to the danger Reuben recognized. The constable turned on his heel and looked at Reuben briefly, curious to know why this Jew was protected by the highest ranking member of the Tzar's secret police, and how a simple tailor in a rural, Ukrainian town even came to know someone of such standing.

"If you're looking for a murderer," Malinovitch continued, "perhaps you might watch for someone who might offer for sale or barter something that could not possibly be his."

The constable nodded in agreement and motioned to his two men to move out ahead of him. He bowed again and touched his finger to his cap.

"It was a great honor," he said.

"It was a pleasure to meet a colleague from the provinces." Malinovitch smiled and nodded. The constable beamed at the cordiality and left.

No one let out a breath.

"He'll not bother you again," said Malinovitch, his hand on the door. He nodded his goodbye.

When the door closed behind him, Reuben sank to the bench. He knew how close they had come to disaster. Had Malinovitch not been there, what might have happened? They all silently thought the question that none dared ask. Reuben took the tea to his lips, his hand shaking. He stared beyond them.

"It's all right now, Mr. Chernov," Leah said, trying to comfort him. She and Jonah and Zeena looked at each other knowing that it was not all right. Leah touched Zeena's fear again and began to know how tenuous their existence really was. Jonah, for the first time, learned his father's newest lesson.

Alexi Malinovitch moved into the crowd and was lost. He turned to the shop. He knew that if he did chose to return, he would have to live their daily fear and become as helpless as they. It was impossible. To return would be to live again, but to die a different kind of death. Now at least he was compensated by power and money and the comfort and security power and money bring. Why give that up? Why choose helplessness? No, he would not willingly choose to be destroyed when he had already sacrificed so much to survive.

CHAPTER 8

Like an uninvited specter, Alexi Malinovitch silently stalked the outer edge of afternoon shoppers and unemployed laborers. He eased his way stealthily into the waiting crowd unnoticed by them, but intently eyed by others who knew his purpose and stood eager to move at his slightest action. Some expressionless men waiting he marked with a poisonous nod; some pale student with invisible venom. Some he stood before briefly, capturing their vague and vacant faces with his basilisk gaze, also marking them as things for beating or arrest. Not one of them suspected him at his work.

The young man stood on the barrel and held up his hands as if to quiet a mob.

"You," he shouted at them, holding the word till it captured their attention. "You are a people oppressed and hated." He waited. Those sitting on boxes who seemed to take their living from the air around them, looked up at the opportunity presented by a new voice and a new face.

"You," he said with more emphasis as he directed himself to the listeners, "are a people cast out and kept strangers in your own land. How long will you be idle and silent at the tyranny that tore you from your beloved homes and keeps you poor and without hope?" He took a deep breath. "Do you remember how you were thrown out onto the roads with only what you could carry and herded to this narrow strip of hell set aside for you? How many of you watched loved ones starve and die until you found a place for your wretched bodies?"

The speaker paused and watched the tattered crowd move towards him. He noticed some heads nodding and remembering. Some looked at him and walked away, choosing not to remember.

Others inched closer and waited silently to recall torn lives and shattered hopes.

"You, whose family once owned taverns near the border, where are those taverns now? Stolen from you because you were too competitive! And you whose families once owned or leased good land, where are your deeds and leases now?" He became animated and pointed to the horizon. "I tell you that treachery and oppression sit on the throne of Russia, and I tell you that treachery and oppression laugh at your suffering in the gilded palaces of St. Petersburg. Look at you!" he screamed in anger and frustration. "Your sacred writings are burned by royal decree, your children are impressed into the army and those who are not are denied schools and universities. Why can only one third of you sit on your own town councils, and why can none of you become a mayor? People of Krivoser," and he opened out his arms to them as if to embrace and plead. "Please, please open your eyes and your minds and act. The world out there is different from the world in here. In other places the people have a right to speak out and rule themselves."

At a distance, Alexi Malinovitch noticed a girl move through the crowd handing out pamphlets. He moved towards her silently.

"Today in the cities," the young man continued, "the nobility hold secret meetings and conspire to cover their own greed and deceit by concocting lies that blame you for all the ills of this country. Why do they do this?" he paused. "They do this because they know you see yourselves as weak and without hope. You are oppressed because they know you will do nothing. They know you will not stand up against their lies, and as long as you allow this to happen, they will continue to present you to the peasants as the cause of all destitution and suffering that they and the clergy create."

Malinovitch nodded. The agents on the outer edge of the crowd, like a family of spiders, threaded their way, inch by inch, towards the speaker and stood close to those forlorn people already singled out for attack.

"You have been accused of ritual murders. Only two years ago yet another heinous blood libel was brought against you. You who throw away a precious egg if it has even a hint of a blood spot are regularly accused of the foul deed of using blood instead of wine. How long will you be silent? What will it take for you to rise up with us?"

The young girl giving out the leaflets approached Malinovitch with one extended. It was Zeena, and he again felt that strange longing as their eyes met.

"You foolish child," he hissed, and he grabbed her arm. The leaflets fell and scattered on the mud. People turned mechanically.

"You're hurting me!" she said loudly and then was transfixed at the moment she recognized her assailant.

"You're playing in a dangerous arena," he said, barely moving his mouth. His action was taken as the signal. The agents, as one, leaped on the unsuspecting listeners with hidden bludgeons and bare fists. Old and young alike fell to the ground in pain and blood.

Malinovitch dragged the screaming girl through the surging crowd, immune to her blows and protest. For her safety, he twisted her arm behind her back and pushed her into a doorway, shielding her with his own body against the force of the terrified mob seeking any way to escape. The speaker ran past him. He could have reached out and caught him but chose to press the struggling Zeena into further security. A barrel splintered next to their heads and Zeena screamed in terror. The mob pushed against them and he struggled to hold the space of her safety. Within it, she turned and saw for herself the brutal melee.

"Jonathan," she screamed into the street, desperate to see the young man safe. "Stop them," she implored over her shoulder. "Please stop them!" and she clawed at his arm. "Don't let them kill him. Please, don't let them kill him!"

Agents looked into windows and smashed open shop doors searching for the speaker. They ran past Malinovitch who turned to shield Zeena from them lest they recognize her as the one who distributed the leaflets and request that she be turned over to them.

When the market was clear, the constable and his men stepped out of an alley where they had been told to wait.

"I've just been informed that the Zhids were making trouble again," he said winking at Malinovitch knowingly. "Luckily," he continued, "we were close by and frightened the trouble makers off. I see you've caught one of them."

"You dare call yourselves servants of the law," Zeena screeched. "You filth, you . . ." Malinovitch put his large fleshy had over her mouth.

"Ah," said the constable, "you have caught one that is on fire, but I'll take her off your hands and we'll see how much she burns when we're finished with her."

Malinovitch shook his head and tightened his hand over her mouth. "She was not involved," he said in a flat authoritarian tone. "You obviously do not remember her. She is the eldest daughter of my friend, Reuben Chernov, and I remind you that I shall hold you personally responsible if any of them are molested."

The constable froze at the mandate and memorized Zeena's face. "It will be as you wish," he said, uneasy at the thought of being ordered by a man of such rank to protect a Jewish family. The thought tore at him with disgust.

"We will take usual troublemakers in for questioning," he continued, changing the subject. "You know you have to watch these people every minute. I tell you Alexi Malinovitch," his tone attempting familiarity, "this is a very difficult job. I've seen these people incite the government and peasants time and time again. They bring these attacks on themselves. I am the legal enforcer here, but I cannot hold the scales of justice impartially between real Russians and these Jews. If they're not guilty of something today, they were probably guilty of something yesterday and will certainly be guilty of something tomorrow."

Malinovitch felt Zeena's body tighten and he renewed the pressure of his hand over her mouth as she struggled to speak again.

The constable gave his hoarse laugh, touched his finger to his hat in salute and waved his men to follow him.

Zeena's captor held her until the men disappeared around the corner and then took his hand from her mouth. She gasped for breath. She wanted to tear at the constable and she wanted to tear at Malinovitch. She wanted to run through the street searching for her Jonathan. But he held her wrist in his powerful grip so she had to remain.

"You're a reckless child," he said moving her slowly towards the safety of a side street. Slowly, shoppers and merchants peered out from their places of sudden refuge and inched their way into the square to salvage what they could of their produce and murmur in small, frightened groups. On the other side of the square the constable and his men questioned and searched those who foolishly chanced to come near them.

"Do you know what could have happened to you if I did not pull you away? Do you know how your arrest could injure your family? Have you any idea of how they would interrogate you to give up this Jonathan of yours?"

"I don't want to hear what you have to say. I do as I like and I don't like being held by my wrist like some naughty child who is not trusted, so let me go!"

"Do you fight to get away from that young man when he takes your hand?"

"What we do is not your business. Now let me go!"

Malinovitch chuckled to himself at her chatter and detected beneath her anger a mild amusement.

"If I let you go, will you promise to walk with me for a short time and listen to what I have to say?"

With the possibility of release, Zeena's expression changed and relaxed. She looked up at the towering man and felt caught between her admiration for the power he possessed and her own fear of being unwillingly held and overwhelmed by anyone.

"I won't run if you let me go," she said.

"Will you walk with me and listen?"

"I will walk," she answered, "but you can't make me listen."

"And what if I have something to say that may be very important for you and your young man?"

"Then perhaps I'll listen." Her body relaxed and she picked up her pace to match his.

Malinovitch slowly relaxed his grip, and as he expected, Zeena bolted like a determined mare. He laughed as he reached out to encircle her wrist again and she looked at him and they laughed together.

"Zeena, I once read a story in a book of myths about a beautiful young woman who could turn herself into the most remarkable monsters to escape capture. But of course, such monsters were only frightful images, and the hero who discovered this was able to hold onto the girl no matter what she chose to become. When the maiden realized that this was no ordinary man, she gave up and granted his wish to marry her."

"I hope he and all the little monsters they made together lived happily ever after."

"You are very like that magical girl," he said, somewhat amused by her sarcasm. "At once you appear a shy, pretty and modest young woman as you did in the shop, and at another moment you're a fanatical revolutionary ready to sacrifice herself and her family for a cause I'm sure you know very little about. I have seen you brave enough to speak back to the constable and frightened enough to scream for the welfare of a young man named Jonathan. Do I have a pretty girl or a monster in my grasp now?"

"If you think I'm a monster, you must have been talking to my mother." She started to laugh. He laughed also and released her hand knowing that this time she would not run.

"How did you get involved with that young man and his movement?" he asked after a moment. "His efforts will lead him and those who follow him only to destruction. You can bring down your whole family by even knowing such a person let alone loving such a person."

"Who said I loved him?" Zeena responded haughtily. "And what right do you have to say such a thing to me?"

"You screamed for his safety when I held you back. I have heard people scream for the safety of loved ones many times before so I know you are in love with this young man."

Zeena slowed her pace and relaxed. Her voice softened and she seemed to forget the most immediate past.

"What's St. Petersburg like?" she said suddenly with childlike wonder.

He glanced at her out of the corner of his eye and smiled. For a moment he was Alta Mitvoy, a young man of the town who worked in his father's store and he was walking with a pretty girl named Zeena Chernov and they were dreaming of a far away place. He reached out and touched her hand and her warmth fed his fantasy.

"Ah, St. Petersburg," he said broadly and smiled at the thought of his home. "St. Petersburg is a beautiful city with broad tree lined boulevards and fine ladies in beautiful dresses."

"And do all the houses really have wooden floors?"

"Certainly," he answered, "and some even have marble. I, myself, live in a house that has a marble entrance foyer," and he heard his own voice speak as that of a youth eager to impress a pretty, young girl. He laughed at himself yet continued.

"How I wish I could go there," she said clasping her hands in front of her. "Oh, how I wish I could walk only on wooden floors and dance with a handsome young man at a party in some house with a marble floor." Zeena did not know what a marble floor was, but she knew that if it existed in St. Petersburg, it had to be something wonderful.

He watched her brighten as her dream unfolded with talk of lace and silk and fur.

"Lace dresses and parties and dances?" he said. "That doesn't sound like the benefits promised by your young man's revolution. That sounds like the dreams of someone who would enjoy the benefits of a privileged few."

"Well," she said, realizing her inconsistency, "just because you don't like the way things are, doesn't mean you have to stop liking other things."

"Zeena," he said looking at her. "Something tells me that you are no more a revolutionary than I am, and I think that you like the excitement because being a revolutionary is something to do. I also think that if your revolution suddenly fell apart, you'd just walk off without shedding a tear, and in a moment you'd be looking for something else to excite you."

"I don't like it when people tell me what I'm thinking!" and she glared at him and quickened her pace.

She had caught him off guard and he was pulled up short and actually pained by her reprimand. He wondered at his curious reaction and called after her.

"Zeena," he said reaching out for her sleeve. He reached into his pocket and pressed two gold coins into her hand much the same way a weak parent might bribe a reluctant or angry child. "Please, Zeena, don't be angry."

She opened her hand and starred with wide eyes at the shining coins.

"Are these really gold coins?" she gasped. "I've never touched real gold coins." She turned them over and over, feeling their warmth and weight.

"For that fine dress and shoes when you come to St. Petersburg to dance," he said smiling.

"But you cannot give me these. I mean I cannot accept them." He interrupted her by placing his finger gently on her lips.

"Zeena, I want you to put them in a safe place. The world sometimes goes mad. You saw what happened today. Only money can buy safety. You tell your father I had to go, and you tell your young man that he is in great danger if he continues speaking out as he does. If he loves you, he will not ask you to help him." He took her hand and held it lightly, never taking his eyes from hers.

"Perhaps I will see you again when I come to St. Petersburg to dance." She laughed and looked up at him playfully. "Don't be surprised if you see me there one day. I know where Papa put your address."

He was loath to let her hand go and he cradled the soft, warm palm and allowed his fingers to memorize its youth. Something warm fluttered through Zeena at the touch of this mysterious older man who seemed to like her enough to give her gold coins.

The rear door of the watch repair shop flew open suddenly, startling Dora and freezing her in place as she turned.

"What do you want?" she stuttered, unable to compose herself. "I have no money."

"I don't want your money," he said brushing past her to close the curtain. "I'm going to stay here until the police pass by and then I'll leave. I promise." He nervously looked around the shop for a place of safety.

"There is no place to hide here," she said in a tight and frightened voice and she wondered if this dark haired youth might be the very person who murdered Putinsky. She began to cry.

"Of all the damn places to come into for help," he muttered in disgust. "God, please don't cry. I hate it when girls cry."

He ran to the back door and opened it a crack. "Damn it," he muttered, closing the door quickly and bolting it. He turned to her. "Listen to me," he said desperately grabbing both her shoulders, "I'm going to get under this counter and if you tell them where I am, I'm going to tell them that you are the brains behind the whole revolutionary movement to overthrow the Tzar."

There was a pounding on the rear door. His eyes implored her and she knew he would not involve her if caught.

"Who is in there?" bellowed someone. "Open the door or I'll smash it down." At the same moment, the front door glass rattled.

Dora's brain raced for a response to both demands. The door shook again. They would surely look under the counter and she and her Zedde would be charged with helping a fugitive. She motioned him to be silent and quickly reached under the counter for the latch. Her grandfather would forgive her. The wall clicked and she quickly pried the door open and pushed him into the dark closet. The front door rattled insistently.

"Make no sound," she whispered, and she turned in time to see the door bulge in its wooden frame.

Trembling, Dora ran to the door and threw open the curtain. A policeman cocked his head like a curious ape and wondered what kept her.

"What do you want?" she asked in her small, frightened voice.

"Open the door," thundered the man as he scanned the shop through the glass pane.

Dora slid the bolt and jumped back before the door could knock against her from the officer's thrust. At the same moment, she heard a loud pounding on the back door. She looked from one to the other and began to cry again.

"What do you want?" she said tearfully, putting herself between the counter and the man who was moving towards her menacingly. The officer passed her and unbolted the rear door. Another policeman entered.

"I saw him come down the alley. He might have come in here."

"Nobody came in here," Dora insisted. "Nobody came in here."

One officer moved around the room opening doors and drawers and knocking on the floor for a hidden cellar. The other grabbed Dora by both shoulders, shoved his face into hers and demanded that she tell him where the fugitive hid. Dora shook her head from side to side and the officer smashed her across the face with his open hand.

"You're a lying Jew bitch and I'll show you what we do to girls who lie to the police."

He pulled her up by the waist and threw her onto the work table. The other, laughing, moved around and stretched her hands above her with one of his hands and muffled her scream with his other sweaty hand over her mouth. His eyes glistened at her terror.

Dora twisted up and away from the insistent hand that reached under her dress and tore at her undergarments and the more she pushed, the more her tormentors laughed.

Suddenly, the door to the shop opened and the men froze as the constable entered. Dora's eyes begged him. The constable said nothing. The hand withdrew from her dress and the other from her mouth. The men looked at each other and laughed the nervous laughter of children caught at an evil game. Dora sucked in a deep breath as the officers met the constable's gaze and slowly backed away from her. The elder officer moved slowly into the room. His jaw tightened and a muscle in his temple twitched. He looked at them contemptuously.

"Is assault on young girls part of our plan to rid the Tsar of his enemies?" The constable's face flushed with rage. "This is one of Reuben Chernov's children. Have you forgotten that this family is under special protection and I will be held responsible if any harm comes to them?"

The two looked at each other. "We did not know that she was one of them," said the younger one with a slight step further away from the sobbing girl. "How were we to know? We saw someone . . ."

"Silence," bellowed their commander as he helped Dora sit up and lower her skirts. "Your brother just married that pretty Shanagrotsky girl. Yes, I remember you from when I visited your house. What is your name, child?"

"Dora," she sobbed, avoiding his eyes.

"Well, Dora, I'm sure you see that this was a grave mistake on these officer's part and I'm sure there is no need to mention this incident to your father. I can assure you that you will not be bothered again." He smiled and nodded his head. She nodded her head also.

"Get out," he said to the men who were already moving quickly to the door. People hurried past them, averting their eyes. Some braver soul peered into the shop. "Go about your business," the constable shouted from where he stood. "Nothing has happened. Get out of here." He turned back to Dora and lifted his fingers to his lips as if to confirm their agreement. She nodded again, too frightened to do anything but agree. The constable closed the curtains before he left and stepped into the street. People fled from him.

Dora sat stunned. Then, slowly, the sensations of the hand over her mouth and the hand tearing at her body overwhelmed her and her mouth opened in a silent cry that was silent until she sucked in her breath. She pushed the skirt between her legs as if to push out the horrible sensation that lingered. When she found it to be of no use, she wept into her hands.

The young man in the closet strained to hear, and the muffled sound of someone crying filtered through the wooden planks. He pressed his ear closer, but there was only silence. His fingers hesitated against the latch and then he lifted it slowly. The door moved silently on its hinges and he peered around the room through the crack. Dora turned suddenly in the direction of the faint click and moved towards the sound in a half daze.

"What happened?" he began. "I could hardly hear anything that I could under . . ." He left off mid word when he saw her face and the blood at the corner of her mouth. He reached out and lightly touched her cheek. "Your mouth," he said with great tenderness and then his eyes flamed. "They hit you. Those rotten bastards hit you!"

He took her in his arms and patted her shoulder gently. Dora had never been touched by a stranger in such a way and she felt confused and embarrassed. Still, she did not pull away. She wept softly on his chest.

"You should have told them where I was. They wouldn't have hit you."

"I couldn't tell them. It would have been like helping them kill you and that would be a great sin."

The young man smiled at the thought. "Oh, they wouldn't have killed me," he said taking a handkerchief from his pocket and dabbing her eyes. "They'd question me, throw me in jail, give me a good beating and after a few days, I'd escape. It's happened before."

"Why were they chasing you?" she asked, new tears balancing on the rims of her eyes. "You didn't kill anybody, did you?" Dora thought of how she would tell her Zedde that a murderer knew the secret place of the watches and tools.

"No," he said, suddenly reminded of his narrow escape. He moved to the window and lifted a corner of the shade. "I was making a speech and those bastards started bashing in the heads of those listening. Those dirty Tsarist bastards don't give a damn who gets hurt. I saw them hit an old woman. Do you believe that? How old are you?" he said suddenly aware that she was a very pretty girl.

"I am seventeen, almost" she said standing a little taller.

He moved past her and opened the back door a crack and peeked out. "I have to go," he said suddenly. "But I really want you to know that I . . ."

"You can't go now," she interrupted. "They'll be watching the shop. I know them." She pulled him away from the door. "You wait till it starts getting dark and people start going home. Then I'll go out and pretend I'm closing up and I'll walk around to the back and see if they're watching. If they're not, I'll knock on the back door and you can come out." She paused and lowered her eyes. "What is your name?" she asked softly.

"Jonathan Metkoff," and he smiled a broad toothy smile and pretended to tip an imaginary cap.

"And yours?"

"Dora Chernov," she replied shyly.

He looked at her briefly as one might glance at a picture in a book before turning the page and then studied her with renewed interest, recognizing something familiar there.

"I think I've seen you before, but I know I haven't."

He moved away from the door, silently concluding that she was correct and that it would be wiser for him to remain there until dark. She watched him survey the room, perch on top of her grandfather's wooden stool and wrap his ankles around two of the legs. She watched his every move and soon became aware of an awkward silence.

"Sometimes I feel like that also. Sometimes I think I know someone I can't possibly know or I've done something I can't possibly have done before."

"That's not unusual," he replied. "In fact there are people who believe that we continue to be born over and over again and those moments are really recollections of having done similar things in an earlier life."

Dora looked at him incredulously and her mouth opened slightly. "How can that be?" she said. "After you die, you stay dead until God sends the Messiah and you get your soul back at the end of time."

"That belief is fine if you're a Jew and you have Jewish beliefs. But there are a lot of people in the world out there, Dora, who believe that you keep getting reborn until you reach perfection and that belief seems as valid as any other piece of religious nonsense people have come up with to explain away their confusion and fear."

"That's a terrible thing to say about people and a terrible thing to say about God and I hope He wasn't listening because something terrible could happen to you."

"Something terrible has been happening to me all my life and it started long before I gave God a reason to get even with me. Now at least God has a reason."

"You sound like my sister," she interrupted, "and I'm not interested in hearing what you have to say about God. Besides, if God is not good, how do you explain that you came in here and not into some other shop where you might have been turned over to the police? I could have turned you in, but God wanted me to help you and that's what I did so don't you go talking bad about God!"

Jonathan looked at her and the corners of his mouth turned upward. "If that's what you've been taught to believe," he said laughing, "and that's how you act, then you are the only righteous person I've ever met."

"Then I feel very sorry for you," she replied, "because I know a lot of people who are good people and behave the way the Torah tells them to behave." Dora suddenly turned away, embarrassed by her forwardness.

He studied the soft sand colored curls that fell upon her shoulders and wondered what it would be like to kiss her.

"I'm nothing of a revolutionary," she insisted, keeping her eyes riveted on the floor, "and I'm also eighteen and not to be preached at as if I were a child."

He laughed. "A few moments ago you said you were almost seventeen which means you are really sixteen. People age rapidly in this place."

Dora laughed, opening her eyes and stepping back from his closeness. She felt a flush rise to her cheek as she looked into his deep, dark eyes.

"I'm seventeen," she murmured softly and lowered her eyes quickly so he could not read the playful lie.

"Dora, I'll tell you a little truth I learned from my father one day." He smiled at the recollection. "My father once looked at me and said, 'Jonathan, don't tell any lies because if you lie, you've got too much to remember.' Then he gave me a sound beating just to make sure I'd always remember what would happen if I ever lied again."

"And did you ever lie again?" Dora said, her eyes dancing.

"Of course," he replied, and they both laughed.

"Your father sounds like a wise man. Where do your parents live?"

"They don't," he said with more abruptness in his voice than he intended. There was a pause and Dora felt his pain briefly.

"Then who takes care of you?" she said innocently.

"Takes care of me?" he chortled. "I've been taking care of myself since I was fourteen, and I've done fine for myself for the past six years." He stopped himself from continuing. "Look, Dora, it's getting late and if I get started on my life, I'll probably end up making a speech. I really appreciate all you've done, but I think it's best that I get back to my friends."

She did not want him to leave.

"Jonathan," she said, moving quickly to the window and lifting the corner of the shade. "Why don't you come home with me? You can have dinner and sleep in the barn and by tomorrow they will have given up looking for you." The thought and the ruse excited her as she spoke. "If I close the shop now, the police may get suspicious. You go back into the closet and stay there until it gets dark and I close up. Then you can put on my Zedde's hat and coat and you'll stoop down, and whoever looks at you will think you're an old man. Mama is a wonderful cook and Papa will like you because you like to talk about ideas." She searched his face for agreement.

"Well," he said slowly, poised between his need to be on his way and the thought and the need of a good meal with a family. "Well, maybe, but only if it's all right with your parents. I wish I could remember where I've seen you. There is something so familiar about you."

"Perhaps we passed each other on the street or you were near me at a stall in the market. It doesn't matter. We've met now and you are coming to dinner."

"Perhaps it was in another life," he teased. "You and I were the Tsar and Tsarina and because we were so rotten to our subjects, we were put back on earth as an orphaned revolutionary and a servant who cleans watch repair shops."

"I am not a servant," she said pulling herself up as tall as she could to reinforce her stature and the indignity of the implication. "This is my Zedde's shop and I am a watch repairer just as he is!"

"Girls can't repair watches," he responded flatly as if his statement was the eleventh commandment.

"That's what you think," she said smugly, and, picking up a tweezer from the bench with one hand and placing the glass into her eye with the other, she lifted a small jewel from the tray and dropped it into place.

Jonathan's mouth opened slightly. Dora saw the expression on his face and realized that she did not have to say another word.

CHAPTER 9

Zeena sat on her bed studying the intaglio faces pressed on to the coins. She had never seen such delicate lines. Certainly, she thought, these coins were meant only for very special people. Only she and such people could know their magic and beauty. Now they belonged to her. They were meant for her and only she could appreciate them.

She lay back on the bed and placed the coins on her eyes. Their weight bore down and in the swirling blackness behind her lids she loosened her hair and let it fall to her shoulders. She stepped into a room such as the ones she had read about in stories, and lifted the train of her white lace gown and draped it over her arm.

Gilt mirrors rose around her into the scented mist and golden cherubs perched on shimmering crystal chandeliers. The sound of violins echoed from unseen halls. She stood silently waiting, bathed in the glow of a thousand candles. A man approached, a man with a neatly trimmed beard and dressed in a short red jacket with gold epaulets and gold buttons. A dress sword hung at his thigh and it swayed as he approached. Then the sword disappeared. He held out his hand to her and she saw herself lift her own hand to his. She watched him kiss it softly, never taking his dark eyes off her. They stood facing each other and he put his arm around her and she felt herself drawn to his body. The buttons of his coat pressed against her as they gazed into each other's eyes. Suddenly, the man became her Jonathan and the music swelled as she danced with him around the fantasy room long into the night. His black eyes caressed her, and she became lost in the intensity of his passion. On and on she danced, alive and vibrant and feeling all there was to feel and sensing every sense at once. She breathed in each second of the dream as if each second were the last. She bathed in each sound and sight and danced through the world and through each book she had ever read. She was each beautiful heroine and each princess. Then slowly, very slowly, the music faded. Her swirling skirts fell limp on her body. Her Jonathan took her face gently in his hands and pressed her lips passionately against his own. She swooned and he lifted her into his arms and carried her into the night. Such was the magic in the gold coins and, at that moment, Zeena resolved that one way or another, she would get to St. Petersburg.

"Zeena, I need you to set the table."

Zeena took the coins from her eyes quickly.

"Zeena? Are you in there?"

"It's Dora's turn to set the table. I clean up." Zeena tried to conceal the annoyance in her voice.

"Well, Dora is late and don't think she's not going to hear from me on the matter when she gets here. Now you come out here and set the table and she'll clean up!"

Zeena stretched her arms back above her head and thought of what it would be like to look up at a sculpted plaster ceiling painted white and gold instead of one that was water stained and rotting.

"I'm waiting, Zeena!"

"I'm coming!"

Sarah moved to the door and took her shawl from the peg, but as she was about to touch the latch, it shook and the door opened quickly. Both Dora and her mother were startled at the sudden confrontation.

"And why are you late? You know I don't like you walking alone when it's getting dark." She returned her shawl to the peg.

"I'm sorry Mama," Dora said, trying to catch her breath, "but while I was working the back door of the shop flew open and a boy who was being chased by the police came in and then I hid him and the police came and . . ."

The spoons fell out of Zeena's hands and clattered on the table. "Where is he?" Zeena took Dora by the shoulders and shook her. "Is he all right? They didn't get him, did they?"

Sarah pulled her away. "What do you think you're doing?

You keep your hands to yourself or you'll feel mine." Sarah's voice shook, and the same sickening fear that had crept over her earlier in the day at the mention of the police, crept over her once again. "Reuben!" she yelled, suddenly realizing that one of her family was again threatened by the police and she was not there to protect her. "Reuben!" she bellowed again, grabbing the wrists of both daughters.

"Where is he?" mouthed Zeena to her sister, her eyes flashing her fear and anxiety.

At that same moment, Sarah noticed a shadowy figure near the door, pulled both girls behind her, and held them there.

"Quiet!" she whispered. "Someone's out there," and she prepared to throw herself between whatever it was and her daughters.

"That's Jonathan," said Dora, innocently discounting her mother's fear. "He's the boy I told you about."

Zeena made a move towards the shadow but was restrained. Dora motioned for the shadowy figure to come into the house. He entered. Sarah released her daughters, scanned the yard and horizon quickly and bolted the door.

"His name is Jonathan Metkoff, Mama," Dora said, hoping her mother would accept him at least for the night. "He didn't do anything bad, Mama. He was only making a speech."

Jonathan nodded. His six foot frame made a half bow to his hostess and his muscular arm reached out to shake her hand.

"A speech?" Sarah echoed, knowing suddenly what he was and what danger he brought with him.

Jonathan's hand hung in the air.

"You bring a revolutionary to my house?" She threw a sharp look at Zeena and made a vague connection between her daughter's reaction and the young man who stood uncomfortably in her kitchen.

"Out," she said pointing to the door. "If no one is going to think about the welfare of this family, I'll think of it."

"But they're looking for him," pleaded Dora. "They won't come here because the constable told the officers that we were never to be bothered. This is the only safe place. Please, Mama. Please let him stay."

"What's going on here?" said Reuben entering from the back door, buttoning his trousers. "What is the yelling and who is this?" His tone of annoyance changed as soon as he saw Jonathan and as soon as he recognized the urgency on the faces of both his daughters and his wife.

"His name is Jonathan Metkoff, Papa, and he has no parents and the police are after him and please let him stay." Dora took a breath. Sarah was already shaking her head at what she knew would be her husband's response.

"Would you give me the courtesy, my dear Sarah, of allowing me to think about and understand what is going on before you make up my mind for me. My daughter pleads for a stranger and my wife wants the stranger out." He prepared his next comment to counter the attack he saw forming on her lips.

"Reuben, the police are looking for him and if he was seen coming here with Dora we'll all go to jail."

"Sarah, we were once strangers in a strange land ourselves and we still are, and besides, Dora is right when she says that the constable gave orders that we were not to be bothered. Here is the only safe place for him."

"Don't give me quotes from the Torah," she shot back. "We are in danger!"

"And don't tell me we cannot help a young man who is in need and probably hungry!" His tone changed immediately as he turned to the uncomfortable young man who nervously twisted the grandfather's old hat in his hands. "Now let's get some food into him," Reuben said gesturing him to the table, "and find out what is going on." Reuben looked at Dora, wondering how she had come to know that the family was under the constable's protection.

"Don't worry, Mama," said Dora following her mother to the stove. "If anyone saw us, they'll think it's Zedde visiting us. That's why I made him wear Zedde's old hat and coat. He even stooped over."

Sarah turned and inspected Jonathan a little closer. Indeed he wore her father's coat.

"Well," she said, her voice less caustic. "At least you had the good fortune to come into a shop with my daughter who happens to be very bright. But," she continued so he would not think she liked or approved of him, "don't think you're going to stay. I don't need any revolutionaries around here," and she threw another cautioning look at Zeena.

Jonathan followed her eyes to the girl he had hardly noticed in his first encounter with Dora's parents.

"You," he said looking directly at Zeena. "That's why I thought I knew Dora from someplace, but it was you I saw in her."

Sarah wondered what Zeena knew about this anarchist and how she was involved, but said nothing. She only looked at them.

"I wondered if they got you," he said. "You were the first one grabbed."

Sarah could not contain herself and turned to Zeena demanding an explanation.

"Oh, it was nothing," she said, avoiding her mother's gaze. "There was some trouble in the market and a fight." She moved to the sink. Sarah stood there not knowing whether to yell or weep.

"Is the world going crazy?" she bellowed. "One daughter brings a mad man home from God knows where and the other lets me know that she was involved in only a minor riot in the market. I'd like to know what's going on right under my nose!"

Reuben scratched his head, and though as curious as his wife to learn of the events, changed the subject to ease the moment.

"Where are Jonah and Leah?"

Sarah scowled. He had inadvertently touched a different nerve. "Your son and his wife may be here or they may not be here," she answered curtly. "They don't take me into their confidence. They ate the lunch I made for them, put their belongings on the cart and with a polite `thank you', left for her uncle's home. They were invited here to dinner, but I got no definite reply. You know as much as I know." Her voice was steady, but rose curiously on the final word of each sentence.

Reuben did not like the inflection, for he had heard it before, and most often as prelude to upheaval.

"I want you to know," he said to her, his voice unusually resolute, "that Jonah is your son and Leah is your daughter-in-law, and they will remain that whether they live here or not. They want to live at Mitvoy's, that's fine with me. They want to live here, that's fine with me. They want to live in the street, that's also fine with me. It's finished," he said flatly, "it's finished, and I don't want to hear any more about it. I want no more accusations, I want no more faces. It's over!"

"Are you quite finished, Reuben? Are you quite happy you've embarrassed me in front of a guest?" She busied herself and said nothing else.

Reuben watched her. He knew his beloved Sarah and knew she would place herself between the mouth of a cannon and her children, but he also he knew it would be easier to reason with the cannon. This silence was only a temporary victory. Sarah was merely catching her breath.

Zeena watched her mother return to the stove and she watched her father take his place at the table. With a calmness that belied the excitement of having her Jonathan in her home, she moved towards him, discounting Dora completely. She knew nothing of him other than his name, and that he appeared and disappeared regularly. But she loved him with an intensity and passion that flowed out of her own nature and her secret, romantic novels. Where he went and what he did, she did not know. She only knew that he had black curly hair, coal black eyes, and spoke like a fearless prophet. She watched him, listened to him, gave out his pamphlets, and hoped so desperately that he would fall passionately in love with her and take her away. Now he would. She would meet him secretly and tell him of her feelings. Together, they would run into the night. Her heart felt as if it would explode, and she thought that he would see it pounding against her dress.

"What happened?" she said in a high, excited whisper. "How did you get here? Are you all right? I was so worried for you!"

"I'm all right now, thanks to your sister," and he looked at Dora and smiled warmly. "She saved me."

Zeena felt resentment rise in her. Normally she viewed Dora as a non-entity, someone who faded into the wall, a fool who played with clocks. Suddenly, she was an opponent, someone with whom she must contend. She looked at her delicate sister and wondered. She, not Dora, should have saved him. She, not Dora should have his gratitude. He should look at her that way, not at Dora. What did Dora know of his goals? What did Dora know of risking everything to give out his pamphlets in broad daylight. She, not Dora should have risked being arrested for him. Dora even knew his full name before she did. How dare Dora receive his affection!

"I'm glad you are here," she smiled masking her budding annoyance. "I'm glad you were not caught."

"So am I," he replied. He paused. "Look, I really feel a little foolish. Your name is Zeena, isn't it? I know I've talked to you a few times and you've given out my pamphlets. I'm really glad you got away."

Zeena's stomach sank. She had watched him each time he came to town, followed him, memorized his words and loved him so deeply that she risked her life and her family for him. How could he not know her feelings? How was it possible that he hardly remembered her name?

"Yes, that's right. My name is Zeena," she said, looking him squarely in the face with tears welling up behind her eyes. "My name is Zeena."

"Zeena, get Ruth and help me serve dinner. Dora, you show your friend where the toilet is in case he needs one. Then show him where he can wash up. Revolutionary or not, we are civilized people in this house and we bless our food with clean hands."

Zeena watched Dora take his hand and guide him to the back door. She watched and tried to imagine what it would be like to touch him.

CHAPTER 10

January 28, 1882

"Yes, Jonah, I am very much aware of tradition," Leah said planting herself down in the chair by the window, "but it doesn't change the fact the I still don't want to go!" For the past year, she had uttered the same complaint each Friday afternoon and her plea had gone unheeded.

"The Sabbath is the Sabbath, and on Friday night we go to my family for dinner." Jonah could hear his father saying the same words years ago when he was a child and he knew the wisdom in the statement that there was 'nothing new under the sun and all was vexation of spirit.'

"Here," he said, sitting down on the bed next to her as he fumbled with his collar. "I can't get this button." Her hands lay sculpted on her lap. "Oh, come on Leah," he coaxed. "Help me with this thing."

He knelt before her. She raised her hands and pulled the collar over.

"You know your mother will start on me. 'Why won't you name the baby after my uncle? When will you give me some pleasure?' You know Zeena is going to say something to her so called betrothed that will make us all want to hide our heads. And he'll snort something stupid, or ignore it and shovel some more food into his fat face. Only God knows why Zeena ever allowed herself to agree to a marriage with someone who is as repulsive as Ezra Bendak is beyond me. Why your father ever allowed your mother to have her way with this so called union, I'll never know. If everybody hated old man Putinsky so much, how can they accept his grandson into the family?"

Jonah bristled, but did not respond. He had heard Leah's feelings about the match for Zeena the moment it was announced, and her comments were a constant reminder to him of his abortive effort on Zeena's behalf. The memory of that evening appeared and disappeared like a recurring illness, and he could still feel the fever of recriminations on his face. All fell apart before his mother's onslaught and Zeena's condemnations. He had tried. He had really tried and he had failed. Now Zeena barely spoke to him. She barely spoke to anyone.

"All right," he said, finally exasperated. "So Ezra Bendak isn't exactly the nicest person in the town, but he'll be a good provider and he'll give Zeena anything she wants."

"Jonah," she said, "I know you well enough to know that even you don't for a minute believe that. All Ezra Bendak can give your sister is money, and though that may be what your mother thinks is the only thing that's important in life, you know as well as I that Zeena wants something more."

"Then why did she accept the pearls, the ring and the other gifts and then parade herself up and down the town showing herself off? I once thought I knew what Zeena wanted, but now I'm not so sure."

From the moment Zeena saw that Jonah had relented and given up on his overt objections to her getting married, she had virtually cut him out of her confidence and out of her life. The wedge she hammered between them as his punishment, cut deeper into his life than even she might have imagined, and he was devastated by her absence. He was also angry at her for having done this to him and to herself.

"Ezra Bendak," Leah continued, discounting his statement about Zeena's responsibility, "is a disgusting boor who thinks because he has more money than anybody else in town, he can belch and wipe his mouth with his sleeve and everybody will look away. Besides, he's oily and his beard grows in patches."

There was a moment of silence.

"Jonah, do we have to go? Why can't we have our own Sabbath

dinner with my sister and Uncle Issac. Aunt Malka is so ill. Who know how many more Sabbaths she'll see? Whatever pleasure she can still take, let's give it to her."

As she spoke, Jonah felt the tightness in his neck. She still did not understand what it would mean not to go to his parents and he did not feel he was being insensitive to her uncle and aunt because they had never invited them to stay. Besides, they lived with them.

He reached behind his neck and took her hands. He held them and looked into the deep brown eyes that sparkled with the expectation that he would hear her need.

"Leah," he began looking down, not wanting to see the sparkle change to disappointment. "Leah, every Friday night we go to my parents because that's the tradition." He felt her hands retract in his but would not let them go. "Leah, ever since we left, it hasn't been good between you and Mama, and me and Mama. She thinks you lead me around and that you forced me to leave her house. If we stop going on Friday nights, she'll only think you're trying to split the family further and further apart and that will cause even more problems."

Leah pulled her hand out of his. "You mean problems for you, Jonah. I don't care what your mother thinks about me, and I'm not afraid of what she'll say about me, either. I wish you could just see her once the way I see her, but you see only what you want to see."

"Let's not start talking again about what I see and what I don't see," and he stood up quickly as if she had burned him with wax. "I see what I have to see to keep food on our table and clothing on our backs. I see what has to be done for us to survive. You are right Leah, as you are always right. There are things I don't see because I don't want to see them. I don't want to see them because to see them means I have to do something about them and the only thing there is to do about them is as unthinkable as cursing God. She is my mother and I will not dishonor her. I love you Leah and I love her. If you force me to choose between the two of you, I will choose you. But don't expect me to like having to make the choice, and don't expect me to like you too much for having demanded that I make it! Damn it Leah, why do you always force me to balance between the two of you?"

"You don't see it, Leah snapped. "I was in the family for one whole day and I saw it. Zeena lives with it, but you don't. Well, Jonah, I think you ought to see it for yourself. I don't have to tell you, but I'll tell you this. Maybe you don't mind being treated like a fool, but I'm not going to let her treat me that way. She's your mother, not mine and I don't have to take her abuse!"

"Well what am I supposed to do about it?" he shouted angrily. "What's abuse to you is just her normal way. I don't see her being abusive. She's just the way she always is. It's you who's too sensitive."

"I'm too sensitive? I'm too sensitive!" and she pointed to herself and moved towards the table so that it was between them. "That's incredible. I don't treat people like they're things. I don't demand from them or make others feel like they're dirt or incompetent. And I don't go back on my word."

Jonah banged his fists on the table in frustration again and she jumped. He did not like himself and he did not like her for what they were doing and saying to each other.

"Leah, we must stop this now. You have what you want. Why are you continuing this?"

"I don't want to fight with you about this any more either, Jonah. You said we'd move back to my uncle's house and we did. You agreed to put away money so we can go to America, and you are. I'm upset because you didn't tell your mother the real reasons why we had to leave and because you didn't tell her she continues to treat me like a servant every time we see each other. Unless you tell her, Jonah, she'll never treat me well."

"I still don't see her treatment of you as being any different from her treatment of anyone one else. If you don't like it then you tell her! What am I supposed to do? Should I sit her down and say, Mama, don't tell Leah to get dishes or clean up because it sounds like you're treating her like a servant? She says what she likes and does what she likes because she is the mother and it's her right. You're the son's wife. One day you'll have your own house and you can say whatever you want to whom ever you want. Pointing out her flaws would be breaking a commandment!"

"But you'd let me break the commandment," she said hurling his inconsistency back in his face.

"Nothing escapes you, does it Leah? You're right. I can't ask you to break a commandment either so you are to say nothing! I am not going to say anything and neither are you."

"But she won't learn anything, Jonah. She won't change."

"It's not for you or me to teach her or change her. It's not our place. Why can't you understand?"

He looked at her standing there. He was all knotted up and he ached to hold her. "This shouldn't be happening, Leah. All this is outside us."

"No it isn't, Jonah. This is between us. She is between us."

He moved around the table and went to her, but when he put his hands on her arms to hold her, she tensed and pulled away. Something inside him collapsed.

He moved the window. "It's almost time to leave," he said, his voice shaking. He turned slowly. "I'm sorry for what I just said. I shouldn't have said that I wouldn't like you. I will always like you." He held out his hand as a peace offering, but she did not move. "Yes, I am protecting myself, but let me remind you that if I wasn't interested in protecting you, we'd still be living in the loft and we wouldn't have the savings I've started for us. Maybe I don't say what you want me to say, and maybe I'm afraid to say it, but I do keep you away from my mother as much as I can, and once a week, just to keep the balance, is not so much to ask."

Leah said nothing but moved to the dresser and picked up her hair brush. Strains of silky hair fanned out and clung to her shoulders. Jonah moved behind her and his hands encircled her waist. "We have to go to your parents and I don't want to be late." The brushing became rapid. "I don't understand you, Jonah. You argue with me one minute and the next minute you act as if nothing had happened.

I don't understand how anyone can just put aside all those feelings as if they do not exist. Things add up, Jonah. Things add up."

His hand slid from her shoulders and hung limply at his sides. He turned and walked back to the window and sealed himself against her words with a sigh. She watched him move and knew he had shut her out again. There was no point in talking about this any more. She knew, if pushed, he would always take her side against everyone and no personal sacrifice would be too great for him to make for her. She knew this, but she also knew he would never see without being told to see, and never act without being pushed to action. It was this she could not and would not accept. Always there would be tensions and heated words before he spoke, and always there were the recriminations after he spoke. Always, she was the one who would force the issue, and always, the blame for his assertion lay at her feet. Yes, he would protect her and give to her and care for her, but always it seemed just a little too late. Always it seemed to happen just a little after it should have happened. Something important was missing, and she wondered if he really loved her. She doubted his love most when he escaped into himself and shut her out.

Cracked ridges of the road broke under his weight and from time to time he would touch her shoulder to keep his balance. Then he stopped, took her hand and walked beside her without speaking.

He kicked a small rock and kicked it again. They passed the cemetery, and he thought of all those silent people wrapped in prayer shawls and shrouds. Who were they? What meaning did their lives have? He was part of them, part of that endless sea of nameless people who were destined to die without ever being known. He did not want their end to be his. Had he not married Leah but had run away as Zeena had asked, he might have changed his destiny. Together, he and Zeena would have had the strength to act against any force, but separated as they were now emotionally, they were powerless. Was that why Zeena accepted the marriage? Was she as powerless without him as he was without her? Why does it have to be so hard, Lord? Do you mean it to be this hard or am I making all the wrong decisions and doing it to myself? Lord, I feel like a baby learning to walk. You know how parents let the baby go and the baby just stands there not knowing what to do? They're afraid to take the next step because they're afraid to fall, and they don't want to sit down. They just stand there reaching out into the air. That's how I feel, Lord of the Universe. That's how I feel. How do I help Zeena, Lord? And how do I make it right for Leah, also? And me and Mama, Lord. Will it ever be right between me and Mama?

"Jonah?" Leah said. Her voice sounded distant though she walked at his side. "Jonah?" she repeated and stopped and pulled his hand. She could not see what visions he saw, nor could she understand why they lived in her young husband, so they continued in silence until they reached the gate to his parent's yard. The goat stuck its head through the slats and Jonah patted it. Leah hesitated as if some unseen presence warned her against entering. Jonah felt her stop and he turned to her.

"Are you all right?" he said softly.

She looked down and shook her head. He did not understand and he never would.

"I told you," Jonathan said, pointing a threatening finger at Ezra Bendak. "I told you they'd murder him. I told you he'd never come to trial and how can you be so stupid as to believe that he hanged himself? He was a hero and now he's a martyr." Jonathan gulped down his wine and continued. "Remember, Bendak, your wonderful Tsar decreed one third of us to die through starvation, one third driven out through expulsion and one third of us disappear through conversion. That's the plan, and believe me that they'd like to kill us all. All our deaths are the silent agenda."

"You can't know for sure that he was murdered. That's all I'm saying." Ezra Bendak did not look at this sometime guest, sometime boarder, whom he had come to dislike for his handsome appearance and his political views. "He was found in his cell and they said it was a suicide. We can't be certain it was not." He put another fork full of potatoes into his mouth so the word suicide was garbled.

"Suicide!" exploded Jonathan again. "They could piss on you and tell you it was raining and you'd believe it, you gullible idiot. You don't want to see because if you saw what was going on, whatever conscience you had left might prod you into acting like a human being and that might interfere with how you make your money." Jonathan Metkoff was very red and very angry.

Reuben threw down his fork and knife as the last words escaped Jonathan's lips and before Ezra could react. "I do not object to political discussions or even heated discussions at my Sabbath table Jonathan, but I will not tolerate profanity or insult. Ruth, stop laughing or you'll be sent outside."

"I'm sorry Mr. Chernov," Jonathan replied hastily. "I just forget myself when I'm faced with people who will not see the truth of what's going on in Russia today and what's going to happen to us if we don't do something soon. Russia will explode, and as long as people, like this idi . . .," and he caught himself, "like this person, refuse to see or act, we'll all explode with it."

Ezra thrust a large slice of chicken into his mouth. "You know, Metkoff," he began, waving his fork in rhythm with his chewing and discounting his host's caution. "For someone who has no trade other than making speeches, makes no real living, other than living off the kindness of people like the Chernov's, for someone who sleeps most nights in a barn, who owns nothing and has nothing to lose, you make a big noise for those of us who do have plenty to lose. If people with skill and wealth are willing to sit and wait out these troubled times and not worry, who are you to do the worrying, and who are you to get the government all upset so they view the rest of us with suspicion? You're a trouble maker and you make trouble for the rest of us who have something to lose!"

"You're missing the point, Ezra," interrupted Jonah, who felt the insult to Jonathan was undeserved and the reasoning faulty.

"The fact that Jonathan has no trade does not exclude him from the ranks of those who are concerned about living. I find it inconceivable that you can discount someone's entire existence and their right to speak simply because they don't own anything. God has given each of us a stake in this and Jonathan's is as great as anyone else's."

"And what stake is that?" Bendak sneered.

"His life and the lives of those people he loves. That's his stake. That's all our stakes because when you come right down to it, Ezra, things can be replaced, but you can't replace a life."

"Nobly spoken, my dear brother-in-law to be," said Ezra mockingly. "I know how the two of you think and I find you both amusing. You, Jonah have almost nothing to show for your years, believe your condition in life is ordained by God's plan, you pray to him and bless his name for the meager survival he lets you eek out. You, Metkoff have less than nothing, not even an honest trade, you believe your condition is caused by the political manipulations of the government, and you call God a myth. One blesses God and has next to nothing, and one dismisses God and has nothing. I neither bless nor dismiss and I have possessions, power and respect in this town. So who I ask you, who is blessed by God?"

"Everybody in town knows how you got your money," fumed Jonathan at the insult, "and never confuse fear and dislike with respect, Bendak. And let me tell you this. I take a perverted sense of pleasure in being absolutely sure that when this world does explode and your agent friends start one of their pogroms, you're going to be treated just like any other Jew only you'll have more to lose."

Reuben watched Ezra gulp down his glass of wine and pour himself another as if Ezra hadn't heard a word Jonathan had said. This man, Zeena's betrothed, was a boor, and Reuben knew this from their first meeting. Also, his strange pursuit of Zeena, despite her obvious distaste for him, discomforted him and made him increasingly aware that he should not have allowed Sarah to badger him into agreeing to the match. Zeena sat in an unnatural silence, separated, unmoved and distant. From time to time she darted furtive glances at Jonathan and then at Dora and then back to her plate. Her father ached for her and for the loss of her spirit.

"And what do you have to say, Zeena?" he asked. "Such a political issue finds you silent? Is this my Zeena?"

"I have nothing to say," she said in a sorrowful, calculated whisper that she knew would pain him, and she lowered her fork to her plate and left off eating. "What is everyone looking at? Don't I have a right to say nothing or have I lost even the right to keep my thoughts to myself? I seem to have been forced to give up everything else. Are even my thoughts not my own?" She glared at her mother and avoided Ezra.

Then, pushing her chair away from the table, Zeena rushed into the back room. Sarah stood abruptly, and Reuben motioned for her to remain in her place and that he would handle the situation.

"Pass the carrots to your brother, Dora," Sarah said a moment into the uncomfortable silence.

"Why does Zeena cry so much?" asked Ruth. "She never used to cry, but now she cries more than I do."

"Nothing is wrong," Sarah replied, looking at the bedroom door. "Brides get nervous. They cry a lot. Eat your dinner before it gets cold."

Reuben sat down on the bed next to his daughter who lay with her face buried in the pillow. His hand hovered over her head and lightly touched her, but the comfort he wished her was not to be accepted and he saw her body retract under its offer of silent consolation. "Zeena, Zeena," he whispered. "Sit up and talk to me. It is not good that you are so unhappy, especially on the Sabbath."

"Then change it for me Papa, change it for me." She turned over and looked at him with such pain, that his very soul ached. "What does it say, Papa? 'Better a dry morsel amid laughter than a feast amid strife?' Change it for me, Papa. If you ever loved me, don't force me marry Ezra Bendak." She put her arms around his waist and held him as she had held him when she was a small child frightened of a storm. "Hold me, Papa," she sobbed. "Don't let Mama make me marry him."

She wept onto his chest, and he felt his shirt dampen with her tears. His hand rested on her shoulder and he tried to soothe her with a gentle touch. A tear rolled down the side of his face and he touched his finger to it before it fell. Caught between his wife's insistence on this marriage, his own belief that tradition had to be maintained, and his daughter's anguish, he could only place his hand on her head and pray for the strength he would need to mend the torn fabric of her life.

"Your Mama does love you," he began again, " as she loves all her children. But she also thinks that the world would fall apart for them if she wasn't there to keep it going. You, your brother and your sisters are a part of her and not separate people. That's why she is always telling everyone what to do and how to do it. Do you understand what I'm saying to you? By doing what she does and saying what she says, she really believes she protecting everyone from some unseen horror that is waiting to tear your world apart. Some mothers are like that. They give everything to their children, but they don't know to give their children what their children need to become independent of them. And when their children get angry with them or push them away, they cannot understand why they are being treated so badly when all they do is give. They give life, they nurture, they suffer and feel they are owed more than they can ever be paid back. Such people see only what they give; never what they don't give." He sat, waiting for some response. There was none.

"I will talk to Mama again," he said after a long silence." Perhaps this time."

"No, Papa, no," and she shook her head. "Mama wants me to marry and the arrangements are all made. She won't listen." Zeena looked up at him. "She hates me, Papa. She hates me enough to be willing to see me married to someone who will make me miserable all my life."

"Zeena, I will not have you say that. Mothers do not hate

their children. Didn't you hear anything I just said? She just thinks you'll be better off married, and Ezra is the only young man who has shown any interest in you."

"Then she doesn't love me enough to want to see me happy. And what about you, Papa? Do you love me enough to want to see me happy?"

He was silent for a moment and then lifted her up and looked at her. "I want you to tell me the truth, Zeena. I want you to tell me why you finally accepted the betrothal ring and his other gifts if you had it in your mind not to marry him?"

"I had it in my mind to get away from Mama because she's killing me. Marrying Ezra Bendak was the only way I could do it without running away and hurting you. I was wrong, Papa. I was wrong."

She had caught him off guard. He had not realized that his feeling had been a factor in this drama. In his heart, he knew very well how Sarah felt about their eldest daughter, but he could not bring himself to acknowledge it.

"We only want someone for you who will work for you and give you a nice home and children. That is what a woman must have. It has always been that way."

"But I want to be more than just a wife and mother. You poured your knowledge and dreams into me. I want to see the world in the books, Papa. Marriage and children are fine for someone who wants that or who thinks that's what they need. But that's not what I need, Papa, and never, never with Ezra Bendak!" Her voice shook, but the intensity of her resolve was clear. "He's stupid, cunning and close minded, and skilled only with numbers. You've taught me to look at the world and question and be curious. He only talks about his money and what it buys and the only thing he wants to know about is what he'll eat for dinner. He doesn't read or talk or listen and he tells me that I don't know what I'm talking about when I say something. Is that what you want for me, Papa? And Papa, he has no sparkle in his eyes and there is no laughter in him. Please, Papa, I will . . .I will . . ." Zeena did not end her sentence.

Reuben could not help but wonder if he had erred in pouring into his daughter what he had poured into his son. But with Jonah, the universe was quiet and abstract and safe. Jonah was a passive thinker. Zeena's universe vibrated and she vibrated with it. Against her mother's wishes, he had shown her more than what was expected of her and he had taken enormous pleasure in her growth and spirit. Now, she would not settle for less than the world he had allowed her to glimpse. He was also responsible for her plight.

"I'll talk to Mama after the Sabbath is over. I did not know, Zeena. I saw, but I did not understand. Now you stay here and I'll make some excuse. If you feel like coming out for tea, come out. If not, we'll talk again tomorrow." He kissed her on her forehead and stood.

Zeena felt limp, like a flower after a heavy rain. She watched him hobble to the door, stop, turn, shake his head sadly, and close it behind him. She desperately wanted to believe that she would not be forced into the hateful union with Bendak, but the reality of her life laughed at her from all corners of the room as she fell back on the bed and wept until she fell asleep.

The Sabbath seemed to falter under his wife's and daughter's tears and recriminations. Their behavior was an affront to God, and for the first time in his life, he wished the holy day away for its own sake. When the ritual of separation was completed, Reuben asked everyone except Sarah to go outside. They looked across the table at each other with apprehension.

Sarah sat on her chair opposite him like some waning deity of old who anticipated yet another encroachment on her domain and further erosion of her power. She nervously brushed crumbs from the white cloth. Reuben put a cube of sugar between his teeth and took a sip of tea. He offered his wife a small square of bread covered with preserves, but she waved it away. He took another slow sip of tea, placed the glass before him, and clasped his hands in front of his face and then to his forehead as if in prayer.

"Sarah," he began, not really sure how to proceed in this. He

was uncomfortable with negotiation and was even more uncomfortable with confrontation. He was better at letting God and Sarah run his world, but the situation with Zeena had become intol-
erable to the point where peace between him and his wife might
have to be sacrificed for the sake of his daughter's happiness. "Sarah," he began again. "I spoke about the betrothal with Zeena
yesterday when she ran into her room."

Sarah's jaw tightened in anticipation and her hand moved to
flatten out a crease. She began shaking her head up and down. "I
knew it. As God is my witness, I knew it was about that!"

Reuben took another sip of tea, knowing full well that
any further statement made before Sarah finished her ful-
mination was useless.

"You know if this betrothal is called off, Reuben, we will not
be able to lift our heads again in this town. Ezra is a powerful man
with powerful friends who can do us harm." She waved her finger
in the air at him ominously.

Reuben weighed her words carefully as he always did, for
though he often minimized her prophecies because they were accompanied by such drama, he never discounted the elements of
truth in them. Ezra Bendak was a powerful and feared man. Of
that there was no doubt. But now, more was at stake than had ever
been at stake before, and, placing everything in the balances, his
daughter's ultimate happiness and his love for her tipped the scales
in her favor. He would have to make an end to this matter even if
it meant repercussions to his business.

"Sarah," he said with all the resolve he could muster. "The
prophet said,`he who troubleth his own house shall inherit the
wind.' You fear an ill wind from Bendak, and the town, if the
marriage doesn't take place. I feel an ill wind from God if it does."

Sarah turned in her chair and was about to speak when Reuben
held up his hand.

"There should be tenderness and affection between two
people, especially if they know each other. We were lucky. It
came to us. I saw it come to Jonah and Leah. But Zeena and

Ezra do not have it. There isn't even the possibility that it might grow." He opened his palms to her and extended them to her. "Sarah, my dearest Sarah," he repeated for emphasis. "She doesn't even like him, let alone love him."

"Love?" Sarah interrupted. "What does she have to know about love? Let her know about survival from day to day and scratching out and making due. I found her a man who will treat her like a queen and give her everything a mother could want a daughter to have. Why shouldn't at least one of my children know what it's like not to bargain for an egg? Why shouldn't we be able to walk through this town and finally have some respect because now we have the ear of someone who's important?" She took a quick breath. "You are a romantic fool, Reuben, a romantic fool like your son. Zeena is no romantic. Love isn't an issue with Zeena. With Zeena the issue is will. Her will over my will. And as for an ill wind from God, you let me and God work it out."

Reuben's face flushed and he struggled to control his voice.

"You are missing my point, Sarah. To force Zeena into a life of misery for some idea that she'll have a secure future or status when we both know she will be miserable is a sin. We know it is wrong. We cannot force her to do something that we both know is wrong. We both want her to marry, but I held her and felt the misery in her. I cannot permit my own flesh such misery." He paused and waited for her response but there was none. "Sarah," he said softly, "I fear what will happen if she marries Ezra, not if she doesn't."

"I promise you, Reuben, nothing will happen. Girls marry boys they don't like or even know every day and the world doesn't fall apart. It won't fall apart for your daughter either."

"Sarah, Ezra is a person who looks at people as if they are things. Look at his business. He buys things from people when they are most desperate. He still has a few of the things we had to sell when we couldn't make enough money to pay his grandfather. You don't re-member? If Zeena becomes his wife, she will become another thing like the things in his shop. What if she runs away or worse? What if she does such a terrible thing as his wife? Would that bring you less shame in the town than if we called off the wedding? Now he has no claim on her other than an agreement. How will Ezra respond once they're married and he loses his most precious possession? Do you think it will go well for any of us? If we end this now, we may feel his scorn, but we have had difficult times before. We will get through them as we did before."

"I am tired of difficult times and scratching to survive," she yelled. Tears rose to her eyes and fell down her cheeks. "We finally have the chance to have some comfort by making this marriage and I will not sacrifice that comfort. We have other children and other marriages to think of. With Ezra's connections, Dora will make a good marriage and don't think I don't see the looks between her and that anarchist you welcomed into this house. Let me tell you that that has to stop, too. And don't you think our Ruth will also benefit from having an older sister married to a wealthy man?"

"But she hates him, Sarah. She hates him and won't marry him."

"And I say she will marry him." She stood and leaned over to table, her fists clenched. "She will do as I say if it's the last thing she ever does. I am her mother and she will do as I tell her!"

"How?" he yelled back as he stood. "How can a mother be so callous to her child? How can you stand there with no hint of dread that this marriage is doomed to fail?" He moved from his place and took a deep breath to compose himself. Then he turned to her again.

"I thought I knew you in your heart, Sarah," he yelled, "but I see I do not. I don't understand what is between you and Zeena, but I do know that if it continues, it will bring down this family." He smashed his fist down on the table. The glass of tea tipped over and poured over the table. "I will not permit this thing to happen!"

"You won't permit it! You won't permit it!" she railed back echoing his final words. "What did she tell you about me? What poison did she pour into your ear that you come at me banging tables? You want to know what's going on between us Reuben?

The same thing that's been going on from the time she was little. Why am I doing this? Why am I doing this? Because I want her out of this house and married the way a girl is supposed to be married. I've lived with that angry, morose shadow long enough and now that somebody has finally taken an interest in her, I want her out. I know what Ezra is, and I know what he comes out of, and I tell you he's better than she deserves. She's lucky he sees the pretty face and her silken hair. Wait till he sees how she wants to be treated like a grand duchess and wait till he hears what she'll say to him if she doesn't get what she wants. If you want to pity someone, Reuben, pity Ezra Bendak and may God forgive me for giving him a shrew who'll make his life miserable. And if you have any pity left, Reuben, pity me for getting gray from her and growing old from her."

There was a prolonged silence as Reuben drank in his wife's fears. In the silence, Zeena stiffened behind the bedroom door and felt her face grow hot. He was weakening. Her mother's tears were washing away his resolve and he would succumb as he always had. She bit down on her lip and fought her own tears with the pain. No, she thought. Neither her brother nor her father was strong enough to win against her mother. She would have to be her own strength. She knew this and for a moment, she hated him as she had hated Jonah for being weak. Always, always she had only herself.

She threw the door open and stood frozen between the posts. Reuben looked at her tearfully and raised his fingers to his lips.

"No, Papa, no," she blurted out suddenly. "I'll not be quiet this time. I'll not become her sacrifice on the alter of her good name, and be torn apart so she can hold her head up high while I suffocate and die."

Reuben stood. "Silence," he bellowed. "I'll not have you speak to your mother like that."

"No," she screamed back in desperation. "I'll not be quiet and no power on earth will make me marry Ezra Bendak. You can't make me do it. Not you, not Mama, not your tradition and not your God."

"Silence!" yelled Reuben again, raising his hand and smacked her across her cheek for her blasphemy. His hand hovered in the air and he looked at it and then into the eyes of his daughter. He had never touched one of his children in anger. They stared at each other, each in his own confusion, and Reuben felt his hand grow hot. He saw her eyes widen and then narrow in contempt. He pulled it to his side as a shameful child might do. Her eyes confirmed what she had decided was true as she stood listening to her parents argue. Neither of them loved her and together they would force her into this marriage. She said nothing, and her silence tore into his heart like claws. She backed away towards the bedroom door never taking her eyes off the two of them. How would she proceed now, she thought? How would she proceed now that she was totally alone? She put her hand into her pocket and felt for the gold coins Malinovitch had given her a year ago. The time was near when she might have to use them to buy her freedom.

CHAPTER 11

Zeena paced the bedroom as if caged, stopping mid-stride to change direction only to change it again. Her movements were abrupt and contracted, as if forced by some malevolent energy to reduce the space in which her body could blurt out her rage and fear. She found herself pivoting to the right and to the left, and finally standing immobilized in the center of the room.

In three short months she would wed Ezra Bendak and there was no way out. Her body tightened as she covered herself with her arms against the fantasized embrace, and saw the past traumatic weeks rise before her like some deadly miasma. She saw herself stealing into the barn to wait until Jonathan returned. In silence, she fingered the shirt he sometimes wore and pressed it to her lips and face to become intoxicated by his lingering scent. She dreamed that together they would leave this place and wander the world. She remembered how his look of surprise at finding her there in the darkness turned to incredulity and then to disgust as she begged him to flee with her or make love to her, or at least, in her desperation, to kill her. His searing rejection and his statement of love for her own sister continued to pound in her head like the clanging of a cracked, iron bell.

She returned to the present, and the hate she felt for Jonathan at that moment returned with her. She wanted to kill him for his rejection of the love she offered him. He did not understand. No one understood. And now, a week later, a week closer to her wedding day, he avoided her eyes and his absolute silence, when no one else was near, condemned her. Her mind raced her to St. Petersburg and it flung her into the open arms of the large, fatherly man who had mysteriously appeared and disappeared without further word. He would protect her and he would care, but that fantasy also faded as Jonathan's face intruded. She would give herself to a peasant in the field or to one of the constable's men. Anyone, anyone but Ezra. The thought of being touched by him, or being opened and entered by him, of carrying a child by him and bearing the pain for him tore at her as nothing had ever torn at her before. To die here without having lived. She moved her hands to her groin and tore at the air in front of herself as if tearing out the reality of what would soon be. Then she sank onto the bed. She did not weep. She had no more tears.

"Zeena?" The door opened slowly, and Ruth hesitantly poked her head in. She was dressed as a little Persian queen. "Mama said you should go to the Purim service and not go near the boys who get drunk and you should wear Dora's costume because she has to help Zedde and can't go and it's hanging on the door." She blurted her mother's dictum in one breath and quickly ran off to meet her friends.

Dazed and drained, Zeena saw a shaking hand slowly reach for the makeshift gown and veil slowly swinging on the back of the door. She was beyond thinking as she lifted the dress to her body and let it fall to the floor. She set the crown of straw and fake flowers upon her head and covered her face with the veil. The mirror threw back an image of a specter, unrecognizable like a hundred other counterfeit Queen Esthers who would also gather at the Purim service. Zeena Chernov disappeared, and in the mirror she saw herself as the faceless shadow she would become if she could not free herself from her own inability to act with the force of her own resolve and vision. She looked at herself a long time and a thought rooted itself in her brain like a parasitic vine. Hidden behind the veil she might move unnoticed, and she could watch and wait and take back at least a small piece of something she wanted for herself. Did not Tamara veil herself and seduce Judah? Did not Lot's daughters go into him when he was drunk? The thoughts of what she might do to take something for herself flew blindly back and forth like dark birds in a cave. Judah never knew Tamara through her veil. Lot never knew in his drunkenness what

his daughters had done and the deed could be done when a man
was drunk. Her plan took form. She would have her vengeance on
him and on Ezra. Her whole body became animated by the thought.
It was Purim and tradition permitted the men to drink to excess.
Jonathan would drink as well. She would watch him, wait, follow
him to the barn and she would lay with him. It could be done.
Ezra would never be the first to enter her, but the man whom she
loved, would. The man who dared to love her sister and not her,
would. She would be revenged on all of them.

She laughed a high pitched tormented laugh and quickly put
on the crumpled dress. Throwing the veil on the bed, she pinned
up her hair so she would not appear as a young girl. Never taking
her eyes off the mirror, she covered her head with the veil and set it
in place with the crown. She looked at herself. In the place of
Zeena Chernov was a woman who could, with anonymity, work
her will. She would look like all the others, but she would not be
celebrating a holiday. Her thoughts swept her to Jonathan's place
in the barn and the soft hay upon which he would sprawl in his
half conscious stupor.

She ran out the door and to the synagogue with the taste of her
resolve in her mouth, trying to subdue her own fear for the act she
would commit. As she ran, she heard the lectures her mother had
dutifully given her on modesty and the laws that sanctified a home
and a woman. She laughed at the thought of the ruse and laughed
away the thoughts of the young girls who were brought all smiles and
blushes to the marriage canopy, eager and pure. She would at least
have this much and she would laugh at Ezra for as long she lived. If
she were to be given in marriage like chattel, the prized goods would
be soiled. If her body was to be torn and entered, she would at least be
the one to decide the man it would be. She would be in control of this
if she could be in control of nothing else. Ultimately, she knew she
would lose, but she at least could set some of the rules to the game she
was being forced to play.

The synagogue glowed. Children and young adults, dressed
to imitate the characters of the ancient Persian court, crowded on

the steps and filled the doorway. She let herself be swept along by the gaiety and the noisemakers, but never entered into it. She pressed her way through to the separation between the men and women and scanned the field of men at prayer. She saw her mother and Ruth and was caught short by a flush when they looked straight at her and then away. She laughed again and continued peering with hawk's eyes for her Jonathan.

Beyond her concern, the rabbi walked up the left staircase leading to the oak lectern built into the balustrade. To his right, the seven branched candelabra gaily flickered the holiday spirit. Parents quieted children and took noise makers from fidgeting hands. Zeena used the old sage as a focal point and traced the line of men first horizontally and then vertically, but always returning to the sage to begin again. Her hungry scan for Jonathan encompassed the entire room and she found him at the rear standing in front of the age darkened fresco of Rachel's tomb.

The old man at the lectern cleared his throat and stroked his white beard, now looking orange from the candle's glow. A solitary noisemaker sounded and a hand was slapped by an embarrassed father. A child's cry was muffled. From behind the lattice screen, Zeena watched, and the world around Jonathan took on a vague, white haze.

"Queen Esther was a beautiful woman who was presented with a burden she felt was greater than she thought she could bear." The rabbi paused for the audience to join him in his thought. "And what was that burden?" the Rabbi asked rhetorically. "To save her people from extinction at the hands of a madman." The Rabbi's voice softened as if only understatement could reinforce the moment, then it rose again. "Mordecai, her cousin, came to her and said only she could act, but to act, she had to tell that she was a Hebrew and come before the king unsummoned. For this she could have been killed." He paused for effect. "And how did she respond?" he asked with drama building in his voice. "She responded with fear. No, she said", and the rabbi's voice rose. "But it was only when Esther realized that she had been placed in her exalted position by God and pushed onto the threshold of a great moment, did she agree." He paused and looked at his listeners. "But understand this, my dear friends. Esther did not agree to risk her life to become great herself. She agreed to risk her life to save the lives of her people. Why did she not agree immediately? Why did she not leap to their defense the moment she heard of their plight? Wouldn't she have been the greater for it?"

Zeena was caught by the questions and drawn into the web. She turned to the lectern for a moment and forgot Jonathan.

"No," he continued. "She was greater because she was at first frightened and thought of herself. Esther was human first before she was a Jew. And because she was human first, her choice to risk her life was all the greater. Was Moses not reluctant to do God's bidding? Did not Jonah flee from the word and work of the Lord? I tell you my dear friends that to act bravely for what is right, especially when you are afraid to act, is what greatness is made of. To go beyond your own real fear and act for the greater good of others, is what a real hero does."

Jonah lowered his head and thought about his broken promise to Zeena. He had acted even though he was afraid of what would be said to him and he wondered if there would ever be a time in his life when he would act and he would not be afraid.

"There are things in our lives greater than ourselves and each day God places us between choices," the Rabbi continued. "God gave Esther the freedom to choose, as God gives us all the freedom to choose. And God gave her the freedom to say no, as God gives us all the freedom to say no." The rabbi took a breath. "God was silent, but Esther said yes. God was silent, but Esther spoke. He paused again. "When God is silent to you, might he not be waiting for your response? We must each speak that response for ourselves. It is the `yes' to the righteous act in the face of fear that God wants us to give. We can all be like the heroes of our Bible if we accept our fear and let that fear be the threshold to righteous action. Fear is natural. You can choose fear and not act and God will not destroy you. But if you choose fear, when beyond the fear is the chance to act righteously, what do you do to yourself? How do you walk without looking over your shoulder? How will you sleep without waking suddenly? God was with Esther when she took courage and God will be with you. Act for the good and God will carry you up on eagle's wings and you shall not be afraid. Shrink from the opportunity to do good, and you will punish yourself by carrying with you that which you did not do. Sin, my children, is not acting righteously when you have the choice and the chance to act. You know this and so does God."

Zeena listened to the old man's words despite herself. She, like Esther, stood at the threshold of a dangerous choice and would step over it also in fear. But for Esther the threshold led to a throne room and the possible adoration of her people throughout time. For Zeena, the threshold led to a pile of hay and the vilification of the man she loved if she could not carry off the ruse.

Then, enshrouded in her secret, the make believe queen, more Tamar than Esther, rose slowly, purposefully, easing her way through the gaiety like a mist, rubbing lightly against skirts and shawls, and moving down the steps towards Jonathan. Her body pulsed with anticipation and tensed in the heat of what she was about. She stood and watched him furtively, glancing back and forth for fear that someone would recognize her.

From where she stood she could see the tables laden with food and drink, and she could see Jonathan and Jonah toasting each other. Glass after glass was drained and with each she grew warmer and warmer as if the wine itself flowed through her own body. She watched, invisible behind her veil. Soon they would both stagger home, but Jonathan would be alone. He would go to the barn and she would be there waiting.

She moved further down the steps and through the crowded foyer. The cool air caressed her like a sculptor's hands and shaped the veil against her body as if she and it were soft yielding clay. She ran past darkened shops, as vacant and empty as the people she knew who worked in them. Zedde and Dora were gone. They would be at the

Mitvoy's with the others for the holiday celebration. She was expected too, but she did not care.

She crossed the little bridge and suddenly, far in the distance, she could make out the outline of the house and the barn. She had seen the sight a thousand times, yet now it was a new sight, a new place. Her steps slowed involuntarily. Again, all the lessons of modesty and decency were pushed away as if they were an assailant. She was resolved to do this thing and be avenged on the man she loved and on the man she hated.

She waited breathlessly and patiently in the darkest recesses of the small barn. Her thoughts alternated between the mystery of the impending act and anger she felt towards herself and towards her family and betrothed for the action she had to take.

Finally, finally, the door opened quietly, and Jonathan peered into the darkness, holding his fingers to his mouth to silence the goat. He staggered and fell against the central support beam sending a milking stool clanking across the floor. Zeena pulled herself further into the darkness as he staggered towards a pile of hay where the stool lay. He picked it up, set it right, and then, arms extended, fell backward on the hay laughing. He laughed his drunken laughter into the eves.

Zeena's heart beat faster and a slow flush rose up her body and centered in her cheek. He lay there quietly for a moment and then began snapping his fingers to imaginary music. She laughed to herself a young girlish laugh, and yearned to run to his side, and laugh with him over his foolishness. But Ezra's image passed before her, and her disgust for him gave her the strength to move closer out of the blackness that held her.

Jonathan's eyes were closed and she softly stepped closer. He snorted and blew his breath through parted lips and his hand aimlessly fell across his stomach. Her eyes softened for him and glazed with tears. He moved again. A torrent of anxiety surged through her. Her knees weakened. She could feel her heart pounding in her chest. She could feel the blood hot in her veins. His breathing was regular in his wine sleep, and she knelt beside him, an anxious Psyche by her sleeping Cupid. Slowly, she positioned herself next to him and reached over to open his coat. He moved slightly and she froze, her hand hovering above him. Again, she lowered her hand to the top button of his shirt and opened it and then another. She tested the depth of his sleep by letting her fingers rest in the soft curls of his chest hairs and by feeling the rhythmic motion of his breathing. He did not stir. Her hand explored his torso as it rose and fell. The heat of his body flowed into her hands and into her arms. She wanted to throw herself on him, to kiss him tenderly and be held by him, but she could only look at him through the veil and feel the tears rise in her eyes. She should have been his wife. This should have been a warm room with a down mattress. She should have been dressed in white and it should have been she who would be touched gently and knowingly. Then she would have been unafraid. She moved her face close to his. Their breath mingled through the gauze and she lightly touched her lips to his. His hand gestured weakly as if to brush away a fly, but it fell again at his side. She lowered her face again, pressing her lips to his parted mouth. A dream, fashioned from ancient memories, took form in Jonathan's brain and he allowed himself to fade into the kiss.

Her pulse quickened as she slid her hand hesitantly towards his stomach and then to the rim of his trousers. Again, he moved. Again, she hesitated. Then, she lowered her hand slowly, allowing it to glide back and forth on the front of his pants. Through the cloth, she felt him respond and she pressed her lips to his again with more intensity than before.

Jonathan dissolved further and further into the dream he dreamed. He had wandered into forest with tall trees arching above him, hiding the moon. A goblet of wine appeared and he drank from it. Two trees appeared before him like a door, and as he moved between them, a beautiful white bird glided out of the night and descended onto his chest with velvet talons. He dreamed himself pushed back on a bed of leaves between the trees as the great bird spread her wings across his body and covered him with the warmth of her downy caress.

Jonathan's eyes opened slowly, and narrowed to focus on the dream image that had suddenly become real. A veiled woman crouched next to him gently stroking his body. Slowly, very slowly, he became aware of the sensation and the warmth that spread across his groin. He could feel himself responding to her touch, but did not pull away or question.

Through the wine dark haze, his brain focused, as best it could, on the rhythmic motion of the stranger's hand and the new and wonderful sensation of a woman caressing him so tenderly. He had dreamed this dream before, and now it was not a dream. He would let it happen.

Zeena's own excitement grew as she raised herself and sought to release the buttons of his trousers. One by one she opened them and she felt his manhood touch her hand. She allowed her fingers to encircle it just to know and then released it to unbutton her own undergarment. Her own dampness and heat surprised her as she ran her fingers through the moist, matted hair until the natural moistness that was hers allowed them to move freely up and back. She quivered at the thought of her next act as tears of regret and sorrow merged with the heightened excitement of anticipation and desire. She lifted her skirt and straddled her half conscious lover, feeling a rush of blood to her cheek as his burning shaft touched the outer rim of her vagina. She leaned back above him, holding him to her soft, yielding opening until her natural moistness allowed him to move into her with some ease. A warm sensation in her groin fanned out to her legs, and crept down her thighs and back again to some secret inner depth of her body. As she moved, the fear and anger ebbed with sweet sensations she had never known. Her breath quickened as she pushed him deeper into her body, deeper to the door only he would open.

He responded to her out of his own need for completion and release as he slowly thrust his pelvis up to meet her.

And then she knew that the next movement would be the one

that would have him enter her fully and keep him locked there forever. Her skirts fell on either side of him and her hands reached down to the earth as if to succor strength from it. For a moment she looked down at him as though they were man and wife and her soul ached for him and his love with all the passion she had ever known.

The great dream bird held his neck with her beak and drew his groin to her downy body. The dream lover thrust downward again and something deep within told him that he must fulfill his part of her rite. A mystery was being performed, and this alter upon which he lay would be for all eternity her private nesting place.

The pain tore her as he entered her fully. She bit down on her lips and paused a second till the pain passed. Again tears rose in her eyes, not from the pain, but because life was such that she had to act as she now acted and because she knew it would always be that way. She pushed back and down again and this time the pain would not stop her. She closed her burning eyes and suddenly, the pain was over. A gush of warmth flowed through her as he slid slowly into the loosening channel, and she was overcome by the sensation inching slowly across her inner thighs to where their bodies became one. He pushed up again, the wonderful sensation building in his loins and his hand reached up her thighs and took hold of her. He pressed himself deep into her body.

She thought to flee now that he had opened her, but the strange sensation building in her combined with the thought of his discovering who she was, was too exciting to let pass. She responded by raising and lowering herself to meet his slowly undulating pelvis and she synchronized her body to draw from him the ultimate pleasure she could extract. What did she care now. She had accomplished her objective. But now, something was taking over that even she could not control, and she gave herself over to it with abandonment never felt before. She would not stop this even if he were to awake or even if the whole town were to discover them. She would have him completely even if she were to explode that very moment. Her breath came faster and faster as she gave herself

up to the shattering pressure that mounted higher and higher in
her groin. The writhing man in his half conscious pleasure beneath her, thrust upward into the feathered creature and opened
his vacant eyes to gaze at the magical white bird or demon that
hovered over him. The unquenchable fire in her, the tensions and
passions that recklessly pulsed through her, shook and twisted her
arched body till it exploded in time to the convulsions of the man
who emptied his life into her at the same moment.

"Love me, Jonathan," she gasped. "Love only me."

For a moment they froze. Zeena, the make believe queen, the
magical white demon bird, hovering over her subject, her prey, her
lover, looked down upon him through tear filled eyes. They were
married now and he would always be hers. That much she knew.
Jonathan would always be hers. She looked at him longingly and
eased a small silver ring from his limp hand and slid it on to her ring
finger. They were married now and it would always be so.

CHAPTER 12

May 2, 1882

Reuben looked up from his work when the bell above the door shook. The setting sun was behind the large figure who stood in the door, and the blackness of the silhouette would have frightened him were it not for the imposing form turning slightly, allowing the scarlet rays to etch out the aquiline nose and protruding lips of the man who wanted to marry his daughter.

"How good to see you, dear Ezra," cooed Sarah as she moved around the counter past her husband. "Reuben, look who's here," and she took Ezra by the arm and led him to a chair near the counter. In her mind, she was already pouring him a glass of tea and offering him small cakes.

Reuben was uncomfortable. He slowly removed his glasses and rubbed the corners of his eyes. Zeena's pleas again echoed in his head, but Sarah's exhortation about Zeena having nothing in life with no husband also weighed heavily. Still, he could not erase the anguish in his daughter's eyes.

Ezra Bendak settled himself into the chair facing Reuben. He did not acknowledge Jonah, but immediately took a large handkerchief out of his jacket and wiped his forehead and neck. Then he blew his nose and put it away.

"So how's business?" Reuben inquired feigning interest and trying to avoid the purpose of the visit.

Ezra stiffened. "Do you mean my shops or what?" he asked almost defensively.

Reuben replaced his glasses and peered over them at the man before him. He had forgotten for a moment that even small talk with a man like Ezra could be a source of accusation and conflict. Reuben was uncomfortable and did not like having to be on his guard when exchanging words with the man who wanted to be his son-in-law. At that very moment, Reuben resolved that Zeena should not be his wife. Even Sarah was caught up short by Ezra's response, but she threw a sharp glance at Reuben as if he had insulted their guest purposely.

"Here's a nice glass of tea," she interrupted, diverting attention from glances that were potentially dangerous. Reuben lowered his eyes, resigned to the fact that Sarah was determined to let nothing interfere with the marriage.

With cautious obeisance, she placed the tea next to Bendak and watched him ignore it. She stood there uncomfortably, as a child waiting for approval that will not come, but Bendak's eyes remained riveted solely upon Reuben. She straightened her back and retreated to the little iron stove. All was out of her hands now. She was not in control, and she was afraid.

Bendak leaned forward, his hands on his knees, and eyed Reuben through horizontal slits.

"Well, Mr. Chernov," he said abruptly. "I understand you are having second thoughts about your daughter becoming my wife."

Reuben slowly removed the glasses from his face and studied them. Sarah nervously straightened bolts of fabric on the shelves. Jonah silently prayed that his father would void the agreement so he would no longer have to feel the accusation in his sister's eyes.

Reuben took a deep breath. "Do you love my daughter?" he asked slowly.

"That isn't what I asked you, Mr. Chernov," Ezra said, but he paused, recognizing that he might have to acquiesce to this evasion. He felt the heat of anger rise for he was accustomed to having his questions answered immediately.

"Mr. Chernov," he continued. "We are both adults. We both know the ways of the world, and how difficult it is to live well. I am a man who likes to live well. With me, your daughter will live very well.

Besides, your daughter as my wife will bring you certain business advantages that might go elsewhere if I decide they should."

Bendak had placed his implied threat carefully before Reuben and Sarah. Both were aware of it and what Bendak could do if he chose to involve himself in their livelihood. Reuben had never considered this as a factor in his decision, and had dismissed it whenever Sarah alluded to it. Now, from Bendak's own lips, a new, ugly truth loomed up and stood before him. Indeed, there was Zeena's happiness to consider, but now Bendak was throwing Zeena's own family's survival into the balance and Reuben was sure the man sitting before him could be very vindictive.

"You make the problem more complex, Ezra," he said, controlling his anger. "You answer my simple question about love with a promise that evokes both good and evil for my family. You have not as yet told me if you love my daughter."

Bendak took the handkerchief from his pocket and wiped his forehead and neck again.

"You want to know if I love your daughter? Well," he continued, placing both hands on his knees, "if it makes a difference to you, I will tell you that I love your daughter."

"See," interrupted Sarah, sweeping around the counter. "Now everything is as it should be." Jonah stood. "So it's done, Ezra," continued Sarah. "I tell you you've not made a mistake, and you'll be like a son to us."

"Sarah!" shouted Reuben suddenly. "Everything is not as it should be. Everything is far from what it should be!"

Sarah looked at her husband incredulously and her mouth opened slightly.

Reuben stood in front of Ezra trying to remain calm.

Ezra rose abruptly.

"Ezra," he began, "I will not give you my answer until I talk to Zeena again."

"Tell him no, Papa," Jonah said suddenly. "Tell him he can't marry Zeena. Ezra glared at him with cold contempt, and Sarah uttered a small shriek as if startled by a rodent.

"I will not be shamed before this town, Mr. Chernov. Every-one knows that I am marrying your daughter." His eyes raged.

"You have nothing to worry about, Ezra," Sarah interjected quickly, trying to reassure him. "You know how these things are. Fathers and daughters have special relationships. Brothers also have special relationships and want everything to be right. It will be all right. I promise." Her eyes darted sparks at her son and her husband.

She ushered Ezra to the door and opened it for him. "You'll see. By tomorrow everything will be all right."

"Tomorrow," Bendak repeated, controlling his obvious displeasure.

"Everything will be all right tomorrow," she whispered so only he could hear. "I guarantee it."

Sarah watched the figure move into the square and disappear into the crowd of workers on their way home. Then she turned.

"Are you both insane?" she bellowed, covering them with a blanket of collective hostility. "How can you do this to me? How can you do this to your family? With a word he can ruin us, and you treat him like a beggar?"

"I don't like him," Reuben said softly, and looked down at the garment on his lap.

Sarah folded her hands over her skirt and stared at him. "You don't like him! You don't like him," she repeated as if the single expression would not be enough to punctuate the importance of her coming thought. "You'd like it better if people stopped coming into the shop? You'd like it better if suddenly the mills in Odessa stop your credit? You'd like it better if we become outcasts and starve in the street?"

"Mama," interrupted Jonah. "How can you want someone in your family who would do such things to people? How can you want Zeena to live with such a person?"

"No one asked you, so don't give what you're not asked for!"

"He is right," Reuben said. "This is a man without honor or learning or righteousness." He stood. "The man you've chosen for our daughter calls the Tsar's agents his friends." His voice rose and his face flushed with anger and resolve. "I will not have this man in my family. I will not force my daughter into a marriage with this person." He saw Zeena's pale blue eyes entreat him as he spoke. "If Zeena wants him, that's her decision, but I will not consign my child to a life of anger and torment."

"Then you condemn us to a life of poverty as outcasts." She paused and took a breath. "Why don't you see what I see? Why don't you believe what this man can do if he decides to do it. We are in too far, Reuben. See reality," she cried, and sank to the chair weeping and shaking.

"I see Zeena's reality and her reality is more important. This is my child and I will not force her into such a life. Bendak will do nothing to us."

"Do nothing to us? Do nothing to us," she repeated. "Oh, God, oh, God, I married a fool."

Sarah stood again, her fists clenched at her sides and her heart pounding. The shop was silent. Zeena would have to agree to marry Bendak, she thought, and above her father's protests.

Sarah moved through the marketplace, consumed by the single thought. Zeena had won. She heard laughter, Zeena's laughter. But how to force the laugh back down Zeena's throat? What did Reuben or Jonah know of the delicate balances of life? They didn't see the world as a place where you bargain for the dregs because that's all that's available. They didn't understand survival as she understood it. They didn't know the pain of seeing others feeding their families the best food available, when her own children had to eat scraps. No more would she have to feel the shame of watching the rich gossips chatter about her behind their hands? Never again would she have to nod agreement to the wealthy who criticized Reuben's work to her face and then discounted it? What it took in bribes to keep Jonah out of the army and all those years of deprivation for her and her children would be paid back in the status of having Ezra Bendak as her son-in-law. It would all be Zeena's, and she would be there to enjoy it, too. Zeena would walk through the town in expensive warm fur and Zeena would preside at a hand rubbed mahogany table decked with finest crystal. Zeena would have the big two story house in town and then she, the mother, would walk in and sit on the velvet chairs as if they were her own.

Somehow Zeena had to be made to see what would happen to her brother and father if she did not agree to the wedding. And the decision had to be made before Reuben told Zeena that he would not force her to marry. But how? How could she get Zeena to marry against her father's wishes when this is what Zeena wanted?

She forced herself forward, not knowing what she would do or say when she got home, but knowing that home was where all would be decided. Each thought of her's hit a wall, and each wall was Zeena. She slowed her pace. She was letting her fear run away with her head. She had to be calm. She had to be in control! She had to move carefully.

The small wooden house seemed smaller and shabbier in comparison with the grand vision of Bendak's home. How Zeena could dismiss such a future was beyond Sarah's comprehension.

Zeena tensed when the door opened, but continued working without turning around. She had been thinking of the child she carried, and how a part of Jonathan grew in her body and would always be part of her. At first, when she had missed her period a month ago, she was filled with fear. But the fear soon gave way to comfort, the comfort of knowing that she at least had something that came from loving Jonathan. But she also came to the realization life in a small town for a bastard child and its unmarried whore mother would be a daily horror, and the shame to her father was more than she wanted him to bear. And where could she run with an infant in her arms? So it was that Ezra Bendak who became the only viable solution to her dilemma and that thought gave her a moment of perverse amusement. The cause of her problem was also the solution to it.

Zeena placed the dishes on the shelf, and poured the dirty water back into the bucket. She dried her hands and turned.

"You're back earlier than I expected," she said matter of factly, breaking the prolonged silence.

Sarah sat at the table, sighed audibly and said nothing. She folded her hands in her lap and lowered her head. Finally, overcome by a sense of profound helplessness, and giving into a genuine fear, she began to sob softly.

Zeena's immediate thought was of her father. "What's the matter with Papa?" she cried.

Sarah took her hands from her face and looked into the terrified eyes of her daughter. Deep in Sarah's brain, something began to connect with Zeena's fear.

"You love your Papa, Zeena?" Sarah asked simply.

"What's the matter with him?"

A possible opening for Sarah presented itself. "If you love your Papa, Zeena, don't let him destroy himself and his family." Her voice implored. Such a conciliatory tone was foreign to Sarah's voice and it increased Zeena's anxiety.

"What are you talking about? Where is he?"

"Tell me what happened!" Zeena demanded, throwing the towel on the table, menacingly.

"Your father has decided against the marriage." The words fell from her lips like measured daggers. She had her plan now.

Zeena stood and looked squarely at her mother. A smile crept into the corner of her mouth, and then broadened. She laughed with her soul, a hysterical laugh of triumph and relief, a laugh of one who has escaped and cheated death. Her father did love her. He would not let her be condemned to a life of pain and torment.

Sarah's eyes widened as Zeena's victory paean resounded through the room.

"Laugh, you fool, laugh and watch your father destroyed. Laugh and watch your sisters starve. Laugh and watch your father kill himself trying to feed his children when no one will speak to him or come into his store. Laugh, you foolish, foolish girl. Laugh him into the grave!"

"What are you talking about?" Zeena shouted suddenly, her mother's fear taking hold of her and pushing aside her triumph. "What else do you know? Did Ezra say something to Papa?"

Sarah had a feeling of impending victory.

"What did he say?" Zeena asked again.

Sarah looked directly into Zeena's face. "Ezra said that if you did not agree to marry him, whether you have your father's approval or not, he will cut off your father's credit line in Kiev and see to it that no person in the town comes into the shop."

Sarah caught her breath and calculated Zeena's response. It could go either way. Zeena could laugh in her face or acquiesce. Sarah had made her final move. She would either win or lose with Zeena's next word.

"That filth!" Zeena said with contempt.

"Call him what you like, Zeena, but he still holds your father's life in his hands."

If it was true that Bendak would destroy her father if she refused to marry him, what might he do when she showed the town that she conceived a bastard rather than have his child? And what might he do to avenge himself? Would he get at her through Jonathan's child? Children mysteriously disappear. Somewhere she could hear Sarah's yammering, but it was vague and far away. The vision of some distant horror perpetrated on the child was presenting itself and taking hold.

The decision that marriage to Bendak would be the only solution was confirmed at that moment, and Zeena again saw how ironic it was that love for her father and love for the child she conceived out of desperation, and hate for Bendak would bring her to the wedding canopy with that man. She began to refocus on Sarah's chattering about the future, and she looked at her mother. None of this would be happening had it not been for Sarah. None of the anguish and tensions of the past months or the past years would have happened had Sarah not connived and manipulated her and her father into this situation. None of this would have happened had Sarah not viewed her own child as an enemy in the house.

" . . .so it's now up to your father, and if I know your father, he'll throw everything away because he loves you." She was careful not to lay any blame or make any accusations. She was careful not even to suggest that Zeena marry Ezra. She knew any suggestion would be hurled back with contempt. No, Sarah had to be cautious. She had to wait and let Zeena take the lead in this. It had to be Zeena's choice, and she was banking on the fact that Zeena's love for Reuben would sway that decision.

Zeena looked at the crying woman before her for a long, silent moment. She moved her hands to her stomach to caress the tiny life growing within her. She would have one last triumph before she capitulated. A sardonic smile etched its way across Zeena's mouth.

"I will marry Bendak," she said flatly.

Sarah gave a small audible shriek that combined victory and surprise, but she muffled it lest Zeena take back her words. Sarah made no other sound.

"But don't imagine that I'm doing this for you." She paused and searched her mother's eyes for that look of question which she wanted to change to shock and horror and shame. She moved her hands over her stomach again and watched Sarah's eyes focus on them.

"I hate Ezra Bendak and I hate you for having created the horror we've all been through." She waited for a response, but there was none. Then, slowly and deliberately, so no word would be lost to her mother's ears, Zeena told Sarah how she had played the whore so Ezra would not be the first man to have her.

"I gave myself to someone else, Mama. I conceived a bastard Mama, by a man whose name you shall never know." Zeena studied her mother's face as an artist studying her creation. She could see the shock and horror take hold. She could see her mother's eyes widen and flame with the passion that only comes from the knowledge that a child has brought profound disappointment and shame. Sarah turned slowly, and her hand smashed across Zeena's face.

"You whore!" Sarah screamed, recklessly forgetting the danger of the moment. "After all we taught you and gave you, you shame us like this?"

"Thank you for that Mama. It's just what I wanted from you," and she laughed contemptuously. Sarah raised her hand again, but did not move it further.

"Go ahead, Mama. Hit the pregnant whore again! Don't worry," she taunted, "I will still marry your wonderful son-in-law to be."

"Who's the father?" demanded Sarah, grabbing her by both shoulders.

"Not Ezra Bendak," Zeena laughed.

"How can I tell your father?" she asked, shaking her head and putting her hands to her lips. "How can I bring him such shame?"

"It's your shame, Mama?" Zeena said. "Do you feel the shame hot on your face, Mama?"

"How could you have done this to your father?"

Zeena laughed. "To my father," she said loudly, and repeated it. "To my father? I didn't do this to my father. I did this to you and your bridegroom. That's who. I did this to myself. The three of us did this so don't involve my father." Zeena's voice grated. Then it suddenly changed.

"Don't you see, Mama," she said softly. "You can't tell anyone, especially Bendak. That's the beauty of it. You tell Bendak and he won't marry me and everyone in the town will know Sarah Chernov's daughter is a whore. You tell Papa and it will really kill him and then it will be your fault. I don't care what they call me, but you do, and you will have to smile, and know, and be silent, even under the wedding canopy."

She read the frustration and disgust in her mother's face and she started to laugh again. She had gotten back at least a small part. She had wounded Sarah and Sarah would have to keep the wound concealed. Zeena felt she had won at least something.

June 3, 1882

Bendák strutted into the room looking like a rare bird who had been lovingly preened, and scanned the assembly for the key figures in the grand dramatic work he had meticulously orchestrated for himself. The good wishes and honor he was purchasing for himself through the lavish show would create and support an image of himself that all would envy for years. He moved through his relatives and friends perfunctorily acknowledging hands and kisses until he reached the door of his house. He turned.

"Rabbi," he said abruptly, "you first and then me." He motioned to the rabbi to move ahead.

The rabbi stepped through the door into the darkening twilight. Ezra followed him and then turned again to his family.

"Look happy and don't let your candles go out," he said looking back over his shoulder. "Mama, make sure the people who join in the procession have candles. If they don't, give them but make sure you remember who they are."

The leader of the klezmer band greeted Ezra with the appropriate deference due someone who was willing to pay the large fee, but Ezra waved him off imperiously with the admonition to play loudly as he walked toward his prize.

Sarah swept into the room all smiles and warmth, the satin skirts of her new dress rustling like autumn leaves.

"I tell you Zeena," she said laughing, "the jester Ezra hired is a real wit. The town hasn't had a jester at a wedding in years. I tell you they'll talk about this wedding for a long time."

"I don't want you near me," Zeena said simply. "I don't want you around me now."

Sarah looked at her. "I thought for just a moment," she said, "just a small moment, you could put aside your bitterness but I over estimated you. Word just came that the procession from Ezra's house started so get yourself ready."

Zeena did not move. Sarah looked at her daughter's reflection in the mirror. The bride's eyes were red. Something in Sarah wanted to take hold of her daughter and comfort her as a mother would at such a time, but only enmity was between them and such a bitterness of spirit that neither could transverse it. Sarah, muttered softly, "hurry," and left the room.

Zeena stood before the mirror and muttered softly to her reflection, "fool."

She came through the door to a round of quiet applause from her family and a few close friends of her parents. She moved to the chair in the middle of the room. She sat, as was the tradition, and the ladies in the room gathered around her and began to braid her hair for cutting. Zeena refused to have her hair shorn, but agreed to have it cut shoulder length figuring that it would have grown back in the two months she was going to give him. After that, she would be gone. So, she sat and listened to clicking of the scissors and watched carefully.

The jester approached her and made a sweeping bow.

Zeena smiled her mocking smile and touched her stomach unconsciously. The jester saw the secret movement and knew the tears that sat on the rims of this bride's eyes were not tears of a nervous and expectant virgin. He had gazed into the eyes of hundreds of brides and he could read their secrets as if they blurted them out. In that second, Zeena saw in his soft gray eyes tender understanding, and she let his sympathy touch her and release some of her burden. He finished his song to her upon his knees. Zeena smiled slightly for his song and sympathy.

The woman gathered around her and placed the wig upon her head and she felt herself recoil within. She rose automatically aching to tear the unwanted burden from her head, but did not. She moved past her Zedde who beamed proudly at his beautiful granddaughter. Jonah stood by the door next to Leah, expressionless. Leah's hand rested on the child moving within her. Jonah silently implored his sister's forgiveness. Zeena moved past them as if they didn't exist.

Far in the distance the bride could hear the faint rhythms of trumpet and drum. Reuben and Sarah moved on either side of her, Reuben feeling that his heart would break for her. Sarah looked straight ahead to the sound of the music.

Zeena glanced at the barn and thought of Jonathan. He was somewhere behind her walking with Dora. She studied the undulating road and the dry weeds that clung tenaciously to the caked sand. She thought how she and Jonah had played their childhood games and how things were then. She thought of how it might have been different if he had heeded her plea to run away. Why was this happening? She only wanted to be free. Had it not been for the child, would she have fled? Did fear for her father's well being dictate her choice or was it something else, something she could not fathom? But she would not have her child branded a bastard, and what better revenge then to have another man's child lay claim to Ezra's wealth. She would never have a child by Ezra Bendak, and as soon as he believed the child was his, she would take it and deny Ezra the pleasure of ever touching it. That would be her revenge. The procession continued.

Reuben thought of Zeena: Why do you condemn me with your silence? Did I not agree to your wishes? Did I not insist that you break off this marriage? I don't understand you. I gave you what you wanted, but you didn't want it. God gave you a beautiful face and a bright mind, but who gave you the anger? Only Ezra wanted you. Ah, Zeena, I do not understand. I do not understand.

Sarah thought of Zeena: I carried you under my heart, but you would never let yourself come into it. It should not have been this way. The world is cruel, and little snatches of comfort make it bearable. I have maneuvered for your comfort to give one of my children some quality of life and yes, I will take a little something for myself. A child should not hate her mother. What did I not give you? Was the food out of my mouth not enough to show that I loved you? Ezra is the only way out of a lifetime of deprivation. He is our way out.

Jonah thought of Zeena: I'm sorry, Zeena. So very, very sorry. I tried, but Mama is so hard. It's not good all the time between me and Leah. She's very like you and like Mama. She lets nothing go. I thought it would be so different. You were right. We should have run away. I thought Leah would make my life better, but I was wrong. I do love, her. I do. And I love you, too. But it's so very different from what I thought it would be. I hold her, but I don't feel safe the way I used to feel in the circle. I know now that you may be the only person who can help me feel safe. I can't forgive myself for not having helped you, Zeena. If you will forgive me, God will forgive me. Please, Zeena. It's so hard being me.

Leah thought of Zeena: It's your own fault, Zeena. You should have run like you said you'd run. Your father wouldn't have died of shame or a broken heart. People don't die from such things. The world is a big place and one can hide. I'm here. I'm married. I'm pregnant. I wanted Jonah. I agreed happily to be his wife. But to marry out of anger and hate is a crime against yourself. Why do you do it? Why submit yourself to a man whom you loath? It's not for his money. You're not like that. So what are you after? What else is there Zeena that no one knows about?

The procession moved over the bridge with well wishers on either side, their candles flickering brightly. Zeena focused on a vague distant point and saw no one until they crossed the bridge. Then, suddenly moving into the line no more than ten feet from her, a candle illumined the face of the haggard old woman from whom she had recoiled the day after Jonah had married. The orange light revealed the toothless grin. A chill surged through Zeena and she froze. Reuben and Sarah felt the tug and stopped. They glanced at each other, but she began to move again. The gray face of the old woman would not dismiss itself, and in Zeena's imaginings, the old crone's twisted boney finger beckoned the bride to follow her in the dance of those who were dead and yet still lived. Zeena's fear, her ultimate fear of becoming like everyone else, of dying here before she had lived, or laughed or danced with a happy heart, would come to pass if she did not run. She had only half a plan thought out, the part that protected the child. From now on she would have to plan her flight. The vision of the old woman disappeared with the new thought. She stopped again to concentrate on the future. She had to focus on that time when she and her baby would be safe. Then she would confront Jonathan with the truth and he would come to her. That was the vision she would keep to give her the strength to endure the next two months.

She and Jonathan at last together with their child. Zeena took a deep breath and walked to the synagogue door.

Sarah, laughing, took Ruth by the hand and beckoned Dora and Leah to follow.

"It's time for the veiling," she said above the bright syncopation of the flute and violin. The groom lumbered down the gauntlet of smiling faces, but kept his eyes riveted on his prize.

Sarah and Ezra's mother, Gittel Bendak, stood in front of Zeena with raisins and hops resting on the bridal veil. They smiled politely at each other, but Gittel did not speak to her new in-law. Sarah was triumphant as Ezra and the rabbi seized the veil by two corners, lifted it quickly, and covered the bride's face. Suddenly, like manna from heaven, a shower of raisins and hops fell upon the bride and groom from the hands of well wishers.

Bendak put out his hand to Zeena. It hung there for longer than was appropriate, but she took it and rose silently. They moved back down the gauntlet with kernels of wheat and corn and sweet meats under their feet. Zeena moved as if in a dream. She had successfully separated herself from the reality of the world for the moment. She saw and did not see. She heard and did not hear. She felt and did not feel.

From the rear, those assembled strained to hear the rabbi's intonations. He raised his hands in the familiar way of the ancient priests and uttered the ancient benediction. They watched Zeena, escorted by the mothers-in-law, circle Ezra. They saw the cup of wine offered first to Ezra and then to Zeena. They saw the veil lifted and wondered at the hesitation before the cup was sipped. They saw a gesture with her hand and knew that it had to be the moment when the ring was placed on her finger. They saw someone bend near Ezra's foot and then a wave of mazel tov, good luck, swept back to them. They, too, shouted their good wishes. The band struck up the most joyous of tunes and the people bent over to kiss each other and wish each other well.

The bride and groom were lifted up in chairs and danced around the square. Zeena felt the cool breeze on her cheek and watched the people clap their hands in the circle below. She was suddenly aware that she was married, and she wanted to die.

Zeena stood in the small dressing room off the bedroom and slowly unbuttoned her wedding dress. She tried to fantasize Jonathan helping her, but reality would not give way. Bendak's image kept intruding and the image sent a wave of nausea through her. She held the table for support. She had to keep her head clear and her emotions steady to plan her next move. She had to learn the routine and fit into it. She had to find where they kept the money box. She would pretend and she would be successful. She took the small vile of beef blood Sarah had collected from salting meat and concealed it in her night gown. She would make him believe she was still a virgin.

"Stupid," she heard her mother say. "You think he won't know you're a whore when he doesn't see blood on the marriage sheet? You think a woman like Gittel Bendak won't demand the sheet to make sure you're a virgin? You think the whole town won't know and that she won't push him to annul the marriage?"

She remembered how her mother had pressed the vial into her hand with instructions on what she had to do. Zeena did not like thinking well of her mother, but, at this moment, even she, dredged up a modicum of thanks for her mother's forethought willingness to enter the conspiracy.

Zeena looked at herself in the mirror and steadied herself for the ordeal of her bridegroom.

Ezra's eyes traced the outline of Zeena's raven black hair floating on her white lace gown. Like lustrous ink on snow, he thought.

She stood in the center of the room, her eyes closed. She felt Ezra's fleshy hand on her shoulder and she contracted. She fought his image behind her closed lids. His hand moved down the front of her dress and rested on her firm breast. He watched her for a reaction and he smiled his mocking smile when she turned her head away. She kept her eyes closed, and conjured up Jonathan's handsome face. The tears rose behind the lids. The hand encircled her breast and she felt it contract upon her. She could not help but open her eyes. The fleshy face peered at her. His dark eyes twinkled expectation. Her stomach moved and she closed her eyes again.

"Why did you marry someone who hates you, Ezra?" she said slowly.

"Ah, my sweet Zeena speaks to her bridegroom. And what does she speak of? Does she speak of love? No, she speaks of hate. Open your eyes and I'll tell you." He waited. She slowly opened her eyes. They glistened like wet coals in moonlight through her tears. "Ah, does my sweet Zeena cry because she is so happy?"

She said nothing. He reached out and first played with locks of hair and then moved to rub his fingers against her cheek.

"Why did I marry someone who hates me?" he began. "Ah, why indeed?"

He placed both his hands on her shoulders and stared at her.

"All my life," he began, "it seemed to me that people have hated me. Even when I was little. Can you imagine that, Zeena?" There was a curious resignation in his voice and vague pain. "I think it was because I was ugly to look at. But now it is no matter, because all those who hated me are afraid of me, and I would rather have them fear me than like me."

A faint, sardonic smile rippled across his mouth as if only he knew a great secret or great truth.

"Now they hate me for good reasons."

His face hardened and his eyes became deadly serious.

"You want to know why I married someone who hates me, Zeena? I will tell you, my dearest wife. To me, you are their hatred made flesh. I married you so I can see the hatred and control it. Now the hatred is mine and I can watch it because I can watch you. I can caress the hatred as I caress you now, and I will come into it and feel it surround me. I can overpower it and subdue it and make it mine." He held her shoulders tightly, and pulled her close against his body.

"When you can see and touch and subdue something that has eaten at you and torn at you all your life, then you don't have to be

afraid of it anymore. Can you understand this my dearest wife?"
He paused.

She hardly heard him.

He forcefully put his arm around her shoulder and moved her
across the room.

A trickle of a smile ran down the corner of her mouth and
she laughed at herself for the deception that had brought her
to this moment. Another image of Jonathan brought her a wave
of sorrow. Jonathan's voice should be coaxing and caressing her
now. He should cover her soft flesh with his strength. Only she
had permitted this to happen. The brief shame her mother felt
was nothing to what she was going through. It was not worth
it. Her mother married off a pregnant daughter. Her mother
could lift her head in town and brag of the good marriage she
had arranged. Later she would even brag about the child. Zeena's
stupidity slowly and agonizingly crept over her. Her mother
had won.

Now an alien hand slid down her stomach to grope her. The
heavy hands turned her and pressed her to sit. Her mother had
won. Ezra had won. Her father and Jonah and their tradition had
won. Everyone was in control except she. Only she had lost. Now
she had to let this man into her or the child would not be protected. A hand moved up her thigh.

She felt herself fall backward and her legs lifted on to the bed.
She would let Ezra have her and she would submit to him for two
months and as often as he wished. She would go to the doctor and
he would declare her pregnant. After that she would leave with
enough of his money for her and the child to live well. Now she
would keep her eyes tightly shut and plan her plan.

She felt the gown pulled up. She bit down until her teeth
ached. She felt the heavy hand touching the inner side of her thighs.
She bottled out all light. She thought of the gold coins Malinovitch
had given her. He would welcome her. An unwelcome finger slid
between her legs and her mouth was covered with moist hot lips.

Her mind raced to Jonathan and the little silver ring she took when she married him and conceived his child. The fingers prodded her and parted her body. She fled to the images of St. Petersburg memorized from the books. They whirled into her brain and she saw herself twirling round and round the glittering hall. The heavy body moved down on her and she voluntarily let her legs be moved apart. Alexi Malinovitch stood before her with a handful of gold coins. The music of the fantasy violins soared. The fingers moved and searched within her with little concern. In a month or more she would run to Malinovitch. He would welcome her. Ezra Bendak tore his way into her dry channel and she screamed a scream of rage to underscore her shame and indignation.

Her husband undulated on top of her and grunted his climax. At least now she had a plan.

Zeena waited a very long time before she reached into the pocket of her nightgown for the vial of blood.

CHAPTER 13

Zeena pretended to be asleep until Ezra left the bed. Her tears slid out of her eyes and ran down her temples onto the pillow as if they belonged to another. She would have to get up. She would have to begin life and pretend to be living.

"You up, Zeena?" cackled Gittel Bendak who was knocking at the door. "Zeena, I'm coming in to change the linen."

The door opened with authority and the short, coarse looking woman with a round flat face and big eyes waddled into the room.

"We change the linen in this house on Monday mornings. You should know this because you will have to do it from now on. Don't think you're going to lay around here like a princess. I know you Zeena Chernov."

Zeena immediately thought of her mother's warning. Her mother was so right. Gittel Bendak was shrewd and equally dangerous.

The chunky figure plopped the bedding on the chair and stood with her short arms on her hips. "Well," she continued, "you going to lay there until the Messiah comes?"

Zeena's immediate thought was of the sheet. She had not expected such an overt and brazen display so soon, but she remained cool. So the old bitch wanted to see if there was blood on the sheet. Well, Zeena knew there was an ample stain and laughed to herself because she knew that her new mother-in-law would believe it was from her ruptured hymen. "Here, look," she said contemptuously, standing and tearing the sheet from the mattress. "See," and she gloated. "Your son got unused merchandise." She watched the woman glance down and look away disappointed.

"You don't put anything over on me," Zeena continued. "I know why you're here and don't think I'm going to make beds in a house where there are servants to do that."

Ezra's mother glared back with equal contempt.

"You'll do as you're told in this house," she said sharply.

"I don't think so," responded Zeena with equal strength. This woman meant nothing to her and held no power over her. If this slovenly hag thought of making life difficult, Zeena would make her life a living hell. Perhaps she sensed this in Zeena, for she turned and moved towards the door.

"Make the bed," she retorted, hoping for the last word, "and then come to the kitchen."

"A black cholera should catch you," Zeena muttered, and she heard her own mother speak through her own voice.

Mrs. Bendak stopped in her tracks at the curse, and turned. But, before she could utter a sound, Zeena had crumpled up the stained sheet and hurled it into her face.

"Here," she shouted. "You forgot what you came for, and you can hang it on the synagogue door for all I care."

Zeena learned the routine of the house quickly, and though Mrs. Bendak eyed her every movement with suspicion and accusation, she, nevertheless, let the woman know at every chance that not only did she not care what Mrs. Bendak thought of her as a daughter-in-law, but also that she was not the only woman in the house with Ezra's ear.

In the mornings she moved around the kitchen mechanically demonstrating little or no interest. If Mrs. Bendak asked her for anything at all, she became even less interested in that aspect, and said there were servants to do that. After a few days, Mrs. Bendak no longer requested anything from her new daughter-in-law. To be sure, they railed at each other with dark curses and gestures, but whenever anyone approached, especially Ezra, they pretended harmony, for each knew that forcing Ezra into a position to choose between them would bring enormous risk.

In the afternoon, when the work Zeena chose to do to relieve the boredom was over, and the old lady took her afternoon nap, Zeena would sometimes make her way to the shop in the front of the house where Ezra manipulated and coerced the needy merchants and townspeople. The store itself mirrored the desperation of the people who frequented it.

But the bulk of Ezra's income came through the lucrative interest he charged on loans to those who were unable to make enough to keep their lives or families together. And, when the unfortunate could not keep up with the payments, Ezra would graciously accept family treasures for well below market value as payment, and place these for sale. When his prey no longer had anything of value to give him, Ezra would accept home furnishings for his used furniture market. Finally, when there was nothing left, Ezra, if he liked them, would offer them work in his mill at starvation wages. His grandfather had begun the work, and his mother had expanded it to the point where Ezra had most of the town in his pocket. Strangers, city people, non-Jews, came into the shop, but they were always ushered into the back room for privacy. Some wore uniforms.

Nevertheless, Zeena wandered around the store fingering the fine things there. One day she found a samovar she recognized as once sitting on the shelf near the stove in her parent's home, a samovar that had disappeared years ago. Now she understood that it must have been brought here in a bad time when her father was paying off the loan that kept Jonah out of the army. She studied the shiny brass object from her childhood, a cherished wedding gift to her parents from her father's parents. It did not belong here she thought. And now, since she was the mistress of the house and had some claim to this, she could do with it as she pleased. She lifted it from the shelf and dusted it off. She wondered why she even cared about it, but could draw no conclusion from her thought other than that the Bendak family had no right to it. They had her and that's all they were going to get. The thought of old man Putinsky taking it from her father angered her, and she could imagine the torment her father must have felt when he stood in this very place and handed it over to that thief. The objects in the room suddenly lost their glitter and value. Their beauty became tainted with the pain one feels in having to part with cherished keepsakes in order to survive. The silver became dross and the cut crystal suddenly became dull. Each told a tale of pain. Zeena wrapped the samovar in a lace cloth and put both in a pillowcase. She rearranged the shelf so it would appear that nothing had been taken, and resolved to take it home with her when the old witch took her afternoon nap.

After dinner that evening, Ezra sat hunched over his daily receipts and Zeena sat on the couch sewing and watching the evening ritual. She hated sewing, but the house was bereft of books and she had to have a reason to observe Ezra's comings and goings with the money box. Two gold coins were not enough to take her to St. Petersburg. Ezra would give her no allowance, claiming that all her needs would be taken care of just by asking. Mrs. Bendak would not give her a kopek either, insisting that at the market she tell the merchant to put the charge on her husband's bill. She was slowly becoming aware of a new kind of power, a power that controls through money. Those who had the money had the power, and those who had the most money had the most power. She was starting to understand the arguments over money her mother would initiate in the house. Her mother understood the power of money because her mother understood survival. She was understanding it also.

The old lady sat rocking back and forth in the creaking chair and peered at Zeena over her spectacles. She knew very well how uncomfortable Zeena was under her gaze and how irritating the creaking chair really was to her daughter-in-law. Zeena periodically looked up, flared her nostrils and then, smiling sweetly, asked the old woman for instruction in stitchery. Zeena knew this angered her because Zeena always asked for the exact instruction she had been given the evening before. Ezra did not realize what was going on and would look up occasionally and smile at the seemingly tranquil scene. This would infuriate the old lady because her own son could not see what a fake his bride was. But, she would say nothing and Zeena would continue to smile.

"Zeena," the elder Mrs. Bendak began, "I was told by a friend that you were seen carrying a large pillow case out of my son's store today. Then I was told by another that you were seen crossing the bridge on the way to your parent's home." The old woman paused, thinking to unnerve Zeena with her knowledge of Zeena's comings and goings in the town. She smiled secretly and waited for Zeena to flush with guilt.

"How nice it is that you have so many friends," Zeena said sarcastically, and smiled through her teeth.

The elder Mrs. Bendak straightened herself and pursed her lips at being foiled. She would have to be more direct.

"So what did you take from the shop?" she said slowly but pointedly. Her voice was calm and calculated to catch Ezra and involve him slowly and carefully in a confrontation with his wife. The woman gloated and did not look up from her work. The only sound was the creaking of the rocking chair.

Ezra, as his mother had hoped, put down his pen and turned for an answer. The chair continued to rock back and forth. Zeena did feel a flush creep over her face, but it was not one of shame and, with equal calm, she told him, in a matter-of-fact way about the samovar she had found and how she merely returned it to her parents.

"Some people might say taking something that doesn't belong to you is stealing," the old woman replied in the same steady voice.

"And some people might say that how it was obtained in the first place was stealing," Zeena retorted with equal calm.

The old lady threw down her sewing and struggled to her feet pointing and shaking her finger at Zeena. "I told you, Ezra, I told you!"

Ezra stood between them. "There is nothing to get excited about." Ezra was annoyed with both of them for the little game they seemed to play with his support as the prize. "We have more samovars than we know what to do with mother, and besides, I told Zeena she could have it." He watched his mother's face for her response and he continued to look at her in a way that told the woman that he did not appreciate what she had created. Feigning support for his wife was his way of letting her know that he did not want to be bothered by such banter. He wanted the same peace in his house that other men had. Gittel Bendak was indeed caught up short, she sat down to her knitting, and did not look up. Zeena appeared to be both astonished and amused.

"It isn't good business to give away things the family has earned through hard work," she muttered.

"Now we'll have no more to say about this," he said resolutely, and he looked from one to the other. Each kept her eyes on her work.

Zeena sewed patiently for a week and watched. Each evening Ezra would rise and disappear with the money box and return later for his brandy. One evening, Zeena slipped out of the room before he left and hid in the hall closet. She watched Ezra climb the stairs to their bedroom and lock the door behind him. He returned moments later without the box. Zeena left her hiding place after he returned to the sitting room, went to the kitchen for some small cakes she had baked and set them near him. Ezra looked at her and smiled without asking where she had been.

A few nights later, Zeena left the room and squeezed herself under the bed. Her heart pounded and she thought he would hear it when he opened the door. She waited and watched. Soon, the door opened and Ezra locked it behind him immediately and moved directly to the wood box near the stove. She watched him push it aside with a little effort and place the strong box into a hollow in the floor. Then he pushed the box back, stood, dusted his trousers and left. Zeena smiled to herself at her cleverness and moved slowly to the door and listened. She opened the door slightly and heard the door to the sitting room close. She quickly let herself out and flew down the steps to the kitchen so that when Ezra realized she was gone and came looking for her, she was already emerging from the kitchen with a tray of cookies and a fresh pot of tea.

"Look what I have for you," she cooed, carrying the tray into the room. "I baked them because I know you like something sweet at night." Tomorrow she would pretend nausea and confine herself to bed. They had been married over a month already and it seemed to her that the nausea would indeed be taken as an indication of her pregnancy. With time, she could help herself to a few coins each day and sew them into the lining of her corset. They would never be missed. And, if she took a few each week over the next two months, she would have enough to face the world unafraid. She would wait for a Sabbath when the old woman slept and Ezra was in synagogue. The old witch had eyes and ears all over town, but on the Sabbath, even the town gossips were too busy with their own families to run and tell tales. Yes, she would tell them she was going to visit her parents and get on the ferry. And even if someone saw her, it would be too late and she would be gone.

The days limped haltingly, and when she could not pretend sleep in the morning when Ezra reached out to touch her, she feigned nausea. She permitted him to take her as often as he liked, but only at night when she could not see him. Afterwards, as he slept, she would leave the bed and go to the small ante-chamber where she would wash herself thoroughly.

One night she returned and Ezra was awake. He spoke to her of his need to end the silent war that raged between them. He spoke of his need to be a husband to her and his hope that she would come to care for him. He wanted not to hate or be hated any longer. He promised her anything if she would only try.

Zeena said nothing but thought of the best time to tell him about the child. In two days she would have taken enough money. Yes, she would tell him in two days. That would give her the time she needed.

Ezra talked about a shopping trip to Kiev to refurbish the sitting room if she liked.

Zeena counted the days that would have to elapse between

her announcement of the child and her flight to St. Petersburg. She counted again the number of coins she had already sewn into her corset.

Ezra's hand reached out and felt for the tips of her fingers. He assured her that he could be a good and generous man and reminded her of how he had taken her part in the samovar incident. Zeena permitted his hand to rest on hers, but there was no response to his touch. She saw herself leaving the house dressed in her best on the pretext of making a Sabbath call on her parents. She saw herself moving through the quiet town to the ferry. Her fantasy leaped her first to the Kiev train and then to Alexi Malinovitch.

"Zeena, please," she heard him say, his voice choked and tearful. "I don't want to hate anymore. I want to be happy."

The vision of freedom and the success of her deception filled her with anticipation. "We'll see, Ezra," she said in a controlled and calculated voice.

She looked to the window. In the outline of the window frame she imagined Jonathan and drew him to her and had him lay down at her side. She smiled at the vision and closed her eyes. The fantasy body pressed against her like a demon from another world, and her mind embraced him.

'Do you not hear the pleading of your husband?' said the vision suddenly.

'He is not my husband. You are my husband. We were married in a barn. Do you not remember the ceremony?'

'He is asking you to love him. Can you not hear his need?'

'I hear him,' she responded.

'And can you have no pity on this man, Zeena? He is opening his heart to you.'

'Do not lecture me, Jonathan. None of this would be happening if you loved me as I loved you.'

'This is happening because you are who you are, and not because I did not love you.'

Ezra blew out the candle. He did not want her to see the tears in his eyes if she turned towards him. She had said that she would see. Perhaps there was hope for them. He did not understand why he was suddenly moved to hope for love and tenderness from her. Her only overt sign of affection was that she baked him cookies without being asked. It seemed to him that he was loving someone for the first time in his life and he wanted this someone to love him also. He wanted nothing else. Even her closeness in bed without response was something to which he could cling. Tonight he risked asking her to love him, to give in some small way the affection he so desperately sought. She did not laugh at him as she might have, and she did not run from the bed or vilify his need. She did not use his vulnerability or ridicule him. She merely said, we'll see. It did not occur to him that she did not care, and barely heard anything he had said.

Zeena waited a little over a month before allowing the doctor to examine her and confirm that she was indeed pregnant. Within hours, the entire town knew that Ezra Bendak was going to be a father. The week that followed was the happiest in his life, but on the following Sabbath, Zeena did not return from her parent's home.

The door to the Chernov house slammed against the wall and shook the dishes. Ezra lurched into the room and, startled by the intrusion, Reuben dropped the spice box he was about to pass to Ruth. The candle threw another shape on the wall, but the wildly gesticulating intruder shared none of the serenity of the other Sabbath shadows.

Ruth stooped to pick up the spices where they spilled. Dora took the wine cup from her lips and passed it hesitantly to Jonathan. "Ezra," Sarah said, moving towards him fearfully.

"Where is Zeena?" he bellowed, stopping Sarah in her tracks. His voice was a mixture of anger and anguish.

"I'm sure I don't know what you're talking about, Ezra," she replied, trying to cover her own confusion and anxiety. "Zeena was here early in the afternoon, had lunch with us and left. We talked about the baby and possible names, she said goodbye and left. That's all there is to tell. Ezra what . . ."

"You're lying to me," he interrupted, shaking his fist in her face. "She stole money and was seen getting on the ferry and I demand you tell me where she went!"

"You are not to speak to my wife that way," shouted Reuben. "Zeena is not here and we do not know where she is! If she comes by, we will tell her you're upset and you want her home. Beyond this, I don't know what to tell you."

"Zeena was seen coming from this house and was last seen getting on the ferry. Now I tell you this and you hear me. If Zeena isn't home within the hour, you'll all be sorry. I swear, as God is my witness, I will bring down this house over your heads if you don't tell me where my wife and my child are!"

They looked at him with a mixture of disbelief and fear.

"But we don't know where she is," Sarah protested again, wringing her hand. "Please Ezra, believe us. We came home from synagogue, had a nice lunch, Zeena ate, we talked, she left, we slept, we read, we ate dinner and then you came in. That's all. We don't know where Zeena is."

"Zeena came here and you know where she went. Neither of you ever liked me. I know all about this family. You tell me where she is, or you get her and my child back, or I'll make your lives such a hell that you'll be begging in the streets or worse!"

They stood dumbfounded. The braided candle that Reuben held threw fantastic images against the wall and ceiling. Ezra's face, distorted in the orange light, was demonic in its anguish. He slammed the door and left.

Sarah sank onto a chair and rocked back and forth sobbing.

"Did she say anything to you, Reuben, anything at all that would indicate where she was going?" She could barely speak from fear.

Reuben searched his memory of his conversation with Zeena that afternoon, but was at a loss to recall anything that hinted of flight. Dora, Ruth and Jonathan looked at each other trying to understand what was happening.

As long as Ezra believed that they knew of Zeena's whereabouts, they were all in danger.

CHAPTER 14

Zeena was surprised that she could close them all off; father and mother, brother, sisters, husband. All shimmered and dissolved in the heat mirage hovering on the horizon. Only Jonathan's image and his child growing within her body, did she happily carry with her into joyful exile. The years of dreaming, anger and pain were behind her now as she stepped into freedom. Ezra would be outraged and agonized. She almost felt sorry for him.

The town spread out before her like a shabbily set table. The little wooden houses of her life crowded together and seemed to lean one upon the other for support. It was a new perspective and she had the fantasy that if she plucked out one of the rickety wooden hovels, the whole place would fall down upon itself.

Zeena tossed her head back and laughed into the hot July air, turned from the back of the boat, and looked down the lake to the distant shore. The bearded ferryman pulled his pole from the mud and pushed it past her, tipping his cap as if she were a fine lady. She lifted her head haughtily just to feel what a haughty response was like, and she laughed to herself at all the remarkable possibilities freedom and spirit had to offer. She would play, and she would dance, she would study and work and become someone. Malinovitch was a nice man who would introduce her to the life she sought. Reaching into her purse, she felt for the two gold coins to reassure herself of his promise. She touched the bodice of her dress and assured herself again of the other coins she had stolen. Zeena felt for the ring she had taken off Jonathan's finger. She took it out of her purse, pressed it to her lips, and forced the simple tarnished band onto her finger with the silent vow that it would never be removed. Then she turned away from the town and looked to the horizon. Now her mind vaulted her to a train station and the clanking and whistling of the engines as they pulled out. She saw herself walking along the broad picture book boulevards until she came to her benefactor's street.

She imagined his grand home and heard one of his servants greet her with great respect, ushering her into an elegantly appointed sitting room where a crystal chandelier shimmered in the afternoon sun and oil paintings of hunting scenes and old ruins looked down from heavy gilt frames. All the picture books and romances came together to construct the dream. Then, he would enter, elegantly dressed in a quilted velvet jacket, and he would take her hand and he would kiss it. He would take her to the ballet and they would ride in an open coach, and when the child was born . . . Her reverie faded suddenly. What a fool she was. What if Malinovitch insisted that she and the child return to Bendak? She shivered in the heat. She saw him forcing her to the train and back to Kiev. She saw Ezra waiting there with his mother to take her back to Krivoser. Panic seized her. She had to think. Perhaps she should say nothing and just disappear when she began to show. She was a little heavier, but to look at her, no one could guess she was in her fifth month. She could buy loose fitting things, but eventually she would have to leave his protection. But where would she go with an infant? She would have to continue or create some charade to survive.

The ferry inched its way down the elongated lake taking what suddenly seemed to be an eternity. Some peasants sat drinking wine in the unseasonable heat. They paid little attention to her, thinking her too well dressed to be one of their own. But when one did wink at her and approach, he was cautioned by a companion that she was married. She heard the statement and her finger curled into her palm to finger the band on her left hand. She had not taken it off. But, if wearing it now served her purpose, might it not also serve her purpose if she continued to wear it? What if Malinovitch didn't know she was married? What if she told him that she despaired of ever finding a husband in Krivoser, and that she and her mother had such arguments that life had become unbearable. Such a story would assure her of not being sent back. But what of his response to the pregnancy? That was impossible to foresee. He could throw her out as a whore, or he could become a kindly benefactor. Everything was a possibility and nothing was sure. The world spun through space in a sure orbit, but life seemed more like the rickety old ferry, subject to shifting sands and hidden shoals. The ferryman knew his river and could change course easily. What did she know of life and about changing course mid stream? The only thing to be sure of was the vision of the goal. The path towards it was always an uncertainty, and if she were to exert any control over that path, she would have to be constantly vigilant. But she could not control chance.

At this moment she was sure that no one knew where she was going, and that no one would know she was married. The trip before her was a long one and would take several days if all went well. She would have time to think and plan. She would have time to test chance as a friend or an enemy. She looked towards the shimmering horizon. The most immediate goal was reaching that shore. Then it would be finding the train to Kiev. From there, there were other trains. It seemed overwhelming, but she did not have the luxury of being overwhelmed and having someone to hold and comfort her. All was behind her and to be forgotten. She laughed at herself and at all the past foolishness. If she said she was not married, who would know? She would have no past and who would tell her differently? She would be free to create a new life. What did she need of foolish circles created in her brother's arms? Jonah was right. It was time for giving up their childish play. Now, she had only herself, the effects of her choices, and a long journey before her.

Zeena sat in a plush compartment of another train speeding to St. Petersburg. Already, chance had taught her an important lesson. She was told by a porter that the line she stood on was for the third class carriage, as he escorted her to a first class waiting room where cakes and tea were served. She thanked him and when she turned, she saw, through the window, the queue of people dressed in their shabby third class best. Zeena's dress, by comparison, indicated a woman of means who obviously had made a mistake. It was this chance observation on the part of a porter that brought Zeena to the realization that even appearances initiate chance happenings. She would have to stop thinking that she was a third class person. But there, in that arena where the wealthy sipped tea and chatted in muffled tones, Zeena, by comparison, felt shabby. She moved to some innocuous corner and sat quietly trying not to be noticed. Aware, after a time that she was, in fact, not noticed, she resolved that as soon as possible, she would purchase a dress that would make her appear the equal of anyone in the room.

Two days of watching endless fields passed in agonizing boredom. Zeena was overjoyed when the train stopped in a small country town south of St. Petersburg and an aristocratic looking man, his wife and daughter stepped into her compartment. The younger woman glanced at her and turned to the window, as if deciding that Zeena was an unimportant provincial not worthy of even the smallest of courtesy. The man and his wife smiled broadly and sat opposite her next to their daughter. Zeena kept her eyes lowered until the gentleman spoke to her.

"You are traveling to St. Petersburg for the birthday festivities?" he inquired.

Zeena smiled and shook her head, not wishing to appear foolish for she did not know of whose birthday he spoke. "It is a tradition with my family that we go to St. Petersburg for the birthday festivities," she said and created an upper class fancy for herself.

"You are from the provinces?" he continued.

"Yes," she said hesitantly. She suddenly felt naked, aware that the image she projected on a ferry from Krivoser was that of a peacock, but on a train to St. Petersburg, she was a dull pigeon. He could tell from her dress and the way she spoke. Speech differences was something she had not considered. She observed the two woman sitting on either side of him. They were fashionable, each with a high lace collar and plumed hat. Their hands were soft and their nails sculpted and polished. She instinctively curled her own fingers into her palms. Her own best dress, by comparison, was unfashionable and revealing. Her speech, her dress, her hands, her everything, blurted to the world that she was a nothing from a nothing town in a nowhere province.

"Your family will meet you then at the station?" he continued.

"Not exactly," she replied. The moment for testing her skill at dissembling had come sooner than expected and she was grateful for the opportunity to practice a lie. "My family could not attend this time, but insisted that I do not miss the festivities."

"Then you are free," he said.

Zeena looked at the empty finger on her hand. "Somewhat," she said, resolving not to say anything else.

"Then you will be returning?" he continued.

"Not immediately," she replied. She did not know where the conversation would carry her and grew uncomfortable with the fabrication. "I will seek employment," she responded simply. She had planned her escape from Ezra, but she had not draped herself in a new identity as a Russian. She was being questioned on a life that did not exist.

"What kind of work do you seek?" he asked. "Do you have an education?"

Her mind raced through her memory for another appropriate lie. "Certainly," she said, with an air of playful indignity. "I attended a school for young ladies in Kiev until my parents died. Then I had to leave to help my brothers run the family business. It was my goal to become a teacher but when they died, I could not continue."

"What a pity that you have been orphaned."

"Yes," she said sadly, lowering her head appropriately. "Father was an army officer and was killed in the service of our beloved Tsar." She thought of her mother and the myriad of curses she had been brought up on whenever the Tsar was mentioned. "Mother died shortly afterward of a broken heart."

"How regrettable," he said nodding his head sadly. "But what business was your family in if your father was an officer in the army?"

Zeena flushed. She was caught. "It was my grandfather's business," she rejoined, making note that if she was to lie, she was going to have a great deal to remember. Somewhere she recalled Dora saying something like that. "It was a large factory on the outskirts of the city."

"Then why did you leave, dear child?" interrupted his wife sympathetically. "It sounds as if you were needed."

Zeena hesitated. "A fire," she said, deciding that only a fire could separate her from this mythical place. "It burned to the ground and my brothers decided to go their own ways, and I chose to go to St. Petersburg to continue my education and work in a shop or as a companion, or even as a live-in tutor for a family with small children."

"I wish you luck, my dear," said the affable gentleman. "It is sad that within such a short period of life, so much sadness has befallen you. Do you not have a young man whose heart is breaking because you are going away?" he laughed, leaning slightly forward.

The skirts of the two women on either side rustled uncomfortably. The hand of the older woman rested on her husband's arm.

"Now, Gregor," she said in a tone that admonished him with a feather. "Perhaps the young lady does not wish to tell you all of her life."

Zeena smiled at her, and took her words as a clue that it was inappropriate to tell a stranger the details of one's life. Sarah would have told her to shut her mouth, but this lady conveyed what was appropriate with a gentle word. The woman's demeanor spoke of reserve and breeding. Perhaps it was not seemly to be as open as she had been, and certainly not as passionate as she had been in her other life.

"I meant nothing," the man laughed to his wife. "Surely the young lady understands," and he winked at her.

"Of course I understand," she smiled reassuringly. The eyes of the gentlemen looked at her approvingly.

The train began to slow. They were coming to the outer most towns surrounding St. Petersburg.

"We will be stopping off at our country home on our way to our home in the city," he said. He nodded to the younger woman to ready herself. She opened a small purse, and took out a delicately sculpted mirror and glanced at it. She touched the tips of her fingers to the perfect auburn curls that protruded from her bonnet, but Zeena thought the movement superfluous. Both she and the girl knew the perfection reflected in the glass. Zeena made note. She would need a purse to match the new dress, and she would need a mirror. She had to project the image of a Russian lady of refinement and means to be above suspicion. The ticket for the seat had cost dearly, but she had learned much already and concluded that one had to spend in order to make a profit, and that spending on oneself was a valid expenditure. She would have to be more reserved in her manner.

Their daughter continued in silence. She had dismissed Zeena imperiously and seemed to regard her father's efforts at light conversation with respectful disdain. She turned from her mirror and looked out of the window. Her deep, dark eyes were fixed on some distant point, on some distant music or banquet. Her head was always held high. Her skin was flawless and like alabaster. Zeena could not help studying her, trying to project herself into her body and life. At one point, Zeena also raised her head and fixed her eyes on some distant point. When the young woman closed her eyes, Zeena memorized the delicate arch of her brows. She had never seen such delicacy in real flesh. The curls covered a high, patrician forehead that was mirrored in the aristocratic air of the older woman to her left. Here was a man who must have everything the world could offer, and he fathered this perfect beauty who was probably the light of his life. There was her own father who had nothing of the world's wonders. Yet, she wondered if this beauty loved this affable man, as she loved Reuben, and she wondered if this man ever sat and read to her or taught her. She wondered if she was ever blessed by him on their Sabbath or if they ever walked together and spoke about politics and literature. Zeena was overcome with a sudden longing for her father. She had not thought that she might never see him again.

The train came to a halt, and Zeena lurched forward. The family before her moved involuntarily and settled back.

"My dear girl," said the portly gentleman, "you do not know anyone in the city so I am giving you my card in the event that you need a friend." He took a thin, silver rectangular box from his waistcoat, removed a small engraved card from it, and held it out to her like a benevolent uncle offering a favorite niece a gift. Zeena smiled up at him as she took it.

She had demonstrated some social skill. Certainly he would not be offering his card had she shown herself to be a rude provincial. She looked at this name. Count Gregor Perowski. He stood and took her hand. Zeena flushed under his gaze.

"Now, my dear child," interrupted the Countess, "if you want to do any shopping for the most up to date and cosmopolitan fashions, you might consider going to the Gostiny Dvor on the Nevsky Prospekt. There are two hundred shops there and the dressmakers often have ready to wear dresses that I must say are as beautiful as those made to order."

Zeena smiled and nodded in deference to her, and again recognized the skill of breeding that enabled her to tell Zeena that not only was she out of fashion, but where she might go to solve her problem.

The Count's daughter stood and waited for Zeena to move out of her way. Zeena stood back, and the young woman swept between them and was gone.

The Countess Perowski paid no attention, but continued. "Of course, some are quite expensive, but believe me dear, in St. Petersburg, everything is impression, or rather, impression is everything." She fluttered a laugh at her mistake, but Zeena quickly noted both expressions as truth. "If you look acceptable, my dear, you'll be acceptable. It's all very superficial, and if you want my advice, you'll go back to your home where the people are honest and real. It's the earth under one's feet that keeps people real, not the bricks. But I've said much too much already. Let me write the name for you." And she took the card from Zeena's hand and scribbled the store's name and street on it with a silver encased pencil she found in her purse.

Zeena unconsciously raised her hand to her waist and felt the coins. There was ample money sewn there to purchase several outfits with whatever accessories she needed to appear a lady of fashion. A new excitement took hold of her at the prospect.

"That's very kind of you," Zeena said. The Countess Perowski smiled and turned. Count Perowski also smiled a lingering smile, and patted Zeena's cheek twice.

"Now, remember," he said, "you contact me if you need any help. Also," he continued, "my wife and I left you a small package of supper. You still have about an hour or more to the city, and we thought you might be hungry."

The thought of food sent a growl through her stomach. Count Perowski laughed and winked at her embarrassment. He cradled her hand, turned and left.

Zeena looked after him and then quickly tore open the corner of the small basket with the relish of a field hand. She sat down and urgently bit into a small single cake and a last wedge of cheese. She sat and watched the endless miles of fields stretch out in all directions towards a strangely luminous horizon and, after a time, lifted the latch on the window and slid it down. The twilight air, though warm, was still refreshing and the breeze from the distant sea swept in quickly, furrowing itself through her hair like the fingers of a comb. She put her face into the wind and closed her eyes. There was a faint taste of salt mixed with smoke from the engine and she fancied herself standing on the prow of a ship like a mythical goddess. She made the rumble of the wheels the roar of the tempestuous sea bringing her closer to an explosion of bright expectations. Indeed, she was to begin again.

In the distance, the city etched itself against a gray purple sky. A huge spire rose like a pointing finger catching the rays of the descending sun on its western side. Smaller buildings fell away in the dusky haze and suddenly other spires appeared on the twilight horizon. She could make out the curvature of a huge dome of some cathedral, and the line of sight moved around the horizon to form arms that seemed to open to greet her. She memorized the darkening silhouettes and returned to her seat.

She had to have some plan or story to keep herself safe, yet she knew that once it was uttered it could not be changed. Thinking of the inconsistency in her story to Perowski, she felt again the flush of fear at almost being unmasked. She did not like that feeling and would not be stupid enough to repeat it. She picked up the delicate wicker basket and traced the intricate weave with her finger. She would tell Malinovitch only part of the truth; she had run away from a brutal husband who had beaten her when he found out she was pregnant. She was unable to tell her parents of his brutality because he had threatened to ruin them if she did. She would tell Malinovitch of the repeated beatings and how powerful this man was in the affairs of the town. Why did she agree to marry such a man? To protect her family from the ruin he threatened if she didn't. How could her parents let her do such a thing? They did not know. The man had approached her privately and made his threats. She had been caught in a situation beyond her control and she would have lived with her choice had he not threatened the life of the child with his treatment of her. Yes, she thought, it was a good story, true enough to be believable and outrageous enough to be believable. She saw herself relating it slowly, and tearfully. She saw herself begging him to allow her to stay at least until she had her baby in safety. She would plead convincingly and he would protect her. She smiled to herself, satisfied that the tale would be accepted as truth. She turned the little basket over and over again trying to trace a single piece of straw through the carefully crafted weave, but the straw became irretrievably lost in the pattern. She heaved a deep sigh, but where such a sign emanated from, she could not tell.

Out of the corner of her eye she caught sight of a building flash by. She flew to the window as another train, heading south, clanked past. Her own train seemed drawn to the distant lights as if hidden there was the same mystical power that draws an insect to a candle. The city was the force, and the train approached it irrepressibly. More and more houses flashed by until they blurred in her side vision into a gray train of their own. And then, magically, it began to slow, for its own survival's sake, and vented its passion in huge outpourings of steam and smoke until it screeched and lurched to a halt at the Moscow station. She tightened her grip again to keep her balance when the train forged forward. There was a sudden silence and then a burst of activity. Sounds of luggage and cartons being lowered from the compartments on either side echoed through the walls. Uniformed men, pushing carts strained against them as they inched along the platforms. Cascades of steam billowed up in front of her compartment window and disappeared. She laughed at the surprise.

A knock at the door startled her, and she moved towards it, lowering the shade and stepping back in almost one motion. A young man stood before her with something in his hand.

"Yes," she said cautiously, remembering her accent.

"My master, Count Perowski, told me to give you this before you left the train." He smiled at her and touched his hand to his cap. "Count Perowski," he continued as if the speech were memorized, "informed me that as a new employee, you are to have these letters transit and that I, his trusted servant, am to see that you are not to be detained or inconvenienced when you go through the check point, and that I am to escort you to the house and let you in."

Zeena flushed again. What gate?, she thought. And, what papers of transit? What else did she not know of this world? What else had she not planned that would rise up before her like a sudden fog? Her hand trembled as she reached out to the young man.

"I can see you are frightened," he said, puffing himself up like some high official. "You are not to be afraid for I, Ivan Ivanovitch Russakov, have been instructed by the Count Gregor Perowski, to escort you through the officials and to see to it that you are not molested."

Zeena relaxed slightly and opened the note.

"Thank you," she replied, realizing that to respond in any way
alluding to relief, would be to raise a question in this young man's
mind of the legitimacy of her being there. She feigned a casual air
and read:

> The bearer of this letter is my wife's personal servant. I have
> sent her before us with my valet to open our home in the
> city at 72 Fyodor Street.
>
> I neglected to give her the official documents, but will
> provide them to the officials as soon as I arrive in St. Peters-
> burg should that inconvenience be necessary. Please accord
> her all courtesy due a member of my household staff.

Zeena's hand faintly shook. In a confident scrawl appeared the
bold letters of the name—Count Gregor Perowski.

"A fine man you and I work for," said the young man, looking
for Zeena's luggage.

"My luggage was sent earlier in the week," said Zeena, sensing
his question and choosing a tact that would propel her into her
newest charade. "I like to travel without being encumbered."

Ivan Ivanovitch Russakov stepped aside and Zeena moved past
him with her head aristocratically high. She had a new game to
play and she felt herself moving into it with relish.

"Count Perowski has instructed me," he continued in his official voice, "to escort you not only through the officials, but also to
take you to supper, give you a tour of the city and see you safely to
your new home."

Zeena stopped and looked at him squarely in the face. He had
a broad grin across his mouth and looked past her to keep from
laughing. His blue eyes twinkled mischief, as he brushed a shock
of straight blond hair out of his face, but it fell quickly back again.

Zeena studied him carefully. He was taller than other young men
she had known in Krivoser, even the peasants. His face was smooth
and not reddened by the sun or by wind or by wine. His nose was
straight and his eyes were like almonds, as if in some distant past, an

ancient tribesman from the steppes of Asia had fathered an ancestor. His lips were full, and had a natural boyish pout. How unlike Jonathan, whose dark, handsome features were indelibly inscribed on her memory. How unlike Ezra in every way.

She was strangely attracted to him. "You are a liar," she said, her eyes laughing also. "You have made the entire thing up about dinner and a tour and escorting me home because you think I am a young, stupid provincial serving girl who will fawn over the first city man I meet because I am alone."

The young man continued to look straight ahead. Zeena studied the underside of his nostrils and chin. His grin broadened.

"You are a rude young man."

"Most of what you say is true," he replied, "except for the part about you being a stupid provincial." He looked down at her and smiled. "I do not think you stupid," he continued softly. "It's just that when you pulled down the shade and I saw you, I thought how pretty you were and how much I would like to walk with you along the Neva. And, I thought how much I'd like to sit at a cafe with you and enjoy a small supper and watch the people."

Zeena briefly considered Malinovitch turning her away. Perhaps this handsome young man and the Count might be of use. Besides, she thought, she was alone, naive of the city's ways and it was getting late. Also, she needed a new dress. She could not allow herself to appear in the city this way. She would go with him and then she would find Malinovitch.

He turned and opened the door for her, and she swept past him down the narrow corridor. He moved in front of her so he could offer his hand when she stepped off the train. She stood poised for a moment, extended her hand and stepped down onto a new stage. She held the small wicker basket as if it were the jewel case of a great lady. Her mouth opened slightly in wonder. The fluted iron columns before her stretched to massive studded girders arching from one column to another to support a filigree roof through which she could see wisps of twilight clouds. Billows of steam swirled around her feet as she was escorted through the elegant people towards the iron gate.

"Are there always so many people?" she asked him, scanning the crowd and noting the style of current fashion.

"It's the Tsar's birthday week," he said proudly, as if the Tsar were a personal friend. "I shall take you to the parades and we shall go to the great fair and we shall have a wonderful time."

Zeena looked at him swaggering proudly next to her. He walked as if everyone looked at them and he had to give his audience a show.

"You presume a great deal." Her amazement was tinged with a coquettish exasperation. "Young men where I come from are never this forward or abrupt." She laughed to herself, remembering the assortment of pale, shrinking youths who had been paraded past Reuben and Sarah by the matchmaker. Only Jonathan would have been this confident and self possessed. She continued to walk, and pretended that the swaggering young man was Jonathan.

"You mean they are more forward and abrupt?" he joked, his eyes widening at the game.

"I mean that if a young man where I come from were to tell a young lady that she was going here or there without even asking her, the young man in question would be sorely disappointed. Besides, a young lady where I come from would have been properly introduced through another person and not brazenly confronted by the young man himself."

"Then permit me to stop one of these men, and I will tell him my name, and he will introduce us properly." He motioned to someone coming towards them, and Zeena pushed his hand to his side.

"Stop being foolish," she said with aristocratic indignation, and she glared at him until she began to laugh.

He turned to her again and walked backwards. "I am Ivan Ivanovitch Russakov," he said, taking his hat from his head. "I am currently one of the Count's valets, always a student, sometimes a poet, sometimes a conductor on a train, and all the time a protector of beautiful young women."

"You are the silliest person I have ever met, and I think that if each of the people and the occupations you just mentioned were to be added together, you'd still not add up to a whole sane person."

"You are as witty as you are beautiful," he laughed with a new delight. "Please let me take you to supper and show you my city."

They reached the line. Uniformed men stood rigidly on either side of the gate. An official looking man, painfully thin in his dark suit and high, stiff, white collar looked up and down at papers and travelers through a spotted pince-nez. Zeena fidgeted. She had not anticipated this and the thought of what would have happened had Count Perowski not taken a liking to her was a consideration that shot a hot surge of fear to her cheek.

"Is this something that usually happens?" she asked, testing her voice for traces of anxiety.

"There are always police watching, but this whole week surveillance has doubled because it is the Tsar's birthday and there have been threats made by a nihilist group." His voice dropped to a whisper as he glanced around to see that he had not been overheard. "Besides, there are always nihilists and Jews trying pass themselves off as true Russians."

Zeena bit down on her back teeth at the new revelation. "And what happens when one of them is caught?" she asked, trying to sound matter of fact.

"The Jews are in league with the nihilists to destroy the monarchy." he whispered. "They are very dangerous and very secretive. They are also very powerful and their power extends all over Russia and all over the world."

Zeena laughed to herself. Powerful? She thought of the Jews of Krivoser and their sad, hopeless trek to the grave with only poverty and faith as their constant companions. If there were powerful and secret Jews, she did not know of them. Even Ezra, considered powerful by the townspeople, here would be less than nothing. Jonathan wanted a better way of life for all, but he never spoke of killing the Tsar. Jonathan could not kill anyone. True, there were Jews like her mother who cursed and wished the Tsar death with every breath. But, between the cursing and the execution of that curse, there flowed a river of philosophy that would prohibit anyone she knew to bridge the utterance of the curse with the action of execution.

"But what do they do with those who are caught?" she pressed.

Ivan shrugged his shoulders. "Exile or death for the nihilists. Fines and prisons for Jews. Maybe exile, maybe death. Who knows what goes on in the Peter and Paul Fortress."

He motioned silence. They approached the stiff little man. Zeena's heart began to pound and she feared the petty official with the pince-nez would hear it. She reached out for Ivan's arm to steady herself and forced a smile.

"Your identification," the man said sharply. Ivan produced his card.

"And hers?" he said peering at her analytically.

"She's a servant in the home of Count Gregor Perowski. I have a paper of transit here."

Ivan presented the paper to the man who took it and squinted at it. He looked at Zeena, and then at the paper, then at Zeena again.

"This is most irregular," he said.

Zeena felt her stomach drop and her cheeks flush.

"This is most irregular," the man said again, shaking his head.

Ivan moved close to him and whispered something. Together they moved over to a large icon on a wall near the exit. Zeena held on to the railing for support. She watched them converse, shake hands and walk back together.

The stern little man looked at Zeena again.

"This is most irregular," he repeated, taking his pince-nez from his nose and pointing it at her. "But since Count Perowski is such a well known figure in St. Petersburg, I will take this most unofficial letter as your temporary letter of transit. But, you must tell the Count that your own papers must be returned to you."

Zeena reached out, her hand shaking slightly, and forced a smile. Together she and Ivan moved past him towards the icon.

"Say nothing," Ivan whispered out of the side of his mouth.

"Just look natural and don't look around because he's watching us."

Ivan kept his eyes on the icon. "Count Perowski is a very smart man," he said. "When he gave me the letter, he also gave me a small sum of money in case the little official needed to be persuaded. The count knows who is who, and what is what in St. Petersburg. The blessed mother must be watching over you also."

He glanced quickly back at the gate. The stiff official was busy checking papers and he and Zeena would not be remembered until he reached into his trousers this evening.

"Little people can be bought with little sums. Big people can be bought with big sums. It is one of the facts of St. Petersburg."

Zeena heard his voice as if through a curtain. She was trying to calm herself. Chance would be a constant companion. Had the train porter not chanced to see her, she would not have chanced on the Count, and she might be on her way to jail. Had the Count not chanced to take a fancy to her, she would now be on her way to jail, alone and lost. People could be bought. Certainly, Jonah had been bought from the army. A new thing to remember. The memory of Malinovitch in Reuben's shop and the power he held over the police came to mind. That was a chance meeting, and did not his money buy her a fantasy and a goal? And what of the power that he had? Count Perowski seemed to command the same power. It was a power that seemed to control life and death. She thought of Sarah's power over her life and of Ezra's power over the townsfolk. She thought of the power she had over Ezra. Power and chance. Twins of the same mother. Power and chance seemed to rule the universe. To have power was to be ready for chance and possibly be in control of it. Having power was the secret, and money was the path to it. In that, her mother was right.

Her companion stood before the icon and made the sign of the cross on his body. Zeena looked at the image of the mother and child painted gold behind the glass, and stifled her laughter. Praying to a picture was even more infantile than praying to the eternal void. Had someone clever conceived a deity that captured the essence of power and chance, she would have lit a candle to it without hesitation. Suddenly, Ivan seemed less than he had been. She wondered at the new realization, but dismissed it feeling that her disdain for his childish mystery was her's, and she was not about to allow it to stem the flow of what promised to be an exciting adventure.

She stood silently next to the young man who bowed his head in prayer. How silly and out of control everything seemed to be, she thought. Here she was a runaway wife, pregnant by a secret lover, just rescued from prison by a kindly stranger who was acting through a handsome alien youth. What she had fancied on the ferry was true. Everything did seem to move along on invisible intersecting currents, and she fancied herself floating with it. Things were moving along swiftly for her, and though there were surprise tensions, they seemed to dissipate. She had no conflicts. Perhaps conflict was an overt confrontation to the current. All her life she had been in conflict. Perhaps, she thought, she had been caught in other people's currents. Of course, she had always been part of her mother's current. She always fought it. But, why? To save herself. That was it. She had been fighting all her life to steer her own life on her own current. She had no conflict now because she was in control of her life and doing exactly what she wanted to do. She felt good. She would float along. She would go wherever the current flowed. Now it flowed to St. Petersburg on the Tsar's birthday.

CHAPTER 15

They left the Moscow Station, Zeena holding Ivan's hand. The immediate fear dissolved as she stepped onto the Nevsky Prospekt. Before her stretched an uninterrupted street as far as she could see; a huge thoroughfare lit by an endless row of brightly flickering lamps. In the distance, she could make out the huge silhouette of the steeple she had seen from the train. It seemed to look down on an endless river of busy shoppers and businessmen like some benevolent and approving god of commerce.

"I give you my St. Petersburg," he said broadly, gesturing towards the street. Zeena laughed a young girl's laugh of expectation and felt the impulse to race into the street with her arms wide open.

The brash young man excused himself and made her promise that she would not move. He shook his head up and down, emphatically reinforcing his resolve that she not disappear. Zeena agreed to wait.

She watched him turn and run back into the station. Then she turned to drink in the city. She wished it to be noon. She wanted to be able to see every detail and memorize every sign. Now she would have to content herself with the strange blue shadows and purple images. Even in her imagination, she would never have seen the sculptured stone buildings stretching above her or the brightly painted signs reaching out to diners and shoppers. So many people. She could lose herself here. Here she would find the excitement and pleasure of life denied her. She scanned the street. Not half a block away she could see a huge sign above a glass entry way that said Gostiny Dvor. "Gostiny Dvor," she repeated, and reached into her pocket and took out the small card that the Countess Perowski wrote upon.

That was the store. She would shop there tonight. She would be fashionable. It would not really matter what it was, as long as it was nicely styled for a city lady. Tomorrow, in the sunlight, she would be indistinguishable from any other young woman of means, and that was her objective. She wanted to lose herself in the anonymity of style. Suddenly she grew impatient for Ivan. She touched the coins near her body. She would need some of them now, though she did not know how many. She had to have the best. It was an investment in herself and since she was all she had, she would not be stingy. Image was all, she recalled the countess saying, and, if everything did float, she would float in fashion.

Ivan appeared suddenly beside her, dressed in a light colored suit.

"You are as handsome as you are charming," she said and brushed off some imaginary soil from his lapel. He smiled broadly and offered her his arm.

"Are you hungry, or do you just want to walk?"

"I'm starving, but I must go over there first," and she pointed to the store as if she shopped there regularly.

"How do you know of that?" he asked.

"Do you think we are unaware of what is good in the provinces?" she retorted with amused indignation. She pulled him by the arm as an eager child might, and they were lost in the crowded street.

When Zeena emerged from the bank of shops, she was in a summer yellow dress with lace inserted into the bodice. She carried a matching parasol, edged in white. Upon her head, also appropriately placed by the shop owner, was a small straw hat with a white feather and net veil. And, oh, the softness of the silken underclothing against her skin. She was more animated than she had ever been before in her life. Her cheeks felt rosy and she could almost feel the twinkle in her eyes. As she passed the window, she threw a side glance at her reflection and smiled at the sight. At last she was where she needed to be. The young man on her arm was not her Jonathan, but he was young and handsome and she liked his brightness. She felt young and alive for the first time in her life. She would not think of anything other than the moment, and all the moments before her.

"I know of a wonderful little place where students gather to sing and talk. The food is good, and cheap, and you can sit for hours outside and watch the boats on the Neva."

Zeena agreed with delight, and they maneuvered through the shoppers, she stepping lightly lest her shoes be scuffed. She was like a child and she could not see fast enough and she could not hear fast enough. Each image seemed important enough to etch itself indelibly on her memory. When they reached the Anichkov Bridge, she could not contain her joy any longer. She pulled him by the hand and dragged him to the ledge to look at the small pleasure barges that slid under them as smoothly as if water fowl. She looked up and was startled. Looming above her, on massive bronze hoofs, a giant horse reared up in like surprise, but was kept in check by an equally strong youth clutching its reins. Zeena's mouth opened slightly.

"You have never seen anything like those I bet," Ivan said proudly. "Tsar Nicholas the First ordered them created by a sculptor named Klodt, and he liked them so much, he had copies made and sent to the King of Prussia and the King of Sicily."

"You sound like a travel book," Zeena said laughing.

"I am," he said proudly. "Everyone in St. Petersburg knows this. We are a very proud citizenry!"

Zeena thought of Krivoser and laughed to herself. She fancied them there and her pointing out the open sewer and the fish stalls.

"What's that building?" and she pointed diagonally across the bridge to a massive dark structure that dominated the corner opposite the bronze equestrian.

"Those are the Veganov Dance School and the Pushkin Theater."

Zeena's eyes widened and strained to make out the detail. "How I should love to see a play," she wished.

"Then you shall," he said with bravado. "I shall take you!"

"And will you take me on a pleasure boat on a canal?"

"I will show you everything as soon as I get back."

Zeena looked at him with a strange sense of loss. Suddenly, she did not like the idea of being alone.

"Where do you have to go?"

"I must make another run tomorrow to the provinces and then, perhaps to Moscow. I don't know yet, but I know I won't be back until some time next week."

"And you leave tomorrow?" Zeena said.

"You are sorry to see me leave?"

"Yes," she said softly. "I am sorry."

They strolled across the bridge holding hands in silence. A warm breeze brushed against them from the river. Somewhere in the distance, Zeena could hear a violin.

The current moved her to a small cafe opposite the river and she found herself looking longingly in to the bright blue eyes of the young man who laughed and spoke of his dreams. More than once during their banter on life, and politics, and books, she wanted to reach out and touch him to see if he were real or just a part of the magic created by the violins and the soft breeze.

They walked slowly towards the street Count Perowski had written on the paper he had given Ivan. Her pulse quickened at the thought of the strange house and the huge lie, and its uncertain resolution. Ivan talked on about growing up in the city, the winter, and how people came from all over Europe to hear the ice crack in the spring when the river thawed. He spoke of the magical white nights when the city was never without light. Zeena nodded and smiled, but more and more her thoughts projected her into that uncertain future.

The Nevsky Prospekt crossed Fyodor Street a block after the Guboyeder Canal, and they turned. In the dim, flickering glow of the lamp, Zeena could make out the lines of great stately houses; severe and classic. She could feel herself drawn closer to Ivan in her intimidation. They reached the house and stood before the gate.

"You are home," said Ivan somewhat sadly.

Zeena lowered her eyes and said nothing.

"It will be wonderful living in such a place," he said.

Zeena hesitated. She did not want to go into the house.

He smiled at her, and pushed the ornate fence open and motioned her to proceed. She felt more comfortable, gave a quick curtsy, and moved onto the stone walk. The soft shadows preceded them and invited them up the steps to the heavily carved wooden door.

Ivan turned the key and the bolts fell out of their places. He pushed down on the handle and the door eased back on its hinges. In the dark vestibule, she could make out another door of etched glass, framed by wooden scrolls. Zeena felt uneasy and realized that she was here, not because she had created the situation, but because someone else had. Someone else was in control, not she. She made the decision to go with Ivan, but the Count had created the scenario. She would leave as soon as Ivan left her presence and go to Malinovitch as she had planned.

The door eased open and they stepped onto a thick carpet that, in the dim light, shimmered with the most intricate designs she had ever seen. Ivan felt for a candle near the door, and lit it. The glow softly radiated down the foyer and echoed back the sound of quiet elegance. They stepped from the rug onto white and black tessellated squares. She did not know that she was walking on marble.

"Have you ever been in such a house," whispered Ivan, as if his voice above a breath would rouse the ire of the Count's venerable ancestors pictured on the walls. Zeena felt like an interloper, but excitement of what might come next in the game urged her hesitantly to the broad oak steps leading to the second story. She paused, her hand on the sleek banister. She did not know where she was going, and she remembered that she had to leave. She turned towards him.

"Thank you, Ivan," she said moving towards him I am very tired and would like to go to sleep. If you show me the servant's quarters, I would be very appreciative. He radiated a strange youthful beauty and she paused and studied him in the flickering orange light.

"Would you like to see the room the Count sleeps in?" he said hopefully. He sounded like a naughty little boy bent on a dangerous adventure with a new friend.

Zeena hesitated. "It's very late, Ivan, and I don't think the Count would like it." She did not sound convincing.

"Please," he said, taking her hand and turning her around to the stairs again. "Please," he repeated.

She felt herself move up the steps. The glow from the candle danced on the highly polished, sleek wood. The portraits along their path looked disdainfully at the commoners desecrating the sanctity of a nobleman's home. Zeena looked up at the fantasy hero, backing up the stairs, holding a candle to light her way.

She knew he had to go so she could leave, but the current on the steps was strong and natural and impelled her to flow with it. It was a new and dangerous insanity, but insanity had been piled upon insanity for as long as she could remember. What was another insanity in an insane world, and in an insane life? Shall I add adultery to my list of sins, she laughed to herself, never taking her eyes from him. Why not? I'm already a whore. Besides, hell was as much a fable as heaven.

He invited her over to the massive carved wooden bed. She protested as she moved towards him. His touch was gentle, but she felt herself tighten. He hesitated, sensing some unknown difficulty, but he continued. His soft blue eyes eased and warmed her and she realized this was not Ezra. She told her skin that this was not Ezra, and she strained for all traces of Ezra's touch to dissolve from her memory. This handsome youth was unlike anyone, even her beloved Jonathan, and the difference in his forbidden looks and forbidden history fascinated her and drew her with an excitement and a danger she had never known. A force from a swirling vortex, somewhere outside of her being, drew her closer with each beat of his heart. She took in deep, measured breaths, and let them out slowly as if to establish some measure of control over something that was beyond control. She willed her body to relax. She willed the tensions of her past lost, and with each exhalation, expelled more and more of her hesitation and fear.

She poured herself into the flesh of the hands that moved in slow, circular motions, over her shoulders and arms. She drew herself into his chest and breathed the salty musk of his body. His hands moved to the buttons on her dress, and he fingered them lightly.

"Zeena, you are so soft and lovely," he whispered.

She raised her head. He moistened his lips and softly kissed the half parted mouth of the trembling girl in the summer yellow dress. Her mouth tightened and he hesitated, letting his lips hover and gently brush against hers until they softened under his gentle insistence. Again, Zeena caught herself responding to another time, and she again forced herself to concentrate on his lips until she felt her own respond. His arms moved down her back slowly, and he pulled her so close to him that the buttons of his jacket pressed her flesh. She felt his mouth move over hers in an easy, moist, glide and she felt the tip of his tongue trace the outline of her lips and gently probe her parted teeth. She felt herself melting and flowing away. A soft, strange heat flowed slowly down her body and settled between her thighs. She moved closer to him as if to ease and stay the pulsating sensation. His arms reached up again and she felt the first button of her dress open and then the second. She opened her eyes slowly and separated her lips from his. They clung as they parted.

"Let me help you," and she reached behind her to loosen the sash around her waist. She did not take her eyes from the beautiful and forbidden face before her. She was as much fascinated by the strange current that flowed around her, and this strange bedroom, and the strange sensation filling her up as she was by this new body. She thought of Jonathan and that moment in the barn so fraught with anguish, longing, and fear. She thought of the agony of Ezra's brutal touch. Now, there was only the softness of the candlelight and Ivan. This was as it should have been with Jonathan had chance favored her. These were the feelings, the dangerous feelings, that would carry her to awareness. In her mind and in her body, the terrible yearnings of her former life cried out to be satisfied. The ache was of such great intensity that it did not matter whose hands or lips or thighs pressed against her own so long as they erased the memory of her marriage and let her taste the joy of feeling love. She wanted to float in time and be swept away in eternity.

She stood in the delicately stitched underclothes with the dress around her ankles. She bent down and lifted it, trying not to break the moment with the practical concern. Her dress was dropped over the chair carefully, and she stood before him unashamed. He was a stranger, yet more familiar than anyone had ever been before. He was without fear and trouble. He was untouched by the trauma of history. He was clever and exulted in life, and he touched those secret longings in her that called her to be as exhilarated as he. He was the man of all her romantic fantasies, and she knew him so well.

He stood above her like a blond tower. She had seen statues in forbidden books on ancient Rome, and thought of the magnificent bronze man steadying the rearing horse on the Prospekt. Now the statue of the demigod was living and he had come down from his high place like the giants of ancient days to the daughter of a man. He would make her immortal. He would free her from the invisible shackles of her past and carry her off to a new world. She pushed herself onto the center of the Count's bed.

Her mythic lover tormented her with long kisses and a slow undulating motion against her body that loosened her and allowed her to give herself up to him with abandon. It was she who pushed against him violently as if to consume him in the fire that burned within her and radiated out of each pore of her flesh. She opened her eyes and looked at the hovering man above as if through the pulsating heat of a mirage. The old world did not exist. It had melted away and she was reborn in the pounding of his body against hers. She reached out to him and pulled him down, and, as he fell, his hips surged brutally towards her and she screamed in the pleasure pain of the massive thrust that placed his pubis against hers. She lost her breath and clung to his body, and began to cry.

She was being touched. For the first time in her life, she had given up her anger and allowed herself the passion, honesty, and truth of touch.

She pulled his face towards her own and her lips devoured his mouth with the intensity of a demon sucking forth the soul of a fallen saint. She wanted to consume him. She wanted to drink in life. She wanted to make each passionate second count for each year of the death she had lived. Now her body was alive as it was meant to be. Her soul tingled. The current swept her along and she did not care where it flowed. Here in his arms, she felt safe, safe from tormented memories and hate. Here she was free to love and be loved on her own terms.

Her hips surged to meet the long, steady thrusts. Each time he withdrew slowly and her body seemed to follow him as if to savor each centimeter of pleasure. There was a strange tension and drawing sensation building slowly in the deep secret recesses of her loins. It tantalized her as it grew. She heard Ivan's breathing become heavier and his thrusts more intense and savage. She rose to meet each thrust with equal intensity and pleasure. The new tensions in her grew in proportion to his lunges and she began to focus on a wave of electrical impulse that seemed to pile up a strange potential energy, and press against a wall within her for release. Again, and again, his groin smashed savagely into her and she rose to meet him each time. Her face burned. He began to gasp in his own agony of pleasure, and he buried his teeth recklessly in her neck. Zeena's mouth opened and through gritted teeth, screamed into the silent room the abandoned scream of a woman who has freed herself from her fear and anger and has given up her body to passion and sensation. For a brief moment, Zeena floated in space. Nothing touched her. Time did not exist. Ivan's body relaxed and he laughed the hoarse, gruff laugh of a young man who knew he had given a woman great pleasure and a passionate memory. His body relaxed and he sank on her. His energy flowed out with each breath he took. He could feel the natural contractions of her inner muscles ripple against his slackening penis.

He withdrew to a wonderful agony. She grasped him and held him close, memorizing with her own body the inches of his flesh. She felt him softening between her leg and wished him there for eternity. She held him tight.

"Don't leave me. Not yet," she murmured and she closed her eyes to fix the moments of their love making. She tried to fix his face, looking down at her in the orange glow. She tried to fix the straight flaxen hair and the muscular ripples beneath the smooth skin of his chest and torso. She tried to fix the way his eyes riveted on her as he undulated inside her.

She held him tenderly and moved her hands over his back. The image of Jonathan's face emerged out of the recesses of her memory. His chocolate eyes, so alert and knowing, looked at her curiously and seemed to question silently the radiance that emanated from her face.

You have no right to question me, she thought.

I am not questioning you, her imagination responded. You are questioning yourself.

I have no questions about what I've done or what I'm doing, or what I will continue to do, and do not imagine that I regret any of this.

I did not say regret, the memory answered, you did.

I carry your child.

I know, you told me months ago.

Is that all you have to say, she thought flatly. The image said nothing. She waited, and still there was no response.

Why didn't you love me as I loved you? she thought. The image remained mute. I would have loved you as no man had ever been loved before. Why?, Jonathan, why? All I have to give I would have given to you without exception. All my passion would have become your pleasure.

You are too much for me, Zeena, the vision responded. You need too much. There is an emptiness in you that I am not enough of a man to fill. There is an intensity in you I cannot ease. There are passions in you that overwhelm me. You frighten me, Zeena, and I am not at ease when I am with you. The image faded.

The word "frightened" echoed in her brain and brought her back to the bed and the man, so different from the fantasy now lost in the shadows of her memory.

Damn you, Jonathan, she thought. Damn you for coming to me now, and damn you for your truth. A tear rolled slowly down the side of her cheek and slipped into the corner of her mouth. She became aware of Ivan's weight and grew uncomfortable. She wondered if the baby felt the weight also. Slowly, the room took on its reality and she felt her thighs wet and the sheet beneath her sticky and uncomfortable. She squirmed slightly and loosened her arms. Ivan opened his eyes slowly and smiled at her. He moved to one side and allowed himself to fall next to her. The bed bounced and he laughed a muffled laugh into the pillow.

Zeena studied the dark recesses of the room. Was she to regret this? Was she to regret any of what she had done? The baby seemed to flutter. Was she to regret this child or the passion for Jonathan that brought her to this place? Ivan lay next to her hovering near sleep. She looked at him and her eye traced his body in the flickering light. She thought of a legend she once read where Psyche lifted a lamp to look at the sleeping Cupid and her Cupid fled when some hot oil awoke him. How, she wondered, was it possible to love Jonathan yet feel so intently attracted to this stranger? She barely knew him other than from her fantasy, and yet she had given herself to him fully and without reservation. She had never known such safety before, and such freedom. Yet, what did she feel for this stranger and what did she feel for Jonathan if she could feel this way with a man she barely knew?

The physical sensation she had tried to memorize faded to a series of silent mental images. How strangely the magic flows away, she thought, and we are left with the sticky wetness of reality and sheets that need changing. She laughed to herself and slid her legs stealthily over the side of the bed so as not to wake him. Her eyes could trace the outline of a door opposite the bed and she made her way towards it, hoping it was a privy closet. The candle faintly illuminated the heavily carved brocaded chairs. A gilt frame portrait of the Tsar hung on a wall closest to the door, and she mused on the Tsar having watched a common valet make love to a Jewess in a Count's bed.

The door creaked open and the light slid into the corners of the small ante-chamber. Zeena was astounded and she stifled her laugh to think that this privy, with its polished black stone walls and washing basin carved in the shape of a giant shell, was larger and higher than the main room of Ezra's home. She raised the candle and looked in wonder at the painted walls. Above the tub a chariot rose out of the sea drawn by horses with curving flanks that swerved into a huge fan tail. Brandishing a three pronged fork, some giant stood erect and in control, as dolphins leaped around him. She opened a small mirrored door, and dozens of towels and sheets lined the shelves. She reached up and took a towel for herself and Ivan, and a dry sheet for the bed. She moved to the shell basin. She looked for a pump, but there was none. Two identical handles with faces and bodies of fish looked at her. She pushed at one hesitantly. Nothing happened. She pushed a little harder and out of a fish mouth in the middle of the basin, fresh water gushed onto her hand. She jumped in surprise and delight. She cleaned herself off, marveling at the wealth and beauty. She returned with a damp towel and clean sheet. Her demigod slept in the pale moon light that filtered in from the half shuttered window. She watched him and her eyes traced the lines of his strong body against the dark shadows of the bed clothes carelessly draped around him. She had to wake him and they had to leave this room. He had to leave and then she would leave and all of this would become an amusing memory to savor and delight in at another time.

She inched towards him and touched his shoulder. He made a muffled sound into the sheet and turned over. She could make out the full form of the sleeping man and could not help herself from savoring him. But she reminded herself that he had to awake and she also had to be on her way.

"Ivan," she whispered. "Ivan, you must get up."

He repeated the muffled tone and she could not keep herself from moving her face to his and kissing him awake, so beautiful did he appear as he lay sleeping. He reached up slowly as he opened his eyes and his arms encircled her body in a tender embrace. Again, she felt herself melt into his lips and chest, and she pulled away.

"No, Ivan," she said softly. "You must leave."

"You are wonderful," he said. "You make me feel wonderful."

"But it's getting lighter outside and the Count will be here soon."

"The light is only the magic of the season," and he reached out to touch her hair. "We have plenty of time."

"Please," she repeated emphatically. "You must go and I must straighten this room or I will find myself on the street tomorrow with no place to live."

"Then we must find a place to live together."

"Ivan, we will be caught."

"If I am caught naked in the Count's bed, I will be beaten and no more. But for your sake and safety, I will get up. Will you promise me that we will see each other again?"

"Yes," she said, tenderly.

"Swear this to me." he said looking at her with a tenderness and hope she had never seen before in any face. "Zeena, you are so different. You are unlike any other girl I have ever known. You are interesting. You can talk about politics and books and dreams. And you want to learn about everything. Being with you is exciting. That's so important to me and so rare in a girl. You are more than any girl I've ever met."

Zeena lowered her eyes, embarrassed by the praise and the sincerity of his affection. She thought of her father and the precious moments near the stove at night or on the Sabbath when he would sit with her and read to her and ask her to question. He had taught her how to be interesting.

A tear rolled down her cheek and she saw his finger touch it and bring it to his lips. She wanted to throw herself into his arms and dissolve there in his strength and safety. He leaned forward and kissed her softly. Her eyes closed as she leaned into his kiss.

"Please, Ivan, please," she said shaking off the desire that was building for him again. "I don't know when they will be home and I must make the bed. I don't think the Count would appreciate knowing that his servants made love in his bed."

"Well, at least someone is making love in this bed," he laughed. "Besides, you are right and I have something to do in the city before the Count and his family return tomorrow. But swear to me that you'll see me and I'll get up and I'll even help you make the bed."

"I swear," she said, wondering where she would be when he came knocking on the door.

"Then I go," and he swung his legs over the edge of the bed and searched for his clothing. She watched him dress, memorizing him as she had memorized the evening and the city. He was part of her new life and the first good memory of the new history she was writing for herself.

She stood and the sheet she wore fell from her body, but she felt no shame before him. She merely laughed and tucked it in. He placed his cap on his head and pulled it down over his face.

"Promise me you'll be here," he repeated through the cloth." Then he lifted the cap and looked down at her. His eyes drew her in. "I need someone like you, Zeena. With you, I sense I can become something. For you I would become more than a valet."

Zeena clung to his words, but knew he was not part of her plan. Yet was not what she ultimately sought, standing before her? With him she could also do and become. What was power and money and control when compared to this feeling? She had to think, or at least, rethink. Even what she felt for Jonathan was different from this. She needed time, but the glow filtering through the shutters urged her to press him to leave again.

"Yes," she lied. "I'll be here, but please go now. Please."

He moved away slowly. "Come with me to the door."

She followed him into the hallway. The blue iridescent light seemed to vibrate throughout the house and they shimmered like ghosts on the stairwell against the mahogany panels. He turned and kissed her again before he finally left. Zeena stood there, her eyes closed and swayed slightly after their lips parted. When she opened her eyes, he was gone.

All she had dreamed of was becoming a reality and the secret longings for magical nights and tenderness could be had. She climbed the stairs. Even if she never saw him again, she would have this night. The portraits continued to look down with disdain upon the girl wrapped in the sheet, and she laughed at them. She felt a strange peace. Something had gone right. Finally, something was the way it was supposed to be and she thought of this as she changed the dampened sheet and smoothed out the bed covering. She was in her own current and it was good. It was right. The room glowed a hypnotic silver blue. The memories infused themselves into the carved bed posts and clung to the tapestry on the wall. She climbed back onto the bed to better feel the memory of his body and as she lay there, a carousel of bright thoughts whirled around in her head. She closed her eyes and soon she was asleep.

CHAPTER 16

"My dear child," a voice said softly. Zeena opened her eyes slowly and then widened them as reality descended upon her. She had fallen asleep and now she was discovered. She reached for the sheet to pull it over her body, but the shadowy figure was sitting on it. She lay there, exposed to him.

"My dear child," she heard him say again. "How delighted I was to find that not only did you accept my invitation to my home, but you found your way to my room."

Zeena could barely speak. "I meant no disrespect. I was just so tired that I fell asleep in the first room I found."

"No disrespect imagined, my dear child," replied the Count in the same affable tone. "I am delighted to find you here and so eager to thank me for my kindness."

Zeena watched his eyes hunger as they traced the line of her body and fix on her pubis. She felt her entire being contract as if Ezra sat next to her.

"My dress is new and I did not want it creased. Please do not think that I am the kind of girl who would give her body in exchange for kindness." She stammered out the words as the fear in her grew. The old feeling of powerlessness began to take hold as she watched his image grow sharp.

"I was hoping that you were exactly the kind of girl who did repay kindness in that way, but if you are not, it does not matter."

"Then I will thank you for your kindness and I will be on my way," said Zeena, hoping that he would remain the kindly man she had met on the train.

"My dear child," he continued, as if they spoke across a dinner table, "you must remain under my protection. St. Petersburg is not a friendly place for Jews who have no legitimate business here. There are prisons, and heaven only knows what, for those who scoff at the Tsar's laws. Surely you did not think me foolish enough not to see through the thin fabrication of your story? You people are always trying to evade the law, or get away with more than you deserve."

Zeena moved to sit up, but the Count pushed her back and held her by the shoulder.

"Now I'll tell you exactly what will happen, my dear. After I leave you, you will get up and dress yourself, and leave. I and my family will go to church. By mid-day we will have returned, and you will come back here. You will present yourself, telling my wife that the people you were to stay with left for summer holiday, and you were wondering if she would be kind enough to put you on the staff. She has a good heart, and will. I shall be supportive of her decision and delighted that you will be part of our household."

Zeena's thoughts leaped to Malinovitch. She would go to him immediately and he would help her. He would protect her. She wanted to beat herself for her stupidity.

"And, my dear child," he droned on, "if you do not come back, I will guarantee that I have enough power to have you hunted down. The government thinks the Jews more dangerous than the nihilists. It is foolish of course, but it would not stop them from putting every available person on your trail to rid holy St. Petersburg of your unholy presence." Zeena watched him smile and wink.

"No, you will do exactly as I say because you are a bright child and probably have a taste for some of the nicer moments of life that would come to you by being the play thing of a very wealthy man."

He placed his hand on her breast. "I have not treated myself to a pretty toy in almost a year, and it is time I did so."

Zeena felt the reality of his words come down upon her as if she were a grape in a press. She would be a slave for as long as he wished, and, after that, he could easily turn her over to the police. The current had become treacherous again and she was being swept towards a whirlpool.

He smiled his amiable smile, as if he were making some magnanimous donation to a favored charity and his hand moved down her breast to her navel. She felt herself contract.

She stood in the early morning sunlight and held the iron gate to steady herself. Ezra, at his worst, had not been so brutal. She cried and staggered down the street. Now was not a time to be without her wits. The threat was real. He would indeed have her hunted down and destroyed. He had that power and all the resources that came with such position. Now she feared for her life. The current indeed had swept her suddenly from a halcyon sea onto treacherous rocks. So swift. So sudden. She, herself, was to blame. She had gone with Ivan. She had fallen asleep.

Malinovitch must know of this. Only he might be able to protect her.

Zeena put her hand to her body and felt the coins for reassurance. She reached into her purse for Malinovitch's address and moved down the street to the Prospekt. She moved through the morning sunlight, oblivious to the neo-classical beauty. All she would have memorized she did not even see.

Zeena walked for blocks in the direction a passer-by had given her. She kept her head down, fearing to meet the eyes of someone who would see through her masquerade. She looked up only to read the names of the streets carved onto the sides of the buildings. Finally she stood beneath one that read Petrovaad, and she followed the numbers. Like the street of the Count's home, the trees were tall and bursting with foliage, but these homes seemed closer together and not as grand; not as ornately carved and decorated. She held the slip of paper in her hand and searched the numbers until she stood before the house. She swallowed and climbed the stone steps to a double glass door. Bells from all over the city pealed their call to the golden dome churches, and she froze, remembering the order that the Count had given that she was not to return to the house until after he and his family returned from church. A pious man, she thought. A true believer and defender of God.

She reached for the chain hanging on the wall, and pulled it. From within the house she could hear the tinkle of a bell. She studied herself in the reflection of the glass. She looked like a young lady of style and breeding. She put her hand to the veil on her hat and poked at it. As she reached for the bell again, the door opened and a stern faced woman studied her through piercing gray eyes. Zeena caught her breath.

"We have no apartments available," and she moved to close the door before Zeena could speak.

Zeena reached out and put her hand on the door. "Please," she said, her voice beginning to crack. "I do not want an apartment."

The woman squinted at her and looked her up and down. "Then what do you want?" she asked abruptly.

"I've come to see Alexi Malinovitch."

The woman's eyes widened and she stepped back with an expression that spoke of both surprise and fear.

At the sight of the woman's reaction, Zeena reeled with the thought that Malinovitch might have moved or died, taking with him her hopes.

"I will see if he is in his apartment," she said curtly. She studied Zeena again with renewed interest and a mocking smile turned down the corner of her mouth as if constructing a choice bit of gossip.

"What is your name?" she said opening the door again.

"Please say Zeena Chernov is here."

The concierge made a short snorting sound and then disappeared. Zeena looked up and down the street quickly. A thousand words of explanation raced through her head. The door opened again and the dour woman stood aside for Zeena to enter.

"I was told to show you to his rooms in a few moments. You are to wait here and I was instructed to offer you tea. Do you want tea?"

Zeena almost laughed. The woman spoke as if she had memorized the lines and could never of her own volition offer someone tea out of her own sense of courtesy. Zeena forced a smile and sat on a frayed sofa designated for her by the woman's finger. Then she disappeared through a door.

This was nothing like the way she dreamed their first meeting would be. Perhaps this once was a grand house. Perhaps the sofa upon which she sat and the rug were once clean. Perhaps the paint was once bright and the wood was once polished. Behind the door, Zeena could hear the faint rattle of cups on saucers. She took a deep breath and tried to relax. She closed her eyes, but the Count appeared and she opened them again. She felt the tears rise in her eyes and silently roll down her cheeks. The door opened and the woman reappeared with a tray of cakes and tea.

"Follow me," she instructed flatly.

Zeena moved up the dark stairwell in the wake of the black ankle length dress.

They stood before a large wooden door that might have been the master bedroom of the house before it became a series of apartments. The woman balanced the tray on one hand and knocked with the other.

The door opened slowly. Alexi Malinovitch stood there facing the woman, and ordered her to set the tray on the table and leave. Zeena's heart sank and she felt the tears rise again. The woman sniffed the air detecting the scent of cologne hastily applied, and again, a sinister smile turned down the corner of her mouth. Her eyes questioned him about the stranger in the yellow dress. He dismissed her query with a quick motion of his head. Zeena did not see the conversation.

Alexi Malinovitch closed the door and turned. Zeena saw him through the blur of tears. She caught her breath and began to cry. He appeared bewildered and his arms, outstretched in welcome to his old friend's child, were lowered slowly to his side, and his face took on the look of one genuinely concerned for another in pain. It was an emotion not familiar to him.

Zeena felt fear for the vulnerable child that lived within her.

He came towards her and gently took her hand, and led her to the settee near the window. "Now tell me what has happened, and why what should be a happy time has become so sad for you."

"May I please have some tea?" Zeena asked softly, trying to control her cracking voice.

He reached for the pot of tea, and poured it into a cup. "Here," he said sympathetically, "a good cup of strong tea will help."

Zeena forced a brief smile, avoiding his eyes, and took the cup in her trembling hand.

"You must think me such a fool," she said, and her last words were lost in the cup of steaming amber liquid.

"Is that better?" he said solicitously.

"Yes, thank you," she responded, and took a deep breath.

"Now," he continued, "tell me why you are so sad and then tell me of your father and family."

"I hardly know where to begin," she said slowly, and she scanned her memory of the train and the story she had decided to tell. Now, she had a sequel as well. "I will tell you from the beginning. A man named Ezra Bendak threatened to ruin my father and brother if I did not marry him."

Malinovitch straightened his back and his eyes widened slowly at the name. Zeena saw the change.

"You know him?" she said.

"No," he responded, "but I knew something of his family."

Zeena paused, expecting something more, but Malinovitch reached over and calmly poured himself a glass of tea.

"I agreed, against my father's wishes, and became pregnant immediately." Zeena studied his face, but could discern only a brief flair of his nostrils. He motioned for her to continue.

"He hated me and the thought of me having his child. He even claimed that the child was not his, and he beat me without mercy. I ran away to save myself and my baby."

"And do you still carry the child?" he said softly.

"Yes," she said.

"And this is why you are so upset?" he said, taking another sip of tea, and encouraging her to do the same with a motion of his hand.

"Yes, and there is more." She had placed Ezra in her history

and could think of him and speak and lie about him with complete justification and impunity. But this other thing, this recent
thing, caused a fear in her so genuine, that at the thought, she felt
herself gasp for air and heave great sobs into her hands.

"There, there," he said, tenderly. "There is nothing so bad
that a good friend cannot make better." He reached over and lifted
her chin. He looked into her pale eyes and remembered the beauty
he had seen through the window of her father's shop. He remembered his own fantasy and the coins.

"Tell me," he said, "tell me so it will not be such a burden."

Zeena swallowed. "I met a man and his family on the train. I
did not know when I came here that people needed identification
papers, so he must have realized this and gave me a letter of passage so I could get off the train. A porter gave his letter to me as
well as a key to this man's house after the man and his family left
the train. The letter told me that the man and his wife invited me
to their home, and since I had no place to go and it was late, and
I didn't know how to find you, I accepted the kindness." She paused
again for breath. "I fell asleep in a bedroom, but did not know it
was the Count's and then he came home by himself."

She saw Malinovitch's eyes widen at her first mention of the
man's title.

"He awoke me and told me that he knew I was a Jew, and
would have me arrested if I did not agree to his demands."

"And what were his demands?" Malinovitch asked in a steady
voice that was like steel. The muscle in his jaw twitched and gave
the lie to the passive expression he wore.

Zeena stifled another wave of tears and sat for a few seconds to
catch her breath and form her next sentence.

"He demanded that I reappear at his home this afternoon. His
wife and daughter are coming from the country today and were to
meet him at church. I am to ask his wife to employ me as a maid."
She paused. "Then he said that if I didn't, he would call the police
and turn me over as a Jew illegally in the city. If I ran away, he
would have me hunted down and put in jail." She paused again.

"Then he," and she began to sob again, "then he," and her mouth formed the silent words that said through gasps, "raped me." She took in a great breath and let it out, and cried quietly.

Alexi Malinovitch also sat silently for a moment. "And what is the name of this Count, Zeena?" he said softly. His eyes riveted on hers as if they tried to scan her memory for every horrid detail of the last day.

"Count Gregor Perowski," she whispered for fear of being overheard.

Malinovitch bit down hard and curled his lower lip into his mouth.

"The Count is a very rich man and very close to great power. You have fallen into the hands of a formidable enemy." He raised his hand to his mouth and fixed his gaze on a point beyond her. "The Count is a very powerful man."

"I fear for my welfare and my child, and I have nowhere to turn. I would leave, but I don't know anyone but you, and I have no papers to get me out of the country."

"Papers can be bought, but they will take a little time and will cost dearly."

"I have money," she said. "I still have the gold coins you gave me." She reached into her purse and held them out to him.

He laughed as he saw her sudden brightness and child-like movement, and he was taken back to the moment when he had pressed the coins firmly into her hand and invited her to visit him. Life as it might have been crept upon him, and that thought, combining with the story she had just told, enraged him and he stood abruptly. He appeared as a man calculating a move on a chess board. He walked to the window and turned to her.

"You must return to the Count's home."

"But I am so afraid of him. I have never before met anyone who can smile at you and destroy you while he is doing it. Even my husband was more honest. This one is a fiend. This one is nothing like what he seems. Please let me stay here with you."

Throughout, Malinovitch had expressed neither emotion nor support. She did not understand his reserve. She knew he was happy to see her, but when she began to tell the events of the past few days, he became as a wall and she was afraid he did not care. Zeena felt her fear overwhelming her again and she knew she was going to cry.

"That is impossible. This is a difficult time. You must go back as you were told." He could feel the resolve in his eyes and sadly watched her childlike expectation fade with his words.

"I, too, have some power and I will get you papers that will legitimatize you in St. Petersburg and enable you to leave the country."

"Perhaps a hotel?" Zeena said. Her shoulders fell.

"I have money sewn into my clothing."

"No," he said. "There are no hotel rooms available at this time of year. You do as I say and keep your money for the future that you face with your child."

"I fear that my money might be taken if I go back there."

"Then I will keep it for you until the papers are ready. But you must return to the Count this afternoon and speak to his wife as he ordered. If Perowski discerns any change in you, you will be in grave danger. I will take care of everything else and by next week you will be on a train to Paris. Then I will take back my coins and use them to visit you."

He waited for her to smile or for some indication that her pain had been eased, but there was none.

"But why can't I stay here?" she said simply. "I would be safe and I wouldn't be a bother. I swear I wouldn't."

Malinovitch pursed his lips and thought of her request. "I cannot tell you why," he responded, "but you cannot stay. But I'll tell you what we'll do." His voice mustered as much brightness as it could under the circumstances and he took both her hands. "There is a ball being given in honor of the Tsar's birthday and I have an invitation." He leaned in and whispered. "How would you like to accompany me?"

She looked up through tears and a faint smile toyed at the corner of her mouth.

"Now wouldn't that be nice?" he said again.

"Yes," she agreed. "But what if the Count goes to the ball also?"

Malinovitch smiled. "There will be many great balls held to honor the Tsar," he said, "and the one the Tsar and his family will grace will be the one the Count and his family will attend. Of that I am sure."

Zeena took another sip of tea and Malinovitch thrust some cakes at her like an indulgent father. Her stomach growled and she was reminded that she had not eaten since the evening before. She thought briefly of Ivan and wondered where he was.

"I do not know what to say," she said, and took another cake. "I feel so ashamed of myself to have gotten into such a stupid situation."

"You could not avoid it, Zeena. You had no idea that papers were needed, and you had no idea with whom you were dealing. The Count is well known for having an evil reputation when it comes to pretty young women. You are not the first to fall into his web."

"But he seemed so kindly on the train and had he not written out that letter of transit, I would have been taken to jail."

"That's exactly what I mean. You could not possibly have known. You did the only thing you could do. The Count will not go unpunished, I vow that to you, but it will take time."

"Please," said Zeena. "Do not do anything that will cause you trouble. It isn't worth it. Let this become a bad memory."

"As you wish," he said, and he reviewed his memory for names and events that would bring the Count the disgrace whereby he might be destroyed. "But you must learn," he continued, "that because someone smiles at you or offers kindness, it does not mean that such people are kind. Now tell me of your father and the rest of the family and whether you continued involvement with that street corner anarchist."

She felt the baby move and she put her hand on her stomach. He noticed the movement.

"When is your baby due?" he said tenderly.

"I think in five months."

"And will you return home to have it?" he said.

"I will never return. I closed that life when I removed my ring and took enough money to take me to the other side of the world."

"And you think you can end a marriage and close out a family by wishing all of it away?"

"It is the only thing I can do. On the other side of the world there are no records and none to point a finger." She spoke softly, trying to keep arrogance out of her voice. She did not want him to dislike her.

"You will learn in time that we carry our past with us, and we deal with it effectively by confronting it. But, you are young."

Zeena looked at him and waited. "I have sewn the money in my corset," she said wishing to change the topic. "You said you would keep this money for me until I leave?" She tried to make her tone business like, but her voice rang with supplication. She had to trust him. There was no one else to whom she could turn.

He nodded his head in agreement.

"May I use that room?" and she pointed to a door.

He nodded his head again and she rose and walked to it quickly. Malinovitch watched her, tormented by her pain, and his own hidden longings. He would deal with the Count in time. The powerful were arrogant, and the arrogant made enemies. The Count already had enemies and had been the object of hatred voiced by many whom Malinovitch had interrogated. Now he would add another rape and slavery to the Count's already impressive list of brutalizations. The Count would be a special challenge. He could feel the hatred he carried with him move to a central place and crystallize as he sat there. The thought of Zeena returning to the Count, of this special young woman brutalized, was a tormenting thought. But if she did not return, the Count was vindictive enough to demand that the police look for her. That would place her in greater danger, and if she were found under his protection, his own position might be jeopardized. He, too, had enemies who would pull him down at the slightest provocation.

The door to the bedroom opened and Zeena emerged with the small pouch in her hands. She brought it to him, and sat. He took it and felt the weight of the coins. He sensed her hesitation.

"Rest assured, my dear child, that your money will be returned to you."

Zeena was startled by the words 'my dear child' but released the pouch. She had to trust him. There was no choice.

"Do not be afraid, Zeena," he said reassuringly. "You will have your papers, and you will have them by next Sunday. Then I myself shall escort you to the train station and send you on your way. Perhaps I might even travel with you for a distance." He waited for her to smile. She did not.

"And Saturday, we shall attend a great ball. You will like that."

Zeena smiled, and her body sank. "I cannot go," she said, wistfully. "How will I get out of the house? What will I wear? How will I get there?" The old dream was offered, but her circumstances crowded in and pushed at it.

"Firstly, only the servants will be at home, and none of them have an invitation to a ball."

Zeena smiled.

"Secondly, I shall send a carriage for you, and it will be at the door of the house at a precise moment, and all you have to do is step into it, and I will be waiting."

"And will you transform my dress into a ball gown?"

"Sophia has many gowns. Take one of hers. She'll never miss it, and she'll never know."

Zeena was caught short by his familiarity. "You know the daughter by name?" she said, her eyes peering at him questioningly.

Malinovitch was thrown off guard. He had allowed his own fantasy to make him less cautious and reveal to her more than he had intended. He cleared his throat.

"Everyone in St. Petersburg knows Sophia Perowski," he said quickly. "She, like her father, is also most formidable."

She also laughed, remembering the disdainful elegance of the Count's only child, but felt uneasy. Could she really trust him? What did she really know of him or his history? Her father was vague on their relationship and would say nothing when questioned directly. Malinovitch headed the St. Petersburg police yet chose to live in a part of the city that was away from fashion and power. His work generated fear in her even though he smiled at her tenderly. Now he had her money. The Count had also smiled. Again, she felt powerless. No, she had to trust him because there was noone else.

He reached into his pocket and pulled out some bills. "Here, take this. You may need some money."

She felt more at ease. She took another cake, and nibbled at it. As uncomfortable as she was, and with all the doubts she had, she felt strangely relieved that there was to be a solution to her problem within a week. Then she would face another unknown. She regretted that she would have to leave St. Petersburg. There was so much to see and do, and many dreams to be lived.

Malinovitch sat now in the smoking jacket she envisioned, but not in the elegance she had dreamed. He was, in reality a middle aged man with wisps of gray in his beard. His blue eyes were intense and cold and studied her through wire glasses that balanced on a straight nose.

"When did you say you will have your baby?" he said suddenly.

Zeena was suddenly uncomfortable and she quickly reviewed what she had already said to see if she had mentioned a time.

"I think five months," she said, somewhat embarrassed.

"No one could possibly guess from the way you look."

Zeena blushed because his tone also indicated that her appearance was pleasing to him. She wondered at the way she was perceived by men. In the space of a day, three men looked upon her with desire.

Malinovitch turned to the door suddenly. Zeena had heard nothing. He raised his finger to his lips and stood.

"Maria," he called out.

The door opened slowly, and the stern faced woman stood framed in the doorway like a stone statue. She folded her arms and waited.

"Well," he said, annoyed that he was once again reminded of her silence, her vigilance, and her awareness.

"It's almost time," she said dryly. She stared at Zeena and asked the same silent question as before.

Malinovitch looked at her. "They will wait."

She tightened her lips and looked at Zeena. With much disapproval, she turned and closed the door behind her.

Malinovitch spread out his arms in an expression of futility.

"Affairs of business," he said broadly, extending his hand to her, as she rose.

"I will have a carriage in front of the Count's house at seven thirty on Saturday. Watch for it."

He took her arm and escorted her to the door.

"Now, you return to the house. The Count will not find it easy to molest you as long as his wife and daughter are home for the celebration week. When they return to their country estate, as they will after the festivities, you will leave for Paris, and be well out of the Count's reach. Until then, make no mention of me and act as if nothing has happened."

Zeena walked down the street with less trepidation than before, but still fearful of the next few days. She watched the people strolling on the Prospekt in the Sunday morning sun. Again, she caught her reflection in the glass of the shops and saw a fashionably dressed girl. Others passed her, walking with family or on the arm of a young man, and she saw them as no more stylish or attractive than she. Men desired her. She smiled at the thought, and at herself in the reflections as she moved past the shops at a slow, steady pace.

From time to time, she stopped and stood among other young

ladies to study the displays. As long as she did not speak, she could not be taken for anyone other than a young woman of means who was in the city for the Tsar's birthday. How she wished Ivan were next to her. How she wished Jonathan stood at her side. She had time before she had to return to the house. She studied the windows with relish, and touched her bodice to feel for the security of her coins, but remembered they were not there. She felt a chill run up her spine.

Maria Russakov opened the door to Malinovitch's apartment without knocking, and waited. Alexi Malinovitch emerged from his bed chamber wearing a peasant shirt buttoned at the side of the neck. She looked up.

"I didn't hear you knock," he said, knowing full well that she did not.

"Who was that girl?" Her question was as direct as her face. "I do not like surprises, and if you have any surprises for us . . ."

"You are as presumptuous as you are rude!" he said sharply. "And I do not have to tell you anything beyond the fact that her visit was as much a surprise to me as it was to you."

The woman's body seemed to relax. "Alexi, Alexi," she repeated with a rare softness, "I did not mean anything by my question. We are so close to our goal, and I am suspicious of anything new that might alter our plan."

"The visit from the daughter of an old friend cannot change a thing. Clear the table so I can spread this out for you to see."

She took the tray off the table and moved the lamp. Malinovitch took out a map and unfolded it on the table.

"Listen, and remember, because you must repeat it exactly as I tell you. Sophia will hide the bombs Friday night under the bridge on Telsnara Street. Sunday, the Tsar's carriage will leave the Michael Palace and move along the Catherine Canal. Yekovsky, Petrovskaya, and Jeliabov will first go to Telsnara and keep people out from under the bridge. Hartmann, and Ivan are to get the bombs at one thirty and take up their positions on opposite sides of the road in front of the palace exactly here," and he pointed to two places on the map. "The bombs are to be thrown exactly at two o'clock. They must watch for Sophia's handkerchief." He watched Maria's face for understanding. She nodded and repeated exactly what he had said.

"There will be a guard of eight Cossacks. They are to wait until they pass. The carriage will be picking up speed so they must act quickly."

"Who else will be in the coach?" she asked.

"Colonel Dorjibky, and the Grand Duke."

"What if they are killed?"

"Two less tyrants on earth," he responded.

She lowered her head and raised it.

"Narodnaya Volia! The Will of the People," she said softly.

"Narodnaya Volia," he said to reinforce her resolve. "The Will of the People." And he smirked to himself.

He folded the map again and motioned her to the door.

"Also tell them that the train leaves Moscow Station for Germany at two forty five. They will be handed the tickets by Michailov as they cross Ekaterinofsy Canal opposite the stables."

Maria Russakov cleared her throat. "Ivan tells me that there is talk about Sophia, and whether or not she will remain steadfast to the cause. There are those who wonder about her and fear her. She is not of the people and too close to power."

Malinovitch did not look up from the papers on his desk. "You tell your son, and whoever else in the Will of the People, that it is Sophia's money that buys the bombs, that keeps food in their guts, and that bought the tickets for their escape. That's all they need to know. Beyond that, she has more resolve and spirit than all of them put together."

He looked up. "We are close to our goal. We have planned and worked for this moment. We have all risked being exposed." He paused to study her face. "You and I have been through much, and I value your opinion. What is your feeling of the rumors?"

"My feeling is the same feeling I had about her when she contacted us. She is the daughter of a Count. She is a noble woman who has everything in the world. There is no reason why she should risk her life and position, and the welfare of her family, to work with us. She knows who we are. At any moment she can turn us over." She paused for breath. "She is a woman of nobility during the day, and she crawls the back streets of St. Petersburg, dressed like a peasant, at night. We cannot believe it is only for the people that she does this. All of us have reason to hate the tyrant. Only one of my children lives, and he would be dead had you not interceded. You have a history of hate that goes back to your childhood. The rest are all disgruntled students or assorted villains who have nothing except the hope of something better than the nothing they have. But she is a mystery."

Malinovitch thought of Sophia, and what had grown between them in the two years they had know each other. She was indeed an enigma, even to him, and the intensity of her affection and profound devotion had made him uncomfortable more than once. Her passions were always more intense than the most resolute of the group, and her rhetoric more inflammatory than the most ardent supporter of the secret fellowship. But the hatred that gnawed at her and drove her to their confederacy, he could not discern.

Once he had asked her why she had involved herself in such a dangerous business, and she looked at him with aristocratic disdain. The first time she had seen him naked, a circumcised lover, she clasped her hands and said, "ah, even better." He knew there was darkness in her life, but he did not ask again. It was she who had first awakened in him desires that lay dormant and atrophied from his early youth, and he cared for her deeply. But his feelings for her were never at ease, and even when she enticed him to bed, he had the strangest sense that her love was an act of revenge. Her objective seemed more profound and more sinister than that of the Fellowship's, and she seemed to revel in a secret contempt that was profoundly satisfied in his presence; a contempt that inexorably linked them in a sinister devotion that was transcendent. Each trusted the other with an incomplete secret that made their relationship at once compelling and dangerous.

"Maria," he said looking directly into her eyes with a strange tenderness for her. "You and I have no secrets from each other. Sophia is indeed an enigma, and I respect your judgment enough not to tell you not to fear what your senses tell you to fear. I will only say that I look at her behavior. She is resolute, and acts with purpose in our cause. She has never done anything that would indicate the slightest action that is contradictory. She knows everyone in the Fellowship, and if she were going to turn against us, she would have done so a long time ago." He paused to see if her eyes accepted his statement. "I know there is a deep hatred in her for something or someone, but my best sense tells me that the hatred is not for us." He paused again. Her eyes softened somewhat, but her lips remained pursed. "She would not do us any harm."

Maria watched him fold the map and place it in a book on the shelf. Her sense of foreboding was strong, but she trusted him, and her devotion was steadfast. She took a deep breath and exhaled slowly as she pictured the handsome, laughing face of her son, Ivan. There were too many questions and too many doubts and she resolved in her heart that he would not be endangered. How she would do this, she did not know.

"As you wish," she said with resignation, "but I have a bad feeling about everything." She closed the door behind her, balancing the tea tray on one hand. She reviewed the instructions and projected herself to the basement apartment on Sadovaya Street.

Zeena's stomach lurched when the massive wooden door to the house opened. A small, kindly faced woman, so different from Maria, smiled at her benevolently and inquired of her business. She explained, as the Count had instructed, that she had met the Count and Countess on the train, and that she had been invited to call upon them if she met with some difficulty. Zeena waited for the woman to respond, but she only smiled again and invited her into a small vestibule to be seated. She nervously stepped into this house for a second time, and seated herself on the velvet brocade covered bench.

The maid disappeared through etched and beveled glass doors that radiated dazzling colors from the sunlight filtering through the transept high above the door. Zeena watched the light play on the wooden carvings. She was startled when the woman reappeared and gestured for Zeena to follow her.

She did, and was led to two doors at the end of the foyer. The woman opened both of them and Zeena stood, framed in the doorway, as the three people in the room focused their attention upon her. The Count stood and stretched out his hand to her. The Countess turned from her stitchery and smiled a surprised and gracious smile. Sophia Perowski looked up from her book and stabbed Zeena with her hostility.

"How nice to see you again, my dear child," the Count said in his affable voice.

Sophia turned her attention to her father, and threw a silent poisonous glance his way.

"How nice of you to call on us," the Countess injected as the Count led Zeena to the brocade couch opposite her.

"What a lovely dress," she continued, quite satisfied that Zeena had taken her advice. She scrutinized Zeena with pleasure.

"Now, how might we help you, child?" she continued, looking back to her stitches.

Zeena cleared her throat and looked at the Count standing behind his wife. He nodded for her to repeat what he had told her. She cleared her throat again and wanted to spit at him.

"The people I was supposed to visit have taken their vacation, and their house is closed for the summer."

"And they left without making arrangements for you?" the Countess asked, almost shocked at the behavior.

"My arrival was to be a surprise," Zeena said quickly countering. "They could not know."

"Oh, I see," she replied.

"I was hoping you might be able to provide me with a place to stay until the celebration is over. It seems that all the rooms in the city are taken. Perhaps I might work for you."

The Count looked down like an expectant bird of prey, smiled, and nodded his head in approval of her quickness.

"What do you think, my dear?" said the Countess turning towards her husband and patting the hand resting on the antimacassar near her head.

"We cannot let the dear child walk the streets," he said benevolently.

"We do not need any more servants," Sophia interrupted, staring at the scene malevolently. "We're already falling over the ones you brought up from the country now."

"Now, Sophia," her mother replied. "If your father feels that it is no bother, then I think we might admire his benevolence and do as he wishes."

Again, Zeena wondered at this woman who admonished with a feather.

"As father wishes," Sophia replied barely moving her lips and she closed her book and sat focusing on some distant point beyond the window.

The Countess looked up again toward her husband and asked him to ring for a servant. Soon the door opened and a girl of about sixteen, in a dark blue dress and white apron, appeared.

"Bring another place setting for tea," the Countess said softly. Sophia rose from her seat.

"Where are you going, Sophia?" asked her father.

"I do not have tea with your servants, father," she replied with restraint.

"We have not decided if she is a servant or a house guest," he replied, stroking his mustache and sensing a battle of wills.

"We both know what she is, father." Each word in the phrase seemed an accusation and Zeena wondered if this daughter and this mother knew of this man's behavior.

The Count looked at her and smiled, pretending not to hear but delighting in the poison.

"Then do not have tea with us, my dear child, but I would consider it the height of impropriety for you to leave. Certainly you were raised with better manners than that, and certainly you were raised not to offend someone to their face."

Sophia's eyes widened at the word. "Offend," she said. "Offend," she repeated. "No," she continued in a controlled voice that might have shook with passion had it belonged to another. "No, we do not wish to offend." She sat down again and opened her book and wished she had the power to destroy them both with her thought.

Maria Russakov looked up and down Sadavya Street even before she reached the entrance to the basement apartment. She knocked twice, and once more. The door creaked open. An eye scrutinized her quickly. The door opened, she entered, and it was quickly closed behind her.

In the middle of the Spartanly furbished room was a table, a lamp hanging above it, and four chairs. Gray light filtered in through horizontal slashes at ground level. Her eyes ran over the men who looked back at her expectantly.

"Where is Hartmann?" Her voice was sharp.

"Where is your mysterious son?" Jeliabov responded sarcastically.

She glared at him. "My son is where he is supposed to be. He does his job, and you will do well to do yours." She stared him down. "Now listen to what is to be done."

She looked at the four men and a sense of dread overwhelmed her. This was the crucial moment when all the months of planning and organizing would come to fruition. Her hatred for the Tsar burned greater than all of their hatred combined, but it was not great enough to risk her son's life for the betterment of the fools assembled before her, or for the cause. She knew that now. She paused and waited for the feeling to subside but it would not. She envisioned him being cut down by a Cossack's saber and dead under the hoofs of a rearing horse.

"Yekovsky, Petrovskaya, and . . .," she paused. She knew she should say Jeliabov, but she did not. They waited. "Yekovsky, Petrovskaya, and Michailoff. You are to go to the bridge on Telsnara and make sure the bombs are not disturbed until they are retrieved. You, Jeliabov and Hartmann are to retrieve the bombs at exactly one thirty. That will give you time to get to the palace gates. There you will take up positions on either side." She stopped and nervously looked at the door.

"Where is Hartmann?" she said again. "He knows we are supposed to meet."

"Perhaps he's in church," said Jeliabov, "or perhaps he's with your son and they're both in church or both safely delivering leaflets to the peasants."

Maria didn't respond. The others looked at each other and laughed nervously to break the tension.

"And what will your son be doing while we are risking our lives?" Jeliabov challenged.

"My son will be doing what he was told to do by the one who tells us all what to do."

"Ah," he said flinging his arms into space. "The mysterious one who tells us all what to do, but whose face and name remain a mystery to all of those who do his bidding. There are too many damn secrets." Secrecy is the key to our success," she shot back. "The fewer the people who can be identified, the safer we all are. When we have done our job successfully, and are safely out of the country, then all will be revealed to you. But, until that time, you will do exactly as you are told or you will . . ." She stopped as the knob on the door turned. They froze.

The obligatory knock was heard. Yekovsky went to the door.

"Who?" he said.

"Hartmann."

Yekovsky looked across the room for silent approval and unlocked the door.

Hartmann looked back up the dim stairwell and entered quickly.

"Where have you been?" Maria said, establishing her displeasure at having to stop and retell the plan.

"I was picking up these pamphlets your son ordered. The contact was late. Where is he?"

"We thought he was in church with you," Jeliabov sneered.

Hartmann looked at Maria, and waited for an answer.

"He will be delivering the word to the provinces. If we are to be successful in the city, we must have support from the people in the provinces. The contacts there must be informed of how to proceed, and quiet those who would rise against us."

"And will he be back in time to stand with us?" said Hartmann.

Jeliabov was glad to have another support his position.

"It was decided that Jeliabov will assist you," she said.

"Jeliabov has never thrown a bomb in his life," Hartmann protested.

"Then he can practice throwing them at you!" she said in a loud, threatening voice.

"I don't appreciate that," he said, waving a finger in her face, "and I don't appreciate that I don't know who is manipulating my life."

"And maybe he who gave me the plan got the plan handed to him. Maybe there are structures in the Fellowship that go beyond this city." She paused and waited for him to relax. "I get my orders, and you get your orders, and I don't know where he gets his orders. I've never had the presumption to ask. I am part of something bigger than I am, and I don't measure what I am asked to do by my own need to control. I am a soldier, and I do. And, if you don't have the heart to do the glorious task given us, I suggest you get out now!"

"And what of the woman whose name we also do not know?" said Hartmann.

"She will be at the gate and you will watch for her handkerchief to signal the bomb. At two o'clock when the coach approaches she will signal you. You, Jeliabov, will throw your bomb first. If it finds its mark, Hartmann will not have to throw his." She turned to Hartmann. "You will count and wait. If the bomb does not explode or does not kill the tyrant, you will throw yours."

"But I've never thrown a bomb in my life," interrupted Jeliabov. "Why must I be the one?"

Maria looked at the fear in his face knowing well that it was her son who had been given the task of hurling the first projectile.

"You would not have been selected if you were not thought of as capable and deserving of the honor," she lied. "Remember, we are writing history. Remember we are changing history. Each of us has a task to perform. Each will do and make any sacrifice needed."

"How will we get out of St. Petersburg?" Petrovskaya interrupted.

She looked around the room. "Kibalschitisch will give out the tickets. You will make your way back to the bridge. He will be there. The train leaves at two forty five, for Germany, and safety."

"Narodnaya Volia!" she said as if to end the meeting quickly.

"The will of the people!" they responded.

Zeena moved in and out of a fitful sleep, and when she opened her eyes again, a tower like figure in a quilted burgundy robe stood framed briefly in the glow of a twinkling corridor gas lamp. The room darkened again and she froze as she felt the presence approach the bed. The bed strained under the additional weight. Zeena tightened her grip on the coverlet. The silver glow of the white night detailed the round face and body of the Count. She could not help but think of how god like Ivan had looked the night before in the same light, and what an obscenity the light revealed only a day later. She felt the blanket being tested against her grip and then torn from her hands with one powerful gesture. She lay there exposed and vulnerable.

"If you scream, my dear child," the Count murmured softly, "no one will hear you, and if anyone did, they would pretend they did not. That is the meaning of discretion among the nobility and among the servants of nobility. Now my dear," he continued as he began opening the top buttons of her night gown, "you have a wonderful body," and she felt his hand encircle her breast.

"Ah, how like my Sophia's," he murmured.

CHAPTER 17

Zeena moved around the opulent prison under the watchful gaze of the servants and the leer of the master. Once she had thought Ezra to be the most odious of human beings, but now she was convinced that this upstanding fraud who pretended to be noble in both birth and nature, was far more loathsome.

Sophia's disdain for Zeena blossomed into a silent rage. The other servants assumed the displeasure of their mistress and treated her with either disinterest, rudeness or cruel laughter. Everyone except the Countess seemed to know why she was there, and Zeena surmised that she had to be just one more in a line of young girls who had suddenly appeared in the home of the Count to assume the duties of a special servant. No one spoke to her or ate with her. It was almost as if they blamed her and hated her for being caught in circumstances created by their employer. Only the Countess smiled a sympathetic smile and looked away, and Zeena had the feeling that the Countess did know and chose to ignore it. These people, thought Zeena, these storybook people, who made the history and literature of the world, by comparison, were not deserving to share the same world as her father or even her mother.

So Zeena waited out the days as instructed and thought only of the Saturday evening when Alexi Malinovitch would be waiting for her in a horse drawn coach. Ivan had not returned and she was thankful of that. She did not want him to know what had happened to her.

Whenever Sophia left the house, Zeena would find her way to Sophia's room on the pretext of cleaning it. Sophia's closet was larger than the bedroom she and her sisters shared and was painted a pale green and decorated with birds in flight. In it there was a full length mirror and a chair. It was bursting with dresses for every occasion. Upon first seeing them, she was astounded by the splendor and workmanship of the garments. Then she became angry that one person should have so much while so many had nothing. She thought of Jonathan and his speeches about the inequities between people, and how just the cost of one of these dresses could probably feed a family for a year. The thought drew him closer to her. She had not thought of Jonathan since the night with Ivan, perhaps because she was ashamed, but when his handsome face materialized before her, she smiled at it.

Which dress would you like to see me in, Jonathan? she mused.

You do not belong here, the vision responded. You must leave this place as quickly as you can. I warned you about this and you did not listen.

You know if I leave, the Count will have me arrested, she said taking a pale beige velvet dress from the hanger and holding it up against her body. Do you like this? she inquired of the vision.

As there are ways of getting into this city without papers, there are ways of getting out, Zeena. You are far too clever a person to believe you could not get away if you made a little effort.

She replaced the garment carefully, and allowed her fingers to caress a line of dresses stitched with delicate applique and embroidery and came to rest on a pale blue ball gown of tulle and lace.

Malinovitch has all my money so you see I can't possibly leave now. You could have walked away from Ivan on the street and none of this would have happened to you. You can walk away now if you really wanted to. What are you really after Zeena? Do you even know?

She took the dress off its holder and held it up. Around the waist was a white satin sash that was pinned by a tuft of white and blue velvet flowers. She turned to the mirror. I like this one, Jonathan. What do you think? How will I look in it?

Will it close?" the vision said. You are beginning to show the child.

How nice of you to notice, she responded. Yes it will close.

The waist is high. It's the French style. And Jonathan, she added. Say our child.

She noted exactly where it was so she could find it quickly. If anyone saw her with it, she would say that she had been instructed to take it to her room to mend it. She would find a way to wear it to the ball.

You are playing a dangerous game, Jonathan said.

I thought you had gone, she responded.

Run, Zeena, run away and desire nothing that is here. These people, these noble people, these people in power, are more than you can handle. There are no rules in the games they play, and there is no moral force in heaven or on earth that they fear. They do as they wish with nothing to check their behavior or desires. You are surrounded by hate and yet you stay. Why do you endanger yourself so, and why do you endanger our child?

Zeena smiled. Because it's exciting Jonathan. I weigh the ugliness and the danger against the excitement, and I still find it better than what I had. I am alive for the first time in my life and this horror will soon end.

And to feel alive you are willing to be enslaved and play the whore, endangering your life and the life of the child?

Stay out of my business, Jonathan. If you loved me, none of this would have happened and now I will find life anywhere I can. Besides, it's just another moment in time and it will pass. It means nothing. Who is to know and who is to care? Another distasteful memory in a sea of distasteful memories and this one is as meaningless as my wedding night with Ezra. But you know all of my memories, Jonathan. You know them all.

The vision faded. Everything softens in time, she thought. Now, she would focus on the ball and the music and the dancing.

Her eyes scanned the rows of satin slippers and she hastily tried on a pair of blue shoes that matched the gown exactly. How nice to know that Sophia's feet were slightly larger than her own. Now she had only to wait.

May 18, 1882

Count Perowski and his family left to celebrate the birthday of the Tsar. All the servants, except for the porter and Zeena, were given the night off to celebrate. The porter started his own celebration as soon as the Count's carriage left the street, inviting a bottle of vodka and a street walker to his room in the basement. Zeena hesitated slightly as her blue satin slipper touched the step of the coach. The footman nodded deferentially and held out his gloved hand to help her alight.

The building before her, in the opalescent twilight, shimmered like a baroque pearl amid the torches and gas lamps. So this, she thought, was more of the opulence and grandeur that Jonathan reviled in his speeches. So these baskets of stone fruits and flowers overflowing onto an endless row of elegant columns, were built with the taxes that kept her people and the peasants of Krivoser in a constant state of destitution.

She was awed by the magnificence. She looked at the hand of the footman and laughed as if she had attended birthday balls in honor of the Tsar as a regular yearly event. Then she raised the lace overlay of her skirt and extended her foot to the pavement. Malinovitch followed like an ardent attendant, took her hand and placed it on his arm. She looked up as the coach pulled away. Statues of white stone with gold overlay heralded her entry. A breeze from the Neva caressed her as she and Malinovitch walked slowly up the marble steps to the arched entrance where an elderly man in a red coat with gold trim, silently looked at the invitation and announced Colonel Alexi Malinovitch and Miss Zeena Bendelevitch. Smiling at her new identity, Zeena returned an imperial smile to him and he nodded them into the foyer.

Zeena stepped into the dazzling world of the picture books. She could not stop herself from opening her mouth. Alexi looked at her and smiled beneficently at her delight. He watched her eyes move up the polished white marble walls to the vaulted, arched, corbeled ceiling resting on capitals supported by sleek, Corinthian columns. He watched her eyes drink in the larger than life statues of saints and heroes of ancient times astride each capital. He saw her focus on the two-tiered massive chandeliers ablaze with a thousand candles under a canopy of gold laurel leaves.

He nudged her slightly and she blinked herself back to his side and looked at him warmly. She thought of the moment she had placed the gold coins on her eyes and she danced away into a dream in the arms of a dashing officer. Now the dream was real and she could hear the sweep of wonderful music that glided down the staircase and swirled around her. The dream was real because she chose to make it real.

Her escort extended his arm, his lips smiling broadly under a mustache flecked with gray. He was a young man again and he was giving his new bride St. Petersburg as a wedding gift. He loved her with the passion that blazed out of a desperate youth. Now he would play at being the lover or if needs be, play at being the fool. But he would savor this new feeling, a feeling he called, happiness.

He led her to a carved staircase. Polished to perfection, the wide banisters, supported by a hundred small columns in the form of eucalyptus leaves, curved upward to the second story. He watched her hand glide and caress the smooth surface until it was abruptly stopped by a huge urn. He laughed at his love's astonishment, and her eyes passed onto a gigantic pair of onyx columns with golden capitals. A pale purple and blue glow that had been kissed by torch light, eased quietly through the arched windows above, shrouding in a faint haze the gods and demigods straining their muscular frames to support the carved ceiling. Strains of a music she had never heard before welcomed her to the huge mirrored hall, and she stood before a swirling mass of color sweeping by her as autumn leaves caught in a whirlwind. She could feel her own body respond to the incessant one, two, three, one, two, three of the music and wanted to glide out onto the floor and be swept away in the violins and flutes. But she had never heard the music in her fantasy and she did not know how to move.

"It is a waltz," he said. "It was born in Vienna and is fashionable enough so everyone does it. Come, I will show you."

Zeena felt his strong arms guiding her and before she could protest that she could not do this, she found herself being turned and swayed in a great circle. Her feet moved rapidly, each trying not to trip over the other. She began to laugh. "But I don't know how to do this dance," she said in mock protest.

"That is why women wear long dresses so no one will see how their feet move. The men are the ones who must know the steps perfectly. I suspect most of these women have wheels on their shoes and are being rolled around in time to the music."

She laughed at the wonderful thought. "But I do not . . ." and he broke her words off.

"You are doing just fine. Just count one, two, three, and I'll do the rest."

She clung to him for fear that she would fall and she kept her eyes riveted on his face so her head would not swim. She felt her body relax and flow as she became accustomed to the repetitive step. He sensed her ease and smiled.

"See," he laughed. "I have taught you how to swim by throwing you into the deep water. That was how I was taught in the army. You had two choices. You could have tripped and fallen, or you could have learned how to waltz. You concentrated, and learned, and now you are as good as any of these ladies."

Zeena threw her head back and allowed her body to float into a current that moved in three quarter time. The man who held her was an enigma. He was older than her father, but his spirit was as young as Ivan's. He was feared for the power he had and for the position he held and yet, he could laugh and dance and gently move a young woman around a ballroom with great ease and grace. He had the audacity to bring an alien to a palace ball in honor of the Tsar, and had even suggested that she borrow the dress from a Count's daughter. He filled her with awe and delight and she felt safe in his arms.

They danced on and she caught a glimpse of their reflections in a huge mirror that hung above one of the great fireplaces. They were magnificent together and she turned and twisted in time to the music just to see, so she could remember. And then the music ended and her skirts continued to swirl as if they wished to dance on and on.

There was a sudden eruption of polite laughter and gloved applause, and Zeena found herself naturally doing the same.

They stood before the fireplace and Zeena looked up to the gilt mirror above her. Around her, like bees on a flower, the chattering ladies hummed their delight, but Zeena paid no attention. Her eyes were on the mirror and the girl in the blue lace dress who looked down at her from a magic glittering world. She noticed Malinovitch next to her and the recognition of an older gentlemen who surveyed her carefully and winked his approval. Zeena laughed to herself and leaned over to inquire as to who he was, but the music interrupted her thought and she was again swept away like a blue feather in a breeze. She pretended to feel the eyes of young officers on her, and the jealousy of the pale, thin creatures near them who sipped their punch.

The music swelled and was finally over. She felt flushed and she waved her gloved hand for cooler air.

"I forgot your condition," Malinovitch said. "I should not have imposed myself on you like that. You should rest."

Zeena smiled at him for his thoughtfulness, but insisted that she was only slightly light headed.

"Then you shall sit right here," and he led her to one of the many large, high back, brocaded chairs and insisted she sit. "I shall bring you some punch," he said and turned, making his way through the chattering crowd.

Zeena sat and was relieved for the opportunity, for though she reveled in the dance and the fantasy, she felt tired. The physical and emotional strain of her flight and the events that ensued had stressed her beyond what even she felt acceptable. But now, here, all seemed well. The promised tickets and official letters would be available tomorrow. Then she would be free and whatever ugliness would fade in the glitter of the memories she would choose to keep. This memory she would keep.

The music began again, and the ladies and their handsome escorts swept into the circle and wound themselves up like a clock. She felt royal sitting there on her throne, watching the light and color glide past her and she was amused at how comfortable she felt. Here was Zeena Chernov, sitting in a grand ballroom, wearing a dress borrowed from a Countess' daughter. There was nothing she would not achieve at that moment. And, she would have continued her reverie had a familiar voice not interrupted.

"Zeena, my dear, I admire your brazen approach to life." Count Perowski looked down on her. "If you were a man, I'm sure you would be very successful in business, but such behavior in a woman detracts from her femininity."

Zeena flushed with fear.

"I see you are wearing one of my daughter's gowns. You have exquisite taste," and he ran his eyes over the line where the lace ended and her breasts began. "I think before Sophia sees you, yes, she is here also, you'd better leave and return it." He waited for her to move, but she sat there, too afraid to act.

"I, for one," he continued in a slow steady monotone, "am outraged that you would steal the garment and insult these people by pretending to be what you are not. But your kind is known for such brashness and affront." He took a sip from his glass of wine and calmly surveyed the room. "Your brashness makes you even more exciting and I shall consider a punishment that will match the excitement you generate." He nodded to a passer-by who deferentially nodded to him. "You are the most interesting toy I have ever had." He smiled at another guest. "You do agree that your punishment should be suitable to the offense? Do you not, my dear child?" He waited.

Zeena sat there barely allowing her breath to escape. Her concern was that Alexi would return and there would be a confrontation. She was so close to her goal now that she could not risk their meeting.

"I'm sure you can find your way home," and he extended his hand to her as any gentleman might do. Zeena sat with her hands folded on her lap for a few seconds and slowly raised her own. She looked up at him.

"I hate you," she smiled.

Count Perowski smiled back, bent his head and kissed her hand. "Of course you do, my dear child. It is important that you do and I would be disappointed if you did not."

For a split second, Ezra, and what he said to her on their wedding night, flashed into her mind. She did not understand them. Why did men such as this one and Ezra exist? The music began again and a young officer approached but turned when she accepted the Count's hand and stood.

"You will leave now, but we will talk about this tomorrow evening, I promise. And you will tell me how you maneuvered yourself into a palace."

Zeena looked at him. By tomorrow evening she would be on her way to Hamburg and then to Paris.

To the casual observer, their silent reflections mirrored back the sight of a pretty girl whose hand had just been kissed by a distinguished elderly gentleman, perhaps her father or a family friend.

Sophia watched the silent scene reflected in the mirror above them, and wished that she could send the hatred out of her body and engulf them both in a conflagration that would not even leave a memory of their existence. How dare he invite his latest whore to the ball, she thought, and how dare he permit this whore to wear one of her own dresses? She shook with rage, and moved quickly to the French doors and onto the balcony. She could not scream into the night, so she screamed within until she had no more scream and no more pity.

The Count looked around the room briefly and moved along the edge of the dancers. Zeena stood as if ossified. Her head swam and ached and she felt the lids of her eyes quiver. She watched him disappear beneath an arched opening.

"I'm sorry to have taken so long, but I met an old acquaintance who kept me." His voice trailed off as she turned to him and he saw how the color had gone from her face.

"Zeena, what has happened?" His concern poured out.

"The Count saw me here and ordered me to leave."

Malinovitch stiffened. In his haste to please himself and ease her stress, he had endangered her further. He had not thought the Count would even consider attending this ball. And if the Count was here, perhaps Sophia was here also.

He quickly scanned the room.

"Perhaps then, to avoid the problem, it would be better to leave." He looked around again and ushered her out, surveying the room as they left. If Sophia saw him with Zeena, he could be destroyed with one spiteful word. With Sophia, all was the intensity of the moment. Her serene exterior belied a seething and passionate spirit that fed on hate. In which direction her hatred was hurled, and for what reason, was a matter of conjecture. It could just as easily be hurled at him and the movement.

He moved down the steps rapidly, abhorring the feelings that surged through his body. They were ancient and fearsome, conjuring up those moments when he lived and moved only among hostile forces he did not control.

They moved out of the palace into a pale purple light that had lost its magical quality. They rode in the coach without speaking until Zeena broke the silence.

"I am afraid to go there. Let me go with you."

Malinovitch thought only of the task set for the following day at two o'clock. If the Count chose to remark to Sophia about the dress and the ball, there was no telling how she would react. Zeena had gone this far and had to continue. He felt for her, but could not risk the assassination attempt on his affection for her. He was a fool to have created this moment. In his effort to involve himself in a dream, he might have jeopardized everything. He was not sure that he had not been seen. He was not sure if Sophia was there. He was not sure if anyone in the same scenario had made any connection between him and Zeena.

"You must return, but tomorrow you will be free. The Count and his daughter must suspect nothing." He was adamant, and his mandate to obey frightened her into silence.

"You will lock the door to your room tonight. They will return early in the morning and he will be too tired to bother you. He will sleep and go about his business tomorrow and by the time he returns, you will be gone."

Zeena nodded, but her fear would not be stilled. Malinovitch placed his hand on hers in a gesture of comfort, but she could not be comforted.

"A message will come to you tomorrow, and all will be well."

CHAPTER 18

"Who is at the door?" Sophia asked as the housekeeper passed her. "There is a messenger here for that new girl," she said, full of an indignation that mirrored the look in her mistress's eyes.

Sophia was curious as to what message one like Zeena would receive and from whom.

"I will take care of this," Sophia said in a steady, methodical tone and the housekeeper nodded slowly as if they were of one mind.

Sophia opened the door and the young man looked sheepishly into the disdainful eyes of the aristocrat, and stammered, "Are you Zeena Bendelevitch?"

"I am," she said, riveting her eyes on him. "What do you want?"

He held out a sealed envelope and, bowing nervously, backed down the steps. Sophia returned quickly to the sitting room, opened the envelope, and read:

"Meet me in front of Dvor at two thirty."

She turned the page over but finding no signature, tore it in half, imagining some lewd rendezvous with another married man of means. Perhaps this man also had a daughter? Anger burned on her cheek at the thought of another daughter seeing her father's infidelity and forced to remain silent. To Sophia, all women who replaced mothers and daughters in their father's hearts were whores and should be destroyed. And the fathers who replaced their daughters with whores should also be destroyed.

She sat at the writing desk and wrote: "Be at the basement apartment of 12 Sadovaya at two o'clock. Wait."

Her malice had given birth to her response. She would have

her vengeance with one confession. She folded the note carefully and sealed it in a plain envelope.

Sophia rang for the housekeeper and moved to the door. "Give this to Zeena," she said, "and do not question her movements."

Alexi Malinovitch nodded thanks to the ticket agent and placed two tickets to Paris via Hamburg in his pocket. He felt for the gold coins Zeena had given him. Already, the money Zeena had given him and his own considerable fortune had been secreted out of the country and waited for them. Now at one forty five, he joined the throngs of festive Sunday strollers to catch a glimpse of the Tsar and his carriage. He walked along the Nevsky Prospekt and smiled broadly as he passed Gostiny Dvor. He was as a bridegroom. I shall raise the child as my own, he thought, and perhaps we will have one of our own together. I shall live life as I might have lived it. It was almost two o'clock.

An hour before Malinovitch looked into his future before the Dvor, and not too far from where he stood, Maria Russakov faced her son.

"We all take orders, Ivan, and we act even if we do not like them." She looked into his impassioned and disappointed eyes. "You have been ordered to take the tickets to the bridge at one forty five, give them to Kibaschitisch and then you are to go to the train station, watch them leave, and return to your employer's home. Take this money and do not argue with me! It must be done this way!"

Sophia dressed in what would allow her to easily blend in with the throngs, and let herself out of the servant's entrance. She looked up and down the street, opened her purse to check for the red handkerchief, and thought of the moment when the tyrant would be dead and when her father would be brought down before all the world.

Then she silently rehearsed what she had not been ordered to do. "Death to the tyrants. Narodnaya Volia," she would scream. She saw herself captured, confessing, and directing them to the basement apartment where Zeena waited. She would insist that Zeena was a key figure in the plot to kill the Tsar and she would refuse to speak to or allow her father to help her. He would bear his shame until it destroyed him.

Zeena told the housekeeper that she was going to church and then to the parade. She left the house breathing a sigh of relief, and never looked back. She wore her new yellow dress and her entire demeanor spoke of new expectations and beginnings.

She felt herself glisten and smiled brightly as gentlemen put their hands to their hats in greeting. The throngs of holiday strollers converged on the Prospect and moved towards the water and Palace Square. The Tsar's cortege had already passed, and Zeena was genuinely disappointed that she had not caught a glimpse of him. She moved along, noting the time as one fifteen on the clock. She had a few moments to spare before her rendezvous with Malinovitch. She quickened her pace even though she longed to stand before the beautifully appointed windows. People chattered around her and she smiled at them and hummed as she moved in the direction of Sadovaya.

The Tsar sat in the gilt carriage, waving and smiling at the crowds of well wishers lining the boulevard. The Grand Duke Michael, and Colonel Dorjibky sat facing him. The Colonel smiled approvingly at the Grand Duke, reached over and picked a flower petal off the Tsar's trousers.

"It is a beautiful day for a celebration, your majesty," he re-
marked and watched the Tsar's face for agreement.

"I am weary of this," the Tsar said through a smile, "and I
would like all of these people to disappear."

"We will be at the palace in a few minutes and you can rest,"
replied the Grand Duke.

The Cossack honor guard trailed in perfect unison on their
coal black horses, past the Kazan Cathedral, and raised their drawn
sabers into the air in salute. The massive bronze bells pealed out
their resonant greeting and crowds lining the Prospekt applauded
them and threw flowers in their path.

Jeliabov and Hartmann eyed each other and hugged the brick
wall of the palace near the central gates. They nodded slightly
when they spotted the woman who held a red handkerchief to her
nose. She stood near one of the city police stationed there to keep
order and control the crowd.

The cheers seemed to move like a rolling wave toward the
conspirators and they knew the Tsar's carriage was approaching.
Each inched cautiously towards the palace gates like crabs eyeing a
delicate morsel. The cheering voices heralded the approaching coach.
To his left, high above the crowd, Hartmann could see the bob-
bing hats of the Cossack guards. Jeliabov choked as his stomach
rose into his throat, and reached into his satchel for the nitroglycerin bomb.

The two faced each other across the space between the gate as
directed, and read each other's fears. The iron gate with the great,
golden double eagles, creaked opened like massive jaws. The crowd
behind Jeliabov suddenly surged, and he almost lost his balance.
The first honor guard trotted past him, and his heart pounded as
if it, too, would explode out of his chest. The coach rolled past and
Sophia waved the handkerchief as signal. He hurled the bomb at
the Tsar's coach and cursed the man's soul to hell. The explosion
rocked him back, but did not throw him to the ground. Shrieks of
terror tore the air on all sides and the crowd shrunk back from him
in confused horror. He stood there, separate, and recognized that

the bomb had fallen short and had done damage only to the coach. He froze, and two Cossacks turned their horses and were upon him. The Tsar alighted unhurt, and when he was seen, a cheer of relief and gratitude rose from the throng.

At that moment, Hartmann, hurled his own bomb at the Emperor's feet, and it exploded on impact, shattering the monarch's legs below the knee. Alexander II clutched at his thighs, his face contorted. His white, silk trousers burst crimson, and he sank in a pool of his own blood, screaming in agony. Jeliabov bolted through the rearing horses into the crowd, but was captured. The force of the explosion pinned Hartmann to the wall, and a Cossack officer leaped upon him with his sword. Three other Cossacks lay dead in front of the gate with their horses torn and thrashing wildly on top of them.

In the mayhem, Sophia Perowski ran into the street screaming, "Death to the Tyrants! The Will of the People lives!"

Amid the pealing bells, Zeena could not hear another tone clang the hour. She knocked on the basement door, but there was no answer. She stood and fidgeted and knocked again. More time passed. She thought she had heard someone move inside, but no one answered. She paced back and forth wondering why Alexi Malinovitch was not there. She sat on a small stool and waited. After a time, she became aware that the bells had stopped. She clearly heard the half hour peal, and then the bells began again, but different from before.

She heard someone on the landing above, brightened with anticipation, and stood.

"Do not move if you want to live!" commanded the voice, and four guns were aimed at her head. The police officer stood on the stairs as his men raced down and surrounded her. One tore her purse from her hands.

"You are Zeena Bendelevitch?" the voice demanded flatly.

Zeena backed away, but was pushed forward by a rifle butt to the small of her back. She nodded.

The man who had taken the purse skimmed the papers and handed the letter of transit from the Count and the note to the officer in charge.

"Yes, this is the link," he nodded.

"But, I have done nothing," she screamed. "What do you want of me?"

"You are a murderer and a traitor and the bitch who worked with you has already confessed her crime and directed us to you. These two pieces of evidence will hang you."

"But I don't know what you are talking about," she protested. "What two pieces of evidence? What murder?"

"Silence, you damn liar!" and he smacked her across the mouth.

She froze, wondering what was to follow. She thought not to speak again for fear of incriminating herself or Malinovitch. What did they know? What was there to know, and how might a foolish word uttered in fear jeopardize her life? Yet, she knew that if she did not declare her innocence to what ever she was accused of having done, her silence might be construed as a confession of guilt.

"You've made a terrible error!" she cried. "I know of no murders. I am not a traitor!"

One pulled her arms brutally behind her back and manacled them tightly.

"Please, what do you want of me? I have not murdered anyone. I did not know I had to have papers. I did not know Jews were not permitted in St. Petersburg. Let me go," she said desperately. "I will never come back. I swear to you I will leave and never come back." The officer looked down at the frightened, sobbing girl dispassionately.

"I do not know what papers you're talking about."

"Our Emperor was assassinated less than an hour ago, and the woman who confessed said we would find her accomplice waiting here."

As he spoke, he motioned for the door to the apartment to be broken down. Two men turned and kicked it in, their guns poised for battle, but they found the room empty.

The others pushed up to the steps and motioned her up with their guns at her back, and then her buttocks. People in the street had gathered around the black van that waited. Zeena was pushed down the dark corridor to the street.

"But, I didn't do anything," she sobbed. "I didn't do anything."

Alexi Malinovitch stood under the clock and watched the hands press on to three o'clock. The drone of the bells rang fear into the streets, as they pealed out their death tale to all the city. He paced off the blocks under his feet again and again, and when the clock struck three, he moved down the street in the direction of his home. He did not understand. Perhaps she waited for him there. Perhaps he had miscalculated and the Count would not let her leave. His pace quickened. She had to be somewhere. Around him people gathered in small groups to share the tragedy. Panic and anger swept up and down the Nevsky Prospekt as he moved. Silent rage and terror engulfed him on all sides.

Maria stood at the window anxiously awaiting his return. Already a message had come from the fortress for him to go to the office at once.

The manacles etched into her flesh with each movement of her hands. The police prodded and kicked her and pushed her along the dimly lit stone corridor with the butts of their rifles, and when she fell, she was pulled up by her hair. A small dry trickle of blood clung to the corner of her mouth and the bruise near her eye began to turn a deep purple. Her hair was matted with dirt from where she had fallen in the yard, and wet with sweat. The corridor was cold and damp from the sea, and the wind that moved down the passageway chiseled itself through the thin shawl she had around her shoulders.

She was being pushed into a dark, subterranean place, and no one knew where she was. She and Jonathan's child could disappear without a trace, and none would know.

The heavy boots thudded against the floor. She moved along with their heavy cadence and her heart beat as loudly. She glanced furtively from side to side. Heavy brown wooden doors, with small barred openings, lined the passageway like upright coffins. She began to feel faint, but struggled against collapsing. She was suddenly a non person without friends or family. Zeena Chernov, Zeena Bendak, Zeena Bendelevitch, Zeena Nothing. She, who had envisioned herself as clever and in control, was suddenly nonexistent. Why had Malinovitch directed her to that basement? What could possibly have happened? But what if he did not care? What if he only wanted her money? She dismissed the thought. It was impossible. He would find her and explain. He would free her. It would be as another bad dream.

A rat ran across her path and she screamed and bolted in terror. One guard quickly stepped in front of her and pushed her against the stone wall with his rifle. She was too terrified to speak, but not too terrified to groan from the pain of the gun against her breast. She opened her eyes to see a black bearded mouth with yellow teeth snarling a warning at her.

"Murderous Jew bitch," he sneered. "There is nothing I'd like better than to put bullets through your eyes for what you did to my Tsar." He pushed her further into the stone wall and pressed his groin against hers. "Soon you'll know what pain is," he whispered into her ear.

She froze. This man, or any man who wished, could destroy her and the baby with a word or a bullet. She went limp against his body, and he eased the rifle constraining her.

The other guard moved further down the passageway and she heard the rattle of a key in a door and the sliding of heavy bolts. The guard pulled back and she fell forward against the wall. The jagged stone tore at her skin and she forced herself into an upright position.

"Move or you'll feel this rifle against your traitorous head!"

Zeena swayed and moved forward into the darkening tunnel. Air, even more putrid and hot than before, touched her nostrils and choked her. In the vague shadows she could make out an even darker opening that shaped her cell. The guard shoved her towards it.

"I can't go in there!" she screamed in terror. "I can't stay in the dark. Please, for the love of God, don't put me in here alone!"

"Don't call on your Jew God to me or I'll smash your face in!"

"Please, please," she begged. "I am afraid and I am sick. I am sick. Please! Please!"

"I'll give you this rifle up your murderous ass," and he pushed her with all his might into the black space and slammed the door. She staggered and fell onto the damp stone floor and the door bolts fell into place with a thud. The little iron door at eye level slid open and the dim light through it was interrupted by blackness, and a voice.

"Please," Zeena begged again. "Don't go. Don't leave me. I'll do anything. I'll give you anything. Please." She crawled to the voice. "I beg you, if you have any pity in you. Please! I cannot stay in the dark!"

The blackness moved away and the faint light reappeared briefly only to be cut off by the changing shut of the little iron door.

Zeena sat enveloped in a sightless, soundless terror and overwhelmed with the true blackness of the cell. When she was little and the darkness made her afraid, she would crawl into Jonah's bed and they would hold each other and pretend it was like before they were born. She was safe in his arms and there, in the fantasy, they created the circle. Now, again, she was a frightened child as she had always been, only no one was there to ease her fear. She pulled herself up the wooden door and felt along the wet, slime covered walls till she found a corner. She turned and faced a blackness where it did not matter if her eyes were open or closed. She slid down to the stone floor and pushed herself into it as if it were a womb. Something scurried near her leg.

"Jonaaah!," she screamed into the silence. "Jonaaah!"

When Malinovitch saw her the next morning, his soul lunged to her aid, but he sat there dispassionate and implacable. On his right sat his clerk, Misha Traranskovich, a small boney man with boney fingers, who was writing before Zeena entered, and continued writing without ever looking at her. To his left sat Nicolai Karpov, an honored officer of the secret police, and second in command to Alexi Malinovitch. His squat frame was motionless as his eyes devoured her.

Zeena was pushed forward by two armed guards and tripped over the torn hem of her dress. She fell to the floor sobbing. She had not slept for fear of the rats, and her body ached from the brutal strip search to which she had been subjected by her first interrogators. The cold tile on the bruise on the side of her face was a comfort and she pressed her cheek into it for relief.

Malinovitch bit down on his teeth and waved the guard to pick her up and put her on the chair before his desk. A round, burly man in a white coat, a Dr. Melkinkov limped into the room and over to the desk. He nodded in deference to Malinovitch and Karpov, and began to whisper. Malinovitch sat, his face showing no response to the news, but Karpov moved in closer and gesticulated with his fist towards the seated woman. They listened for a time. The fat man took out his handkerchief several times during the secret talks and wiped his forehead. At one point, Malinovitch signaled that he had heard enough. The clerk looked up but continued to scratch on the paper. The fat man backed off and withdrew through a side door. Karpov riveted his eyes on the soiled creature whose head was being held up by the nozzle of a rifle.

Zeena opened her eyes slowly and allowed the dim light to gather itself onto the shadowy figures seated at the table. Her eyes widened to assure herself, and she leaned slightly forward in disbelief. He had not abandoned her!

Malinovitch recognized the danger of the moment and covered his lips with his pointing finger as her father did to inform her to be silent. He rubbed it up and down pretending a gesture of thought in case the others noticed it, but Zeena understood. Her thoughts raced over the brutality of the interrogation, and the agony of the body search. Why had he allowed it if he knew she was there?

"You are accused, Zeena Bendelevitch, of complicity in the murder of Tsar Alexander the Second," read Karpov. You were found at the conspirator's headquarters, and the letters in your possession link you with Sophia Perowski who was captured at the moment of assassination."

Karpov's dark eyes bulged behind his wire rimmed glasses and he walked toward her waving the charges in front of her.

"All this cries out against you, and yet you will not confess your treachery. You are to sign these now and confess to the world not only your treachery, but the treachery of your people."

"There is nothing to confess," she moaned in a broken voice. "I have done nothing."

"Perhaps there would be more incentive to respond if you had your man take the manacles from her wrists," suggested Malinovitch.

Karpov motioned to the guard. One pushed Zeena with his rifle butt to stand, and Malinovitch marked him with a poisonous stare. Zeena rose slowly and painfully. The other guard took her hands and unlocked the iron bracelets. Malinovitch, his face never changing, took hold of his desk to keep him from running to her and cradling her in his arms.

"There," Karpov blurted, thrusting a pen into her hand and dragging her to the table. "Now sign!"

"How can I confess to something I know nothing about?" she screamed.

"Damn you, you Jew bitch!" Karpov yelled. "We know you planned it from the beginning, and we know you were put up to this by the heinous murdering crew who gave you birth. You are a traitor from among a race of traitors bent on destroying Russia!"

"What are you saying?" she cried again. "I am no traitor and no conspirator. I don't even know traitors or conspirators. I cannot confess to something I know nothing about."

"We know about the child you carry." he spit out through his teeth. "If you don't sign this, you will die and the child you carry will die with you!"

The words crashed against her ears and Zeena covered her stomach with her hands to protect the life within her. She looked to Malinovitch for help. He remained as stone.

Karpov thrust the pen into her hand and forced it onto the paper. Again she searched the face for guidance. She could sign it, and she and Jonathan's child would live. If she did not sign it, she and the child would die. What did her people have to do with this? For a brief second she thought of the old rabbi's sermon at Purim and Queen Esther before the king's threshold.

"Perhaps she cannot sign her name," said Malinovitch calmly.

Zeena looked at him again, and this time he shook his head indicating that she was not to sign the confession. She paused and the pen fell to the floor.

Karpov moved his arms as if crazed. Malinovitch called him over, and whispered to him. He appeared to protest, but Malinovitch stood at his place behind the table, and Karpov backed off, motioning the guards on either side of Zeena to follow. The clerk took the papers from Zeena's lap, placed them on the table, and also left. For the sake of the others, Malinovitch picked them up and also waved them menacingly at her, but spoke only when the room was clear.

"I have little time," he said so softly she could hardly hear him. "Sophia Perowski implicated you as a conspirator."

"But why?"

"I do not know, but I will find out. Karpov has convinced the Count that Sophia's life can be saved if he swears that you had set up the chance meeting on the train to gain entry to his house and corrupt his daughter. He will do this. This young man you met is the only witness for you, and will be in grave danger if and when he steps forward. Do you know where he is or his name?"

"Ivan Russakov," Zeena whispered.

Malinovitch's eyes widened and Zeena began to cry.

"I am so afraid. Why are you allowing this to happen to me? I am innocent."

"I know you are, Zeena, but you have been caught up in history. It will be a national scandal that the daughter of a Count would involve herself in the assassination of the Tsar, and they must shift the focus away from her. Your unfortunate placement at the apartment provides them with an opportunity, not only to focus on another, but to implicate the Jews of Russia in the murder. That is more important to the government than anything else."

"Why did you ask me to meet you at the apartment?"

"I didn't. I asked you to meet me at Dvor."

"Then how, and why?"

"I don't know, but I will find out." He thought of Sophia and knew that it was she who had to be the catalyst in the drama.

"You must not sign the confession no matter how hard Karpov presses you," he said quickly. "To do so will give the government official sanction to wage war on your people."

"But what of me?" Zeena pleaded. "Am I and my child to die?"

Malinovitch was silent.

"As long as there is life in me, I will not let them kill you. Your pregnancy is known only to the doctor, my clerk, Karpov and me. Secrecy gives Karpov the upper hand, but he will not have it for long. I can make no overt moves to save you now, and you must not look to me. I am your chief interrogator and you must fear me more than anyone else." He heard the door rattle.

"When I push these papers into your face, bite my hand and curse me!"

"But . . ."

"Do as I say, now!" Malinovitch pushed the papers into Zeena's face, and her teeth found their mark. Malinovitch yelled, and the guards, the clerk, and Karpov came running. The papers floated to the floor and Malinovitch rubbed the marks made by her teeth.

"Die, you bastard!" she screamed, and Malinovitch's hand came down across her face.

"Throw the bitch back into her cell," he bellowed, twisting his handkerchief over his hand to cover the faint marks. "I'll attend to her later."

The guards dragged her out. Karpov waved the clerk out of the room and turned to Malinovitch.

"You know as well as I," he said venomously, "that if she does not confess and implicate her accursed race, the daughter of a Russian Count and a noble family will be the focus of the world. How will the world and the Russian people perceive that?"

"I was under the impression that our task was to bring the nihilists to justice. When did our task become that of implicating the Jews of Russia to save the good name of a Count?" Malinovitch busied himself with the confession to control his anger.

"The nobility is Russia, and the Jews are not innocent. This girl is the link we need to rid ourselves of them once and for all time. Through her confession, they will all be damned and destroyed."

"You're starting to believe our own propaganda," Malinovitch said looking up at him. "I believe she is telling the truth."

"Truth has nothing to do with this," Karpov bellowed, forgetting to whom he spoke. "The image of Imperial Russia will be soiled before all the world if it is proven that Sophia Perowski is the chief criminal."

"Either way, the Count's daughter is guilty," Malinovitch replied. "She was there, she screamed her joy at the moment of the explosion, she directed the police to the apartment, and she confessed. On top of that, there are dozens of witnesses. Will you kill innocent witnesses, good Russians? Dozens of them? Will all of them agree to your little plot and remain silent?"

Karpov's eyes questioned his superior's loyalty, and when Malinovitch looked up again, Karpov quickly averted his glance.

"The evidence against this Bendelevitch woman is circumstantial. The letter of transit she carried was written by the Count and will no doubt be confirmed by this young man when he is found. I have no doubt the Count had ulterior motives for giving her the letter. You and I both know the Count's penchant for pretty young girls. The worst she is guilty of is being an unauthorized Jew in the city."

"Then why was she at the conspirator's meeting place?"

Malinovitch paused. "In this you are correct, Karpov. We do not know why she was there and I think we might make the effort to find out. But, I think the focus in this matter must be with Sophia Perowski since she is the only one we have interrogated who seems to know this Zeena Bendelevitch. Does that not seem strange to you?"

The blood vessels in Karpov's cheeks strained. This was disloyalty enough to pour into the ear of the nobility, bring Malinovitch down, and raise himself up.

"You are a very valuable and loyal servant of Russia, Karpov, but you have forgotten or perhaps never understood, that the truth has a strange way of finding the light, and to blame this young woman for masterminding or even representing the nihilists, will perhaps gain Russia and you some time, but eventually will be found to be a lie. Russia and those who were involved in creating the lie will be branded for eternity. Study history, Karpov. Our lives are transitory, but history goes on forever. Our place in history is our immortality. You and I have twisted the truth and perverted justice in our time, but it was on a very small scale, and no one took notice. Today, you and I have been thrust suddenly onto the pages of the history books. How shall posterity find us, Karpov? As tellers of lies, or seekers of the truth?"

"Then let her die before the truth be known to the world. Let her die with the truth. The world will believe anything we tell it, and we will tell it what it wants to hear. When there are none to counter the charge, who is to stop us from writing history as we need it to be?"

"And would you destroy the child along with the mother?"

Malinovitch was struck by his own words. They were strange, yet familiar, and something out of another time and another life.

Karpov looked at him directly. "I would destroy them all with my own hands if Our Blessed Lord would give me the power."

"And you think Our Blessed Lord wants you to murder a young, unmarried woman and her unborn child to protect the image of Russia? In you we have, it seems, a new Herod. Please, Karpov, do not sully Our Lord by rationalizing that by killing an innocent girl and her unborn child you are doing His work. If the girl is to die by your hand at least accept the responsibility for the murderous act yourself."

"Why is this one special?" Karpov bellowed. "You've not stood in my way before when the good of Russia was at stake. Why is this Jew special?"

Malinovitch's back stiffened. He had to be very careful. "She is not special. I told you why I am responding to you this way. We are dealing here with history, not with the little lives of little people. I believe she is innocent and, in the face of history, I will not dip my fingers in her blood and be branded. I have interrogated enough people in my life to tell the innocent from the guilty, and there is nothing to accuse her except circumstantial evidence."

"But if there was hard evidence and someone to accuse her, would you agree to do away with her?"

"If there was a reliable witness and hard evidence to accuse her, then she would stand trial with the others and, if found guilty, the court would sentence her to hang along with the other conspirators."

"You cannot permit Sophia Perowski to stand trial before the world. She is of noble birth."

"There is nothing to be done," Malinovitch finally raged. "She was caught and confessed! He formulated his next step as he glared at the squat figure before him. He would send Maria with a message to an American reporter covering Russian events. The unsigned note would inform the correspondent that an unmarried, pregnant Jewish girl was being secretly held in the Peter and Paul fortress and that she was being falsely accused as a conspirator for the purpose of implicating her people.

"We'll see what comes our way in this," he said to Karpov. "We'll see what comes our way."

Again, as with Zeena, Malinovitch ached to assist her, but again, he was compelled by his office, to sit impassively. Karpov rose and made a slight obeisance when Sophia entered the room escorted by her guards.

Other than a bruise to her cheek, caused by a guard prior to them knowing who she was, her imperious beauty remained untouched.

"You have implicated yourself most willingly in the gravest of matters," Karpov began, "and you continue to hold your confession as if you are actually acting of your own will."

Sophia studied him with mild amusement, and looked at Alexi with a question that inquired as to who this funny little man was.

He read the question, but raised his finger to his mouth for her to remain silent. She returned her eyes to the squat man who moved cautiously closer.

"What would you say if we told you that the Jew we caught at the apartment has confessed to being the force behind the assassination? And, has further confessed to having entered your father's employ to mesmerize you and involve a noble family in an event that would bring them down?"

Sophia threw back her head. "I would say that you were a fool to believe her."

Malinovitch swallowed a laugh and applauded her with his eyes.

"I am talking about Zeena Bendelevitch who has confessed to masterminding the assassination. We sincerely hope that her confession will go some distance to free you and the good name of your family from disgrace."

Sophia stood abruptly. The guards moved, but Karpov raised his hand. Malinovitch said nothing.

"You cannot believe," she began, " that a provincial little tramp that my father picked up on a train, could mesmerize me to murder the Tsar. You forget that my deposition involves me with the Fellowship for well over two years. Do not dare diminish my role or my beliefs because you need to implicate the Jews to meet your political ends."

"Then how can you explain the fact that she was at the very location the conspirators used as a meeting place?" Karpov folded his arms as if he had won a point.

"She was there because I sent her there," she laughed.

Karpov dropped his hands and turned white. Malinovitch leaned closer in dismay, his hands clasped before him. He felt a flush rise to his cheeks.

"Why did you do this to this person?" he said slowly.

"For spite," she retorted. "The little whore is merely a symbol. She was one of a long line of little whores who enticed my father. It was her unfortunate lot to be there when I decided it was time to punish him. By chance, a letter came for her from someone to meet him at Dvor. It was perfect. I intercepted it and had a servant deliver her an altered note. Had the letter not arrived, I would have sent her there to wait anyway."

Malinovitch's jowls fell. He felt his anger rise slowly at her senseless destruction of an innocent girl and the ramifications that would follow.

"Are you saying that Zeena Bendelevitch is innocent of the charges of conspiracy and murder?" He said very slowly.

"Zeena Bendelevitch is a whore who is guilty of enticing my father to bed and must be punished!"

Alexi considered the response and sensed the danger of its intensity. He could not fathom the depth of Sophia's hatred, but knew that she was as unstable as water and could just as easily turn it on him. He could make it a dangerous moment if he pursued his defense of Zeena.

"The Bendelevitch woman is guilty," interrupted Karpov, "and we will produce evidence to prove that it was she who involved you!" His eyes were riveted on Sophia.

Malinovitch mentally smashed Karpov's face. He was relieved that Sophia did not respond. He did not want to hate her.

"What if I tell you that under oath your own father will swear that he was duped and that you fell under that woman's power through drugs that robbed you of your will? We will produce such drugs." Karpov waited.

"Again I tell you that you are a fool to believe that, and my father was lying to save his honored name and his only legitimate child. No, you will not rob me of my sacrifice or my revenge. I will share my glory with that little nothing for my own reasons, but all I hate will go down with me."

Sophia had chosen to be captured and had chosen to die, not for the cause she embraced, but to punish her father and the women who came to his bed. She would continue to spitefully implicate Zeena knowing her to be innocent, and as long as she held to that lie, Zeena could not be vindicated. Malinovitch needed time, but time was against him for he knew that the longer Sophia sat in a cell, the sooner she would realize that her sacrifice for the peasant rabble and the disenfranchised was a meaningless and unappreciated gesture. Then, she might recant and actually blame Zeena to save her own life. Karpov would continue to pour that poison into her ear, and all of Russia would await such a rationalization and applaud.

"The girl is still under the influence of the satanic bitch!" Karpov screamed in disbelief. "That devil's spawn has taken this girl's soul. This may be a matter beyond our control," he said, carefully plotting his next step. "There are holy people among us who understand such matters and who can break the hold that binds the Countess to the other. There are darker powers at work here. I can see it in her eyes."

Malinovitch considered ending this idiocy immediately, but thought that it might provide him with just the time he needed. Sophia would be treated well as long as Karpov believed his own nonsense.

"If you feel she is under some sort of spell or demonic influence," Malinovitch said abruptly, "you may call in whoever you want to rid her of it."

Malinovitch heard the world laughing at Karpov's design. If he knew anything about the world, he knew what it laughed at. He also knew that it would not stand idly by and allow a pregnant woman, even if the woman were a Jew, to be murdered or hung before giving birth. He could keep Zeena safe until the child was born.

CHAPTER 19

Karpov thrust his hat at the housekeeper and confronted the physician on the stairs.

"I insist," he said, "that the Countess attend this interrogation!"

The physician looked at him scornfully. "Her state of mind precludes her from any meeting. I have confined her to bed under heavy sedation. She does not need to be interrogated again. You have done her enough harm."

Karpov snorted and turned towards the sitting room. He waved a servant away and opened the door himself.

Count Perowski sat in the darkened room facing a personalized portrait of his friend, Alexander II. Karpov stood in the shadows briefly, contemplating his opening gambit. Here was nobility brought down, a delectable morsel for his palate. Till now he had glutted himself on the indigent poor, students, or corrupt petty officials. But now, chance had placed an aristocrat on his plate. He smiled a peculiar smile that seemed to mock the Count and himself as well. The scenario to be played out lay before him, and its marvelous potential tantalized him. He would have to proceed slowly, for though there was great confusion as to his station, the Count still held great power. Who would stand by him and who would desert him was still unknown. The man might still be a force to respect and one to handle with care.

Karpov moved to the Count's side and waited. When the Count made no response to his presence, Karpov cleared his throat.

The Count looked up. Karpov knew enough etiquette to act well, though he held the Count and his personal tragedy in contempt.

"I have nothing more to say," the Count said, looking into a vacant and silent abyss.

"I have come to you with an idea," Karpov said softly, "an idea that might, if you agree, save your daughter and your name."

The Count sat there motionless and then looked up slowly at Karpov and questioned him with empty eyes.

"This idea concerns the Bendelevitch woman. I believe she is a fiend who has enticed your daughter into this madness. Now, tell me this. Did you ever see her before the train?"

"No," the Count replied.

"She was in the compartment waiting for you. Is that not true?"

"It is true that she was there when we got on the train."

"Then it is possible that she could have planned this so called chance meeting?" He waited. "I ask you, sir, is it not possible that she might have intended to be in that compartment knowing full well you would enter it?"

"I suppose it is possible, but unlikely. It was a chance meeting."

"These people have ways of knowing everything. They have spies all over Russia," Karpov injected.

"No," repeated the Count. "It was chance. I saw her, I recognized her helplessness, and I desired her, so I gave her a letter of transit. Actually, I gave the key to a servant but he has disappeared."

Karpov's eyes widened. There was another witness who could speak for the Bendelevitch woman.

"Do you know his name?" he asked, taking out a pad.

"Ivan Russakov, if my memory serves. A tall, blond boy about twenty."

"Listen to me," said Karpov in a sinister whisper. "You think she was in the compartment by accident, and I know she was there by design. I think she beguiled you to give her an invitation to your home just to implicate a great, noble family in a crime before the world."

"But my daughter . . . my daughter confessed. She was there. How is that explained away?" The Count took his glass of brandy and began to weep.

Karpov's contempt grew at the man's tears, but he waited.

"Tell me about what happened in the house after she gained entry," he continued, trying not to appear impatient. "Did she try to get information about the celebration? Did you not discuss the route of the procession with her?"

"Zeena was a servant in the house for a few days. Of course there was talk of the festivities. I used her for my pleasure. It was nothing more."

"But you do not know if she used her body to be able to gather that information. I believe she did."

"But who would believe that even if I agreed to say it that way? The Tsar's route was known by everyone. It was in the newspapers."

"She was at the conspirator's meeting place," he retorted. "Was that a coincidence? Was it a coincidence that she was in the same compartment as you and your family? Was it a coincidence that she actually accepted your hospitality?" Karpov waited. "No," he continued, "my dear Count. I believe the Jew contrived and manipulated her way in here, and bewitched your daughter. It was this evil spirit she sent into your child that led her to murder our beloved Tsar. Now, listen carefully to me." Karpov lowered his voice still further. "I know a priest who specializes in such things and can tell in a moment if your daughter was bewitched and possessed. But, it will cost a great deal of money."

The Count drained his glass. "Are you saying that if it can be proven that my child is possessed, her life may be spared?"

"Her life will be spared."

"You must be a fool to think that people will accept such superstitious nonsense. They will laugh at us from around the world."

"Not necessarily, Count Perowski," Karpov said, moving next to him. "Such matters belong to the Holy Church and none would dare doubt its wisdom. Besides, when you place before the Russian people the life of a noblewoman or the life of a heretic Jew, the Russian people will know what to believe."

The Count moved towards the fireplace and considered the thought.

"But how will this charade come about, Mr. Karpov?"

"I will need a written statement from you that you believe that this Zeena Bendelevitch plotted to get into your home to implicate your daughter through her sorcery."

"They will laugh at us," the Count said, shaking his head.

"The people who really matter in this world will not laugh, and the girl will be taken care of long before any trial. Long before those who oppose us can rouse themselves to her defense. Then, like all things, time will pass and she will be forgotten, too. Your daughter will be saved. The Jew will be found to have committed suicide in her cell and it will be put to the world as punishment from a righteous God."

"Yes," the Count said as his despair clutched at Karpov's offer of hope. He moved to his desk and took out a piece of stationary. "It shall be as you say, and my Sophia and my name will be saved." His demeanor changed and his eyes brightened. "Yes, it shall be as you say. Tell me what I must write."

Karpov smiled and began to dictate the indictment. The Count wrote, blotted the paper, and signed his name. Karpov thanked him and placed the paper carefully in a pouch.

Gregor Perowski poured himself another brandy, and then another.

Karpov turned back from the door. "This Ivan person is the only person who might be a witness against us. Can you tell me anything else about him?"

The Count shook his head.

"It is no matter," Karpov said. "With his name and description he will not be difficult to find."

Karpov paused and waited until the Count finished his drink. He moved back towards him.

"You will recall that I said this will cost a great deal of money to make things appear as they must. I will need a flow of cash to whet the appetites of certain people. We could hasten the process if you were to allow me to make withdrawals on a special account. In this way, our meetings will be infrequent and suspicion kept to a minimum."

"Let me know how much you will need, and an account in your name will be created."

"Thank you, thank you," said Karpov, calculating his needs.

Outside, the street was empty. Karpov waited and watched, and when he was sure that no one would see him, he picked up a rock and hurled in through the sitting room window.

Within, the Count leaped to his feet and spilled his brandy. He glanced out the broken glass and backed away in fear.

Karpov waited a moment and then ran up the steps. He opened the door without knocking, and burst into the sitting room, feigning breathlessness. The Count froze.

"Some men ran down the street. I was afraid this would happen."

"Who would dare do such a thing?" demanded the Count, shocked that the sanctity of his home and person had been violated.

"There are people out there who will take vengeance upon you and your family before they know the facts. Those fools do not know of the treachery that brought you to this moment."

Karpov reached into his carrying case and took out a hand gun and laid it on the desk.

"I do not know if they, or some other madmen, will be back to avenge the death of the Tsar on you and your household. I will leave you this gun. It is loaded and you will be able to protect yourself and your wife."

"Thank you, Mr. Karpov, for your concern. It shall not go unrewarded."

Karpov smiled obsequiously and backed out of the room.

The veins in Karpov's neck bulged against his shirt collar and his black eyes flashed rage. He threw open the door to Alexi's office and, brandishing a newspaper in his hand, entered the room waving it threateningly.

"How did they know?" he bellowed.

"How did who know what?" said Alexi, looking up from the new deposition. The face he presented to Karpov was expressionless, but belied his own rage at the lie that lay before him in the Count's own hand.

"The paper, the paper," Karpov roared. "Did you not see the newspaper?"

"No, I have not read the paper today. I have read only the Count's newest deposition." He looked at it as it lay before him, and then looked at Karpov. "It would seem you had a good day." He studied Karpov's face for a response to his sarcasm, but Karpov's eyes only brightened at the reminder.

"Yes, yes. It was a successful day for Russia."

"What did you promise him for his support?" Alexi knew the answer already, but was hoping to glimpse something of Karpov's plan that would allow a counter move.

"His daughter's life and his honor. It did not take long, though he didn't leap at my offer immediately. He actually dismissed my suggestion of bewitchment as laughable."

"But you were skillful enough to create a witness for the state. I must applaud you," Alexi said as he fingered the document.

Alexi Malinovitch's life had taught him that everything was expendable for a purpose. Whatever had been placed in his soul prior to his abduction had been secreted away in the recesses of memory, or excised by the hatred of those who brought him to manhood. At one point in his life, he had forgotten where he had left his humanity. But that was before he had returned to the town of his birth. The secret package that he had hidden away and forgotten had been found, and opened itself when confronted by Karpov and his mindless hatred for someone he loved. And so, Alexi created a game that he and Karpov would play; a game whose objective was to frustrate and destroy Karpov's designs. In the past, it had made no difference whom Karpov tried to destroy. Saving a life was not what excited Alexi. What made the game tantalizing was frustrating Karpov. The excitement was intensified because he and Karpov were colleagues in destruction, and Karpov never knew what he was about. So, each of Alexi's counter moves had to be planned and executed with meticulous secrecy. Karpov's own intensity in a particular case was Alexi's barometer for becoming involved, and the greater Karpov's intensity, the greater Alexi's desire to frustrate him.

But this case was of such magnitude and of such danger, that had Zeena not been involved, even he might not have proceeded. It was only Zeena's chance involvement that made his involvement an absolute necessity, and the danger to himself and his position was dismissed. To Malinovitch, most everyone he had ever encountered had been guilty and not worthy of pity. Year, after year, through his judgments and behavior, he had secretly punished Russia for what she had taken from him, and his secret retribution on her was a sweetness in his mouth.

Now, he had entered the lists in the most dangerous joust of his life. For the first time, his victim was not guilty, and her life mattered to him as no life had ever mattered before. This game mattered as no game ever mattered before, and the fear of losing the game, and the emptiness that would replace the love he felt, engulfed him as no emptiness had ever engulfed him before.

His secret was that he stood among men with neither empathy nor sympathy for their sorrow or their joys, and as long as he kept himself free of feeling, he could not be touched or injured. Now he had to risk being touched and destroyed.

Through the veil of thought, Karpov droned on about the newspaper report. Alexi smiled that his counter parry had successfully frustrated Karpov's initial design, and smiled to himself at the gesticulating man before him. Public opinion, world public opinion, would not permit a woman to be hanged while she carried a child. Zeena was safe for four or five months and that might give him time to orchestrate her defense. But Karpov had already obtained the Count's deposition and had probably made contact with the spiritual mendicant who would certify that Sophia had been possessed.

"Do not let the blood of an unborn innocent child be on the hands of the state. How dare they write this? Who dared tell them?"

"How am I supposed to know? Since you believe her invested with supernatural powers, perhaps she sent a spirit out to the newspapers to let them know her whereabouts and of her pregnancy."

"She said she knew no one in St. Petersburg."

"You called her a liar each time you questioned her," Alexi shot back. "Will you believe only those parts of her story that suit your purpose?"

"I will believe whatever it takes to keep the name of a noble family clean, and you will not stand in my way . . ."

For a brief moment, Karpov had forgotten to whom he spoke, and Alexi saw the sudden fear in his eyes as one sees the eyes of one who had imperiled himself and was suddenly aware of it.

Alexi was pleased at the fear he saw and chose to use his silence. His cold blue eyes froze Karpov, and their intensity seemed to push Karpov back a step.

"My dear Karpov," Alexi began, discounting purposely Karpov's affront to him. It was a calculated move that registered with his adversary. "Ultimately, our job is to ferret out the truth. You have already decided that the truth is not the truth, and that a lie is the truth. But in your hasty leap to convict the Jewess, and blame her people to save a noblewoman who has confessed, you continue to miss the wider picture of a conspiracy to bring down the monarchy and our way of life. I am where I am because I see wider pictures. You are second to me because your scope is limited to what is before your eyes. Karpov, there is a much wider conspiracy here and your focus on this woman allows the true culprits to breath a sigh of relief. Karpov stepped back as Alexi rose from his chair. Alexi held out his hand and Karpov knew that the gesture demanded him to pick up the newspaper he had thrown to the floor and place it on Alexi's desk. Then, in silent rage, he backed up another step, turned, and left the room.

CHAPTER 20

Zalman Yavna closed the door to Reuben's shop, shaking his head sadly and thanking God that his life and his children had not brought him to the sorrow that now confronted his old friend. He turned and looked through the window at the sight of the man clutching the two week old newspaper to his face and sobbing. Mr. Yavna lowered his eyes from Reuben's shame, remembering that a man's shame should be hidden from the face of his friend. He wiped a tear from his own eye and moved silently away.

The letters danced and squirmed through Reuben's tear filled eyes. The pregnant Jewess the paper spoke of had to be his Zeena. Zeena in prison. Zeena, alone and afraid and charged with murder.

Suddenly, St. Petersburg had been brought to his doorstep. His brain tore in all directions at once, searching for some thread of hope to catch on to, some thimbleful of promise.

He frantically searched the drawer for the neatly folded paper with Alta Mitvoy's address on it. Alta would respond and save his daughter's life. He wrote quickly begging, in the name of friendship and in the name of pity, and for the blessing of God. He asked if he remembered Zeena, and he asked that he save her. There would be time. The paper said she would not be executed, if that were her fate, until she gave birth. All was now in the hands of God.

Reuben closed the shop and moved as quickly as he could to post the letter. Then turning, and praying with all the intensity his soul could muster, he limped home to tell Sarah.

Reuben read the paragraph again, slowly, fighting back his tears. His voice shook with fear and incredulity. He picked up the sentence in the middle . . . 'and a pregnant Jewess, one Zeena

Bendelevitch, is also condemned to die for complicity.' He sank on to the chair and buried his head in his hands, and again, wept openly.

Sarah turned from him, her cheeks flushed. Since Zeena's flight from Ezra, Sarah was consumed alternately between her anger for Zeena for having jeopardized the family, and a genuine fear for her child's safety and welfare. Now the evil she had feared was upon them.

"They'll come and they'll kill us for this," she blurted. We'll be murdered because of her."

"The paper is two weeks old," retorted Leah angrily, as she struggled to her feet, "and if they were going to murder us, they would have done it already. Besides, Zeena isn't so stupid to tell anyone there where she is from. She isn't even using her real name. So perhaps we should think about Zeena's welfare and not so much about ourselves." Her tone was a clear indictment of what she perceived as her mother-in-law's selfishness.

Leah's words coiled around Sarah's neck and constricted her throat. Her inner turmoil deepened.

"Another enemy in my house," and their eyes met openly and contemptuously.

Reuben was oblivious to all but the horror of his daughter awaiting death in a Tsarist prison. Jonah stepped between the outrage leaping between his wife and mother and took the paper from near his father's feet. He scanned the page and interrupted the hostile silence.

"Read the part again about America," Ruth said, not fully aware of the gravity of the moment.

Jonah scanned the columns of background data on the trial for the section on foreign responses to the ruling of the court.

> "Four thousand American citizens assembled in a mass meet-
> ing to protest against the possible execution of Zeena
> Bendelevitch. 'Let not this woman's blood be on your hands,'
> the article warned the Tsar."

Ruth began to interrupt again, but Jonah continued.

> "The dispatch was read at a mass meeting of Socialists in
> Irving Hall last evening to protest against the execution of
> Zeena Bendelevitch. Seven or eight hundred men, and per-
> haps fifty women were there."

John Winston was the first speaker. He compared the young Russian Jewess with Judith who slew Holofernes.

'We protest,' he said, 'against the military order for charg-
ing Zeena Bendelevitch. We should hold ourselves guilty of
complicity in the proposed crime if we did not enter our protest against it while there is still time. We have the right as
men and women to protest whersoever and whensoever such
crimes are ordered. We protest to the Tsar of Russia and to all
the world. Be warned, thou steel clad Tsar! Let not this woman's
blood be on your hands.'"

Jonah swallowed and took a breath.

"I don't understand," said Dora shaking her head. "How can
America have rallies against the Tsar for Zeena's sake, and we are
only learning about her now?"

Jonah smirked. "Mr. Yavna got the paper from a friend in the
city and the paper is from outside Russia where governments don't
keep their people ignorant."

"No revolution talk in this house!" screamed Sarah. "Look what
it's done to us already."

Jonah looked at his father who sadly urged him to continue
reading.

> "While we sympathize with Zeena Bendelevitch, we do not
> expect that her life will be saved for us. We do not send out
> prayers before the throne for her. We send out our heart felt
> and deadly curses to her murderer."

Sarah sobbed into her apron. Reuben moved towards her.

> "The revolutionists of the world will never be content until
> the last king and the last emperor is swept away. The Em-
> peror of Russia may be able to make his army fifty times as
> great as it is, but we know how to make bombs quicker than
> he can make soldiers."

"Zeena, Zeena," wept Sarah. "We'll all be dragged away and murdered for this."

Jonah lowered the paper and looked at his mother who voiced
the silent fear of all.

"Sha, sha," murmured Reuben, who moved to hold her shaking body in his arms. He looked from one child to the other.

"Sarah," he said reassuringly. "Like Leah said before, if they
didn't come yet, they won't come. Zeena isn't a fool. If she told
them anything, it was a lie."

He looked at his children as he spoke, but he himself was
not reassured and he knew he offered little comfort to them or
his wife. "Now," he said, "it's time to think of Zeena and the
baby, and how they can be saved. Zeena is safe until the baby
is born so there is time. If such support comes from America,
perhaps they and countries in Europe will also rally to her help.
Perhaps we can do something. There is still time."

"Time," laughed Sarah hoarsely. "Five months. Maybe three
or two. Maybe less," and then, recovering, "who knows when?"

Jonah listened to his father's offer of hope, and as he listened,
something began to gnaw at him. It was a vague, but persistent
feeling that moved from his brain to his throat to his stomach. The
thought that caused it would not take shape, but it was a dangerous thought nevertheless. He looked at the faces of the people who
sat at the kitchen table and suddenly realized that life would never
again be as it was yesterday or last week or last month. How?
Why? Suddenly and without warning the world collapses in on
itself. He felt his throat tighten and his stomach lurch. He had

broken his oath to her and this was the punishment. His sister lay in a prison waiting to be executed. He had pushed her to destruction because of his own selfishness, fear and shame. Because he had not acted, Zeena had acted. It had come back to lay at his feet as he had once feared. He had to make it right. But how?

CHAPTER 21

"Yes, Leah," Jonah sighed, "we'll go to America. I will tell Mama and Papa and I will buy the tickets when I go to Kiev."

Jonah's eyes fixed on the bedpost beyond her and he felt his shoulders sink in resignation. In the space of a blink, in the space it takes to sip tea, he had changed his world and his history. In the space of raising a hand and lowering it, he had created a void called tomorrow. He would either have to carry his yesterdays and his traditions with him, or leave them.

"Why are you crying?" he said, sinking even further into himself. "I said we'll go."

"I am crying because you do not see what I see. I am crying because you do not see how dangerous the world is."

"Leah, I cannot see what you see," he said, trying not to sound exasperated, "because I'm not you. Why do you always add that little bit to make me feel less than I am. We'll go to America. Let it be."

He moved around the bed and blew out the candle. He lay down and turned his back to her. Why, he thought, did she always have to add her own extra little truths? He would do as she asked. And why did he always have to ask her why she looked that way? He would stop that. He felt her hand on his shoulder, but he was hurting inside and very angry. He did not respond.

Several days later, Jonah sat near the window of their room. The air was still and hot, and he looked at the cloudless sky and prayed for rain.

Leah sat in bed watching him with her hands across her stomach as if protecting her child. She was clearly upset.

"I do not understand how your mother can respond that way

to Zeena's situation. I don't understand how your father can just sit there when his own flesh and blood is being tried for murder. Doesn't anyone in this family have anything more than prayers and tears? I'll tell you Jonah that if Zeena were my child, I would have waged war against that city to be with her and protect her."

Jonah closed his eyes and sighed. "Not now, Leah," he said softly. "I've had enough for one day."

"Not now!" she repeated emphatically. "Not now? Let's see, Jonah. How does the saying go? `If I am not for myself, then who will be for me? But if I am only for myself, then what am I? And if not now, when?'" she paused. "What are you Jonah? You sit there and say, "not now." Your sister is laying in a prison alone, abandoned, with a baby coming, and the threat of death over her head, and all you can do is wring your hands and muster up a "not now?" Is this what I could expect from you if I were in trouble?" She waited for a response. There was none. That angered her even more, and she repeated her question. "Well, is that what I can expect from my husband, a not now?"

Her words burned him. She was pushing him harder than he had ever been pushed before; to act in a way totally alien from any action ever taken in his life thus far. He wanted to run into the hot, still night, run away from this wife who pushed him and shamed him, and from the mother who always made him feel less than a man. He wrapped his arms around his chest urgently and squeezed himself as if in pain. He needed to be held, but there was no one to hold him. What was he expected to do? Wage war against the gates of St. Petersburg? Ride up on a horse and demand his sister be turned over to him? He'd be put in prison as an accomplice.

"I need you to tell me what you will do."

"I'm not a hero, Leah!" he screamed, and all the passion and anguish that had been bottled up for so long poured out of him. "I don't know what to do. I'm a nothing tailor."

"Nobody's a hero, and nobody is a nothing," she screeched in her own fear, "but we don't have to be cowards either." Her tone became sympathetic. "Nothing will happen unless someone acts.

Yes, there are people in the world writing letters, but that may not be enough. Zeena needs a miracle. Somebody has to wade into the water before the sea will part."

He remembered and turned to her and let his arms fall to his side. He looked at her. Her eyes pleaded with him.

"Jonah, it's not just for Zeena. I don't want to be afraid anymore. I need someone who is stronger than I am. I need someone who will protect me when I need protection." Her eyes could not read either resolve or fear on his face, but she knew him well enough to know that he would act. For some reason, unknown to her, he could not initiate action himself.

"I have to go to Kiev for Papa. Papa knows people in Kiev who may be willing to help Zeena if they knew who she was." He spoke softly, building resolve. He heard the words, but they seemed not to come from him. He had no idea of what he would do or where he would begin. He had to say something to Leah to stay her fear and save his own dwindling sense of self. He imagined himself on a promontory above a raging sea. He saw himself walking to the gray black water and standing on the edge of the turbulence. He would have to enter the water whether he could swim or not. He had to save Zeena if only to save himself. If she died, he would never be whole again and he could never find forgiveness.

Time slowed under the weight of summer heat. The fishermen, their lined faces straining under their nets and wet from sweat, moved through the haze, silently. Some walked along the mud banks watching the placid lake, wondering at the sin or offense that had been committed to have God shut up the heavens against them. The catch of fish had grown meager; barely enough for survival. They were robust men who normally did not fear. Now they were afraid.

Jonah held Leah by the arm watching the earth for any rut or stone that might be in her path. When he returned, he would have tickets to America and they would begin to pack. He had given his word. Also, he would meet with a Mr. Brodsky whom his father said would be able to put him in contact with the people who were supporting Zeena. He was fearful of the contact and had a strong sense of danger, but he had to do something. He had spent sleepless nights in anticipation of the meeting; nights filled with visions of deprivation and loss.

Jonah turned towards her. "Now it's only till Sunday," he said, "and Mama feels that with Aunt Malka so close to dying, it's better that you shouldn't be there. You know how superstitious she is and it's only for a few days." He looked at her and raised her face to him. "Please, Leah, smile. It's only for a few days and I'd feel so much better if I knew you were with my parents and they were looking out for you. Rebecca will be there to care for Malka."

She closed her eyes and shook her head in agreement, and forced a half smile.

Leah opened her eyes. "Now you take care of yourself and don't let those merchants in the city talk you into anything you and your father won't be able to use. You know what sells and what doesn't. Be careful when you find Brodsky and when you meet with his people. Find out what we can do but don't do anything until we talk."

He glanced to see if anyone watched them, and kissed her.

Jonah picked up the small suitcase, and backed away towards the plank over the mud to the barge. In spite of the turmoil within, he tried to feel taller and important, a man with some responsibility. He looked for a brief moment at the water. He had not waded in, but he would be riding on it. He was torn. He did not want to do what he had to do in Kiev, yet he knew he had to act for Zeena's sake and for his own sanity and well being. He did not know what lay ahead, and he alternated between fear and expectation.

He looked at Leah. "Take care not to lift anything heavy, and stay in the shade as much as you can. And don't worry about me," he added reassuringly.

Seeing tears in her eyes, he caught himself before he could ask her why they were there. Immediately, he felt bad for not asking, but he had promised himself that he would never ask again. This was the first time he had withheld his concern. It did not feel good.

"Don't worry about me," he repeated, though he knew that her worry was not only about him.

The plank between the shore and the barge was pulled away as a ruddy faced man looked around for a last minute fare. Satisfied that there were none, he untied the rope and taking a long pole, pushed it down into the mud until the boat slid out of the shallows. His task was easy. The water was lower than it had ever been in memory, and no wind fought the slight current. The boat glided silently as if both boat and surface were oiled panes of glass.

Jonah looked back to Leah who stood waving with one hand as she rested the other on her stomach. Only she seemed to vibrate life in the uncomfortable, heavy silence. A sudden rush of anxiety filled him. Perhaps it was because he was alone for the first time with a frightening task before him, or perhaps it was that she was standing on the shore and he could not be with her. He moved towards her, but his gesture was stopped by the railing. He thought of jumping into the water and wading to shore, but he did not. He had to do something to help save his sister, buy tickets to America, and negotiate for cloth.

He watched her until she turned and left. Now there was only the town to watch. He saw a place divided in half as God must have divided light from darkness. The half closest to the lake was the world of his parents and ancestors. It was a wooden world of rickety houses with dirt floors and chickens being shooed out of bedrooms by overworked and overburdened women. It was a world that had inched its way imperceptibly in its own effort to establish itself and survive until it reached that cornfield and was abruptly stopped. Fearful of even harsher rebuffs it was certain to suffer if it dared intrude beyond even this small allotted space, the little town learned to stand quietly and its outstanding virtue became patience. The years came and went. Tsars came and went. Clergy, constables, and peasants came and went. And Jonah's people came and went and rested in prayer shawls and shrouds on the hill. Still the town stood, and it was that very virtue of patience that reminded Jonah that if he were patient also, and allowed time to pass, he, too, would survive.

Jonah's eyes continued to move upward. The air shimmered on the distant, yellow stalks and seemed to burn menacingly as they stood watching the equally parched wooden village. Jonah did not understand why it would not rain. He had prayed. Everyone had prayed. He thought of God's promise to close up the heavens if the people ran to do evil and served other gods, and he wondered if they now suffered for some collective offense or perhaps for the offense of one individual who had truly offended the Almighty. He thought of the spring and how the early rain and lush, rapid growth animated the peasants with joy. Then he saw their joy turn to fear and anger when word came that the Tsar had been murdered. The rain did not fall again, and the corn in their silken cradles shriveled and cracked and died as had the peasant's hope. Jonah could taste their fear when they came into the shop and then they stopped coming altogether. He thought that Ezra had something to do with that, but he also noticed that fewer and fewer peasants came to the Jewish village for any reason. He had heard that the church had told the peasants that God had cut off the rain because a Jew had killed the Tsar and as long as the Jews were permitted to live among them, God's wrath would be upon Mother Russia and upon them. But Jonah could not understand why they could not see that the Jews suffered as much as the peasants suffered, and non-Jews had actually confessed while the Jew accused continued to deny any knowledge of the crime. Jonathan had ridiculed him for not being willing to see that it was to the advantage of the clergy and government agents to keep the peasants fearful, and that the Jews were an easy answer to the economic and political turmoil caused by the drought. Now, this drought and the assassination shook the tenuous peace that had existed, and both the parched town and the dessicated corn stood in silent witness to a disturbance in the natural laws of nature and a disturbance in the delicate balance that kept peace between the children of the same Father. Jonah thought of this and despite his desperate need to help his sister, he regretted that he had not gotten off the boat when his instinct told him to do so.

At another time he would have delighted in the streets and sounds of the city. But now, as he moved through the busy, crowded streets, he seemed pressured and confined.

He looked at the crumpled paper at regular intervals as if to assure himself that he was going in the right direction. He had taken care of business. He had negotiated and purchased good patterns and good weaves, all within the financial boundaries his father had set. Ezra had also worked some of his evil in Kiev, but Jonah had cajoled and convinced some if not everyone. Also, he had purchased two tickets to America and wondered how he would tell his parents.

Now his pulse quickened as he looked for a sign that read, Epstein and Grushansky . These two men had been to his wedding and to Zeena's, and he knew them slightly. He was to deliver a letter to them explaining Zeena's plight and he was to beg their assistance, and do exactly as he was told. Jonah was concerned, especially about this unknown. He touched his jacket pocket to assure himself that it was still there, for he knew full well how important and dangerous that letter was. Should anyone other than these two men read it, the entire family would be put in jeopardy. At this point, no one linked Zeena with them, or with Krivoser. But, if the family knew, and Mr. Yavna knew, then Ezra certainly knew by now and God knows who else in the town knew. His eyes darted furtively for signs of his being watched.

The directions from the mill merchant had been clear. Jonah had asked only for the street and was evasive when asked about a number. He thought himself clever for his caution. Now he was on that street, hurrying towards his destination before sunset. He looked at the address again and scanned the store fronts for numbers. He was about a dangerous business and he was not a dangerous person.

On the next street he could see that a small crowd had gathered. Others near him rushed to the same place. He moved along with the curious, but was stopped abruptly and pulled back to the outer edge of a circle in front of a store. The sign above read, Epstein and Grushansky. He could feel a rush of heat over his face and down his back. There was a commotion in the doorway and he could see two men in dark suits holding the arms of a well dressed elderly man. A third walked behind them and closed the door with an admonition to those within that Jonah could not hear.

"What's going on?" he blurted to a man who stood in the doorway of the next shop.

The merchant blinked into the sunlight. "That's old man Grushansky. I always knew that Jew bastard was an enemy of Russia." The he spit into the street and went back into his shop.

Jonah could feel his heart beat speed up and sweat trickle down his back. Whatever Mr. Grushansky's connections were, they were of no use even to Grushansky himself, now. Jonah felt for the dangerous letter. What if the crowd turned on him because they thought he might be a Jew? What if they imagined his mission? He froze where he stood. The crowd moved slowly away without noticing him. Jonah stood there until he realized that only he stood and watched. Was Mr. Epstein inside? But, if he went in and asked for Mr.Epstein, perhaps he would be suspect. Were the police in there dressed as customers and clerks? He would be searched and they would find the letter and the entire family would be taken away. Yes, if he went in and asked for Mr. Epstein, he could destroy them all.

A sudden pain in his stomach almost doubled him over and he heaved as he staggered past the store window. There were people being questioned. He was sure of that. He moved down the street and sat down on a bench. He slid his hand into his jacket pocket and slowly took out the letter. He tore it in half and then again and again. If the police stopped and questioned and searched him, he and his family would be held as accomplices. He let one piece fall to his feet to be lifted away by a breeze. Another floated in the opposite direction.

Jonah buried his face in his hands. I can't do it, God, I can't help Zeena. I want to, but I can't. I can't risk all their lives. But what will I say to them? What will I tell them? They'll say I was a coward for not going. What's right, Lord? What's right? And Zeena? What shall I do about Zeena?

CHAPTER 22

Sunday, July 8, 1882

A government agent dressed in peasant garb rose slowly and made his way past the worshipers to the rear of the church. He scanned them, his dark fierce eyes looking to others who watched him with the same intensity. An imposing figure in black linen with a long gray beard and towering cap, moved slowly through a cloud of incense shaking and swinging a lamp in a measured cadence. Sweet soprano voices from the choir rose in unison, to the icons of the saints and holy family frozen in tempera and gold leaf on the painted wooden walls.

The man with the fierce dark eyes inched closer to the door. The peasant's voices rose to join the choir in solemn praise of the dark eyed deity painted in ascending glory over the altar. Private wordless prayers reached up for rain and blessings in the breathless heat.

A government agent, dressed as a priest, took up a holy icon in one hand, and a portrait of the slain Tsar in the other, and moved from the altar towards the assembly. He stopped, turned and looked at them for a long moment.

"Behold our beloved Tsar," he began. "Behold how gentle like our Father in heaven was his face. Behold how his love for us sustained us and how his life brought blessings to the earth." He paused and mused on the sweat drenched faces.

"Behold the land since his murder," he bellowed. "Behold how his innocent blood was shed as was the innocent blood of our Savior. Behold how the guilty still live and how they have not bled

for their crimes against your little father and your Father in heaven."
Again he paused and his eyes measured the fear before him.

"God has shut you off," he raged with finger pointed menacingly at the sky, "because you have not avenged the blood of his
anointed on earth. God has cut off the earth from the blessed rain
and caused the fields to wither because you allow them to go unpunished!" Again he paused. Again the assembly groaned at the
implied excommunication of their souls. He stopped. His eyes
burned into the impassioned faces and fixed on one old woman.

"Feel the fire of his rage in your body! Feel the shame of guilt
in your own soul!"

The woman shrieked and put her hand to her face to wipe
away the intensity of his gaze.

"For years," he continued, "you have bled, not they. You have
been bled by their insidious presence. You do not see the blood
pouring out of your souls, but God permits me to see it. You do
not see how faint and pale are your souls because you permit them
to dwell among us. But now, God's patience with you is over. The
earth dies under your feet. The heavens withhold their life as punishment. You see the earth die and you will see your children die.
God knows and God sees. And God lets me know and see. He
watches you. See how sad He is that His son was murdered. He
condemns you for not avenging the crime. See how sad He is that
his own children permit his enemies to live in peace and prosper."
He turned from them with a massive sweep of his robe. The altar
boys fled his path. He reached the top of the stairs, and turned
back to them.

"Shatter this sacred day. Shatter it with the wrath of God.
Shatter it so your souls can be redeemed. Shatter it with scythe
and pike, with axe and club. Heal your souls with their blood. You
pray for water and you pray for rain. Pray for strength to rid yourselves of pity. Pray for . . ." and he pointed directly at an agent in
the front row. The man rose and waved his fist in the air.

"Death to the murdering Jews," he screamed. The agent in

the back, near the door, took his cue from him as he had taken it from the priest. "Death to the Tsar's killers," he shouted.

Another raised his voice. "Death to the traitors among us. Take what you need to live!"

The agents at the rear moved to the great doors and threw them open to the blinding sun. Three others stood quickly and exhorted the peasants to their feet.

"Take your children," he screamed to one mother clutching her crying child. "Take him so he can remember how the wrath of God was brought down on Russia's enemies."

The agent's prodding, the heat, damnation stinging their ears, and the terror that gnawed at them, suddenly, like invisible hands, grabbed them in a grip of nameless fear and pulled them to their feet.

"They do not starve," called out one agent. "Their shops are full of goods while you do not have enough to feed your children. Do their children starve? Do their children cry themselves to sleep empty?"

"They have come and they have taken from you what is right-fully yours," bellowed another. "Take it all back from them and drive them out so God will smile on you again!"

A third agent picked up a stick and waved it above his head as he raced towards the cornfield. The crowd surged toward the door in the holy belief that punishment of the Jews on the other side of the cornfield would appease their God's wrathful judgement on them for the murder of his earthly son.

Some men pressed their wives to take their children home to wait for the great mysterious bounty that had been stored up by the enemy. Others grabbed their sons and daughters and pulled them towards the cornfield so they could also be God's agents. Some women pushed through the hesitant elderly and found rocks. Children cried in fear. Men screamed to each other to bolster their resolve and their manhood. Some, for the sake of their soul's sur-vival, conjured up images of Jews they knew and searched for some offense, real or imagined, large or small, to give reason for their impending act. Some went home to pray.

They stood poised in a jagged line on the rim of the corn—field. They breathed in the hot air as if a large bellow that needed energy for its impending explosion. The parched corn stood silently in the brutal sun and moved only when some pitch fork or scythe was brandished against it. Some men pounded their pitch forks on the earth in cadence with the pounding in their chests. Fear and anger poured out of them with their sweat as the agents pushed their way to the front of the line with axes. Then, as one, they stepped forward, and the cracking sound of the desiccated stalks rose up from the earth into the still air like a frightened bird.

The juggernaut moved forward. The corn stalks bent and snapped under the irresistible force. The agents veered the multitude to the right and left, to the town and to the line of little houses bordering the field. Those in front were silent and determined. Their eyes squinted at their destination and burned from the salt in their sweat. Towards the rear, there was laughter and chatter as if going to a festival. Mixed throughout were shouts of courage and the promise of having more than they had yesterday.

Sarah took the compress from Leah's forehead and dampened it again. "You shouldn't get yourself so upset like this," she said trying to be a comfort. "You wake up screaming as if a thousand evil spirits are in the room, but you won't talk."

Leah looked at the woman standing by the wash stand and tried to wipe away the anger and frustration that she felt towards her. She understood her too well and though she recognized that Sarah was not an evil person, she also recognized that Sarah was the type of mother who gave with one hand and took twice as much with the other. With Sarah Chernov, there was only one way and it was her way. There was no discussion or negotiation or compromise in the woman. Leah even felt sorry for her for not seeing how much more she would get in affection from her children had she just allowed them to have the right to thoughts and feelings that were different from her own.

Sarah looked up. "Do you hear thunder?" she asked.

The last wave of peasants and agents from Krivy Ossero disappeared into the cornfield, but from Krivoser, all that could be detected were a strange din and erratic movements of undulating corn stalks as they bent and straightened. When the din of the angry machine became audible to the people of the town, they smiled at the thought of distant rain and a prayer finally answered by God.

Sarah took the steaming kettle off the stove and carried it over to the table. "Leah," she called to the back room. "I'm making tea. She put two of her best cups along with jam and cake on a tray and went over to the door. "I thought we'd sit and talk about the baby. I assume you'll name the baby after your mother or father. I think that's only proper."

Leah forced a smile, surprised that her mother-in-law had dropped her request to name the baby after her uncle. She thought of America, and Jonah, and how she would finally find a place where she would not dream her fearful childhood dreams. It wouldn't matter if they would be poor. She was willing to struggle as long as she and her child and husband would not have to be afraid.. Now, over tea, she would tell Sarah about America because she was not sure if Jonah would.

"No, you lay there and rest," Sarah insisted. "You look terrible." She put the tray on the dresser and moved to the wash stand for another damp cloth.

Ruth had just closed the gate and moved slowly towards the town carrying her father's and Zedde's lunch. Like her brother, she balanced on the dry ruts in the road and wondered at the shimmering road further down where the town glistened in a magic sea of water. The dry ruts collapsed under her light step and she laughed each time as she had laughed when she had played there with Jonah.

Dora sat with a jeweler's glass to her eye trying to concentrate, but Jonathan kept blowing on the nape of her neck. He laughed his young man's laugh as she shivered.

"Don't do that," she giggled and twisted in her chair to face him. She took the glass from her eye and held it to the back of her head. "I need an eye here, too, when you're around."

The love that grew between them grew silently and sustained itself on soft, tender glances. They exchanged few words. Being in the same room was enough and they both knew that.

"Now let me work. Zedde needs this watch this afternoon and you should be with your students. You shouldn't even be here." She pretended to be annoyed but could not help herself laugh. "Now please leave because I have work to do."

"Do you remember the first time I came in here?" he said looking at the counter. "I was really scared. I never told you how scared I was that day."

"We were both scared," she said softly.

He ran his fingers over a mantle clock on the counter. "My whole life has changed since the day I first saw you." He paused and laughed at himself. Here was the great Jonathan Metkoff, street orator extraordinary, mover of the masses, savior of the downtrodden, stammering to find just the right words to say to the girl he loved.

Reuben took a bolt of gray wool and moved it to a lower shelf, making space for the new stock Jonah was to order. He thought of what Jonah would select and whether his son had negotiated well. He was proud and somewhat nervous. He stopped for a moment and moved to the window. He thought he had heard a sound but returned to his place. His stomach growled and he looked at his watch. Ruth would be here shortly and so would his father-in-law. He put down his tea and as he cleared the table, he hummed an old tune softly to himself.

As Jonathan spoke, Dora became less and less interested in the watch she held, and it began to blur through her glass as his soft, hesitant words drew her in.

"I think about you all the time, Dora." He watched his fingers tap on the counter rim. "Each moment we spend together becomes more precious than the one before."

Dora took the glass slowly from her eye and sat with her head lowered. She memorized each word. Jonathan stood behind her and placed his hands gently on her shoulders. She closed her eyes and leaned backward into his touch.

"Dora," he said, "I . . ."

The door flew open and Zedde staggered in gasping for breath.

"Quick, Dora, Jonathan, take the tools, quickly and say nothing."

"But . . ." she protested.

"Silence!" he shouted, pulling the eye piece from her hand and the tweezer from off the bench. Dora and Jonathan looked at each other dismayed. Zedde thrust the tool box into her hands and pushed them both to the secret cabinet.

"You are to say and do nothing!" he whispered emphatically. "No matter what you hear, you are to remain silent."

"But what's happening?" Dora said, her voice shaking.

"No questions, and do not come out until it is dark. No matter what you hear, do not come out!"

He reached for the secret lever and pulled it. In the distance there was a shattering of glass and shouts. Jonathan began to move to the door.

"No," shouted the old man. "You must protect Dora!"

He slid the door open. The silver and gold watches danced on their pins in the dim light. "Get in and make no sound no matter what you hear. Swear by God you will not make a sound until night." He grabbed Jonathan and shook him.

"I swear," he replied, finally understanding the passion and fear in the old man's face.

Then Zedde pushed them into the closet and closed the door. They were enveloped in hot darkness. "Remember to be silent!"

The old man turned and moved as quickly as his body would permit. He pulled down the shades and locked the front door. He had seen the line of peasants break in upon the town as he walked to Reuben. Now that his Dora was safe, he would have to get to Sarah and the children. He could hear the peasants in the street smashing in doors and dragging out the merchants. He opened the rear door as a boulder shattered the glass window in front.

Jonathan moved at the sound. "No," whispered Dora, tearing at his shirt. "You swore to Grandpa."

"But something terrible is happening and he may need me." Another glass shattered and the front door flew open. Dora grabbed him tightly and shut her eyes as something shattered against the wall that hid them from the marauders. He, too, stiffened in his own fear and held her close. She listened to the angry voices and the shatter of glass but could not discern the voice of her beloved Zedde. He had gotten away, she thought. He was all right. She pressed herself to Jonathan and could feel the pounding of his heart. His body made her feel less afraid. If they were discovered and she had to die, she wanted to die with him.

At first, Ruth stood transfixed by the strange noises coming from the cornfield, and she took a few steps closer and peered into it. Slowly, she perceived the awesome danger and froze before the few men and boys who suddenly emerged. Her presence surprised them, giving her enough time to step backward and bolt toward the house screaming. A flaxen haired man with large hands leaped after her for a few yards and lifted her easily into the air with his powerful arms.

"We have our first prize," he shouted above Ruth's cries for her mother. They all laughed, each realizing each had the power to do exactly as he pleased with none to stop him. God's messenger on earth had given them permission.

"Mama, Mammmma," she cried, pushing back at the laughing man's face as he ran with her in his arms to the barn.

"Now you will see what it is like to be a man," laughed one father to his young son."

Reuben fell across the table dazed from the force of the blow. He opened his eyes to see drops of blood fall from his face onto the white lace wedding gown he had been stitching. Slivers of glass fell around him as three cackling women reached through the broken pane for the bolts of blue cotton. Another rock shattered another window as the door smashed open and the mob surged in tearing at this and that and fighting with each other over cloth. Two men ripped the small sewing machine from its bolts in the floor and carried it out over their heads. Reuben fell to his knees as a winnowing pole crashed across the side of his face. He shrieked in agony as cartilage in his nose cracked from yet another blow. A white hot pain rocked his side as the prong of a pitch fork pierced his lung. He choked on the blood that rushed into his throat. Then, like a child's toy doll, he felt himself being lifted and thrown under the cutting table. He gasped and opened his eyes and the wooden planks above him took him back to the moment when he was a child playing there under his father's feet. He closed his eyes against the terrible pain and died. The dry floor boards hungrily drank in the blood that poured out of his frail body until there was no more left to absorb.

"Get the old Jew," shouted a woman when Zedde stepped into the alley behind the shop. They were upon him like wolves. A pitch fork tore at his skin and a rake, thrust up against his throat, held him against the wall.

"Let's see what the old bastard looks like without his beard," and someone tore a handful of hair from the old man's face. Zedde's gray eyes bulged and rolled back in his head as blood collected in the hollow of his cheek.

"More," shouted a sweaty woman brandishing a scythe to the glory of her dead Tsar.

The old man choked and sank to his knees clutching his face. Another agonizing pain tore from his throat as a heavy boot crashed down onto his groin. He lay on his back trying to form the words of his final prayer and confession when another boot found his chest, shattering his breast bone and tearing open the chambers of his heart.

Sarah lifted her head suddenly and ran to the window. "Leah," she screamed. "Leah, quickly, get up and climb up to the loft. Don't ask. Quickly, quickly!"

Leah picked up her head and fell back in exhaustion.

"You can't lay here," Sarah screamed again pulling Leah by both hands and forcing her up. Quickly! There are people outside! Faster!"

Leah moved to the ladder. "I don't think I can climb it, Mrs. Chernov. I don't . . ."

Through the window, Sarah saw the man carrying Ruth towards the barn. She screamed in her horror and ran to the door, yelling back. "Climb for you life, Leah! Climb and pull up the ladder after you!" She picked up one of the Sabbath candlesticks and ran to the barn waving it in the air.

"Oh, my God, my God! My baby! They have my baby!" A crowd of men and women moved towards the house from another direction.

CHAPTER 23

A gray, pulsating sky in the distance lifted his spirit. Finally, he thought, rain had come to Krivoser and they would not be afraid anymore. Jonah stood and watched the distant shoreline, but as the boat crept closer, the image of the rain cloud took on the appearance of a boney fist menacing the sky. He squinted and leaned slightly towards it, trying to define it. He wiped the sweat from his eyes to make sure of what he thought he saw. Awareness became comprehension and comprehension became a nameless ancient fear that rose out of his soul and strangled him in a silent scream. For a second he felt himself falter and his heart pounded in his chest. He pushed through the passengers who were pointing and screaming at the horizon. He scrambled, hand over hand along the railing towards the prow and leaned forward as if this movement would hasten the boat to the shore.

The boat inched forward. Orange flames licked the darkening sky and the acrid smell of the burning town reached his nostrils. Particles of ash began to fall and his rigid fingers curled in anguish around the railing. He bit down on his lip to fight back his tears, but he could not. He was as helpless as one who stands before a dying friend. His body wavered back and forth in desperation.

Somewhere in that smoldering ruin, somewhere in that charred ruin that had been his home, was his wife and his baby. Somewhere in that smoldering hell was his mother and father and sisters and grandfather. And all he could do was stand there shaking and crying.

Why had he not gotten off the boat when his instinct prompted him to do so? The thought grabbed him like a vise. "Oh, my God," he said as the image of her standing on the shore with her hand resting on her stomach came back to him.

"Leah," he heard himself scream into the thickening air. "Leah," he screamed again and pounded the railings with both fists.

All around him people jostled each other, their faces contorted in their own personal agony of what might be. The boat suddenly stopped. The mass of people surged against the rail and pinned him to it. Then it gave way under the crush and he and other passengers fell into the brown, ash covered water. The boat steadied itself on a sand bar. The ferryman pushed his way through the screaming crowd and exhorted the men in the water climb onto the sand bar and push the boat as he dug his pole into the marshy bottom.

All the air in Jonah's lungs had been expelled with the scream he uttered as he fell into the lake, and when the water filled his nostrils and clogged his mouth, he thought his chest would burst. His fingers tore at the water and he pushed himself upward. He could not die here. He was being judged and he could not appear before God weighted down and condemned by his own inaction, fears and cowardice. He coughed and gagged himself into the air and thrashed his way onto the sandbar. The ferryman called to him to help, but he staggered away from the boat. As he put his hand before his face to shield his eyes from the ash, he fell and got up and fell again, until he was able to swim and thrash and finally scramble to the muddy bank and climbed out of the water.

Then he began to run, more afraid of what lay before him than of the carnage around him. He could feel the heat from smoldering and burning buildings on his back and the soot, mixed with the salt in his sweat, burned his eyes. Through the bleary haze, the setting sun sent explosions of vermilion to the underbellies of gray-purple clouds. He cursed the beauty in his heart. Why was beauty pouring out of the sky and not vengeance? He could see the peasants carrying household goods above their heads and disappearing into the cornfield. He ran past Yavna's tavern. Drunken men and women wallowed near broken vats, laughing at the chaos. He ran past burning homes and women screaming for their children. He ran past the marketplace. The stands and stalls

had been pulled to the center and set aflame. The caked ruts rose
and fell under his urgent stride, and he cursed them and everything. The house and barn in the distance shocked him by its
solitary silence. He gagged and tasted the acid in his mouth, and
the taste was his fear of what he would find. The withered wall of
corn clicked against each other in a mocking dance. A dry wind
blew against his face. An alleyway where the stalks had been
trampled down lay open like hell's mouth and he peered deeply
into the darkening twilight suddenly comprehending the horror
of how such a space came to be. Then he cursed the space, and the
air and time itself.

He was no longer Jonah. He was that other person, that secret
person kept hidden. The Jonah he knew and understood wept and
felt his heart pounding against his shirt till it was like to smash
through, but this other Jonah exploded with a hatred that had
festered in his blood for centuries. Jonah saw the pickets scattered
under his stride and the down from torn mattresses swirl around
him. Crockery he had known all his life, his mother's pride, lay
smashed against the house. His memory raced through the years
that lay on the ground. He ran over things used only on the Sabbath. He ran over things used only on the Passover. The rage surged
through him as he placed his hands on the door jamb and looked
into what only two days ago was the bedrock of his life. Wherever
his eyes rested in the dim gray light, he saw the torn pages of the
beloved books. His fingers dug into the wood until the pain shook
him to another reality at the far side of the room. A stranger crouched
over a silent form. He could make out the anguished profile of
Leah. Out of a dark place in his soul, the thing that also lived in
him lunged up and contorted his face. His eyes burned with the
other's hatred. He could feel his lips silently stretch over his teeth
and his hands reach down for a leg of the table at his foot. Like a
stone-age savage brandishing his crude weapon above his head,
the other Jonah, the savage Jonah, held the table leg aloft and
raced toward the crouching figure, screaming an animal scream of
outrage and anguish.

The stranger turned automatically to ward off the first blow, but the savage was too quick. The club found its mark and Jonah could hear the cracking and splintering of a skull being crushed by a massive blow.

The stranger was dead and fell forward where he kneeled, his eyes open, staring in incredulous wonder. Again, the savage let the club fall again and again and somewhere in its torment, Jonah cried because he had taken someone's life.

He dragged the body to the door and ran back to Leah. He stood there helplessly, his arms hanging limply at his sides. He sank to his knees and sat back on his haunches. He was weeping softly, his hands hovering over her body, not knowing how to touch her and not knowing how to heal her. He rested her against his chest and rocked her back and forth to a silent lullaby as he wept. The room became a vague haze. He looked down at her bruised face. The cracked dried blood on her lips moistened under his tears. How would he live without her? And then, suddenly, he realized that she was not dead.

He put his ear to her breast. He heard her heart beat. He, again, was alive, too. He put his face to her stomach. The child moved against his cheek.

"Leah," he said urgently, "Leah, my darling, Leah." He looked and waited. He listened again. He put his ear near her nostrils and felt her shallow breath.

"Leah, please," he begged, "please, Leah, live." He watched her face for any sign and her lids fluttered but seemed not to have the strength to open. He watched her intently. He raised her hand to his lips and kissed it softly and held it against his cheek. Nothing mattered now other than she lived. How suddenly nothing else in the world was of use. Only her life mattered. The books, the house, his parents, sisters, friends, all thrust out as if his entire life, every element of his conscience and unconscience being, were needed to focus its energy on the one ultimate prayer that she live. He wished his own life out of his body through his hands into hers. He would gladly die if he could save them. She moved ever so slightly. He looked around the room. Tables and chairs were broken shadows. Dishes smashed, feathers everywhere. And the innocent books lay torn and violated like victims of war. Then, his life crowded back. Where were his parents? Where were his sisters? Leah's eyes fluttered and opened to sudden recollection, but her focus was not on him. She screamed and thrashed against imaginary blows.

She pushed at him, not looking at him. "No!" she cried, "I'm going to have a baby. Don't you see . . ." and her voice trailed off to a soft whimper. "No, no, please, for the sake of God, don't hurt my baby." She slowly opened her eyes again.

"Jonah, Jonah," she moaned. "I tried to get away. I tried to climb the ladder when they came in. It was so hard to climb." She hardly paused for breath.

"Sha, sha," he said softly and rocked her gently in his arms. She would be all right now. She was alive and that was all that mattered. "Don't, Leah, don't talk now. Later, we'll talk later."

"They broke through the windows the same time they broke through the door." She continued, oblivious to his plea.

He wanted to hear it all and to hate them completely. Suddenly he remembered that a man lay dead by the door, killed by that hatred. Leah caught her breath and opened her mouth in a soundless cry until all breath was expelled. Then she cried loudly.

Jonah could feel his body shake and he held her closer to calm her. He had to get her to the bedroom. He had to find his mother and father. He had to find his sisters and grandfather. And the man he had killed had to be hidden.

"Leah," he said gently into her ear, "try to get up."

He moved back slowly and carefully to his knees never letting go of her. She was limp.

"Leah," he said again. "Please try."

She cried softly. He looked towards the bedroom door anxiously, and lowered her to the floor. She opened her eyes and clutched at his arm.

"It's all right, Leah, I want to fix up the bedroom so you'll have a soft place."

She relaxed her hold and let her hand slide limply to her stomach.

He stood slowly and looked at her bruised body floating on a sea of torn pages. He picked up the page closest to his foot and reverently pressed it to his lips. A new rush of anger followed by a profound sadness took him as he folded it slowly and put it into his pocket. He would cry over it later.

There was no light in the house and no light from the moon seeped into the room to guide his feet. He moved blindly, feeling totally abandoned. A few embers glowed in the stove and he let them guide him through the maze of broken furniture and crockery to where the candles might be. The flame he lit sent out a tormented light that shook because his hand was shaking.

He was thankful he could not see everything at once. His heart pounded as he pushed the bedroom door aside. He did not want to find anyone in there. He did not know if he would be able to handle more than his pain for Leah.

His parent's bed lay overturned, and the mattress was slashed and thrown against the wall. He set the candle down and his eyes followed it's glow fearfully. He was relieved that the room was empty, but that did not stay his fear. Perhaps they were well hidden, he thought as he pushed hand fulls of feathers into the mattress and placed it on the bed. His crouching shadow startled him. It seemed the shadow of another person, another being, a stranger who had come into the room and overwhelmed the frail image of Jonah Chernov.

He left the candle and moved back through the door for Leah. His eyes quickly accustomed themselves to the darkness. He found her clutching her stomach and whimpering.

"I'm frightened, Jonah, I'm so frightened."

Jonah heard her words but again, thought of the dead stranger. Time had passed and moonlight inched its way through the shattered window making weird roads of light that crisscrossed the room and led his eyes again to the body of the man by the door. What had been done so thoughtlessly, so rashly had suddenly thrust all his tomorrows into the fear of constant discovery.

"Don't think about tomorrow," he heard himself say. "I'm going to lift you up and take you to the bedroom. Put your arms around my neck."

He slowly pulled her to her feet and he thought of how they had stood on the dock only two days ago. Now the whole world had changed. Had he been there to protect her, this would not have happened.

"Oh, Leah," he confessed. "I'm so sorry I went."

He felt her stiffen in his arms. He felt it, and locked her judgment into his sadness as punishment.

"I'm so sorry," he repeated softly, looking back over his shoulder at the silent figure near the door.

He helped her to the bed and she lay down. He sat next to her trying to think of something to say that would ease her fear and quiet his own, but he could not. A dead man lay in the revealing moonlight. His family also cried out for him.

"Leah," he hesitated, "I have to do something important."

She opened her eyes and they looked through him. "I need you, Jonah. What can be more important than me? I'm afraid. Don't leave me."

The image of the man on the floor began to grow in proportion to his fear of discovery. No one must know. It had to be his secret. In secrecy he would find safety for himself and for his family. In secrecy he could buy time to save himself. Anyone who knew of his crime could destroy him with that knowledge and anyone of his family who knew about his crime could also be destroyed.

"It won't take long," and he opened the delicate fingers that clung to his wrist.

"Are you leaving me to look for your mother?" she groaned, and her question, to him, was an accusation and another more lethal judgement.

He begged her silently for her understanding, but she turned away.

"I'll be back soon."

He felt his way back to the other room. He was less concerned about the scattered pages now. The moonlight continued to silhouette the silent figure on the floor. He moved cautiously. Even if the deed were never known, he would still feel like a fugitive. The thought strangely mixed fear with exhilaration. He was a man protecting his wife. He had no choice. A man protects what is his. Finally, he had acted recklessly, but it was without fear. If no one knew of his crime, he would be safe and the deed would be left behind when they went to America. He knelt down to silent shape, secretly hoping it would move, but also fearing it would move. The body was lifeless. He had broken a commandment and he wondered if God would ever forgive him.

'If a man comes to slay you, slay him first.' Could he sustain himself with that? But, had the man come to slay him? There was a gasp from the other room. He moved towards the sound, but stopped himself. Instead, he moved behind the dead man and locked his hands across the man's chest. He struggled and dragged the weight towards the door. Smoke hung in the air and ashes still floated in the haze. He looked around the yard before he continued. No one was there. He dragged the body to the safety of the shadows cast by the barn. Something cracked behind the old wooden slabs. He froze. Cold sweat rose above his lips. His head jerked to the right and to the left. Somewhere in the cornfield low voices sang a drunken paean.

Jonah's eyes shot fire toward the sound as he lugged the body towards it. Now he had to move quickly. The moon was high and its light could witness against him. What if someone hid in the barn? What if his parents were there and his crime was discovered? What if a peasant was still there and accused him of murder? A secret was a secret when only one person knew it. Again, a cracking, as if someone staggered over broken wood. His heart pounded harder, straining against the weight at his chest. He could hear the stranger's black boots make a thumping sound as they dragged across the corduroy road. The cracking of the corn stalks under his feet sounded a new alarm of discovery. Yet, he had to risk moving deep into the field so the body would not be associated with his parent's home.

The field was awash in silver light. When Jonah let the body drop, he saw that at his feet lay the smashed skull of the constable. His eyes widened. His fear and anxiety mixed with regret. Was this man hurting Leah or had he murdered someone who had come to help?

But how could he have known? Now there was no hope of staying. A peasant's death in the horror of the day might be overlooked, but this man's death would not. He lugged the dead man further and further into the field toward the singing of the drunken revelers. He and Leah would have to run. He felt for the tickets in his pocket. He would give her a ticket and keep the other. There would be time. She would be able to travel in a few days and meet him. There would be confusion and she could get lost in it. He would run to Kiev and send for her to meet him there. She would come to Kiev and they would travel together to Copenhagen. It was a good plan. And, perhaps they wouldn't find the body. There would be time.

A cracking again at some distant place shook him back to his need to separate himself from the dead man at his feet. He turned towards the sound and turned again so he would leave the field at a place different from where he entered. If anyone saw him come out, they would not be able to retrace his steps.

He steeled himself against the beauty of the silver light on the dead stalks. He must not see the beauty. He did not want the horror of this night tainted with beauty.

He felt suddenly weak. Whatever strength was there to drag the dead man into the cornfield was gone, and he faltered, staggered, fell, stood again and froze. From behind the stalks, he could see a man moving towards the house. Again, Leah was in danger. The other Jonah grew bold again and would act. Little else mattered. He had killed once to protect her, and he would

again if he had to. He emerged from the sea of barren corn
stalks different from the person who entered it. He could not
change what he had done nor could he earn forgiveness. But if
God could let this horror be unleashed on those who believed
in His goodness with such passion, was this a God of forgiveness? And who would forgive God for having seen and heard
and not interceded? What was the offense? What offense could
have been so great as to have turned God from them? The
thought pressed in on him like a boulder on his chest, and he
felt his faith pushed out of his body and into the ash laden air.
He trembled at his emptiness and staggered on. The corn stalks
became the backdrop, each drenched in a bleached white light;
grim silent spectators to a life suddenly and violently destroyed.
He did not know how to be a criminal. He did not know how
to be a murderer. He no longer even knew how to be Jonah
Chernov. Yet, he stood there against the evil setting, a murderer, a criminal, a potential fugitive from the law and from an
angry and cruel God. Everything was happening so quickly.
Suddenly, there were no choices except the choice to live and
protect what was his. Nothing could wait and he had to be
unafraid for all of them. He would stay and protect them. Yes,
that was a better plan. When the body was found, he would
pretend surprise. As long as only he knew his secret, he could
be safe. He would have to move deliberately and with stealth.
He would have to monitor all feelings and all reactions. Anything might give him away. It would have to be the secret self,
the other Jonah who would help him survive.

He took a deep breath, closed his eyes and opened them again,
trying to find the other presence within. His eyes looked in a new
way and measured and calculated the distance. He scrutinized the
darkness and the outlines of shadows on shadows as an animal
might. A shadow moved. Jonah constricted. The shadow became a
man. Jonah clenched his teeth and breathed deeply. He did not
move in his fear but the shadow did and the shadow became the

shape of his brother- in-law. Jonah released his breath and relaxed. He would not have to test himself against a marauding peasant.

Ezra's face was contorted with pain and fear. The sparse beard was matted with soot and sweat poured out of him.

"I swear I had nothing to do with this," he stammered in his fear. It became more than they said it would be. You'll tell them when they ask you. Won't you, Jonah? Jonah barely heard him through the yammering. Had Ezra had seen him with the body?

Ezra grabbed him by the shoulder suddenly as if confronted by a harsher reality. "I didn't know this was going to happen," he said, his eyes flashing a desperate earnestness. "I didn't want this to happen." His grip tightened and he shook Jonah as if to make him believe. Then Ezra stopped abruptly as if he suddenly realized that he was revealing a secret of his own, a secret that could destroy him.

"I saw you drag that body into the cornfield," he said suddenly waving his finger menacingly, "and don't you think I won't tell them if you tell them what I told you. You've always hated me," he said backing away from Jonah's face, "but you won't hate me anymore. Now you'll fear me for what I know about you, and that witch I married will hang, and I'll find a way to have my child and none of you will ever hurt me again."

Jonah looked at his first true enemy and sifted the words for understanding. How long did he know about Zeena? What confession was he making? Who were the "they" he spoke of and what did he mean by saying, "I didn't know that this was going to happen?" But the questions were overshadowed by the one screaming reality. Ezra had seen him. Now Jonah had to choose to either run to save his life or kill again. But if he killed now, it would be a calculated act and not one at the moment of fear or passion. No rationalization would free him from the truth; he would truly be a murderer. There would be no excuse and no defense. Either he would have to stop Ezra or he would have to run.

"You're crazy, Bendak. You saw nothing!" Jonah peered at the fat, sweaty face hoping that some confusion would register. "I wasn't even in the cornfield."

Bendak let out a shrill laugh. "You want me to think that, but I know better. I saw what you did and I'll tell. Don't imagine I won't. You'll all pay for what you did, Chernov, not me."

"I don't know what you're talking about," Jonah screamed in exasperation as he desperately searched for a plan.

Bendak stiffened and drew back. "I still have what's mine."

He backed away from Jonah and shook his finger at him again. "Yes, yes, I was a fool to have come here thinking I could explain to you and you would understand. You never wanted me in your family. None of you ever wanted me."

Ezra's crazed, disoriented ranting continued as Jonah's thoughts flew blindly back and forth in search of another plan.

"You shouldn't have hated me," he repeated. "Now you see what hate does. Now you see what I can do to people who hate me and soon you'll see what they'll do to you."

Bendak continued to back away from Jonah recognizing he had already said too much. He turned slowly and began to walk and then run.

Jonah watched him and slowly pieced together meaning from his yammering that in some way Ezra Bendak had his hand in the horror that surrounded them. If Ezra could turn on his own people, Ezra would bring the police. He said as much. All were in jeopardy.

He picked up a heavy piece of wood that lay at his feet. Bendak was a pursuer and out to slay him. Ezra had to be stopped. Jonah could not name the evil in Ezra, but he knew it was great. Jonah could not even name the evil within himself, but he knew that if God could choose to watch the evil that befell them today without stopping it, God would not stop the evil that was about to befall Ezra either. Time. He had to buy time. Everything was suddenly thrown into the balances and there was only one choice to make. He did not want to kill again, and Ezra had to be stopped. Everyone's survival depended. His thoughts raced to Leah in her pain. She needed him now. Again, he was the other Jonah, running towards the retreating pursuer, brandishing a club high above his head, screaming out his fear and rage. The blow was struck and Ezra fell and tumbled into the ditch that ran along side the road.

Jonah moved past the barn. At the house, a scream tore the silence, and he bolted into the bedroom. Leah's fingers clawed into the torn mattress beneath her and her screams came between rapid successive explosive breaths. The realization of what was happening hit Jonah like a blast from a furnace. He needed help. He knew nothing of birth. He felt his own stomach rise as he watched her small body agonize from side to side. His mother should be here. She would know what to do. Someone should be here. He could not do this alone, not even for Leah. What if he killed the child? What if he killed Leah? He moved towards her helplessly as another shriek tore from her throat. He tore a piece of cloth and wiped the sweat on her face. She opened her eyes and peered at him in a tortured daze.

"The baby is coming," she gasped. "The baby is coming."

"It will be all right," he replied, trying to assure her, but as always, nothing was right and he could neither make it right, nor ease her pain.

Her face relaxed between contractions, but the pallor of her cheek, and the bruises, spoke of an inner pain he could not even imagine. He watched her closely, pressing her hand tightly to his lips. She was quiet and his mind raced to find his parents and sisters, but he recalled how she had condemned him before, and he was too unstable to risk another judgment. He tried to summon up the other Jonah so he would not feel as afraid or helpless, but it would not come. He thought of Zeena and the circle in the hope that he could link in with her strength, but he remained empty.

Her hand tightened in his and her eyes opened wide with a new agony. "Water," she blurted out. "Get me some water," and she bit down hard and groaned through her teeth.

He could use the moments away from her to look for the family. He moved quickly to the kitchen. He could find nothing amid the broken crockery. He went to the yard. The pump dripped quietly.

Again he could hear the drunken peasants singing in the cornfield and again he cursed them. The tin cup was motionless in the stark moonlight. The creaking pump handle startled him and his hand froze in the fear of being discovered. It was a new fear. He began to pump harder and kept looking over his shoulder.

"Here is the water," he said softly. Jonah knelt and raised her head with his arm. She sipped it and winced when the water touched the cut on her lip. She drained the cup and sighed.

"Please, more, Jonah. Bring more."

He remembered he had seen a pot in the corner of the kitchen and he went there. Another agonizing cry reached through the door. He raced back. Her small body was being shaken again by another contraction.

Jonah took a piece of mattress cloth and tore it. "Here, bite on this."

Her pain subsided and she relaxed her grip on his arm.

"I'll get the water now," he said and got to his feet.

"Find your mother," she moaned. "I need your mother, Jonah. I need your mother . . .I asked you before to find your mother."

Jonah felt his body relax. Her earlier statement was not an accusation.

He moved cautiously to the barn. Flames still licked one side of the outhouse. Again, as before, he stood in the doorway blanketed by the fear of what might be in the darkness and heard a startled gasp and muffled cry. All the skin on his body contracted. He fought his instinct to flee and he leaned into the silent barn.

"Who's there?," he whispered into the blackness with great urgency. There was no response. He leaned further in and stepped forward cautiously. He eyes accustomed themselves quickly. He stumbled and fell to his knees against a soft body. He gasped in terror. He looked down and the shadows etched out the silent form of their little goat. Tears welled up in his eyes at the memory of his old pet and its antics, and his hand stroked the lifeless form.

A muffled sound from the rear of the barn startled him. He tightened his grip on a broken piece of wood and moved towards it hesitantly. All was silent again. He inched his way, straining to focus. Suddenly a figure leaped at him and caught him by the neck. A scream emanated from the figure's throat, the summation of agony and hatred of a lifetime in one guttural cry. The hands closed around his throat and nails sank into him till he let out his own cry of pain. He dropped the club and struggled to pry the hands from his neck. And, as he did, the powerful hands relaxed in recognition.

"Jonah?" screamed Sarah. "Jonah?" she repeated, tearing her hands from his neck. "Jonah?" and she grabbed his face and overwhelmed him with kisses and tears. "You're alive. Thank God, my Jonah is alive. Thank God my son is alive."

Jonah did not move. He was overjoyed but suddenly her hands slid from his face and she covered her own. "Don't look at me," she wept, and she turned away from him.

Jonah did not understand. He reached out to the sobbing woman and touched her. Her shoulders were bare and as he let his hand fall, his fingers felt that her back was bare also. He pulled his hand away.

"Mama, where's Papa and Dora and Ruthie?" he said, his voice urgent. There was silence and then a low, tragic moan that crawled out from the depths of her memory.

"Jonah?" questioned a quiet, tearful voice from the darkness.

He turned towards the sound as Sarah dropped to her knees, asking God how she would live.

"My baby, my baby, my little, little baby," she moaned, clutching her face and babbling at the image of Ruth being held to the ground, her young body violated by a dozen men and boys.

Jonah followed the voice and found his little sister cowering in the corner of the barn.

"Jonah," she said again, as if that was all she could say, and when he bent down towards her, she clasped her arms desperately around his neck as if only her brother's touch would erase the terror of the afternoon.

He knelt and lifted her naked, trembling body in his arms. He recoiled at the caked and still sticky slime on her stomach and thighs, but held her fast. A deeper hatred in him welled up as it had never done before and he forced himself to imagine what must have happened. He wanted to see it. He would not push this away.

"Sha, baby, sha, you'll be . . ." and he cut himself off. "Sha, Ruthie, sha." He moved past Sarah and stopped briefly.

"Mama," he said firmly. "Leah needs you. The baby is coming and I don't know what to do." He spoke with the dispassion of another person.

"Mama," he repeated with more force than urgency. "Leah needs you now!. Mama, I need you!"

He waited. His words fell around her in the silent barn and somewhere found a chink in the wall of Sarah's memory and penetrated. She wiped her eyes with the back of her hands and turned, covering her breasts with her arms. The blood from the crosses slashed onto each, was dry. Her thought was of Reuben and that she could never allow him to see her breasts again.

Jonah averted his eyes as his mother moved past him. He watched her stagger toward the house, stopping now and then to catch her breath.

Jonah turned to his sister. He was numb. Such horror was beyond his comprehension, beyond humanity. He did not believe such behavior possible from human beings, and yet Ruth stood before him, her frail body naked, bloody, and caked with semen. And his mother had been forced to watch her child's body violated over and over again.

The moon sent silver shadows through the cracks in the wood. Krivoser burned and the peasants sang their drunken song of triumph in the midst of the dead cornfield.

Ruth's arms tightened around his neck. He carried her towards the pump in the yard.

"Ruthie," she said gently, and reassuringly. "Let me go so I can wash you."

She clung to him and buried her face in his neck. She began to whimper again. He tightened his hold on her body to reassure her and then released her.

"Ruthie," he said again, remembering with urgency all he had to do. "I want to get you clean. The water will help you feel better." He felt her arms relax and her grip loosen on his neck. She pulled back and looked at him through bruised and tear filled eyes. He could feel his own tears as he looked into the child's tormented face.

"It hurts me, Jonah." She was barely audible. " I hurt all over."

"I know, Ruthie." He did not know what else to say. "I want to clean you off so you'll feel better. The water will make it feel better." .

He spoke to her in a steady and deliberate voice and he concentrated on his words to control the anger that began to rise in him again. He put her down and took the handkerchief from his pocket. The caked blood reconstituted and ran in trickles down her thighs. She seemed not to be aware of what he was doing; as if she had hidden herself away from the memory. She stood empty, like a vacant house. He ran his fingers over her stomach and thighs to make sure the semen was gone.

The image of grunting animals tearing into her defenseless body came to him, and he saw them laughing and sweating as they pushed for their turn on her. And they forced his mother to watch! And what had they done to her? To slash crosses on her breasts! There were no words. He had no words.

Again, in the distance, the rollicking verses of the peasant song rose with new gaiety. Again, Jonah questioned the offense. Again, he hurled the silent question into the void and again, there was no response. He moved a short distance away from her and stared into the blackness. Then he turned and looked back at the child standing silhouetted in the moonlight.

"Why?" he suddenly raged into the endless void above him as the savage within him found its voice. "Whhhhy . . .?" he screamed again and all the fear and pain and anger for Leah and his mother and Ruth and himself tore out of his throat like a frightened beast about to attack. "Whhhhy . . .?" he exploded a third time, hurling his fierce anger towards heaven and the cornfield. His scream of anguish was the same as Zeena's scream poured out years ago in this very same field and this very same void.

He ran to the smoldering outhouse and picked up a burning piece of timber. Now, the savage in Jonah had a new weapon. He ran to his hill, brandishing the burning taper above his head and screaming his mindless outrage at God for the brutality of the judgment.

"I curse Your name!" he shrieked into the night. "I curse You for Your silence and for Your lies to us. I curse You for Your outrageous vengeance and I curse You for watching and doing nothing!"

As he reached to top of the mound, the part he had always imagined closest to heaven, he flung the burning stick as high into the black sky as his power would allow. He wanted heaven to explode in flames.

"Burn!" he screamed. "Burn!"

He stood there shaking, his eye stabbing the night with his anger and his teeth bared in defiance. The burning stick turned over and over against the blackness.

"Why did you let this happen to us?" he panted, and watched the torch fall unceremoniously a few yards away. Suddenly, he recognized, in this foolish act of defiance, his own impotency to effect anything in the world. His hands fell limply at his sides and he wept. Heaven had not caught fire, and if there was a God that saw or heard, He would not be moved. The earth rotated silently and the stars remained oblivious to passion. He was caught and powerless and insignificant and had only himself and a brutal reality. He did not yet know how to deal with this, but he did know that if he allowed the despair of being totally alone and helpless to overwhelm him, he would be lost and useless, and those who were even more helpless than he would be deprived of any hope. He turned back towards his sister.

Taking Ruth by her hand, he led her to the house. His foot touched the tattered Sabbath cloth and he picked it up reverently and touched it to his face. He wanted to cry but he dared not. He merely placed the shredded cloth around Ruth.

Another agonizing scream tore at his ears as they crossed the threshold. He led Ruth to a corner and sat her gently down.

From somewhere, Sarah had found candles and placed them around the room. A fire burned in the stove and he could see his mother move from Leah to somewhere else and back again.

Jonah came into the room.

"Find the bucket and put water on the stove. Then go find your father." Sarah's voice was direct and filled with authority and Jonah felt strangely comforted by it. He watched her wipe Leah's brow again, and turned to the door as another guttural explosion tore through his wife's clenched teeth.

He picked up the pot where it had fallen and moved back into the night and he was suddenly confronted with his hatred. Before him lay a blazing cornfield. Like fiery serpents, the fire he hurled up to heaven had coiled itself around the dead corn stalks and squeezed each into burning submission. The fire then inched down and spread to the right and left around the drunk and sleeping peasants until its poisonous viper head flicked its tongue on its own tail. Inch by inch by inch, the inferno had constricted upon the empty space, and the space where they lay was slowly displaced by the searing breath of Jonah's fierce retribution.

His mouth dropped open. Above the cracking and the sizzling of the flames, he could hear the shrill cries of people surrounded by walls of inextinguishable death. The pot fell from his hands and he moved forward instinctively to help them, but he stopped. For an instant he regretted what his hand had done out of hate, but it was only for an instant. He threw away the image of those out there as people. They were beasts who raped his sister and forced his mother to watch. They were animals who beat his wife. Jonah would not let himself imagine anything else, but took a strange pleasure in knowing that the same God who looked away when His followers brought their savagery through the cornfield to Jonah's people, would also look away with disinterest as these servants writhed in the agony of feeling their flesh burned on their bones. And Jonah became sure of this: God looked down with disinterest as His suffering servants butchered His other suffering servants. Jonah suddenly knew that the world was insane and that God chose not to make it sane. He no longer knew what would dictate the direction of his life. If God chose to be silent, one could expect either good or evil and do nothing for it. But one could not do nothing, even if one was terrified to act. Jonah knew that. He had not acted for Zeena, and this is what had happened. It had nothing to do with God. It had to do with his inaction and his mother's anger and Ezra's hate. People caused the chaos. His own rage had made him kill and kill again. The world was suddenly empty, like Ruth's eyes. God had nothing to do with it.

An urgent voice called from the house. He picked up the pot and raced to the pump. His eyes followed down the wall of the raging inferno before him and in the distance, like some black demon etched in orange flame rising out of hell, he could make out the rotund figure of Ezra Bendak struggling out of the ditch and staggering down the road towards the town. Bendak would bring the police. He had to be stopped. But Leah needed him, and his mother's voice was insistent. He pumped for water furiously. It splashed over his hands. He saw his hands holding the pot and he saw himself moving towards the house. Destruction belonged to others. The horror should have taken a life time to happen, not an hour. He was just a tailor, a young foolish man who should have been happily welcomed home by his wife and family after a trip to the city. The shrieks from those entombed in the flames pierced the night and tore through his head. He had no time. Ezra would bring the police and they would charge him with murder. They would believe Ezra's story about him lugging a body into the cornfield because they would want to believe it. He would be killed standing in the yard. They were all in danger. Perhaps Ezra also saw him throw the fire into the field. They would charge his family as his accomplices. He could take no chances. He had to run at that very moment. If he saw Leah again or looked into Ruth's eyes, he would not have the courage to leave them. No one could be accused with him if he was not there. Bendak would be thought a fool and dismissed as a angry husband wanting to get even with his wife's family. Jonah would run and everyone would be safe. He would be of no use to anyone dead. Something or someone inside him repeated that over and over and his thoughts became random and ran in a thousand different directions. He would run to save Zeena, and he would run to save his family. But, it was not really for Zeena that he would run, nor was it really for Leah or Ruthie or his mother's safety. He would run because he did not want to die.

He would remember the suddenness of insanity and how everything that is dear can suddenly be lost in the face of possible death. He would choose life, even if his choice might brand him a coward in their eyes. Alive, he might be able to be of value to someone and make something right. Dead, he was of no value to anyone.

CHAPTER 24

When Jonah could run no further, he fell back against a tree so his legs would not buckle. His sides ached and he gasped for breath. The distant sky glowed a faint orange and he turned from it quickly, like Lot, daring not to look on it and daring not to think about what he had done. He tried to comfort himself with the thought of Leah, but her face contorted in pain, accused him for abandoning her. Ruth's vacant eyes, wondered at him. His thoughts raced to Zeena again, but his image of her just added to his belief that he was responsible for the horror.

The stench of smoke clung to his clothing and he could feel the soot on his neck mingling with the sweat running down his back.

He moved into the black break of trees for concealment and pealed off his grimy shirt and undergarments. He hung his trousers and jacket over a branch and moved slowly down to the lake, cradling the rest of his clothing. A chill ran through him though the air was hot, and he turned from side to side to see if anyone lurked in the darkness.

He waded into the rippling, moonlit water up to his waist and knelt down. He floated his clothing and rubbed them between his hands, dipping them again and again until the soot was gone. Then he rubbed his hair and skin until he felt the grime float away. He took a deep breath and lowered himself so he was totally immersed. He thought of the ritual bath near the synagogue. Now he truly had sin to wash away in the rippling silver water. He wanted to emerge cleansed of his last hours, and the sin of murder. He stood up. The water silently cascaded down his body. He waited to feel something, but only the emptiness and fear engulfed him.

He gathered the floating clothing and out of his shirt floated the square prayer shawl. He let the other clothing fall from his hand as he clutched the fringed piece of cloth, brought it to his eyes and wept into it. He was alone, more alone than he thought anyone could be. He was unclean and there was no power on earth or in heaven to cleanse him or make him whole again. He slowly lowered the prayer shawl from his face and let it float out of his hand. A sudden rush of anger filled him and he picked up a boulder near his foot and smashed it down on the fringed square. He was at a funeral, a funeral for something he had dearly loved and lost. The prayer for the dead sprang to his lips and a few words shattered the hot, silent air but again, he shook it out of his mouth as he had shaken the images of his wife and sisters out of his mind. The anger stopped him. He would not mourn this thing that died. At another time, perhaps, he would decide what had been lost and what needed to be uttered, but not now. He kept his eyes riveted to the place where the prayer shawl had disappeared. His eyes darted over the water and whatever in him that was innocent, ached for it to rise up and be a sign to him that he had been forgiven and that God still controlled the universe. But the water rippled over the place and in a moment he was not even sure where it sank out of sight. Then turning and picking up the rest of the clothing, he waded back to the shore.

He dressed. The wet cloth against his body chilled him but was welcome. He felt better, but knew that neither reality nor sin could be washed away. To be clean again, to be whole again, he would have to do more than splash a little water on his body.

He moved cautiously through the trees, stopping from time to time to listen. When he turned to look back, there was barely a glow in the sky. He thought of leaves that were driven before a wind and saw himself swirling and caught up in the chaos. The short distance and brief period of time he had put between himself and his loved ones suddenly became a vast, unpassable chasm over which he would always see that vermillion sky. He had made the only choice he could have made. He had chosen to live. That was the supreme commandment. He did the only thing he could have done. He clung to the thought for the shred of comfort it briefly provided.

The shadow of the depot building was stark in the moonlight. He would wait and hide and jump on any train moving to Kiev. Hours later, a freight train slowed and he lunged from his hiding place and ran towards it. He could barely pull himself over the ledge of the open door as it chugged past the station. Within, he found a soft pile of clean hay and flung himself onto it. Every part of him ached. A rush of air through the slats encircled his body as the train accelerated. He felt somewhat safe. He closed his eyes to concentrate on the wind, to calm himself and be carried away, but the image that leaped at him in the darkness was not of the peace of the black night, or the moon or stars, but the rage of the fire and his imaginings of people being consumed. He pushed himself to his feet as if to defend himself against the terrible thought that whenever he would close his eye, he would see the flames. He felt himself constrict. Were the tormented screams of those surrounded by flame and death to ring in his ears all the waking moments of his life and torment him in his dreams? Would this be his punishment? He pushed himself against the slats and looked out at the stars. There was no order or reason and anything might be true.

"Damn You!" he screamed into the blackness when he could control his rage no longer. "You watch people destroy each other and you do nothing! Nothing! Is the judge of all the world not to deal justly?" he demanded. Jonah's fingers clutched the horizontal slats of the train and he pressed his face against the opening. "Where is Your righteousness and Your responsibility to us? Jonah gasped for breath. "You have to be responsible, also. You cannot free yourself from your obligation with silence!" he screamed defiantly.

Again, as before, there was no answer and the stars looked down upon the moving train in all their luminous grandeur. Jonah again recognized the futility of his rage and turned slowly and put his hands deep into his pockets and sank back on the straw. He felt a piece of paper and remembered the moment he had placed it there. Again, he saw the room and began to weep. He slowly withdrew the single leaf from his trousers and moved back into the silver light. He opened the torn page and held it so he could read.

"Have I not commanded thee?" it began, "Be strong and of good courage; be not afrighted, neither be thou dismayed; for the Lord thy God is with thee withersoever thou goest."

The Hebrew letters squirmed through tear filled eyes. The sliver of paper fell from his fingers and was whisked up by a gust of wind and carried out into the night.

Jonah awoke suddenly when the train lurched and switched tracks. Dawn was breaking over the buildings in the distance. He heard voices outside moving along the cars and he pulled himself into the far corner covering himself with straw until they passed. He held his breath and did not breathe easily until the train began to chug its way towards the city limits. When it reached the most outlying buildings, Jonah crept over to the door and slid it aside. Somewhere in the distance a whistle blew announcing its arrival into the station. Again, it slowed. Jonah stuck his head out and looked to the right and left. He saw no one and climbed down.

A sudden breeze stirred up some dust and he put his hand over his mouth to stifle a cough. He looked up and down the tracks again and followed close to the train as it rolled towards the station.

Jonah made his way to the mercantile area and sat on a bench until the shops opened. He heard a clock bell strike six. He closed his eyes and dozed as the morning breeze caressed him. A pigeon cooed and flew up. The clock tower struck seven. He opened his eyes. People walked along the tree lined boulevard. He watched them. A small dog ran up, looked at him, and ran off at its masters voice. An old woman appeared and scattered crumbs. The pigeons returned and clustered around her feet. She gave a toothless grin to Jonah and he smiled back. The clock tower chimed eight.

He stood and dusted himself off. He took a breath and slowly walked in the direction of Epstein and Grushansky's. He was hungry. He approach the store, having already decided that if he appeared as if he had business there, he would not be suspect. He tried the door. It was locked. His knees felt weak.

Jonah turned and walked to the edge of the street and sat on a bench. He waited. In a short time a well dressed man, not much older than his father, strolled down the street and up to the door and opened it. Jonah stood and watched the man enter. He looked up and down the street, but there was no one there. He walked quietly to the store and followed the man in. A bell above the door announced him. The man turned in surprise.

"I am not open for business yet," he said, studying Jonah over his glasses.

"Good, good morning," Jonah said hesitantly. "I am looking for . . ."

"You look familiar," the gentleman said cautiously. "You are Reuben Chernov's son." He held out his hand in greeting. "I am Abraham Epstein," he said, taking Jonah's hand warmly and shaking it.

"I am Jonah, Mr. Epstein.

"Well, how can I help you, son of my friend?" he said, looking at Jonah's disheveled appearance. "My young friend," he continued, "what has happened to you?"

"I need your help, Mr. Epstein. My sister is in terrible, trouble."

"But she is a happily married girl. I was at her wedding. What kind of trouble could she be in?"

Jonah swallowed hard and looked through the window to see if anyone was coming. He moved closer to the man in front of him.

"My sister, Zeena Chernov is the Zeena Bendelevitch who is being held in St. Petersburg by the police."

Mr. Epstein looked at him incredulously and backed up against the counter.

"Are you sure?" he said looking past Jonah at the door. The elder man seemed to shrink before Jonah's eyes.

"Yes, sir," Jonah replied, "and my father said you might know someone who might help her."

"I am watched by the police since my partner was taken," he said nervously moving to the door to see if anyone was there. "I cannot help you." He shook his head as he spoke.

Jonah felt his insides collapse.

"But you and I are the only people who can help her," Jonah pleaded. "I must help her! You must help me! You are the only person to whom I can turn."

"I cannot get involved in this," the old man countered and he moved around the counter so it separated them.

"But my sister will die if I do not do something to help her. In America there are Socialist rallies and petitions to save her. There are rallies in other countries, too. I read the papers. They believe in her innocence."

"People rally for their own reasons and your sister's guilt or innocence may or may not be a factor. The Socialists believe in Socialism, and would rally behind anyone who would supply them with a reason to destroy a monarchy."

"Then I don't care what they believe in," Jonah said quickly. "I know only that they are trying to save her and I cannot stand here and do nothing."

"You are either very brave or very foolish Mr.Chernov, but I cannot help you without risking my life and my family."

"Then who can help me?" Jonah demanded, his tone urgent and bordering on threat. He was beyond his quiet respect for age and beyond his fear for his own safety. This man was his only vehicle to whatever secret powers existed out there and he refused to be hindered in his efforts or overwhelmed by despair. He could feel the rage building in his chest, a rage against a man who shrank from the obligation to help someone in need. The old man saw the transformation in Jonah's eyes and became frightened.

"If I tell you who to contact," he said quickly, "will you promise never to come back here again?"

"I swear I will not come back if you help me."

Mr. Epstein looked at Jonah and saw the features of his old friend in the son's face, and his fear became shame.

"Find a man named, Serge Dagillov. He owns a cloth mill on Petrochka Square. Go there and talk about buying a special cloth. When he asks you the type of cloth you wish to purchase you will tell him it is cloth to make uniforms for your workers. He will ask you the color and you will say, red. He will say that it will be a difficult color to get, but you will say that it is the will of the people that they have that color. Then you will tell him what you have told me. He is the only person I know who can help you here."

Jonah looked at him, shook his head and backed away. "I need some money for food and lodging. I will make sure you are paid back."

The man put his hand into his coat and pulled out several bills. He pushed them across the counter towards Jonah and backed away slightly as if from a thief. Jonah picked to bills up without taking his eyes off Mr. Epstein.

"My regards to your father," the old man called as Jonah went through the door. Jonah turned slowly but said nothing. A moment ago this man would have stood idly by as his sister died and now he calls out greetings to the girl's father. Suddenly all people in the world became suspect. He turned to the left and began to walk. He had been on Petrochka Square with his father before. It was about two miles away.

"You must understand, Mr. Bendelevitch," Serge Dagillov continued, considering Jonah more an opportunity than a person, "that I am sympathetic to your situation and your sister's plight, but if I am to plead your case before my associates, I must have some commitment from you to do something for us in return. Perhaps you will agree to speak of our movement and generate support for us as well as for your sister. Mr. Bendelevitch, we are not a charity organization. You do for us and we do for you. Those are the conditions."

"But she is innocent and I know she supports the Socialist movement. Surely that is enough to want to help her," Jonah protested. "Besides, I know nothing of speaking in public. I have never spoken in public. I'm a tailor."

"My fine young man," Dagillov said, putting a heavy hand on Jonah's shoulder. "Let me be perfectly clear about this so we do not misunderstand each other." He paused and heaved a sigh. "You and your sister are totally unimportant. Young people such as yourselves die each day under the hooves or blades of the Tsar's soldiers. Sadly, we are all expendable. Only the cause is of value. If you can accept this fact, and the fact that we are all fodder in the cannon of history, then I will bring you before our committee and place your offer to plead our cause, and your sister's cause, in eastern Europe. If you cannot accept our conditions, then I will shake your hand and wish you all good luck in your efforts." He paused for a response.

Jonah wanted to strike him across his face for his brutal insensitivity. No one was expendable. No one was fodder. How could a cause be raised above the lives of individuals? He wanted to leave, but he knew he could not. He had no alternative. He had to do as this man wished because it was his only way of helping Zeena and himself.

"You speak and read German?

"Yes," said Jonah, thinking of his father.

That evening, Mr. Dagillov stood before a long rectangular table upon which stood a single candle whose light illumined only hands. Jonah, like the others assembled, also sat in darkness so the identities of those he heard shifting uncomfortably in the shadows would remain a secret. Dagillov addressed the seven men who had hastily gathered at his request.

"Gentlemen," he said rather formally. "The preliminary inquiry into the murder of the Tsar was concluded yesterday and our old friend, Colonel Karpov, will be one of the state prosecutors before the tribunal."

Jonah could make out that two of the men squirmed and straightened in their chairs at the name, and another made a guttural sound of disgust.

"It is also reported that Jeliabov, Yekovsky and the Perowski woman have confessed."

"The idiots!" one of the men exclaimed. "How could they be so stupid as to confess? They hand themselves over to the hangman and put the rope around their own necks."

"I heard there were others," another said, "a person named Michailoff and a pregnant woman named Zeena Bendelevitch."

"I never heard of her," another said. "She is not one of us."

"None of us have heard of her," replied Dagillov, "and that is why I have called you this evening. Of all of them, she alone maintains her innocence, which tells me she has been placed in this position for political reasons. This Count Perowski, the father of the other woman, implicates her and swears she bewitched his daughter."

"To what purpose?" challenged a man puffing a cigar.

"Because he wishes to shift the blame from his daughter to this other woman."

"I would do the same for my daughter if I had the choice," he said blowing a large puff of smoke toward the candle. "Besides, I hear she's a Zhid and as for the Zhids . . .well . . .one less Zhid in the world is . . ."

"You are without principle," interrupted a man who stood suddenly.

Dagillov rapped the table. "We are not here to fight each other, gentlemen."

"If you knew Karpov as we know Karpov, you would understand. And keep your attitude toward the Jews out of this!" He took his seat.

"Gentlemen, please. General Karpov is the fist of Alexi Malinovitch and a sworn enemy of the Will of the People Fellowship. Karpov is a virulent Jew hater and was the force behind the recent attacks on Jewish towns in the Pale of Settlement, as well as the author and enforcer of the letters of transit for Jews traveling outside the Pale. The little Colonel will use the Bendelevitch woman to institute additional repressive measures that will strangle us as well."

"Why do you persist in being concerned about the damn Zhids?" said the man with the cigar.

"We worry," said Dagillov, "because we are all struggling against the tyranny and the Jews will be with us because they have nothing to lose. Furthermore, the Jews are the traditional target, and treatment of the Jews is the barometer for the treatment of others. If they begin heavy persecution because of this Bendelevitch woman, the next persecutions will be of the peasants and workers. It has always been that way."

"Then the Zhids are a good buffer between us and the government. Let them bear the fist."

"What kind of idiocy is this?" another shouted. "Our aim is to eliminate hate from the world and the barriers between groups. How can you say you support our cause and hate one of the groups our cause seeks to free from the tyranny?"

Jonah wished he could see the man who was speaking and he wished he could see the man whose cigar smoke hung over the table like a shroud. He was angry that even here where people professed to believe in making a better world for everyone, there were still those who would or could not give up their hatred. Jonah wondered what a Jew had done to the man with the cigar that he would so hate. He wondered if he would ever understand.

"Gentlemen, we must always remember that it is the Tsar and his government that is our enemy. He paused. "Now I would like to propose something to you. There is a young man waiting here who is the brother of this Zeena Bendelevitch. He has agreed to bring our message directly to the people in eastern Europe who may be supportive of our cause in exchange for our supporting his effort to save his sister. I, for one, think it's something to consider. Because he is related to this woman, he is a curiosity and people will flock to hear him and be sympathetic. If he is, at the same time, delivering our message along with his own, well, it seems to me we can spread our word more easily. I see it as a good investment."

"What does he know of us or the Fellowship?"

"He will be given speeches as he arrives in each city. He has agreed to read them as they are written and he has agreed to carry our resolutions from place to place."

"And how will he be financed?" Jonah heard someone say.

"By the usual methods, only the money we currently put into pamphlets we will transfer to his expenses. I have always told you that unless we begin to develop a sympathetic ear outside of Russia for our cause, nothing of meaning will happen here because the outside world will not know of our plight, or care."

The man with the cigar struck a match, lighting up his reddened fleshy face. "And what makes you think this person is a good speaker and why should he have this extended vacation when we sit here in Kiev and sweat?"

"I will vote for him because you will vote against him," one of the men said quickly. And again there was a murmur around the table.

"He has several things in his favor," Dagillov replied. "First, and foremost, he has a sister to save and a compulsion to do it. That compulsion to save a life matches any motivation here to overthrow the Tsar. We, gentlemen, meet secretly, and disappear without knowing the name or face of the one who sits at our side. He will be in the light wherever he goes and will be known to the authorities. And finally, gentlemen, as we return to the safety of our homes, and the warmth of our families, he will move from city to city. Not one of you around this table can assume such a role for us."

"I still think it's a waste of money," said the man behind the smoke.

"Then gentlemen," said Dagillov, "shall we vote?"

Jonah sat in a numb silence and felt like a thing.

CHAPTER 25

He awoke suddenly to the darkness of a strange room and lay there in the residue of an evil dream of Zeena that would not leave him though his eyes were opened. The images of the past days mixed with it.

And, there was something more that he could not speak of or identify. It was as if the thing he had always feared, the thing that lived secretly within him, the thing he had always suppressed, had climbed out and wrapped itself around his body and clung to him with steel talons. He trembled within and he trembled without.

A soft knock at the door startled him and he felt his body constrict as if the thing that clung to him took a breath. He lay there in the silence, too frightened to move.

He heard it again and stood up.

"Who is there?" he whispered with his ear to the door.

"A friend of the people," came the response.

Jonah's hand hesitated as he reached out for the latch and then for the knob. The door creaked back and a satchel was thrust through the opening.

"All you need is inside. Do not be late for the train." The man disappeared without allowing Jonah to see his face or know his name.

Jonah locked the door quickly and opened the satchel. Within was a new suit of clothes, shirts, underwear, a hat, coat, tie and several collars. An envelope containing money, a letter of introduction, one of transit, and an Austrian passport with the name Jonah Bendelevitch, fell onto the bed. The train ticket was in the inside pocket, as was a note to him.

"You are to be on the evening train to Vienna tomorrow.

You are to speak to no one. When you arrive you are to stand under the clock near gate eight. You will be contacted with your speech, where you are to deliver it, a hotel address, money, and a ticket to the next city. You will not receive further instruction."

Jonah felt strangely excited. He had stepped into political intrigue and passion far removed from his life and understanding. This new stage upon which he had placed himself would either prove him or bury him. Again he threw everything into the balances. The image of seeing himself beaten and killed, continued to confirm his belief that the action he took was the only reasonable one to take. Dead he would be able to do nothing for anyone and he believed this with all his heart. Yet, his shame was very real despite his belief. Leah would have to understand the nature of balances and the extremes that the balances sometimes hold. At the very bottom, the choice to live had to be the ultimate weight in the scales.

There was a pocket watch in the vest pocket and he thought of Zedde and Dora. It was time to dress and take the next step. He was unsure of what new feelings and events would fall upon the balances as he moved forward, but he knew that whatever he was able to rectify, the past choices would weigh heavily.

He dressed quickly and looked in the mirror. His old clothes were in the satchel, still faintly stinking of smoke and death. He would toss them from the train.

He opened the door and looked up and down the hallway before inching his way to the stairwell. The bill had already been paid, so he avoided the desk.

On the streets of Kiev, he was dressed as any gentleman, so he did not feel as he had felt when he arrived. He passed the bench that only two days ago he had sat upon as a frightened child wondering how he would proceed and if he would survive. He picked up his pace as if to put distance between himself and the recollection.

Kiev swirled around him in all her excitement and wonder . He thought of how he would have liked to visit here with Leah and sit at one of the little cafes watching the people stroll by. He would have dressed Leah as one of the ladies and she would have outshone the most beautiful of them all. Together they would have attended the theater or listened to the music of the great Tchaikovsky.

At the entrance to the train station, he bought a newspaper and hungrily scanned the pages for any word of Zeena.

ST. PETERSBURG, August 2.

"One of the chief organizers of the attack upon the Tsar, Jeliabov, freely confessed his complicity after being shown the corpse of the German, Hartmann. A cheese shop in the Little Garden Street has been discovered as a secret repository of Nihilist weapons and propaganda. As soon as the police appeared, a male occupant of the apartment, named Petrovskaya, shot at the police before turning the gun on himself. The police found a number of bombs, grenades, and a proclamation stating the assassination had been accomplished by Hartmann, Jeliabov and Perowski. A man named Kibaltchitich has been taken into custody and confessed to having made the bombs. He will stand trial with the others. A student, Ivan Russakov, lurking nearby was taken in for questioning as he carried inflammatory proclamations."

Jonah folded the paper and moved to the gate to wait. His heart pounded when a police officer passed and he lifted the paper to project the image of one lost in the business of the world.

"Your ticket please," the uniformed man said.

Jonah handed it to him along with his passport. The agent looked briefly at Jonah and then back to the papers.

"Will you be returning to Russia?" he asked flatly.

"Perhaps in a week, perhaps two," Jonah answered, feeling his face flush.

"On business?" the man continued.

"Yes, on business," Jonah said somewhat relieved that the officer neither looked at him, nor seemed to care.

The man touched his hat and handed Jonah back his papers and nodded to the woman behind him. Jonah quickly climbed to the train, and finding his compartment empty, quickly closed the door and sat in silence. He watched the people on the platform wave to loved ones and follow them as they moved down the corridor to compartments. Again, he was aware that he was very much alone with no one to wish him well on his journey. He thought of Leah as she waved to him a whole lifetime ago, and he pulled his jacket tight around himself and put his feet up on the seat in front of him. It would be a very long ride. He wanted someone to come in, but he was also fearful that conversation might cause him to reveal something. He waited, but no one entered. Soon he fell asleep.

The next time he spoke to another person, beyond monosyllabic responses to assorted minor officials, it was to a Mr. Schwabb, owner of a beer hall notorious for its open welcome to those expounding revolution and liberalism.

"Well, Mr. Bendelevitch," he said, his voice louder than necessary. "Our friends in Russia seem to think that you may have something to tell us about how to overthrow governments." He laughed and poured Jonah a beer.

"No, sir," said Jonah, feeling uncomfortable. "I am not a revolutionary. I've come primarily to speak on behalf of my sister and enlist the aid of people to help me pressure the Russian government to release her. She is not guilty. Others, perhaps, are to speak on revolution, but not I."

"Oh," Schwabb said. "Perhaps I've misunderstood," and he laughed again, a laugh that Jonah felt mocked him.

There was an uncomfortable silence as Mr. Schwabb drained his glass.

"Mr. Schwabb," Jonah said. "The man who gave me the ticket did not give me my speech. I was told I would be given something." He paused, feeling somewhat foolish. "I have never spoken before a group before and I was hoping that someone would be here with the speech I was promised."

"It just so happens that I have it right here," he said, and took some pages from the inside of his jacket. "I hope you read German, Mr. Bendelevitch, because that's all I write."

Jonah shook his head as he took them.

Mr. Schwabb moved around the counter to a large bell hanging behind Jonah, and rang it. Jonah jumped.

"Gentlemen, gentlemen, your attention, please!" he called loudly.

"Mr. Schwabb," Jonah whispered, "I haven't had time to read or understand this. I need a few minutes to . . ."

"No time, no time," he laughed and started clanging a large brass bell that hung next to Jonah's ear.

"Gentlemen, tonight we have with us a young man from Russia who is the brother of the woman who helped strike the blow for freedom."

There was an outbreak of applause and calls of approval. Jonah reached up and put his hand on Schwabb's arm to silence him, but the large man continued.

"The glory of the nineteenth century was consummated in St. Petersburg. Do I rejoice in the death of the Tsar? Of course I rejoice in his death and every man with correct thoughts, every man of intelligence in both hemispheres, rejoices in the event. It is the tyranny; it is an epoch in history; it is the grandest deed of a hundred years!"

Schwabb raised his hands above his head victoriously, but his eloquence was interrupted by shouts for beer, accompanied by boisterous laughter and applause.

"We know what you've got to say, Schwabb," someone yelled.

Schwabb laughed and waved his hands at the motley, late night gathering.

"To the death of the Tsar and all tyrants like him," another shouted, and half the group raised their beer steins in the air and guzzled the contents.

Jonah looked at them. He was uncomfortable and did not like these people. He felt very much out of place.

"And now I give you Jonah Bendelevitch," and he turned to the thin, pale, uncomfortable figure.

Jonah cleared his throat with a feeble cough.

"I have come here this evening," he began, "to tell . . ."

"Louder," came an interruption, "speak up!"

Jonah cleared his throat again and yelled, "Gentlemen!"

People laughed and those who had not taken notice of him looked up. Jonah laughed also and felt a bit more at ease. Mr. Schwabb stood by the beer barrel, his shirt sleeves rolled up above his elbows. He motioned for Jonah to continue and laughed with a man near him.

Jonah looked at the pages and began to read loudly.

"There can be no regret," he began, "for the world, or the suppressed people of that world, that a tyrant has died. Like the ancient king, Tsar Alexander had been put on the scales and found wanting."

Jonah was interrupted again by loud shouts of approval. In that moment he realized he did not want to say this. He did not believe that anyone should rejoice in someone's death. They applauded him for telling them that it was good to kill! What terrible people they were. Schwabb motioned him to continue with fatherly approval on his face.

"He was executed," Jonah said hesitantly, "by the progressive spirit of the nineteenth century which he tried to smother. He has sent thousands of the best and noblest and most brilliant men to Siberia and the gallows. He had to be stopped."

There was another explosion and calls for more beer. Jonah's contempt for them grew. He quickly scanned the page that dealt with how much more the Tsar should have suffered. He would not read it. It was a brutal thing to say and he was not a brutal person.

"The Tsar is no more," he continued in his own words, "but the back of oppression is not broken. Another Tsar sits on the throne in St. Petersburg." Jonah was surprised by his own words and the passion with which he delivered them. "You are not to rejoice," he screamed at them, "because my sister is being held by this new Tsar without cause. No change has been brought about through the murder of the father. Now there is the son who has quickly demonstrated his skill at injustice."

Jonah paused. He sensed something was happening. People were starting to listen to him. There was no demand for beer and there was no raucous laughter.

"I come before you to ask your help." Again he waited and began to sense the importance of space between thought. "My sister is not a murderer though you would have her be one. I do not know why or how she was taken into custody, but I know that she had no contacts in the Nihilist movement. And I know she would never have killed anyone. I can tell you that she is being held for reasons other than the murder. Perhaps she is being accused because she is weak and provincial and of the people. Perhaps she is being accused symbolically, and with her all the downtrodden people stand accused. Perhaps they want to kill her as the symbolic act of killing us all."

Jonah watched them. They seemed to lean in and hang on his words, and he felt a strange sense of power. "By putting her on trial, they put us on trial. By convicting my sister they convict us all. If we stand by and do nothing to save her, we are placing the rope around our own necks as well."

The beer hall again exploded with applause. Schwabb also applauded him. Jonah stood there not knowing what to do next. They wanted more and he had no more. He had no idea of how he dared say what he had said. Schwabb urged him on.

"I need your help," he continued. "My sister needs your help. All powerless people need your help." He looked at Schwabb who pointed to the papers. Jonah saw on the third page an announcement of a rally to be held in two days.

"You can help me and my sister by coming to the Germania Garden Meeting Hall on Thursday at eight o'clock in the evening." He quickly scanned the page. "Speeches will be given in German,

English and Russian. Come and rally for Zeena Bendelevitch and for the cause of justice and freedom for all the powerless people in the world. Let all Socialists join hands the world over and show them that the powerless can become strong."

Schwabb moved into Jonah's space while continuing his applause, encouraging the others to follow. They rose to their feet. They would help him. They only needed to hear the right words, his words. He did have the right words to save Zeena! His father had given them to him.

CHAPTER 26

A cordon of guards stood before the heavily carved door to the courtroom and watched as each person holding a ticket was scrutinized, questioned, and allowed to enter. The fifteen journalists admitted were again reminded by an official standing near their seats that they were to confine themselves to the external circumstances of the case only. One leaned over and spoke softly of the life sized portrait of the late Tsar, draped in black, that hung prominently in the hall. The space usually occupied by the jury held invited guests, Prince Pierre of Oldenburg; General Milionton, Minister of War; M. Abaza, Minister of France; M. Solski, the Imperial Controller, and General Alexi Malinovitch, head of the police.

When Senator Fuchs of the High Court of Causation entered with four assisting senators, all stood and waited, as he and his assistants seated themselves in the gilt chairs on the high dais.

Michael Turchenko, Prosecutor of the District Tribunal, and Colonel Karpov murmured to each other and scrutinized the priests of various faiths who had been summoned to administer the oaths to the sixty-five witnesses and eleven experts of their respective creeds.

Gendarmes with drawn swords stood close to the prisoners dock. The prisoner's faces, save one, were impassive. Zeena, alone, looked drawn and sallow and fearful. She stood wedged between Jeliabov and Michailov. Sophia sat at the end of the row near Kibaltchitich and Yekovsky.

The Prosecutor of the District Tribunal, Turchenko, rose and walked to the dais, and after bowing to Senator Fuchs, turned to begin the reading of the indictment.

"You are charged with belonging to a secret society . . ."

Jeliabov leaped to his feet. "Your Honor," he interrupted, "I object to a portrait of the dead tyrant hanging in this courtroom. Its presence is a condemnation before we are tried, and a statement that there will be no justice here."

The gallery of spectators croaked their outrage at his audacity, and Fuchs rapped for silence.

"Are you suggesting that you will not get a fair trial in this courtroom, Mr. Jeliabov?"

"That's exactly what I am saying, and furthermore, I demand that we be judged by a jury of Russian people, not by puppets of the Tsarist tyranny!"

"You do not ease your situation by such outbursts," the Senator continued, rapping for silence. "The press is to disregard this outburst."

"Yes," Jeliabov cried, "disregard everything! You are looking at dead people. We have already been tried and convicted!"

"Silence," the judge bellowed.

Karpov motioned for the guards to move, and one stuck a rifle barrel into Jeliabov's throat.

"That's right," Jeliabov yelled. "Get it over with fast. Order the world to forget what is going on here!"

Fuchs stood, obviously shaken. "If you do not sit and be silent, I will have you taken out. Now, make up your mind."

Jeliabov stood silently for a moment and nodded with a look of smug superiority as the newspaper reporters wrote feverishly.

"And you, Mr. Karpov, are never to allow one of your men to touch a prisoner in my court," Fuchs continued, glaring over his wire rimmed glasses at the squat officer.

Turchenko cleared his throat again, and looked at Fuchs for a sign to begin. Fuchs nodded.

"You are charged with belonging to a secret society for subverting the existing order of things, and you are charged with complicity in the assassination of the Emperor of all the Russias."

The indictment continued with Jeliabov taking furious notes

so he could speak to each charge. Zeena watched him with wonder. She was spent. The months of her prison confinement, the agony of the interrogators, and the indignity of the body searches, had excised most of her anger and spirit. But her mind never rested, and every fiber of her being focused on surviving so the child would be carried to term, and she would live. Death was not an option while the child moved within her.

The indictment droned on. At times she heard it, and at times she did not. She was aware that it was over when the President of the Court asked each prisoner, in turn, if he or she wished to say anything at all. Yekovsky stood first.

"It was never my desire to do anything other than to agitate peacefully," he began, "but I found I had to enter into a conspiracy because peaceful agitation was met with contempt and beatings by the police. If you do not give the people a forum by which they can speak to the powers unmolested, you have only yourselves to blame for the horror of the social order and the Tsar's death!"

A smattering of applause broke out in the gallery, and Fuch's eyes widened as he hit his gavel. Guards near the steps poised for action.

"I will clear the gallery if there is another unseemly outburst! Proceed, Mr. Yekovsky."

"I have nothing more to say at this moment, your honor."

Yekovsky sat.

Jeliabov smirked and Senator Fuchs nodded to Michailov, who stood.

"Do you have a statement?"

"I say only what I said at the preliminary hearing. I belong to The Will of the People because it is the only outlet you have given me to voice my displeasure with the way the Russian people are treated. All other vehicles of protest are ruthlessly put down. I did not plan or participate in the assassination. I was contacted by a woman whose name I do not know and she told me what I had to do. I am a soldier under orders in the people's army."

Fuchs glanced at the gallery for a sign of disturbance, but there was none. He nodded to Kibaltschitish.

"I can add little to what has already been said. I make bombs. It is the only way I can earn a living since I and my family were thrown off our land by the government for not being able to pay our taxes. I learned how to make bombs in the army. After the army, I had nothing. It occurred to me to protest my treatment, but I was beaten by the police and I reluctantly was obliged to adopt the measures of a terrorist. I am not sorry I provided the bombs. They were good bombs, made of glass tubes with Bartholdy salts." His eyes glazed. "I took India rubber tubes with fulminating mercury and nitroglycerin and . . ."

Senator Fuchs hit the gavel twice, and then again, until the bomb maker became aware of where he was. Then he was suddenly silent. The murmur in the courtroom subsided.

Fuchs took a deep breath and looked at those left to speak. Public curiosity centered around the women, especially the Perowski woman. He studied the proud, aristocratic face. He viewed the woman as something of an anomaly, for she had waived her right as an aristocrat to be tried by her peers, preferring to stand with the others in a public trial. Her motivation continued to remain a mystery.

Jeliabov, eloquent, and volatile, waived legal aid and chose to defend himself. And finally, the pregnant Jewess who, from the beginning, denied any and all involvement with the conspiracy and whose presence here rested on the deposition of a man trying to save his daughter's life, a sworn statement of another man, a known informer who mysteriously disappeared out of the Fortress, and the story of Sophia Perowski who continued to insist that this woman was a key figure, though all the others denied having ever heard of her. All against her seemed circumstantial, except that she was at the basement apartment.

His voice resounded with appropriate disinterest.

"Zeena Bendelevitch," he said.

Zeena pulled herself to her feet and struggled to establish her balance.

"I am innocent," she began. "I do not know why you have charged me with this crime. I was living in the Count's home and I received a note to come to that apartment to meet someone who would give me a train ticket to Hamburg. I do not know why you don't believe me. I do not know why Sophia Perowski continues to implicate me when she knows my innocence."

Sophia straightened her back and fixed her steel eyes on the clock below the gallery boxes. Senator Fuchs saw that she neither heard, nor cared to hear, the other woman's plea.

"I am not guilty of anything other than being in St. Petersburg without the proper papers. Punish me for that transgression if you must, but do not charge me with a murder about which I know nothing!" She looked directly at the Tribunal. "The indictments against me cannot be substantiated by those who made them, and Sophia Perowski is the only one of these people who condemns me. I beg you to see through the lies and let me and my baby go free."

"No freedom for the murdering Zhid!" yelled someone from above.

"Silence," shouted the Senator, "or I will clear the gallery. I will not tolerate such outburst from the prisoners or from the spectators." He waited, and turned to Sophia.

"Sophia Perowski," he said. "Do you wish to speak?"

Sophia did not stand immediately. She waited appropriately, as an actress might wait for applause to subside, before she delivered her awaited lines. Senator Fuchs clasped his hands and, leaning in, took a deep breath. Sophia slowly rose as if being introduced to royalty. Again, she stood quietly, extracting from her audience exquisite anticipation.

"I and my brethren are prepared to brave torture and death and, though we know we are to die, we take pleasure in knowing that there are those whose names you shall never know who are waiting for the next glorious moment." She did not look at the jury box where Malinovitch sat, but knew his eyes were on her, strengthening her and loving her.

Above, some angry voices, and again the rapping of the gavel for silence.

Sophia continued. "I confess freely my actions. I stand in history, and history shall justify our glorious deed. It was I who pointed the way of the imperial coach, and it was I who dropped my handkerchief as a signal for the glorious deed to be performed. What I did, what we did, we did because we were able to rise up above the tyrannies imposed by a corrupt church and a corrupt government, to see the vision of a world where people rule supreme. I believe in the people only; their verdict is the only one I recognize as valid. And, it is in their cause, that I give my life gladly."

Her words resounded throughout the room. Had it been a theater, the audience would have been on their feet, applauding in wild appreciation. But there was only an uncomfortable murmur of wonder and anger.

At the rear of the room, Count Perowski, well dressed and proud in his bearing, closed his eyes when Sophia finished. He sat there for a moment with tears rolling down his cheeks and then left.

"Your honor," said one of the defense attorneys. "I rise to protest these statements. The bravado we hear from Sophia Perowski must not be applied to others on trial."

"Your honor," said Turchenko, rising to his feet, "each prisoner was given the option of speaking or not speaking. Each chose freely to speak."

"Objection sustained. The prisoners, if they choose to make a statement, will confine their remarks to their own involvement." Fuchs looked at Jeliabov. "Do you wish to make an opening statement, Mr. Jeliabov, or relinquish it?"

"No, I shall speak," Jeliabov replied with a broad smile.

"Then I caution you that is a privilege to speak in my court, not a right. Since you have chosen to defend yourself and waive your right to counsel, I warn you that I will not tolerate inflammatory remarks to the spectators or disrespect to the court. I shall also not allow you to turn this trial into a vehicle for your propaganda."

Jeliabov rose and nodded agreement.

"Your honors, and gentlemen of the press." He paused and scanned the courtroom. "I will be brief because I deny the efficacy of this court. To that end I will not, at a future time, call any of my own witnesses for that will mark them for prison as traitors. I will say that our objective, from start to finish, was to terrorize the country, disarrange the machinery of government, and bring about a socialist order. We, I mean I, was pledged to this task. And as far as this pale, distraught woman here, I have no knowledge of her and can only say that I believe she is the object of someone else's conspiracy to implicate the Jews, as a convenient way of transferring to them the blame you will not fully admit belongs to those among us who belong to the Orthodox Church, and who were in the forefront of overthrowing the Orthodox Tsar. But that is a matter for the conscience of this court, and the conscience of Russia. I, for one, believe in God, but not the God the church has created for us. But that is also another matter. I am a revolutionary. I live for the people I serve, and you will put me to death for the service I have rendered them." His eyes burned with pride and his voice shook as it rose in intensity. "This trial is a travesty of justice, and I demand that our judge be the people or their legally elected delegates. We demand that we be tried by a jury . . ."

Karpov motioned to a guard who ran to the prisoner's box and smashed the butt of his rifle into Jeliabov's stomach. The court exploded!

"Silence," bellowed Senator Fuchs to the courtroom. "How dare you attack a prisoner in my courtroom! Clear this courtroom. Clear this courtroom!"

That evening, on a quiet, tree lined street of majestic townhouses, Count Gregor Perowski took the gun given to him by Karpov for protection, and put a bullet into the right side of his brain.

CHAPTER 27

November 22, 1882

Only the train rides between cities gave him time to rest and time to feel safe. From the moment he revealed to the world that he was Zeena's brother, he knew his only real safety lay in moving with groups of people and in train compartments with only one seat left. Even if no one spoke, he at least welcomed contact with people who neither knew him nor wanted anything from him. It was also warmer.

The newspaper became not only his assurance that Zeena was alive, but also a source of camouflage. Usually, he would buy several in different languages so people might think he was a foreigner and not engage him in conversation. He would pore over the articles about the trial and memorize new words or phrases that would help his own speeches become more effective. But mostly, he pored over the dispatches so he could measure the progress of the trial and the value of his effort to help her.

Jonah knew that it was impossible for Zeena to have known the conspirators, and it was incredulous that educated men could believe that in a few days she could have gotten involved in such a scheme. He had never heard of an Executive Committee, and he had never heard of The Will of the People until he went to Kiev. If Zeena ever did know of them, it would have been a guarantee that she would have mentioned it if only to aggravate their mother. Jonah was now certain that the government wanted her charged as guilty so they might shift the blame to the Jews. Why the newspapers had not picked up on the lie and forced it back down the government's throat, he could not understand. Certainly, the newspapers were obliged to speak. He folded one newspaper and opened another.

ST. PETERSBURG: Special dispatch to the Times

One can only wonder at the compromising revelations made during the pre-trial hearing and the information gathered at the hands of Colonel Karpov, chief prosecutor. The information seemed so readily available that we might assume that the conspirators were either traitors to their own cause, or pressures were brought to bear in the Peter and Paul Fortress where they were interrogated that were formidable. Many persons naturally suspect the means used to induce these depositions. It is stated that in one quarter without qualification, It is a well known fact that a Nihilist named Presnickov was tortured to death. I can only say that very few well informed persons in St. Petersburg believe in his death at all, it being well understood that to escape the vengeance of the party for his revelation, he stipulated that his death should be reported while he was privately shipped off to a distant continent and provided with means of livelihood. Readers will recall that it was Presnickov's deposition, taken by Colonel Karpov himself, which implicated the Bendelevitch woman and was the only deposition to support the Perowski charge.

As to other charges of torture, I cannot say. The student, Ivan Russakov, bore no signs of torture and those on trial for the murder of the Tsar had ample opportunities to denounce it if it had been practiced. The only prisoner appearing distressed is the Jewess, Zeena Bendelevitch, but we can safely ascribe her countenance more to her condition than to her treatment. Of this I am sure, it is only in keeping with the well known character of the late Emperor and Empress, who take such solicitous interest in all the works of benevolence, to desire that increased attention be given by the high officials worthy of their confidence to temper the treatment of all prisoners with humanity and mercy.

"In all the works of benevolence," Jonah laughed to himself as he read the line about Zeena over again. Was she really all right or did the reporter discount her appearance because he did not want to generate sympathy for her? Certainly the line following was geared to generate sympathy for the Tsar. That bastard reporter, thought Jonah. He's probably paid by Karpov to whitewash the trial and the government.

"Humanity and mercy," he murmured under his breath. "A black cholera should catch him!"

The train sped northward towards Danzig. Jonah pulled down the window slightly to taste the late November air. He shivered at its icy touch and shook his head as if to clear it. He had been on the train for more hours than he could recall. He filled his lungs to capacity and released the air slowly, feeling his body tingle. He pushed the window up and sat wondering who would meet him and where he would speak this time. The past months seemed like a parade that began in Mr. Schwabb's beer hall in Vienna and would end in Danzig. The papers had reported that Zeena was close to giving birth.

In Danzig, he would wait and consider his next action. The forces around him moved him as they wished, but at least he no longer felt as much a pawn as he had when be began his odyssey five months ago. The faces in Vienna, Bazel, Prague, Warsaw, and Berlin merged into one, but the excitement of standing before this sea of faces who looked to him as a vocal expression of their hopes, was as exhilarating as breathing the cold air. For the first time, he had a sense of achievement never felt before. He was part of something important and of great value. It was where he felt he should be. This was a vibrant existence so unlike the pallid, tedious days of Krivoser. He carried a message that went beyond his sister's plight and, as he spoke of it, he began to comprehend it. Once he had said that there were things greater than he and Zeena, and that individuals had to subordinate their own needs for the greater good. Now, he was experiencing exactly the same thought, but not for the sake of preserving a tradition. Now he was calling for an end to oppressive monarchies and governments that drained the life-spirit of its citizens. He believed that as fiercely as he believed his sister to be innocent. But what continued to gnaw at him was that Zeena was still not free. All the petitions had still not freed her. He did not understand.

The train stopped and huge clouds of steam enveloped him as he walked to the designated clock. In a few moments, a man approached and thrust an envelope into Jonah's hand and hurried off. Jonah smiled and stepped into the morning frost. In the safety of a doorway, he opened the envelope and scanned the lines. The words he was instructed to speak were cruel and treasonous. He would not use them. Tonight, he would speak as the words came from his heart. It was close to the end.

Jonah entered the double door. All around, men stood in noisy little groups gesticulating and bellowing approval or disapproval over this or that. A few men turned towards him and then back to their conversation. A small man wearing pince-nez spectacles pushed through those assembled and moved directly to Jonah with his hand outstretched.

"I am Josef Schweicz," he began. "You must be Mr. Bendelevitch. We are pleased to have you here," he said gesturing broadly.

Jonah smiled and followed Mr. Schweicz as the little man pushed his way to the speaker's platform. There was a rap of the gavel and a call to attention. Mr. Schweicz cleared his throat, took a drink, and cleared his throat again.

"If an emperor murders his father that he may reign," he began suddenly, "why should not a nation kill an emperor that the people may reign?"

The audience became aware of him as he said, 'kill an emperor' and exploded with cheers.

"I remember witnessing a tax collector come into a village in southeastern Russia. Twenty Cossacks rode into the village and the police officers called out to the peasants commanding them to pay the taxes. The poor people had already been deprived of all their substance and because they could not create money, each was stripped, laid down and whipped."

A murmur of indignation ran throughout the hall.

"I say," the little man on the dais screamed out, "absolutism died the day Alexander breathed his last. Socialism is about to fully develop. The new Tsar will gladly make concessions to the Nihilists or the same fate awaits him. The fate of his father stares him in the face and he may well tremble." He paused for breath. "Within a year in Russia there will be a popular congress in which the down trodden people will be fully represented!"

The assembly erupted again. Schweicz raised his hands for silence.

"We have with us tonight, as promised, the brother of the innocent who languishes in the Tsarist prison. We have read of her bravery in confronting the government and we have heard her plea. We are one with her and her cause. She is a symbol of us all. We all languish in the prison of tyranny. We are all symbolically innocent of shedding a tyrant's blood and we are all symbolically guilty. If innocent blood for a tyrant's blood must be shed before the people can be free, it will be shed gladly. I give you the brother of Zeena Bendelevitch."

There was thunderous applause again. A few stood, and then others, until all stood and expressed their sympathy and support. Jonah climbed the three steps feeling the same flush that he felt each time he heard his name announced and each time he heard the applause. He straightened his back and took a deep breath. What ever uneasiness accompanied his speeches, fled with the sense of control he had come to feel. He waited and felt himself grow as the room was enveloped in respectful silence.

"How is it possible," Jonah began, "for freedom loving nations to continue to offer sympathy to the government of Russia? It is as disgraceful as it is dangerous in the extreme, in as much as it encourages tyranny and oppression everywhere, and discourages every effort of the oppressed to secure for themselves those rights and freedoms these nations enjoy. These nations of the world, these freedom loving havens for the oppressed, these islands of liberty in the seas of despotism, were once themselves ruled by tyrants. Have they forgotten so soon the nature of tyrants that they will even hint at sympathy and support?"

The word tyrant seemed like a code, for the audience, as one, began to applaud and call 'no!' to the speaker. He had drawn them into the magic of his words.

"Yes," he continued, "they say the assassination of an emperor is a tragic thing, but I say to you, is the murder of an innocent woman any less tragic? I say it is more tragic, for you and I have felt the injustice of tyrants, but what injustice against humanity did my sister ever commit? Civilized people and civilized governments do not murder innocent people because they are convenient scapegoats and will further their political aims. Civilized people do not do things like that. We do not do things like that!"

Again, applause broke out from all sides of the room and surrounded Jonah like an embrace. He basked in it and seemed to be nourished by it. He allowed it to continue and interrupted it again to speak before the applause faded.

"You may well ask as you do," Jonah continued, "why the great ones of the imperial Russian government so relentlessly and recklessly pursue an innocent woman and risk the condemnation of the entire western world?" They knew the question was rhetorical. "I will tell you why," he shouted. "They do this because they will not admit that one of their own, a countess, also saw the yoke under which the people suffer. They believe they can shift the blame from the countess to my sister, but they cannot as long as there is a righteous world outside that knows their evil and judges their evil. I want my sister to be free and I take the idea of freedom **beyond my sister. There are other types of freedom and it is no crime for anyone to want to be free, no matter what their concep**tion of freedom is. My sister, you, and I rot in a prison. Help me free Zeena Bendelevitch and we free ourselves. Help me free Zeena Bendelevitch and we all crawl out of our despair into the glorious light of freedom."

The crowd rose to their feet chanting, "freedom," sucked in by Jonah's intensity and the eloquence with which he voiced the aspirations of the people in the room and the down trodden of the world. He had become a transformed being, a protean figure, an inexperienced and profoundly sad human being suddenly recreated by applause and lights.

Jonah stepped off the speaker's podium smiling and nodding to the well wishers.

A young man with intense, dark eyes and black hair watched and listened and took furious notes. When the shouts of applause and support subsided, he approached the platform with a look of wonder on his broad, angular, bearded face.

"I was hoping to speak with you," he said. "My name is Theodore Herzl and I'm with the Vienna Free Press."

Jonah moved back slightly. He had come to know how newspaper people could badger and extract information better left a secret.

"I was assigned to write a story about you but missed you when you were in Warsaw and in Vienna. I'd really appreciate some of your time."

Jonah liked the rush of words and the confidence that sat regally around the stranger's broad forehead. He looked something like an Assyrian statue Jonah had seen in a museum in Berlin. His tight, short, curly beard, and his deep set, intelligent black eyes, his height, gave him a presence that appeared years beyond his youth. Jonah wondered how one became so free and confident.

"I don't give interviews," Jonah said trying not to appear rude and began to move past him.

"Then perhaps you'll listen to me. I have an editorial piece I'm writing on how your sister is being used."

Jonah stopped mid-stride. All around him there were shouts for beer. Jonah watched Schweicz thrust the resolution and petition before small groups clustered around the room. Together he and Herzl moved to the door, and as they moved further from the lights of the podium, Jonah felt the admiration and recognition fade and wondered if he affected anything or anyone at all.

"Did you ever shake your hand in a bucket of water, Herzl, and then take it out and watch the water rest?"

"Yes," Herzl answered. "When I was a child."

"I feel like that. You stand up there and pour yourself out and come down and feel yourself drained and empty. It's very sobering to move quickly from one place in the world to another and realize what you really effect. Look at them. In a moment they won't recognize me on the street."

"Anonymity in certain situations is more desirable than notoriety," said Herzl. "Hope for such a response when you get to St. Petersburg."

Jonah was again reminded of the task and danger that lay ahead. He buttoned his coat and moved into the chilled air. The clock in a distant tower chimed nine.

"Are you hungry?" asked Herzl. "I am famished," and he motioned to a dimly lit cafe on the opposite side of the street.

"Very much so," said Jonah, eager to sit across from someone and relax over a hot meal. Perhaps this man was not one of the dangerous ones. Perhaps he might learn something and understand why he had not achieved his goal.

"I have a stop to make at the news agency." he said with an apology in his voice. "It will take but a moment. I pick up my mail and messages from my newspaper. It's not far."

They turned their collars up against the cold and moved down the street. A dusting of snow swept around their feet.

Herzl spoke first.

"We know nothing about you," Herzl began. "You've been speaking for months, but all we know is that you are the brother of the woman held, and that you are a Jew." He waited for Jonah to speak, but Jonah remained silent. "You are protecting your family then by not speaking? Yes?"

Jonah nodded. "My parents, sisters, wife and child would not be safe if I told anyone where I came from. When I last saw them . . ." Jonah began to stammer from the recollection, "there was a pogrom and I . . ." Jonah closed the conversation. Herzl sensed a profound pain and secret.

Taking him by the arm, Herzl motioned him to a modest building whose sign read Reuters News Service. A cold wind blew down the street and Jonah was pleased to be in a warm place again.

A small bell rang above the door and a plain woman looked up and smiled an obligatory smile.

"My name is Theodor Herzl of the Vienna Free Press. Do you have any messages?"

His eyes captured hers and a flush rose to her cheek. She averted her gaze and turned to the row of boxes behind her back. Somewhere behind the boxes, a telegraph key clicked and voices were raised and lowered in friendly banter.

She turned again, her indefinite face composed and ready to repel the eyes she sensed burned with the fire of damnation. She thrust a packet of letters into his hand and turned away quickly.

"Thank you," he said warmly. She did not respond.

He looked through them and opened the largest one first, tearing it carelessly. Then he stopped. In the envelope was a letter addressed to Jonah Bendelevitch. A note from Herzl's editor was attached. 'This enclosed letter found its way to us through one of our contacts. It is several months old and has been opened and resealed several times by people unknown. It cannot be traced back to its source either. Give it to the person you are to contact, but do it in a private place. The news is not good.'

He looked quickly at Jonah and then away, putting the letter into his pocket. He smiled weakly at Jonah and opened the door. Another blast of cold air hit them as they laughed the hardy laugh of young men.

Herzl opened another letter and read it. "It seems that in four days you will be speaking in Riga."

"It never fails to amaze me," said Jonah, "just how much the press or the world in general knows about where I am and what I'm doing. Does it say what I will be speaking about?" and he laughed an uncomfortable laugh.

"Actually, Herzl interjected, "it is really good that the press, at least, gets this information. As long as the press is interested in you, certain hostile forces might not act. The Russian secret police for example, would not dare touch someone the press follows. Russia has all the bad press it needs."

Jonah laughed again at the vastness of the web that was spun around him and the intricacies of the weave and the sense of balance he needed to maintain in order to move across it without becoming entangled and destroyed.

"Did you ever feel like a puppet, Herzl? Sometimes I wonder if I really need to go to a toilet, or if someone else has decided it is time."

"We are all prodded by one thing or another," he laughed. "Who does not have strings attached to his life, and who is lucky enough to have his fortune and love come to him without strings? I will tell you, Mr. Bendelevitch, that I resent having others push and pull at me. What hotel are we staying at?"

"Doesn't your letter go into that detail?"

Jonah's sarcasm was not lost on Herzl but Jonah did not wait for a reply. "It's called the Europa. Have you heard of it?"

"I have heard of it," he said. "It is one of those havens for the dispossessed of Europe who are fleeing from one place or another, or fleeing to one place or another. How appropriate for the Socialists to have selected it. There's a small restaurant down the street here where the servings are plentiful and the brandy is outstanding."

A dancing fire in the stone hearth cheered and warmed them as they were ushered to a seat by a window. A light snow began to fall. Jonah took off his coat and hung it on a peg. He sat and looked at the heavy oak beams and the chandelier made of antlers. There were dark frescos of hunting scenes on the walls. A woman came over, took their order and returned with two brandies. She paused, classifying them as strangers, and smiled the artificial smile that was good for business. The two young men looked at each other and muffled their laughter as the dour woman disappeared into the kitchen. There was a short silence as Jonah studied the brandy in the glass.

"You said you were writing an article on how my sister is being used."

Herzl swallowed and his eyes narrowed in recollection. "I don't know if you are familiar with the history of the assassination or the ensuing events," he said leaning towards him, "but when all of these meetings and speeches started, I thought they were of a genuine humanitarian nature. They appeared to have been set up to get petitions for the pardon of your sister, but at each meeting, someone always speaks about regicide as the first right of every citizen. Now this certainly does not incline the imperial heart towards clemency, and virtually assures the alienation of a sovereign who could be disposed to be friendly to her in the face of world opinion. I saw the contradiction immediately. It's almost as if someone hadn't thought the thing out, or had thought it out and had something else in mind from the start."

He paused and studied Jonah's face for a response, and Jonah's eyes urged him to continue.

"Then I thought that someone indeed was in control of this from the beginning and was using this tactic to bring about a more sinister plan."

"What plan?" Jonah interrupted, his throat tightening.

"Simply this," Herzl continued, his eyes flashing with excitement. "The Tsar extended the trial period until your sister was close to delivering her child. Now that it is close to what they believe is her time, they are pushing speedily ahead. But, it seems strange to me that they would prolong the torture which she might have suffered in prison, only to culminate it with her execution. Something is going on that we don't know. The newspapers have been gagged and the telegraph operators are warned to be careful what they transmit."

"Forgive my ignorance," said Jonah, "but I still do not see this plan. I see only that she has been saved because even Russia would not dare hang a pregnant woman, and that the Socialists are using the events to further their own objectives."

"But that's exactly it," he said, pointing his finger. "I'm afraid that one of the motives of the Socialists, or Nihilists if you will, is to exasperate the Emperor by their insults and drive him to the commission of an act which must be regarded by the civilized world, let alone by Russian revolutionaries, as an atrocity. Besides, outsiders have lost a great deal of sympathy for the Socialists. It seems that every time a reform is instituted, it is immediately followed by some upheaval created by the Socialists, followed again by Tsarist repression. The world is beginning to wonder whether or not reform is really the objective."

"Are you saying that the Socialists keep this cauldron boiling to generate sympathy for their cause, and that Zeena's death will actually advance public opinion in their favor?"

"Yes," he said. "That's exactly what I am saying."

Jonah sank back on his seat, incredulity written on his face. The conversation between the man in Kiev and himself came to mind. That man had actually said that he and his sister were insignificant in the great struggle of ideas. He had forgotten that, and he had forgotten his response to it. He, too, had come to understand the greater ideas that could be placed before the needs of the individual. Once he had called on Zeena to sacrifice her desires for the sake of perpetuating a tradition. Was that different from the Socialist expecting her to die to perpetuate their economic system?

"If lives are to be lost, they are to be lost to the greatness of the struggle." The words escaped his lips and he was barely aware that they did.

"I see you know the doctrine of the Socialists," said the reporter.

"I have been asked to speak it often enough," said Jonah, his mind racing with the new perception, "but I do not accept it! I cannot believe they would be so cruel as to allow an innocent human being to be hanged. The Socialists know she is innocent. They would not sacrifice an innocent life."

"Then you do not know politics, my friend, and you do not know human nature or human causes." He paused. "Look at yourself."

Jonah stiffened in anticipation of his words.

"You are handed speech after speech by people who have been at this game for years."

"How do you know this?" Jonah interrupted.

"Because the Socialists tell us. They tell us anything that will keep their cause in the papers. We have a great number of informants."

"What else do you know of me," Jonah asked urgently.

"We know you are as innocent as your sister, but they put sedition into your mouth. You carry the brunt of the burden. You, not the Socialist leaders, are in the limelight." Herzl paused as Jonah's expression darkened.

"I am sorry for being so frank," Herzl said. "Please do not be angry with me."

"The truth is the truth," Jonah replied. "You are correct in your regard for those who allow me to speak, but your perception about my sister's situation is a new and frightening revelation that fits a piece of a puzzle too well."

"What's done is done," Herzl replied. "The thing to consider now is how you will proceed. Your purpose is to save your sister. The Socialists gave you the forum you needed. Without them, you didn't stand a chance of keeping your sister before the public. You did what you had to do. The point is, what will you do now? The scenario seems to have you going to St. Petersburg to rescue the child. The Socialist leadership certainly will not do that for you. They'll give you a ticket to your sister and hope you will be taken as a traitor. That will give them an additional sacrifice so the Tsar will again be judged as a barbarian."

Jonah felt a sudden surge of heat throughout his body at the thought. He had never counted on Zeena not having been set free by this time, and he had never dreamed that he would actually have to go to St Petersburg. He never dreamed he would be viewed as a traitor.

Herzl studied his reaction.

"You mean you never considered these things?"

There was a brief silence as Jonah took a deep breath and expelled it. Herzl realized that he had given this chance companion a devastating perception.

Jonah stared through him, suddenly more aware of brutality, of people, and of his own ineptness and innocence in the area of human affairs.

"Perhaps I should leave," said Herzl.

"No," blurted Jonah, suddenly recognizing that this man's perceptions and honesty could keep him aware of his alternatives or at least, alive. "No," he repeated. "I have no one who does not use me to further their own ends. I need a friend." His eyes pleaded, and Herzl returned the gaze with sympathy.

"I will go with you and stay with you."

Jonah felt a sense of relief. He took a breath and exhaled it slowly, thinking of Zeena. He would choose St. Petersburg because that was the only choice he had. He would not flee from his obligation again into a lifetime of shame.

CHAPTER 28

For the most part, the walk to the hotel was passed in silence. Jonah's thoughts bounded from the potential danger of his trip to St. Petersburg, to the frustration of being manipulated by unseen forces. Herzl walked next to him, understanding that silence was the only support he could offer his troubled companion. What the profound secret was, and what the compulsion was that drove this young tailor forward, regardless of obvious danger and potential destruction, remained a mystery. Certainly, he did not need to be the fulcrum of a cause, or the focus which made him carry the enmity of a powerful government. He was either an extremely courageous and righteous human being or a naive fool, for continuing to point out the excesses of a despotic monarchy while still believing he could expect mercy from it for his sister. How could he not know that her death was inevitable? Was he allowing himself to be used, or was he using the Socialists for a purpose beyond his sister's plight? What were this man's needs and what was it that pursued him? Of this Herzl was sure. Jonah Bendelevitch did not burn with the fire of revolution, so ideological philosophies did not impel him. His sister's release was a lost cause to even the most casual observer, but still a cause. Do reasonable people pursue causes in the face of overwhelming odds? Is hope such a power that one would begin a flirtation with death just to keep it aglow? Hope was probably an answer but it was too simple an answer. Other factors existed, and the overwhelming question remained. Was Jonah Bendelevitch a hero or a fool?

The hotel was shabby, a shabbiness reflected in the concierge who squinted at the two men whom she saw as young businessmen or students passing through, and as she turned for a key, she

further classified them as Jews and uttered the word in Polish under her breath. She turned to them again and smiled because it
was her job to smile, but the corners of her mouth returned to her
comfortable frown when they turned.

"Wait," she called. "There is an envelope for you, Mr.
Bendelevitch."

Jonah froze. This had never happened before and as he reached
for it, his hand shook. There was no name or address on it other
than his own. He looked at it and put it into his pocket, wondering and fearing who else might be a puppeteer.

"We do not permit smoking in the rooms," she called after
them, "or women!"

Herzl's hand paused at the elevator button and then pushed
it. He disliked the place and he disliked being there. The engine
began to grind below them and the elevator descended. Jonah
watched him open the iron gate and slide the next. He had not
lost his wonder at the wonderful machinery and gadgetry people
used daily, and the excitement of experiencing one tantalized him
with the expectation of the next.

"I will tell you, Herzl, that when I first encountered this con-
traption, I was so afraid of it that I would walk up the stairs."

They reached the third floor and found the room. Like the
concierge, the room was spartan in its amenities. Herzl put his bag
on one bed and Jonah put his bag on the other. Herzl reached into
his pocket and pulled out a small cigar from a silver case. He offered one to Jonah.

"I don't smoke," he said and wondered why someone like his
companion would disregard the request made by the woman downstairs.

"Perhaps you are wondering," said Herzl testing out the softness of the mattress, "why such a seemingly law abiding citizen
would deliberately discount the request of the sour woman downstairs?" He had sprawled himself out with his boots on the coverlet. Jonah knew that the question was rhetorical and he watched

the smoke curl out of Herzl's mouth in the direction of the curtain. "I am thumbing my nose at her hostility."

"What hostility?" Jonah asked innocently, thinking that her demeanor was not particularly different from anyone else he had encountered.

"What hostility?" Herzl responded with a strange tone in his question.

Jonah immediately felt foolish.

"The hostility towards us as Jews," he said with certainty. "If you didn't hear her, didn't you feel it?"

"I felt nothing different from what I have always felt before. You are a Jew?" Jonah asked hesitantly. "You are like no Jew I have ever met," he hastened to add.

Herzl laughed. "If I were not a Jew, do you think I would be sharing a room with you, or do you think I would have shared my perceptions with you, or would have been sympathetic? A non-Jew does not respond in such a way to a Jew." Herzl paused. "I am what you would call a secular Jew and though I know I am non observant, I am always reminded that I am a Jew. The woman downstairs insists that I remember my origins."

Jonah looked at him and felt less alone. Here was someone who appeared to know everything and have everything and yet also wrestled with his past and his history.

Herzl reached for his overcoat and felt the letter, but decided the bad news could wait a bit longer.

"Then we are alike. You and I believe in ourselves and in our power to effect the world. This much I know about the faith of our ancestors: prayer without action will always prove itself worthless. The Bible is replete with God telling us to keep our prayers and sacrifice and to do what is right."

"For someone who is secular, you seem to have a traditional understanding of what God wants from us. Why do you not practice?"

Herzl paused for a moment and looked directly at Jonah. "Because I chose to be successful in the world that rejects our version

of God and the faith of the people who gave the world that God.
The gentile world does not easily allow success to overt or to practicing Jews. Practicing Jews who are successful make non-Jews feel
uncomfortable. It raises the ultimate question of how can a Jew be
successful and yet reject the true faith and the Messiah? Are you
ever going to open up that letter the concierge gave you?"

Jonah was caught off guard with the shift in topics, but opened
the envelope though he would rather have continued the discussion. Their talk reminded him of home and the Sabbath dinner
table. He looked at his name boldly written across an inner envelope and a ticket to St. Petersburg fell out along with a letter written in the same bold hand. There was no salutation.

> "The birth of your sister's child is imminent. I know you
> have followed the events of the trial as closely as St. Peters-
> burg has followed your efforts on your sister's behalf. The
> ticket and the money contained here will bring you to St.
> Petersburg before the birth of the child so you can take it
> safely. You will be in the greatest danger from the moment
> you enter Russia until the moment you leave. Your bene-
> factor has arranged for newspaper reporters to get on the
> train at Danzig and you are urged to keep in their company
> for your entire stay in Russia. Others will meet you, and you
> will make yourself known to them.
>
> Never be alone. You will be brought to the place of
> your sisters incarceration."

"There is no signature," Jonah said.

Herzl took the letter. "It is not easy to manipulate the people
of the press this way. Someone, someone very powerful has gone to
a great deal of expense and planning to preserve your welfare and
life. Do you know who this can be?"

"I haven't any idea," Jonah responded.

"Would you mind if I accompanied you on your journey?"
Herzl asked.

Jonah's eyes widened at the prospect of transforming the certain boredom of endless miles and endless fear into something to be enjoyed. Jonah nervously played with the ticket as the full message of the letter became clear.

"Be of good cheer, my friend," Herzl said. "You have a guardian angel who drops train tickets, money and reporters out of the sky. Who knows? Perhaps the God of our fathers is apologizing to you for having made a mistake."

"I only wish it were over." Jonah replied. "I miss my family and I want to go . . ." he cut himself off. He sat down on the bed and thought of Leah. Herzl saw the pain and for a while, he said nothing.

"I saw something in you tonight that I hadn't seen before," said Herzl, when the silence began to disturb him. "You seem to be two very different people."

Jonah lowered his head and made a laughing sound of sorts. There was a pause and a reflective sigh.

"Lately, the only time I feel alive, or feel anything for that matter, is when I'm talking to a group of people. All the other times, I'm afraid."

"Jonah, please don't think me forward, but I am curious about something. It's my nature. May I ask you a question?"

"Ask," Jonah said, and he smiled.

"Now I do not believe you have any formal education, yet you spoke as if you've been trained in rhetorics. You actually moved those people, not only with your words, but with the spaces between the words. How did you learn this?"

Jonah thought of his father and the years they had studied and argued over points in the Talmud. That's were the persuasion came from. Other words had been memorized from the other books he and Zeena shared and secreted into the house; Tolstoy, Pushkin, Victor Hugo and Balzack.

"I can't really explain it. I get up there shaking, and as soon as I start speaking, I become someone else. The words are there almost as if they are in a different person. I actually feel myself stretching from within. The ideas about freedom and human rights come mostly from the Torah and other things I've read. Things about people's rights and being honest and free of fear mix together and just come out. I will tell you a secret, Herzl," he whispered and he paused and smiled and lowered his voice. "I do believe I'm two people. I am Jonah the tailor, whose life will ease him into oblivion along with the great faceless masses of humanity who live and die and inch themselves forward by reproducing. And then I am the Jonah of my father's dreams, the scholar who will push humanity forward because he produces something of great worth. Each wages war against the other. The tailor is married and obligated. He has no formal education or degree, no money, and no prospects other than the possibility of being taken as a traitor the moment he walks back into Russia. Once the tailor took comfort in the idea that God had planned it all out nice and neat for him, but then the tailor discerned that God was not in control of the insanity. When the tailor found that he could not explain the insanity, he was left without comfort and the terrible feeling that he had only himself to rely upon. It is not easy being a tailor." Jonah cleared his throat. "You see, Herzl," he continued, "if I slide into oblivion, it is my doing, not God's. It's a burden to be totally responsible for yourself and your life without being able to shift responsibility if you don't like the way things turn out. Where does a tailor go without a belief that God does plan, does direct, and does protect? Where do all the tailors go, Herzl? Where does anybody go? What I carry with me now is a profound feeling that I am inadequate to meet any and all of my responsibilities with any degree of satisfaction."

"You are more than a tailor, Jonah, and thus far I have seen no inadequacy in you," Herzl said in his effort to bring back the Jonah he had glimpsed earlier in the evening. "You have the ideas and you have the words and you can move people to act for the good." His black eyes peered intently into Jonah's face, but Jonah looked down. "Your trouble, my friend, is that you don't believe in what you are capable of achieving and you are letting the darker side of your mind take over. I saw you in control this evening. I saw you loving every minute of being in that light. One does not have to abandon a positive view of life with a loss of faith. Lots of people lose their faith, but what you do with that loss is the test of a human being. One can just as easily choose to affect control over a world that is in chaos. We affect a lot more than we think we affect! You are right, Jonah. You are two people and before me sits a depressed little tailor. Your problem is that you are comfortable being that tailor even if you hate what the tailor experiences. You need to combine the qualities of the two Jonahs and use that combined energy and intelligence to take control of your life. At the very least, we have a choice and you guarantee yourself a well deserved oblivion if you don't choose to act. We may get oblivion anyway, but we must strive for something more. A person can be more than what his history or society says he must be, and as long as we have choice, we have the power to exert some control. You have a heart and you have a mind. Dreams can become realities if you believe they can become realities."

Jonah thought of Leah and the conversation they had so long ago. She had said almost the same thing to him. Why could they see this strength in him when he could only see the helplessness?

"What's wrong?"

"My wife and . . ." He broke off for he did not know if the child even lived.

Herzl watched Jonah withdraw behind something mysterious. He studied Jonah. He was an enigma, a complex, bright young man with visions and aspirations and yet so devoid of confidence and so helpless in his own eyes, that Herzl sensed a profound danger to this young man's life and spirit. There were secrets lurking here and fears that could easily destroy a noble spirit. Herzl heard his own father admonish him once with a line from Job, 'The evil that I fear is upon me.' "Fear begets fear, Theo," he heard him say, "and fear sends out messages to the predators of the earth who sniff the weakness and rouse themselves. When you are afraid, my son, do not let the world know you fear. Cover it at all costs for if you do not, the evil will be borne to you in the teeth of the predators."

Herzl also withdrew and they unpacked. He thought of what he had said to Jonah about power, choices, and control, and any human's ability to effect the world despite hostility. He had never verbalized it before and he silently thanked this quiet, young man for crystallizing within him something of his own spirit.

Jonah sat on the edge of the bed and reread the letter from St. Petersburg.

"I have only one ticket here," he said.

"My editor will not complain if I go over my expenses. He told me to follow the story from the human interest point of view, and he will be very happy to know that not only am I following the story, I'm sleeping in the same room as the story. I hope you did not find me abrupt."

"No," he said. "It is good to hear another voice. A person alone can only rework his own perceptions. Sometimes I think I just scare myself because I only see myself as being limited. I don't know if we ever see ourselves as others see us."

Herzl shook his head and fingered the envelope he had taken from his coat. He was not sure how his friend would respond. His brow furrowed in concern.

"Jonah," he began slowly, "when I picked up my packet at Reuters today there was a letter in it from my editor along with a letter for you."

Jonah brightened suddenly and then seemed to contract.

"The letter was open," Herzl continued, "but I did not read it. My editor's note said the news was disturbing."

Jonah's hand hung hesitantly in the air, and fell slightly as he took the letter. He looked at the postmarks. "This has really been around," he said, to prolong the inevitable. "I really don't know if I can take any more, Herzl."

He turned with the letter and sat on the bed. Herzl sat next to him and put his hand on Jonah's shoulder.

"I am here if you need me, my friend. You are not alone now. Would you read the letter to me, Jonah? It may be easier to share the news than to bear it by yourself."

Jonah nodded, not lifting his head, and took the letter from the envelope. "What's funny about this, Herzl, is that this is the second letter I have ever gotten. The first one was only a few minutes ago. The first of anything should be good, but it doesn't always work that way, does it?"

He recognized the handwriting. "It's from my younger sister Dora. She repairs clocks and watches. I think you'd like her."

Herzl nodded his agreement.

> "My dearest brother, Jonah,
>
> Mama and Leah did not know where you went that terrible night and we still cannot understand why you left when you did. When Jonathan found a newspaper from Austria that told of a Jonah Bendelevitch who was speaking on behalf of his sister's life, we understood a part of why you left, but we do not understand it all. We are glad you are still alive.
>
> There is much to tell you and I'm glad we did not receive that paper for a month because I do not know how I would have told you when it first happened. Even now, months later, I cry whenever I think of them. I miss them so."

Jonah tensed and his fingers pressed into the page and the page began to shake. Herzl's hand moved and Jonah motioned that he would be all right.

> "I do not know what to tell you first so I will start with the least important news. Jonathan and I are married and I am going to have a baby. Sometimes I feel guilty about my happiness, so I keep it silent.
>
> You know of Ruth. She misses you. Some days are good for her and some are bad. Sometimes it seems she goes into herself and we have to shake her to make her speak. It's like she gets lost. We took her to a doctor in Kiev, but he said that her sickness was not a physical thing. He told Mama that she should take her to a doctor in Vienna who is dealing with such sicknesses. Ezra said he will pay for everything, but I fear that she will never be right again."

Jonah's upper lip curled into his mouth and he shivered, remembering how he had found her.

"They raped her," he said, barely able to say the word. "She's only eleven. I don't know how many men, and they made my mother watch."

Herzl closed his eyes and visibly shuddered. Jonah took a breath and continued despite the memory.

"Leah is well now, and you have a beautiful daughter."

Electricity bolted through his body. "Herzl, I'm a father. I have a daughter."

"Mama delivered the baby after you left. Leah was happy to know that you were alive, but she's still very upset that you left her to help Zeena. She has not said as much, but I hear her telling her feelings to the baby. She cries a lot when she is alone. You should have written."

Tears filled Jonah's eyes when he looked at Herzl. "I didn't leave her because I wanted to. Believe me. I had to leave. I really did. I couldn't write either. What if someone watched me post a letter and then went to my family and punished them for what I'm doing now? I could have destroyed them all."

Herzl wondered at what power on earth or what fear on earth could have caused a man to abandon his wife at such a moment. Indeed, here was a character far more haunted and tormented than he had imagined.

"There was a pogrom, and I . . ."

Herzl waited.

"It's my fault Zeena is where she is," he murmured. "I broke my word to her. I knew what I had to do and I didn't do it. We create our own evil, Herzl. My cowardice created mine. We never know what we do."

He let the letter fall from his hands covered his face. Herzl knelt and lifted it. Jonah motioned for him to continue.

"And now I have to tell you something terrible and I have no good way to tell you. Our beloved Papa and Zedde are dead. They murdered them and Mama will not be comforted because of what has happened to her family. The only pleasure she takes is in your daughter. I think she has saved Mama's mind. Mama calls the baby Rachelann because the sound reminds her of Papa and Zedde. I miss them so I think my heart would break if I didn't have my dearest Jonathan to cry on."

Jonah lifted his head slowly. He hadn't even heard the last words about his mother. His mouth opened and he leaned forward as if to speak, but no sound came out. His lips quivered and he shook his head from side to side as tears rolled down his cheeks. He clutched his sides, fighting back his despair and rage and fell forward with his hand over his face.

"Shall I go on, Jonah?" Herzl said, fighting back his own tears. Jonah nodded.

We are all living in Isaac Mitvoy's house and Ezra is supporting us. He has been very kind. Everything was lost. Ezra also paid for Papa's and Zedde's funerals and Ruth's doctors. I think he is doing this because he wants you to help save Zeena and their baby.

He promised that he will take us all to America where we'll all be safe. He wants you to bring Zeena and the baby to meet us in Paris as soon as you free her. They found the constable's body near our house and the police wanted to talk to you, but Ezra protected us from them also.

I know you are doing whatever you can to reunite him with Zeena and the baby after it's born. Ezra said that the world is watching you so you are the only one who can help. Please, Jonah, he has done so much for the family.

I do not know when we shall see you again. Ezra says
that the family can all be reunited in Paris after Zeena gives
birth and you bring them there. He says that as soon as he
hears that you are in Paris, we'll meet you there and then
we'll go to America. Ezra sends Jonathan on trips to the city
with things to sell and he promises to pay him handsomely
when we're all together. We look forward to seeing you again
my dearest brother. God watch over you and our sister.

> Love, Dora"

Herzl handed him the letter and rose to put another log into the
stove. Jonah stared blankly at the floor. Somewhere Herzl remembered that the only proper comfort for a grieving person was silence. He retreated to a chair in the far corner of the room and sat
down.

"I'm sitting here," Jonah began, "trying not to cry again and
trying not to feel. I think that if I feel what is in me, I will explode
or die. My Papa and my Zedde, . . .Herzl? Such good people.
There was nothing in their lives to earn this . . . My Papa used to
say God made him a king every week. I see him standing at the
head of the table and lifting the kiddish cup. The candlelight is
dancing on his beard and he is singing the blessing. He always
finished with a resounding l'chaim instead of amen!" Now Jonah
wept openly. "And they murdered him. They murdered my Papa
and they murdered my Zedde and I wasn't there to help them."

He sank to the floor, heaving and choking back his breath and
crossing his arm over his stomach as if holding back a great force
that would tear him apart. He fell forward over his knees.

"If I were there I might have been able to protect them. Mag-
nified and sanctified is the name of the Lord through all the earth,"
he groaned, reaching into his soul for the only expression of grief
he knew. "Papa, Papa, I will be your kaddish. I will be your kaddish.
It is all I can do for you. It is all I have to give."

Jonah gasped for air and moaned like an animal watching its
young being slaughtered. The anger in Herzl's eyes blazed at the

injustice in the world and the blind hatred that had been inflicted upon this man and his family. He knew the world would not give up its hatred, but there had to be a way to protect this people.

Jonah closed his eyes and after a time, fell asleep. Herzl sat and watched. Whatever metamorphoses proceeded within his friend, it proceeded silently. Jonah had spoken of his rage and fear and confusion and all were being poured into the crucible of his mind along with his honor and compassion to be fired and changed into the form that would ultimately make him into the man who would travel the next day to St. Petersburg and possibly prison or death. He leaned over and covered Jonah against a chill. How unlikely a friend. How different their worlds and how different their responses to it. Jonah embodied all the fears and frustrations of the people from whom he had separated himself, a people he had only glimpsed from the windows of his aristocratic home. He had never touched them or was touched by them. Now there was Jonah, and Jonah was real and not to be denied. Jonah, his family, their sufferings were the vague, shadowy figures referred to at the charity banquets he attended. Charity could not ease Jonah. This Jonah, this frightened young man who believed he affected nothing, had profoundly affected him.

He sat there for a long while and then wept for the first time since he was a child. It was the only thing he had to give his friend.

CHAPTER 29

Zeena pushed herself back on the cot and pulled the blanket up to her face so only her eyes were visible. The sounds stopped in front of her cell door and she heard the bolts shift.

"Not Karpov, please, not Karpov," she whispered and her breath curled before her in the chilled air.

The door creaked open and two dark figures were outlined by the torches behind them. They entered.

"It is very cold in here. Get some more wood."

Zeena constricted at Karpov's voice.

"Certainly we can provide additional fire for our guest." He snapped his fingers, a guard disappeared into the corridor and returned with an arm full of wood.

"You know, Father, that because of her condition, we moved her to one of the best cells we have. After all, she is a world famous dignitary."

He knelt before the small stove, the embers barely alive and thrust in several pieces of wood. In a moment they leaped into a bright flame. "Now that's better. Come and warm your hands." He turned to Zeena.

"Ah, my dear Miss Bendelevitch," he began, "you must not keep yourself from the fire's warmth."

The warm glow beckoned through the chilled air like sweets offered to a child. She did not move.

"I have brought you a visitor," he continued. "He is Father Menkovich, a renown scholar and authority. We have invited him here to help us with your problem." He paused and rolled his hands in the heat. "Of course, we are concerned that being here with you is not safe for one of his standing."

"If he has anything to fear, it is from you, not from me."

"Now," Karpov continued. "You must not show our guest that unpleasant nature of yours. He has come a long way and might be able to help you in your difficult situation. Father, will you wait outside?"

Karpov waited for the priest to withdraw and motioned to the guards. Zeena pulled herself back until she could go no further.

"Don't touch me, I have hidden nothing. I have nothing to hide!"

"We must be absolutely sure you have hidden nothing. You are a member of a very devious people. There is no telling what you are capable of doing."

Two guards grabbed her by the wrists and pulled her off the bed, standing her in the center of the room.

"Please," she begged, "Not again. Don't search me again. It's so cold."

Karpov sat on the table with one leg dangling.

"Lift up your dress above your head or I shall have them tear it off you," he said, his eyes playful and eager.

"Why do you degrade me like this? Day after day you come with your filthy hands. Where is your compassion, you hypocrite?"

"Lift your dress," said Karpov again, only this time his voice was sinister, like a parched man demanding water.

Zeena closed her eyes, as if not being able to see them eased her shame, and lifted her dress. Karpov jumped from the table and pulled the skirt over her head so her face was covered. Zeena instinctively moved to cover her breasts and pubis, but Karpov pulled her hands away.

"Now spread your legs wide," and his foot tapped the inside of her ankle until he was satisfied.

One of the guards approached and knelt down beside her, as he did almost daily.

"Remember, she is tricky," said Karpov, "so be careful. We have an important guest with us who must be protected. A weapon may be hidden anywhere. Be very thorough. Begin at her feet and go up each leg. Search the folds of her skin and the inner thighs. Find the dark spaces and see if anything is hidden. Do not be afraid to probe."

Zeena's scream of indignation was muffled by the skirt.

"Bend over now, Miss Bendelevitch, so we can see if you've hidden anything there. Just turn around and bend over. It will be unpleasant for you if you do not."

Zeena began to weep as her hands reached behind to spread her buttocks. Karpov took a rifle from the guard and slid the cold barrel on the inside of her legs. It was a new terror.

The gun site scratched at her labia as he drew it forward to her arms and up her spine.

"Please stop this!" she shrieked.

"I would judge that a bullet here would shatter your spine and pass through the brain of the bastard you carry."

Karpov cocked the rifle. There was a long silence.

"No!" she screamed, "No, please, no!"

Karpov pulled the trigger. There was a loud click in the frosted silence. The guards began to laugh. Karpov snorted and laughed also and tossed the empty rifle back to its owner.

"Stand up," he said contemptuously. "I am convinced at this moment that you have concealed nothing that would endanger our guest, but of course there are other moments."

Zeena lowered her dress and gazed at him through her tears. "If I had a weapon, it would be you who would be in danger, not the hypocrite who waits outside the door."

A guard moved to strike her, but Karpov held up his hand.

"You know that it would not look good in the court if Miss Bendelevitch were to have any marks on her, or was to say that she was beaten," he said to the guard. "A search for harmful objects is necessary and routine," he continued. "It seems that our tribunal will not tolerate physical abuse."

"You continue to look robust," he said, turning to Zeena again. "If I discover that someone is giving you food beyond what a prisoner is to get, I shall make sure that person never feeds anyone again."

Zeena thought of the food Alexi brought with him on his bi-weekly interrogation sessions with her. She would tell him about this new horror with the rifle. The thought of telling Alexi gave her a feeling of hope. She moved back to her bed and wrapped the blanket around her shoulders. A guard opened the door, and the solid, black cowled figure moved forward in the darkness like the angel of death.

Karpov rose from the table. "I'll be outside if you need me. She has no weapons," he added, as he threw another log into the iron stove.

The priest waited for Karpov to leave, and then extended his hand for Zeena to sit by the stove with him. He threw two more pieces of wood in to insure some degree of warmth. Sparks flew up and out of the opening and were consumed. Zeena inched closer to the flame, her distaste for the bearded figure repressed by her need to feel the warmth of the fire. She warmed her hands and then placed them over her face as if to wash it with the heat.

"It is not healthy for a pregnant girl to be in such a place and it is not healthy for her child."

"Tell Colonel Karpov," she said flatly. "I know what this hole is like and I know how it feels."

"I am told Colonel Karpov will have his way sooner or later. He wants your confession."

"I did not kill the Tsar. Sophia Perowski killed the Tsar, not I. Go talk to her about my innocence."

"I have examined her carefully. She is possessed by the demon of arrogance and pride, a demon that I believe was conjured up by an equally demonic person and let loose onto her. She is possessed by an evil force and this will yet be revealed."

"Didn't they laugh that other priest out of court with that piece of insanity? They'll brand me a murderer, but even the most ignorant in the court rejected the accusation of witchcraft. Are you still trying to prove Sophia was bewitched or has Karpov created a new piece of insanity to get me to condemn myself and Russian Jewry?"

Father Menkovich's hand felt for the cross that rested on his lap. Zeena saw the move and laughed to herself.

"If life were granted you and your child, would you confess?"

Zeena was startled. Never before had anyone spoken of life, or even hinted at negotiation. Alexi had warned her that a confession would seal her fate and bring down the nation's wrath on her people. Now she was close to giving birth and she was still not free. Alexi had not done as he had promised, but only said that things took time. She knew of Jonah's efforts through the lawyer's visits and Alexi's, but even the stacks of petitions from all parts of the world had not persuaded the new Tsar to free her.

"You know that Colonel Karpov has great power, but so does our holy church. You see," he continued, "there is, shall we say, an unwritten agreement, that enables the church to grant, shall we say pardon, in exchange for a confession."

Zeena's eyes focused on his mouth, not wanting to miss a single word when he responded to her next question.

"Are you saying," she said very slowly, "that you have the power to free me and my child if I take up your cross?"

"The holy church does have the power to intercede for those who seek life through our Savior. You see, the government recognizes that if a prisoner, who is also a non-believer such as yourself, confesses her sins, converts, and takes up the way of the cross, there are unwritten agreements and precedence which indicate that in certain cases, it might be disposed to reward that person by forgiving their crime." He paused for a reaction.

Zeena's mind bounded from Alexi's awful admonition to the reality of how close she was to death.

"But are you saying that if I confess to the murder, take up your cross,, and convert to the Orthodox Church, I will go free? Yes or no?" She paused for his assent.

"Now, of course," he said softly, "the murder of the Tsar is a very different matter. Here, the church may not have the power in this life, but you see my dear child that the church will accept you to life eternal if you confess and take the cross."

Zeena pulled back as she absorbed his meaning.

"My child," he said with great benevolence, "if you accept the cross and separate yourself from the sinister people who put the murdering demon in you in the first place, you will be guaranteed life eternal. I, myself, will offer up prayers of intercession for you with our Father in heaven. Then Jews all over Russia will see your conversion to the light, recognize their own error, and follow your path to redemption through the blood of our Lord and Savior."

He smiled benignly at her, secure in his faith and in his power to bring her and everyone to the light.

"Oh, this is wonderful," Zeena said, clasping her hands in front of her, with full understanding. "Oh, you are a crafty son of a bitch. You are nothing like the priests at home. They would come into the shop or the yard and berate us for not loving your gentle Savior. No, you don't berate. You are all sweetness. First you dangle the hope of real freedom and life for me and my baby before my face if I kiss your cross, and then you tell me that you will guarantee me life eternal in the arms of your loving God! you bastard! you sinister, unfeeling bastard! You come here to torment me with the dream of life only to destroy me with despair and the absurd fantasy that the likes of you can actually intercede with God on anyone's behalf? This is really so unbelievable! Do you think I'd really consider exchanging one mythology for another if this life wasn't the reward? Kiss your cross? I'd kiss your ass if it got me out of this rat hole!" Her contempt peaked. "Come to your cross! The only thing your cross has ever meant to me or anyone I know was persecution, death and despair. Despair is the gift your church gives the world quite freely. That is what your church and cross symbolize to those who do not follow it. You and the likes of you have dipped that cross in my people's blood for centuries and you've smeared your Savior's hands with it. Why should I or any Jew go near your church or Savior? Some sweet, gentle Savior you offer me! Some holy church you offer me! Watch another Jew be murdered for the glory of the holy church. Come and be saved by the Jew's blood! Come dip your fingers in the Jew's blood! Come wash away your sins in the Jew's blood! Is that it, holy Father? Is there salvation for you in my blood and the blood of my baby? Is that another one of your holy mysteries? If your gentle Savior is watching, he is weeping for what you have done in his name and for what you are doing now! Get out of here! Get out!"

Zeena picked up the stool she sat on and hurled it at the priest. He lifted his arms to ward off the blow.

"Guard!" he yelled, backing away from her, blessing the air between them repeatedly.

"You are possessed by the devil and so is the child you carry. You are the devil's spawn and damned to eternal fire."

The two guards, followed by Karpov, ran in, their guns ready.

"What are you ignorant fools afraid of?" she yelled. "Do you fear an unarmed, pregnant woman, or do you fear I will send out my evil spirit to destroy you?" She laughed at them. "If I am what you say I am, I would have destroyed you the moment you touched me, you fools."

"I take it you have not brought her to the light of the holy church?" said Karpov in a soft sarcastic tone.

"She is the spawn of the devil and her evil is very great," replied the priest who was retreating in fear. "Look at the hate in her eyes even when she beholds the cross. And the cross does not make her look away or turn back in shame. The demon in her is very strong!"

The guards backed up slightly and blessed themselves. Only Karpov did not move.

CHAPTER 30

The train slowed, stopped and expelled huge billows of steam. Jonah's face filled with apprehension. A light rain clicked against the window and blurred those standing on the platform. He knew he would be met and he knew he would be followed and watched and taken if found alone. But he also knew that a person of great power worked for his safety and for Zeena's. He buttoned his coat and lifted his case, looking to Herzl.

"There is nothing to say, my friend," Herzl began. "I take what I feel for you as a statement of what you feel for me. Nothing else is needed." They smiled at each other, shook each others hand warmly and left the compartment in silence. The other members of the press who had traveled with them, followed closely.

Lines of travelers crowded the gates.

"I am to go to gate ten," Jonah said, feeling for his letter of transit. He looked around, trying to identify anyone who watched him. He felt his heart speed up and he began to perspire as the letter of transit of each passenger wishing entry was scrutinized. The line inched closer to a desperate unknown. He wanted to turn and run to the train.

"Look, Jonah, beyond the gate!" and Herzl's eyes widened with delight. "There's Pierre Bouchard from Reuters in Paris, and there's a friend named Josef Baumann from Berlin. Your guardian angel did not lie about reporters meeting you either."

"Herzl!" shouted Baumann, moving to the gate. "Are you here for the executions?"

Herzl did not reply, but averted his eyes from Jonah's gaze.

"Why are you at the station?" Herzl called back.

"We all received letters to be at gate ten at this time today. We were promised a major story about the Bendelevitch woman and were told we would get it from the brother if he's mad enough to come here. Do you know anything about this? Please don't tell me that all we're going to get is Theodor Herzl arriving in St. Petersburg." They all laughed, and Herzl laughed with them.

"What is going on here?" he shouted back. I've never seen so many police and soldiers in a time of peace."

"There's a private war going on between the head of the secret police and the Socialists," Baumann shouted. "Houses are searched daily and people are being held without being charged. They're rooting out all traces of subversion. No one can move anywhere without letters of transit or without their papers being in perfect order."

"Next," the officer called.

Jonah stepped forward and handed the guard his papers.

The officer studied his face and his name and motioned to a man standing a little way off.

"You may pass," the guard said.

Jonah saw the officer motion to two other men who converged towards him. He froze and perspiration exploded all over his body.

"What's wrong?" Herzl said suddenly.

"There are three men waiting there. I know they are here to take me to prison."

"Where is your letter of transit?" the guard said to Herzl.

"I am with the Vienna Free Press. Here is my passport and identification."

"Without a letter of transit, you cannot enter."

"But I am with the press," Herzl insisted.

"I do not care if you are an emissary from God. With no letter of transit, you do not enter."

Herzl watched the three men stop and then make their way toward Jonah who had stepped through the gate.

Herzl ran to the bars. "Josef, Pierre, that young man those men just grabbed is Jonah Bendelevitch, the brother of the woman on trial. He is your story, and if you don't stay with him, he will be killed. Protect him at all costs. That's why you are here. He's your story."

As one, the reporters raced down the platform to the men who had accosted Jonah and began hurling questions at him. Herzl ran along the bars as all beyond moved down the platform.

"Stay with him, Josef, or he's as good as dead!" he screamed.

Jonah was pushed along and turned towards the frantic voice, but his vision was blocked.

Herzl raised himself as high as he could on the gate. "I'll be in Paris, Jonah. Contact Reuters and look for me in Paris."

Jonah tried to turn, but could only hear the words, Reuters and Paris.

Herzl lowered himself to the ground and held on to the bars. He wondered if they would meet again.

A short distance off, Alexi Malinovitch watched his men surround Jonah and in turn, be surrounded by the reporters whom he had also summoned. He was not at ease. Now, for the first time, he was forced to play the game from moment to moment. His men would bring Jonah directly to him and the reporters would create the world opinion that would demand Jonah's security. There were no certainties in this particular game and Alexi still did not know how he was to save Zeena.

Alexi Malinovitch had always lived on the edge of destruction, and his secret dance with death and danger gave impetus to his waking moments. In the Janus-faced games of vengeance he played, the advantage had always been his. Now, forced to be on the defensive, and finding his efforts sometimes thwarted, the supreme scrutinizer was now under scrutiny. Karpov was hacking at the tightrope Alexi walked, but falling was not an option.

This much he knew. Karpov had, in the past months, lavished upon himself a life style that only a vast sum of money could provide and only Count Perowski could have provided it. But what else Karpov had done with the sum, he could not detect. Who was bought with that money to act, and who was paid to remain silent, was a tormenting mystery. As the birth of the child approached, the death of the mother became more and more certain. Alexi's pain was so profound, that even tears could not express it.

Now, Jonah stood before him, trembling, and Alexi could not even assure him. To Jonah, this man who had known his father in the distant past, was a powerful and fearful mystery. Alexi saw the fear in Jonah's eyes and could not even extend his hand though he yearned to comfort and strengthen himself and his friend's son with a warm embrace.

To protect Jonah, he would have to appear cruel. Though they were alone, Alexi knew that someone listened from behind a door.

"Let me read to you the highlights of this, and you will see the danger that your friends in Europe and America have created for you." Malinovitch took the paper and folded it in front of him and put on his glasses. He looked over them at the young man who lowered his eyes under his gaze. He cleared his throat.

> "To the Tsar, St. Petersburg: December, 1881
>
> Four thousand assembled in mass to protest the sched-
> uled execution of Zeena Bendelevitch. Let not this woman's
> blood be on your hands. The fact that there is no signature
> to this dispatch will no doubt make it all the more mysteri-
> ous and terrible in the Tsar's eyes."

Malinovitch looked up. "'Mysterious and terrible', indeed," he said. "Cowards," he continued, "not to sign their names."

Jonah moved uncomfortably, waiting.

> "John Swinton," he continued in a dry voice, "was the first
> speaker. He compared the young Russian Jewess with Judith
> who slew Holofernes. 'We protest,' he said, 'against the mili-
> tary order for the hanging of Zeena Bendelevitch. We should
> hold ourselves guilty of complicity in the proposed crime if we
> did not enter our protest against it while yet there is time. We
> have the right as men and women to protest against the per-
> petuation of such a crime against manhood and woman-hood,

wheresoever and by whomsoever it is ordered. We protest to
the Tsar of Russia and to the whole world.

Be warned, thou steel-clad Tsar: let not this woman's
blood be upon your hands."

Jonah took a deep breath. He knew it would not be to his advantage to speak. Malinovitch looked up at the sound and paused. Then he continued.

"While we sympathize with Zeena Bendelevitch and her
brother, who is seated here, we do not expect that her life
will be saved to us. We do not send our prayers before the
throne for her. We send our heartfelt deadly curses to her
murderers. The revolutionists of the world will never be
content until the last king and the last emperor are swept
away. The Emperor of Russia may be able to make his army
fifty times as great as it is, but we know how to make dynamite bombs quicker than he can make soldiers."

Malinovitch threw the paper onto his desk and leaned back in his chair, looking exasperated. Then he leaned into Jonah.

"These people," he said, "have not done anyone a service except for themselves. How do you think the Tsar responds to such threats? Do you think he looks kindly on those who threaten his life? Do you think this rhetoric softened his view to your sister?"

Jonah remembered Herzl's perception about their motivation. "I had no control over what was said or written," he said weakly in his defense. "And I learned only lately what moved them."

"I am quite sure of that," Malinovitch responded in a voice so soft, Jonah strained to hear him. "But by lending your presence to their meetings you have recklessly endangered yourself. Oddly enough, your only salvation rests with the newspaper people who report this trash." Jonah was confused. "As long as they are near you and watching, the police can do nothing but watch you and wait."

"And now," he said as loudly as before, "your Socialist friends have manipulated you into a position where you deliver to the Tsar's representative a list of resolutions that would guarantee you your rightful place next to your sister as a traitor!"

He paused, aching to ease the frightened young man. Jonah felt his hands tighten.

"You are a very clever person, Mr. Bendelevitch. To surround yourself with reporters was inspired. Even the Tsar dare not touch you for fear of world opinion. There are even traitors at home who would support your freedom. But never doubt for a moment that as soon as these reporters leave you, we will be all over you. As soon as your sister receives her punishment, you will be old news. We' know your plan, Mr. Bendelevitch. You will surround yourself with reporters until you are safely over the border with the child. We are not fools."

Jonah could feel the sweat running down his back. He was totally confused by the man who paced before him, who sat down, stood up only to pace again. He was being fed information, but to what end and why? Was this man telling him what he must do under the guise of threats? Was this man the guardian angel to whom Herzl referred? Impossible! This was the head of the Tsar's secret police. This was one of the most feared men in Russia! Still, this man was a friend of his father's.

"Well, let us see what these latest pieces of seditious trash say to us," and he lowered his glasses to the bridge of his nose and focused on the carefully written lines.

"RESOLVED: That we shall regard the execution of the young Jewess, Zeena Bendelevitch, by the Tsar of

Russia, as a capital crime against justice and an unpardonable wrong against human nature.

RESOLVED: That even the military court by which she was condemned to death did not procure any evidence connecting her with the deed through which the late

Tsar lost his life, and that four of the five conspirators

publicly declared to the court that Zeena Bendelevitch had
no knowledge of or part in the scheme of the Tsar's death.

RESOLVED: That the circumstances of nature which
led to the postponement of the hanging makes the order for
her death peculiarly shocking to every generous mind.

RESOLVED: That her sacrifice under that order will
be a thing of horror to mankind and womankind everywhere, and that we, as men and women of American citi-
zenship, warn the Tsar to desist from this atrocious act.

RESOLVED: That a telegraphic dispatch based in the
foregoing resolutions be sent from this meeting with the
remonstrances he has received from the Republic of
France, and Switzerland, as well as from other countries."

"Wonderful, wonderful, wonderful," Malinovitch said sarcastically. "You are alive and permitted here because we are not the
barbarians American and western European newspapers say we
are." His voice was loud enough to insure being overheard by those
in the ante-chamber.

Again his voice dropped and he whispered rapidly. "Zeena is
under great stress, but never did she reveal who she is or her parent's
home. I only recently learned what happened. The pogrom did
not originate with the central government."

Jonah felt himself recoil into the chair and concluded that it
was imperative that he view this man as a friend. He felt the muscles
of his face relax.

"Then why was our home brutally attacked if not in retalia-
tion against Zeena?" Jonah whispered quickly.

Malinovitch put his hand to his lips. "One of our operatives was
contacted by an informant in your town who arranged that your
family be intimidated. I read of the incident long after it happened. A
man named Bendak pointed the finger, but it seems that the regional
government agents brought in took the opportunity to use the town
as a warning to the Pale against sedition in the provinces."

Alexi saw Jonah's eyes blaze as if hell's gates suddenly flew open, and he found himself on the road facing Ezra again. Now it was clear what Ezra was yammering about. And now that bastard was tantalizing his family with hope of America in exchange for his child. He vowed in his heart to destroy Ezra Bendak. In some way, yet unknown, Ezra would be destroyed for his evil.

Malinovitch raised his voice again.

"If we were the barbarians the press say we are, do you think we would allow you to be with your sister when she gave birth and then take the child? Do you think you would be sitting here? Do you think you would be still alive? We are not barbarians! Now, what do you have to say for yourself to that?"

Alexi put his finger to his mouth cautioning Jonah not to speak in the hope that the ensuing silence would be interpreted as Jonah's response.

"Those who want your sister and her child dead," he whispered, "also want you dead. They are without morality and know that nations now wave a fist, but will lower it rather than fight over the rights of insignificant people. Jonah," he continued, leaning in, "You are caught in a world where the standards fluctuate at whim. People like me and Karpov are given free reign so long as we move in directions the rest of the world secretly supports. You and your sister are caught in an event that captured the imagination of the lethargic world and they have pulled themselves up an inch or two to murmur their righteous indignation. It roused the sleepers, but I assure you, they will sleep again soon, so it is left for us to rescue her. I still have hope that we can do this. She would have been murdered long ago, had she not been pregnant. She would have been murdered by those who accused her even if she had been exonerated. Had she just been a Jew, the world would have snored and rolled over."

"I assure you, Mr. Bendelevitch," he said loudly again, judging that an appropriate time for Jonah's response had passed, "that the thing of least value in Russia is the life of a Jew."

"Pregnant Jewish women have been murdered by the Russian police before," Jonah interjected.

"Yes, certainly, but not while the world was actually watching. The world is composed of secret murderers. People are good only because they think they are being watched. Put a mask on the saintliest of them and they will pervert themselves in a moment. Turn their faces to the sun where they are known, and each will become a saint once more."

Jonah did not understand this man who moved in and out of voices and in and out of identities. Who was he or what was he? Guardian Angel or Angel of Death?

"Speak up if you can answer this charge," Malinovitch said suddenly and leaned over his desk.

"Had you come into St. Petersburg by yourself," said the quiet Malinovitch, "one of the secret murderers would have dispatched you before you left the gate. Had that happened, there would have been a brief outcry for a few days and then you would have been forgotten. If I allowed anyone to deliver your sister's child, other than you, both she and the child would die in childbirth. People will murder an infant and its mother for money. Some will do it for the pleasure. These are such people." He paused, searching for the next words. "It is with profound regret that I have not been able to win her release after I saved her life initially. She has suffered great indignities at the hands of other murderers and I am helpless to stop it without upsetting the balances that exist."

Jonah understood balances, but had only glimpsed the ones that held Alexi Malinovitch and his world. Yet, Jonah felt pity for this man who was torn between his effort to keep Zeena alive, and the tasks expected of him from his office.

Malinovitch reached under his desk and pulled out a bundle. "I am told that your sister's labor has begun. I have kept you surrounded and waiting these days until her labor was hard. She is due anytime. You will be a comfort to her and perhaps knowing that the child will live will comfort her."

Jonah detected that the steady voice was beginning to crack.

"I have here," he continued, "clean linen, a warm blanket, and infant clothing. You will take this to your sister."

"Is there no way of saving her?" Jonah asked, softly pleading.

Alexi Malinovitch heaved a deep sigh of pain. "I want you to know that I tried, and I continue to try. I told you that the murderers watch and wait until they can murder. I tell you also that they will keep others from saving a life. I am far from being a righteous man and I have done more evil than most. I did try. I did try." He lowered his head sadly.

"Why do you say this to me?" Jonah said. "I did not come here just to save my sister's child. I have spoken all over Europe. Europe and America are behind me. Russia must release her. The world demands that she be released."

"The world can demand what it likes. The Tsar and his court and his hangmen will say what the world gets. Your sister is in their power. I am working to keep her alive as carefully as I can, but I tell you, I will take some pleasure just to be able to save the child. Never give the midwife a moment alone with the infant or the child is dead. I know she has been paid to kill the baby. There will be murderers around you. If you are vigilant and strong, you will thwart their efforts. You must thwart their efforts!"

He made his voice very low. "In the bundle there is a sum of gold your sister gave me and a ticket to Hamburg. I have sent the remainder of her money to the American Express office in Hamburg. It is there addressed to you. Once you have it, you are free to do as you please. The reporters will be with you. They are aroused from their slumber. They have followed you for your story and they will continue until you give it to them. Say nothing to them until you are safely out of Russia with the child. Your story is their payment. Make them work for it."

Jonah's jaw tightened and his teeth were like a vise. "I came here to save my sister's life. I was promised that public opinion would save her!"

"And I am telling you that those who told you that have no control here. Your sister is too valuable a symbol for either side to permit her to live. To the Socialists, she must become a martyr. To the Tsar, she must hang as a warning to assassins and a reminder to

Jews of how tenuous their lives are here. Her innocence is not even an issue." He paused again, and leaned in closer, capturing Jonah in his hypnotic gaze.

"The child is the priority now," he said very slowly. "I will accompany you under guard to her cell. Under no circumstance are you to speak to me or to anyone. When you are there you are to deal with the midwife as you see fit, but she must not touch the baby. After the child is born, you will make your peace with your sister and call the guard who will call me. I will be close by. I am your only safety while you are there and I must act as if I hate you. The danger will lessen when you are outside. The newspapers have been already informed and those who accompanied you here and now wait for you, will triple in number. You will get into the third carriage and be taken to a hotel. All will follow. You will go to room 306 where you will meet a woman who will nurse the child and care for it. She will accompany you to Hamburg so you will appear as just a man and wife with their child going for a visit. Do you understand? Do you have any questions?"

Jonah nodded slowly.

"I thank you," he said quietly, "for protecting my sister and her baby." He paused and swallowed as tears glazed his eyes and fell over the rims. "Must she die?" he asked simply. "Is there no hope for her life?"

Alexi held his breath and choked back his own anguish. "I shall not give up trying as long as she takes breath. Death ends all, and she is not dead. Perhaps tomorrow there will be a better answer."

"Guard, guard," he bellowed. The door opened quickly and four guards rushed in.

"Accompany us to the cell. I have already searched this bundle. The midwife left it when she was here with Karpov. Watch him. He is capable of any treachery!" He threw the bundle at Jonah. "Carry it!"

Alexi, at that moment, waited for the door to close and for the sound of boots on the stone to fade before he approached her.

Even in the dim light of her cell, Sophia appeared regal and the simple chair upon which she sat could have been her throne. Her pale beauty always surprised and delighted him and though there with the gravest of hearts, he could not help but smile within. She appeared placid as she had throughout the trial.

"You know, when I was captured, one of your policeman offered to let me go for fifty rubles," she said laughing at the memory, "but I only had thirty eight, and he wouldn't trust me for the rest." She laughed again and watched him move into the circle of light.

"I read in the paper that the body of a middle aged woman was found floating in the Neva." She studied his face for a response but she could only discern a jaw muscle twitch.

"You murdered Maria, didn't you, dear Alexi? Was she not happy with her dear Ivan not going free? Did she threaten to cause difficulty? I wondered what would happen to her after they caught Ivan. You did a good job getting him exiled, but I'm sure that if Ivan knew who you were and what you did, you and I would be sharing this cell and the gallows together."

"Why wouldn't you let me save you?" he said. "You have done everything I counseled you not to do."

She lowered her eyes and closed the book she was reading. He felt the old warmth reach into his heart for her. She raised her head slowly and looked at him towering over her. Her eyes were crystal clear.

"You did everything you could to save me, my dearest Alexi, and I am grateful. I am beyond being saved. My own sins condemned me before my confession. My confession merely expedited my fate."

She paused and took a breath, and continued to speak in a manner so methodical that it was almost as if she had rehearsed the response and awaited only for someone to ask.

"My poor father is dead and will not see me hang. My purpose, you know, was to have him watch me hang. Did you know that Alexi? I wanted to know that he would be tormented, but he killed himself and deprived me of my triumph." Tears rolled down the sides of her face, but they appeared to be involuntary, almost as if someone else cried for her. "There is really nothing to live for," she continued. "I am a regicide. I am a pariah among my own and I don't choose to live in notoriety. I shall go to hell as I deserve, and it will end the hell of my life on earth."

Alexi heard but did not fully understand. She would always remain a mystery.

"How I wish to free myself of this isolation. How I wish that whore did not carry a child. I did not foresee that. Had I known, I would have spared myself the endless hours of loneliness and memories that have become my hated companions. I am eager for death's caress."

Malinovitch lowered his eyes sadly and made sure his voice was soft.

"Before your father died, he gave Karpov a large sum of money to buy your freedom. Do you have any idea what Karpov has done or intends to do?"

"Ah," she said. "Dear little Colonel Karpov. He's very common, you know. Do you know, Alexi, what he said the last time he was here?" She laughed and rocked back in her chair and clapped her hands. "He actually asked me to marry him after he saved my life. He told me that a vast sum had been deposited for us by my father, but it would take both signatures to get at it. Can you imagine," and she laughed again, "announcing Colonel and Countess Nicolai Karpov? Can you actually imagine that he believed that I would prefer marriage to him over death? Do you know what I told him, Alexi? Can you guess?" Her laughter filled the air.

"No," he said softly, "what did you tell him?"

"I told him that my ancestors would never forgive me if I soiled their name with that of a mongrel's, and that it would be better to die than to risk peopling the world with little Karpovs who might take after us." She laughed again. "You should have seen his pitiful face."

"A man like Karpov who is in love with a woman, and who can taste a great deal of money, knows that death will end his chance at making life as he wants it. Karpov will save you in the hope that you will be grateful to him."

"Perhaps, but the whore has probably dropped her litter by now, so it's too late for him unless he will attempt to rescue me under the hangman's nose. No, my dear Alexi. All will proceed quickly. Happily, they will hang us within a day or two."

He watched her stand and move behind him humming an old Russian lullaby. She rested her hands on his shoulders. He did not move. Every muscle, every tone had to be perfectly calm lest he give away his mission. Yet, he could feel his throat tighten and his cheeks flush. He formed the question carefully, and asked softly.

"Sophia, there is something I do not understand. Throughout you have maintained the guilt of this woman you call a whore. You know she had no part in the assassination, yet you will see her hang. Why will you waste this life needlessly? It is so unlike you."

His conflict had to remain secret, or her vindictiveness, if she suspected his feelings for Zeena, would destroy him. Throughout the trial she was silent because she loved him and believed that he loved her. Throughout it was he who insisted that she let him save her with never a word about Zeena. She moved before him again, and he could see the anger in her face.

"She is guilty!" she raged as if suddenly overcome by some demonic force. "She is as guilty as any of them. They were all guilty. Every woman who ever laid herself down on a bed for my father and brought him to shame is guilty, only this one will pay for all their crimes. She is every woman and every child my father ever touched. He was weak and they all tempted him, Alexi, yes even little girls. I loved my father, Alexi, and he loved me. I was his only little girl. Mother never understood what a man like my father needed."

Her fingers curled around the back of the chair and tightened, turning red under the pressure.

"You see, Alexi, Zeena Bendelevitch is my father's sin made flesh, and she is my sin made flesh. There must be a sacrifice if my father and I are ever to be forgiven and come to God. Prayer and faith alone will not help us, Alexi. Her death alone will atone for our crime."

He watched her move closer. She was possessed by the thought.

"Her death chastens us. Father and I will be clean again." As she spoke, her eyes glazed and she peered up at the small window as if seeking eternity. "The unholy will make us holy again and we will not be damned eternally for our sins. I have confessed this to the holy Father who came here and he said that it would be just as I had spoken."

Sophia retreated into her insanity and belief, a belief and insanity that were beyond the comprehension of a sane man.

Alexi knew not to proceed any further. Her hatred and resolve were all, and at any moment capable of consuming even him.

"You see, Alexi, I loved my father. I always did, but it was wrong of us to . . . it was a sin to . . .love." She stopped suddenly. The color drained from her cheeks and she backed away and felt for the chair and slowly lowered herself.

"Now what were we talking about, Alexi?" she said, smiling as if none of the past revelation had taken place.

"Nothing important, Sophia. Nothing important. I must tend to some business now."

"Then I shall see you again soon," and she extended her hand for him to kiss.

"Very soon, my dear Sophia. Very soon."

CHAPTER 31

The murmuring crowd grew silent and made signs of the cross in the air as if to create a wall of safety between themselves and the cowled figures in the carts rolling past.

Cossacks rode on either side and at times moved their stallions into the jeering mob to maintain a proper distance between them and the condemned. Next to the cart walked the secret police, each assigned to prod a prisoner into an upright position if and when one lost balance or collapsed.

Alexi Malinovitch had assigned himself the task of accompanying the cart and walked slightly behind the officer who walked near the trembling Zeena. He did not reveal himself to her, though he longed to let her know that she was not alone.

Zeena was oblivious to all, and it was only when the carts veered onto the great Chompsky Plain and she could see the black platform above the heads of the people, that she wavered.

Alexi prodded her escort to steady her and silently begged her forgiveness for not being able to secure her life. Karpov had proven too crafty and now he was missing from his place next to the cart. Alexi's eyes sliced the masses for that singular being whom he knew was in the process of buying Sophia's life. Karpov had succeeded where he had failed. Now, his only hope was to discover Karpov's plan and in some way work it to his advantage. But he did not know what it was or who had been bought.

In the distance, the slow measured cadence of large drums boomed out the cart's approach. Alexi's heart began to pound and he could feel the tears in the corner of his eyes trickle and freeze on his cheeks. He wiped them off quickly. Before him loomed the gallows, stark against the low, gray sky. The angry crowd around him spitted their curses and waved their fists menacingly. Their voices were as a distant echo.

"I am innocent," Zeena screamed suddenly in pulsating gasps that froze in the air. "I am innocent. Let me go to my baby." He saw her shoulders sink as she began to weep and he longed to reach up to her and carry her off.

A woman who had heard Zeena, laughed at her plea and spit on the ground. Alexi memorized her face and hated her as he had never hated in his entire life. He wished that they all were one being so he could murder them with one thrust of his knife.

The drums grew louder and louder, each beat accented by the hesitation between. The cart lurched and stopped. The robed figures fell forward, but were steadied by their escorts. The drums pierced his fantasy and pulled him back. He was suddenly aware of an awful silence.

"I don't want to die," Zeena screamed again, and her words cut him like the frozen wind.

He had gambled and lost. He had gambled that public opinion would have pressured the Tsar to acquit her. He had not counted on the depth of the hatred or the politics and his misjudgment had brought about her death. Again, in desperate hope, his eyes devoured the faces looking for Karpov, and suddenly, Karpov was there. He focused on the little man with all the intensity of his being and watched him shake the hand of one of the doctors standing under the gallows. Alexi looked up at the ropes being tested, each by a separate hangman.

Each in their turn, the four men stepped from the cart. Jeliabov faltered and a cossack's sword prodded him to his feet. Karpov moved closer. Sophia stood next in the cart and waited for assistance to step down. Karpov motioned to the officer near her to move away so he could take his place. Now, Karpov took Sophia by the elbow and steadied her. Zeena moved onto the small step and then to the ground. Alexi was four steps behind, never taking his eyes off Karpov and Sophia. Karpov slowed.

The drums began a mournful, deliberate roll of death.

Karpov and Sophia stopped. Zeena's escort seemed confused. Karpov turned and whispered something to him as he and Zeena drew near. Suddenly, he stepped aside and waited until Karpov and Sophia passed.

In that second, Alexi knew that the exchange of places held the key to Karpov's plan and Zeena's life. But he did not know what that plan was. Jeliabov was already mounting the steps and the next was on his heels. There was no time to think. There was only time to act.

Alexi raced a few paces past Zeena and, grabbing a bystander by the arm, whipped the terrified man into Karpov and Sophia, and all fell to the ground.

"Stop that man," Alexi cried, pointing at the innocent stranger who was now set upon by armed Cossacks.

In the confusion, Alexi pushed Zeena and her escort ahead so she was again in her original place. Some Cossack grabbed Sophia by the arm, pulled her up and pushed her up the steps behind Zeena. Her escort followed.

All eyes were on the platform. Alexi kneeled down.

"Are you all right, Karpov? This man jumped out at you and the prisoner. Give me your hand," he said, solicitously and helped him up. "You have a nasty cut from your fall."

Karpov pulled a scarf from his pocket and covered the bruise.

"I'm all right," he said and began to push his way to the gallows steps.

The cowled figures stood, trembling in the frozen air. A bitter wind suddenly whipped at them and the slackened ropes began to sway. A priest paraded before them with a crucifix, and each kissed it except one. The crowd hurled more invectives at Zeena and Karpov's eyes widened when he realized that the one who refused the crucifix stood in the place he had designated for Sophia.

The crowds surged toward the gallows and let up a roar of approval as each hangman placed the noose around the neck of his charge. The Cossack guards moved to push them back. The drums began an agonizingly slow roll.

"No!" screamed Karpov, as he lunged towards the steps. But Cossacks blocked his path and their swords threatened him. Karpov staggered under the realization of what had happened, and tore through the crowd in the direction of the gallows's physician.

Suddenly, the plan was clear. Something had been done to the next to last rope and the attending doctor had been paid to declare a living woman dead. Karpov had to be stopped.

Alexi circled around, the death drum roll pounding in his brain. Above, prayers were being chanted for the souls that would be tormented for eternity.

Karpov broke through the chain of Cossacks ringing the gallows. Alexi had anticipated him and was already there waiting under it.

The crowd surged again and a din went up as the priest descended the steps. Each hangman approached his own prisoner with a hood. The crowd protested that they would not be able to see their faces in the throes of death.

Zeena looked through a blur of tears into the black mask of her hangman. He lowered the hood over her head, and as he did, he thrust something into her mouth.

"When I lower the hood, count to three, and bite down."

Zeena silently thanked him and welcomed the poison that would bring her a sudden death. She would be dead before the trap door opened. She would have no pain.

The drum roll stopped and, for a brief second, everyone riveted their eyes on the gallows as the trap doors dropped open.

Alexi thrust himself in front of Karpov. "The world would do better if you and I were dead," he said, his lip rising in a terse snarl. "But you shall precede me to prepare my way in hell, my dear Colonel." A surge of white heat rushed to Karpov's chest and a shrill gasp tore out of his throat and hung in the air. His eyes bulged at the agony of feeling steel cutting through his flesh and twisting into his heart. His fingers coiled around Alexi's shoulders for support, but it was Alexi who held him up in his powerful arms and continued twisting the knife so all the chambers of Karpov's heart were torn open.

The conspirators hung above their heads. All but one felt the agony of air suddenly cut off by a rope being tightened by his own weight. All but one felt the pain of having his lungs stretching for air and finally collapsing. All but one felt the darkening of his ears and eyes and brains screaming for breath. All but one danced the macabre dance of death.

The crowd broke the Cossack ring and surged forward for a closer look at the lifeless forms. Alexi put one of Karpov's arms around his neck and carried him over to the base of the gallows and propped him up. The crowd surrounded them and pushed against them. Alexi released Karpov and the dead man was carried along until he fell under their feet and Alexi returned to the hanging bodies. The Cossacks pushed the crowd aside and wheeled the cart into place under the gallows. Each hangman above cut the rope and the bodies fell to the ground. The doctor stepped forward to examine each corpse.

"Yes," said the physician, when he came to the body he believed to be the Countess. "This one is dead."

As if through a wall, Zeena could hear the words, but could not respond. She could not feel her legs or arms and she was enshrouded in blackness behind the eyelids she could not open. She was not dead, and her neck ached. She felt herself being lifted and thrown onto the cart.

The doctor watched where she was placed, took her hand and marked it with a dab of ink. Alexi Malinovitch nodded to him as if he were part of the plan, and the doctor nodded back.

"When it is safe," the doctor said, "give her this," and he thrust a vial into Alexi's palm. "Where is Colonel Karpov?" the doctor asked. "Shall I follow our schedule?"

Alexi did not know what he meant or who else was involved.

"Yes, you are to do exactly as agreed and I will assist you."

The doctor smiled, feeling even more secure that the chief of the secret police was part of the duplicity.

"We are to place the Countess in her coffin, and the Countess will supposedly be put on the train to her ancestral home. In truth, we will put the Countess's coffin on the train to Hamburg and another woman's body will be substituted in a duplicate coffin for transport to the Provinces. Will the good Colonel meet us at the station?"

"Yes," said Malinovitch, "but he asked me to proceed without him. He will take a later train. There are others to reward."

CHAPTER 32

Krivoser
December 16, 1882

Crescents of snow lay frozen in the lower corners of the small attic window. Leah stared beyond them to the white flecks that swirled above the lower gable like tormented wraiths. Her eyes moved up to the dried parsley that twisted above her head. A draft whistled in through a crack in the wall and she raised the quilt to the face of her baby who alternately dozed and nursed at her breast.

It seemed a life time ago that she looked up at swaying parsley in the loft and wondered at her future. Now, she looked back on the dream and hope of that time and a great sadness filled her. Her eyes traced the top of Rachelann's head as the wispy ringlets rose and fell in cadence with the suckling. Her hand reached up from her side and, twirling the sandy colored curls, she thought of how she used to do the same with Jonah's as he slept. The thought of Jonah sent a flush of anger to her cheek that immediately mixed with pain and sorrow and longing. The months of waiting and the horror of not knowing if he were dead or alive flooded back and brought with it the tormenting questions of why he had fled from her that night, and why he had not written to her in all those months, and why he had chosen Zeena over her. She closed her eyes as if to cancel his face, and the thoughts, and opened them to refocus on the baby who had twisted away from her and slept peacefully in the chilled air.

The latch on the door clicked and Dora stood there balancing a tray of tea and cakes.

"Are you feeling better?" she said softly.

Leah looked at her pregnant sister-in-law through a blur and forced a smile. Dora had become her friend, the only gentle voice of compassion and reason among a family of distraught and anguished women.

"Ezra called for Jonathan to go and meet another buyer in the city," she said brightly, "and it may be the last time because Jonathan says that most of Ezra's things are sold. Perhaps we will be able to leave soon." She hoped the thought of leaving would bring a smile to Leah's lips. It did not.

"How can I leave without Jonah? How can I leave my sister? She has no one left here now. My uncle and aunt are both gone, now."

"Ezra has promised to provide for us all," she hastened to add, "and I'm sure he will take Rebecca with us if we ask. He's been so good to us since he learned that Zeena was in prison. We're the only family he has, except for his mother, so I'm sure he'll continue his generosity."

Leah lifted the baby and placed her gently in her cradle. "Yes, yes, yes," she said as if she had agreed a dozen times before. "Ezra has been good to us and we owe him our lives. Yes, yes, he has been our strength in our time of trouble."

"Why can't you think well of someone just once," Dora said in uncharacteristic anger as she put the tray on the table. "I see only a man who came to us the day after the pogrom and comforted us in our tragedy."

"Well I see a man who provides for us minimally so we have to go to him every other day with our hands out. And I see a man who almost destroyed your father and brother by closing off their line of credit at the mills when your sister first ran away. We could have starved and died before the pogrom and he wouldn't have given a damn." Leah took a breath. "So I ask you, Dora, what happened after the pogrom to change his mind? Ezra Bendak is not a kind or generous man. It stinks. The whole thing stinks and we are being used. Didn't you ever wonder why Ezra's house escaped with only enough damage so no one would question him?"

Dora sat next to Leah on the bed and took her hands.

"I only know what I see," she said, lowering her eyes.

"I'm sorry," Leah responded, genuinely saddened that she had turned the smile on Dora's lips to a frown. "It's just that to me, he turned too quickly. I just think that he is using us to get his baby. I just have this feeling."

"But look at what he has done. He has given Jonathan the responsibility of meeting with people in other towns to sell the things from his house and shop. Ezra is paying Jonathan now for his work and has promised him more as soon as we're out of here. We are Ezra's family. Where is the profit in his injuring us? We need him to get us out of here."

As she spoke to Leah, the horror pushed its way into her thoughts like an assailant. How she and Jonathan had found Zedde's mutilated body and how Jonathan carried him home, crying as he went. She thought of her mother racing from the house to the town, wild and uncontrollable and how Jonathan ran after her and how he had to pry her off her husband's corpse. She saw Ruth, like wilted flower, sitting for days at a time, humming an unrecognizable tune and then coming back and not remembering. And she thought of Leah who sat day after day waiting for some word of reason as to why she had been abandoned by her husband when she needed him most.

"How can I go anywhere?" Leah interrupted. "Do we know that he ever got that letter? Do we know anything? What if he comes back here? What if . . ."

"Jonah can never come back here," Dora countered. "When he leaves Russia, he must leave forever. He is in constant danger here. And even if he didn't get the letter, we will know where he is because the newspapers will tell us."

"Why did he choose Zeena over me?" Leah said suddenly.

Dora looked up, startled. Leah's intense look repeated the question.

Dora sat back and her shoulders sank as if someone had pushed her down and held her.

"Who can tell what was in his mind that night," Dora said, desperately gathering her thoughts in the space of a heavy sigh. "Finding Mama, Ruthie, you, the town in flames, the cornfield. Who can tell what was going on in him? And when the police came looking to question him the next day? Had he been here, what might have happened? Did he know something that we didn't know? And had Ezra not talked them into going away, what might have happened?"

"But I was giving birth to our child and he left me. How can a husband do such a thing? What kind of man would do such a thing?"

Her voice was tight and controlled as if she had asked the question a hundred times, and her eyes narrowed as if the actual events of that awful night suddenly confronted her again.

"But to leave his wife to help his sister . . ."

"Leah," Dora began very softly. "They are twins. None of us have ever been able to understand what was really between them. No one knew their secrets. Perhaps there is something we still don't know."

Dora raised her hand to Leah's cheek as Leah closed her eyes. A tear splashed on Dora's finger.

"Let the anger go, my dearest Leah," she said. "Think of the baby and what your anger will do to her. Think of the future and what your anger will do to it. Forgive him for the sake of the baby and for the sake of the future."

"But he left me," she said shaking her head. "He ran away without a word. Your father and Zedde heartlessly murdered and then, Aunt Malka and Uncle Issac die, and me not knowing if I had a husband or my baby had a father. Not a word from him and then a newspaper story about a brother speaking to save his imprisoned sister. Still not a word to me! All these months and not a word to me! No, Dora. There are too many questions to be answered before forgiveness."

Leah's breath was coming in short, angry blurts. Dora felt Leah's hand curl into the quilt and she knew to withdraw her own. Leah would not listen until she stood face to face with Jonah and heard his reasons from his own lips.

"Please, come downstairs. Jonathan will be back from Ezra's soon. Ezra told Jonathan that when he hears that the baby is safe, we must leave at a moments notice. He also said that if Jonathan is away at the time, he'll leave money and a train ticket for him with Mr. Yavna. Please come down, Leah to say goodbye. Do it for me."

Ezra Bendak's right hand held back the lace curtain as he peered at the figure of Jonathan Metkoff struggling against a bitter eastern wind. In Ezra's hand was a crumpled paper describing Zeena's death and how his brother-in-law had been spirited out of Russia with a new born infant girl. Ezra smiled to himself, but his thoughts were suddenly interrupted by a shrill voice. He pulled his jacket tighter against the chill as he turned to his mother.

"You are a trusting fool!" said Mrs. Bendak, rocking back and forth. "You give him valuables to sell and you don't even know if he's giving you back the full price."

"I'm buying their trust," Ezra retorted, opening the stove and throwing in another log.

"You don't need another log. You're wasting money," she yelled.

"We're leaving in two days for Paris. We can't take the wood with us. We can at least be warm. Now be silent."

The creaking of the rockers against the wooden floor echoed in the chilled, empty room. Then Ezra spoke.

"If Metkoff shaves some money off the top, it's worth it. I give him very little for what he does for me and he will get even less. He is the man now in the Chernov family and if he is beholden to me for his survival, that family will be beholden to me also and do as I say when he is gone." He moved to the steaming samovar and poured a cup of hot water.

"You risk too much for that woman's child."

The cup shook in Ezra's hand and his eyes widened with rage.

"You're talking about my daughter!" he screamed. "You're talking about your only grandchild!" He hurled the cup at the stove and turned in fury as it shattered. "She is mine! She is all I have and I will risk anything to have her. I have sent a great deal of money to the Socialists to make sure that my dear brother-in-law would have everything he needed to keep his sister's name before the public. I have paid people off at the highest levels to make sure that my child would be brought safely to Paris. My daughter is on her way out of Russia and I will follow her in two days!" He looked menacingly over his glasses at the dark figure in the corner.

"And how do you expect to get back that money? Do you think that luckless bunch of parasites you feed and clothe will pay you? Can we eat their gratitude?"

"They have given me everything they had from the sale of their property for safe keeping and I have been spending that on their upkeep and that's what I use to pay Metkoff. I will keep what is left, and as soon as I have my daughter, I will have everything and they will have nothing! They will suffer for what she did to me. How they will suffer!"

The wind jerked the door inward and Jonathan had all he could do to hold it back from smashing against the wall. Dora felt the wind at her feet and turned from her work at the stove. Her thoughts caressed him even before he was through the door.

"I hate the cold," he said through chattering teeth. Their lips met as he passed her and he moved her, lips still clinging towards the warmth of the stove.

"Ezra hasn't heard anything about Zeena yet," he said in a low voice, "but he said that everyone should be ready to leave within the week. I should be back in plenty of time."

At that very moment, it became clear to Dora that as soon as word came for them to leave, it would mean that Zeena was dead. Tears washed her eyes and she fell into Jonathan's arms and wept without restraint. He held her close and buried his face in her hair and covered her head with kisses.

"Please," she said softly, "please don't tell Mama anything about Zeena. I don't know how much more she can take."

"But she'll know," he said. "She'll know when we tell her we're leaving."

"She'll know, but she won't know. As long as it's not mentioned, she won't say anything. I know how she is now. Leah will know but Mama won't."

"I'll do as you think best," he assented and enclosed her in her arms.

"She should be buried with Papa and Zedde," she said into his chest. "It's her right to have a decent burial."

"I know," he responded, "but if we claim her, we can all be sent to jail, Dora. That's why Jonah never wrote to us. He knew that any letter he mailed would be traced to us and we would be taken as accomplices. Jonah has been protecting us from the moment he left us. I'm sure of that."

"Jonah? Did I hear you say,`Jonah'?" Sarah said in a husky voice as she entered from the bedroom she shared with Ruth. She looked spent and suddenly old, like a faded etching with dark lines and shadows for her eyes and cheeks. Grey hair peeked out of a woolen kerchief she had bound around her head for warmth.

"Jonah?" she asked again as if in that word, Jonah, she had captured the totality of her anguished life. "Do you mean the Jonah who left his wife and mother and sisters when they needed him most? Do you mean the Jonah who should have been standing at his mother's side saying the prayer for the dead at his father's and grandfather's graves? Is that the Jonah you're talking about or is it a different Jonah?"

"Mrs. Chernov," Jonathan said taking her gently by the shoulders so she could not avoid his eyes. "Jonah could not have prevented what happened. Do you hate me for staying hidden with Dora while Zedde was killed? There are moments, terrible moments when life becomes so important that heroic and cowardly things are done to preserve it. Jonah made sure he found you so you could help Leah. He didn't leave her alone. That has to count for something. Women were beaten and raped and men were killed where they were found. Would you rather he stayed and was murdered when the police came so you'd have another soul to mourn? We don't know what allegations were made or who made them. You don't know what he saw or what he did. You must give him a chance to explain before you condemn him for doing what anyone of us might have done if we were faced with the same horror and choices."

"Where's my Rachelann?" Sarah said suddenly breaking away from his grasp. It was as if Jonathan had not uttered a word. He and Dora exchanged worried glances and sighed at the futility of trying to bring reason to a mind steeped in shadows. "Are there enough blankets on the baby?" she called upstairs. "Everything I have to do myself. You leave an infant in a freezing attic? Everything I have to do myself." She moved through the door to the steps.

Dora ran to the warm embrace of Jonathan's open arms and pushed her face into the musky smell of his chest. He was her strength and her love and as long as she could be with this man, she would remain strong and hold the family together. Yet, for herself, she would rather have dissolved into him, disappeared and become one in the eternal safety of his body.

"Why, Jonathan, why?" she murmured into his warmth. "Why must things like this happen? It isn't fair. It just isn't fair."

"I do not know," he said, softly stroking her hair.

"Then will it get better, Jonathan? Will it get better?"

"Yes," he said lifting her tear streaked face and looking into her eyes. "We're making it better. We're doing something by leaving this place. Doing something is the beginning of making something better."

CHAPTER 33

The train to Hamburg waited for last minute passengers and the wait seemed interminable. Jonah watched the baby root on her fist and he smiled. Then he focused on the rain washed window. He tried to trace a single droplet as it ran down, but it disappeared as it joined with others. Through the condensation on the window he could make out the blurred figures of several men wheeling a coffin down the platform towards the baggage car. A solitary, tall man followed. Jonah squinted and rubbed the pane. He was sure that man was Alexi Malinovitch. He pressed his cheek against the freezing pane to see better. A whistle blew and steam spit out of the engine. The car lurched forward. Jonah's thoughts jumped two cars down the track. The feelings he had as he cradled his niece were old, comfortable feelings; more something sensed than physical, and he attributed those feelings to holding Zeena's child. But another thought came to him and though he dismissed it knowing Zeena was dead, the thought was compelling.

He looked at the young woman in the seat opposite him and then at the three reporters who were seated in the compartment with him. The corridor was also crowded. He could not be sure if any of them were Tsarist agents who would shove a knife into him if he moved out of the safety of the compartment. But if Malinovitch was on the train, perhaps one or more of the men around him were in his employ and there to protect him from an assassin. He would have to wait and see.

He projected himself to Paris and felt a surge of ambivalent feelings. To hold Leah again and to see his daughter. To see his family again and to sleep in a place where he would not be startled by every sound. Jonah felt Marta's eyes on him and looked hesitantly into their secret strangeness. Suddenly the image of Leah sat in Marta's place, an image whose countenance accused him silently of cowardice, betrayal and abandonment. He shivered before the angry gaze and for the first time realized the awful possibility that the reunion might be one of bitterness, filled with recriminations instead of the love and joy he so desperately sought. He turned from the harsh vision of what might be, but the image of Leah's unforgiving and desperate eyes persisted on the rain streaked window pane.

He thought of Malinovitch and the coffin. He accompanied a coffin. The newspapers said that the conspirators were to be buried in unholy ground and only the Perowski woman's body would be returned to her home in the provinces. But that was in the south. This train was headed south west. Something in Jonah insisted on knowing and whatever that something was, also dared him to hope that the body in the coffin was Zeena's. At least he would be able to give her a proper burial and the comfort of knowing where she was. But that didn't make any sense either. Why would a man like Malinovitch accompany a dead body?

He carefully handed the sleeping infant to Marta and stood. Immediately, two of the reporters stood and Jonah knew he would be safe.

"I need to go to the toilet," he said. They followed him out of the compartment and down the swaying corridor in the direction of the baggage car. One of the men pushed in front of him to open a path. Questions were thrown at him as he moved through the gauntlet of reporters but Jonah insisted that they'd all have part of the full story when they reached Hamburg, and the rest when he and the child were safe in Paris. The man who preceded him stopped at the toilet, but Jonah pushed beyond him with authority. The two men looked at each other and followed.

Jonah opened the door between cars and a rush of frozen air filled his nostrils. He could smell the sea in it and it refreshed him. He slid the other door open.

"Where are you going, Mr. Bendelevitch?" shouted one of the men above the rush of the wind.

"It is too dangerous," said the other, pushing his way past Jonah to scan the empty corridor.

"I must speak to a man in the baggage car," Jonah said, disregarding their caution.

The baggage car rocked in front of him as he pulled on the handle. It was locked.

The train did a serpentine movement around a hill and Jonah held on to the chain with one hand to assure his footing all the while pounding with all his strength against the glass with his other.

The wind whipped at him with frozen blasts of air and his face and hands started to hurt. Finally, a curtain slightly moved and an eye and cheek looked back at him. He swallowed hard and forced his fear and expectations back down his throat. Over the clanking of the chains that danced on either side of him, he heard a clicking and the door sliding. He entered.

The air was heavy with tannin and musk from the trunks and crates piled along the wall and a single oil lamp dangled from a hook over a writing desk and its light cast elongated, rectangular shadows wherever he looked.

In the center of the car, resting on four small crates was an ornate coffin appropriate for nobility. The door behind him slammed shut against the two other men and a chill quickly ran down Jonah's spine. He turned, not knowing what to expect. Alexi Malinovitch stood like a black tower etched by the light behind him. He did not speak. Jonah's eyes become accustomed to the dim room but he could not see Alexi's face.

"When I saw you on the platform," Jonah began, "I dared to feel that in some way Zeena was alive." He waited for a response, but the tall figure remained immune to the plea and hope in his voice. "Zeena and I could always feel things and see things when we were together that no one else could see or feel. I could not have felt what I felt if Zeena were dead. I thought it might come from holding her child, but the feeling is so strong in me now that I know it is not the infant." He paused again, building as much resolve as he could.

"You must understand. I know what I know, and I know that Zeena is in that coffin and alive. I could not be feeling what I'm feeling if that was not true."

The dark figure moved forward into the faint orange glow of the swinging lamp and past Jonah to the coffin. Jonah pivoted and his foot hit something soft across his path. He looked down and saw the face of the baggage handler staring up at him with the same anguished question he had when Alexi put his knife through his ribs. Jonah recoiled.

"He worked for Karpov. The conspirators will be dumped into a communal grave and lye will be poured on them. By the time word comes back to St. Petersburg that the Countesses' coffin sent to her home was empty, the lye would have done its work and your sister and I will have disappeared."

Jonah's heart raced. "Please, let me see her, please," he said.

"She will appear dead to you, but I assure you she is not. The drug she was given was swift to take effect and potent. The antidote is slow and I am not sure of the effects. This so called baggage handler was really a physician hired by Karpov. He administered the antidote before recognizing the ruse and then became a threat. I will throw his naked body from the train as soon as we are out of Russia. The wolves will leave little more than bones.

Jonah was consumed with the thought of his sister being alive and barely heard Malinovitch. He had tried to save her, but saving her was beyond his ability. Malinovitch, through whatever power or magic at his disposal, had succeeded. Zeena was alive and whatever the cost, it was worth it.

Malinovitch raised the lid of the coffin. Jonah could see the air holes that had been skillfully punched through as part of the ornate design.

Zeena lay there with her eyes closed. Her face had been dusted with white power to give the pallor of death and her black, lusterless hair accentuated the mask. He bent over her and kissed her cheek. It was warm and he began to cry.

"Forgive me, Zeena. Please forgive me."

She lay there motionless. She heard senseless, disjointed frag-
ments of words and felt the dampness of his tears. There was an
image of her brother behind her eyelids and colors that wove themselves around the image, but she could not open her eyes nor could
she form any words. He took both her hands and wished his life
into her body. The circle was closed again and he wasn't afraid or
ashamed.

He raised his tear streaked face and looked at Malinovitch standing over them. "We will all be in Paris together," Jonah said. "We
will nurse her back to health and you will be part of our family."

Malinovitch frowned at his old dream and shook his head.

"She must remain dead to all," he said without the slightest
hint of passion in his voice. "If anyone knew that she was alive, the
arm of the Tzar would reach out into every town or city for her life
and for mine, too. I gave up everything I had and everything I was,
and I have already murdered two men so that she might live and
that I might be with her. She must be dead to all; even to your
mother and your wife. Secrecy is her only shield and hope. My
money is already on its way to Hamburg and it will buy us time
and distance and new identities.

Jonah sank under the weight of the expectation. "How can
you expect me to pretend that she's dead? How can you expect me
to allow my mother to believe that one of her children is dead.
Was everything I've done for nothing?"

Malinovitch's eyes riveted him where he stood. "You will swear
this to me on the lives of those you love, or there will be two naked
bodies thrown from this train for the wolves."

Jonah stiffened and backed away. The man's voice spoke of a
reckless desperation that had no bottom. His voice rose and embodied in it all the authority that his stature and position held.
Jonah shuddered with fear. This man had killed twice that day.
Another death would mean nothing.

"Jonah, you are still alive because you are my dead friend's son. I,
too, shall be hunted if it is discovered that Zeena lives. Karpov is dead
and my absence will be noted shortly. The connection might be made."

He paused. His voice seemed more human. "Your sister and I shall get off this train in Hamburg. I will be dressed as a priest and walk behind her coffin. No one will question me. The doctor explained what was to follow. I shall merely take his place and the driver of the hearse who will be waiting for us will be also killed as soon as I feel that we are safe. Only you, my young friend, have my secret and my plan and I am asking you to swear, for the sake of your sister's safety and for my safety, that you will keep that secret. I know it is a great deal to ask, but great events in a person's life often require great sacrifices. Remember, Jonah, that you and the baby are alive and will continue to live because of what I have done. Please don't make all that effort go for nothing."

The car jerked and clanked and rectangular shadows rose and fell against the walls like waves on the sea. The last time Jonah was confronted with the very real possibility of his own death was when Ezra stood before him yammering and wildly gesticulating about his own involvement in the pogrom. Ezra knew Jonah's secret and was a threat to him as long as he lived. He understood what Malinovitch demanded. Jonah knew Malinovitch's secret and was now a threat. Secrets. Everyone had secrets and secrets, if known, could destroy. Once, he had chosen to live even if that choice had branded him a coward in his wife's eyes. Now he would have to make that very same choice. Again, his life was thrown onto the balances and weighed against the knowledge he would keep. Perhaps, this time, if he kept the secret, he would be truly able to save Zeena's life. He could save her life by keeping silent, and he could save his own with the same silence. As before, he would choose life.

Jonah took a deep breath and slowly let his breath escape. His shoulders went limp and he looked down at his sister and then at the man who was demanding the impossible from him. "May I kiss her goodbye?" Jonah asked. Malinovitch nodded.

Jonah bent over her and lightly touched her forehead with his lips. She seemed warmer than she did before. "Goodbye, Zeena," he whispered. "Everything will be all right from now on. You are alive and that's all that matters."

"Then I can be assured that you will keep this secret?" Malinovitch asked.

"I swear it by those I love, and may I never see them again if I break my word to you."

Malinovitch relaxed and smiled slightly. He moved towards Jonah but Jonah had already turned towards the door.

"Wait," he began. "I want you to know something before you go. That man, Ezra Bendak who was instrumental in your family's tragedy, will not go unpunished. I know a great deal about him and his family and their holdings. I have left papers that reveal some very ugly things that link him with agents who also sought to overthrow our beloved Tzar. And for these crimes against the Russian people, all his holdings in Krivoser, Kiev, and Odessa will be impounded and seized for the crown. It's rather ironic and a fitting fate for such a beast, don't you think? The papers are wonderful forgeries and he will never be able to come back to Russia to prove his innocence. It's just a little bit of justice. There's so little justice in the world. I would have left word that he be assassinated, but to have that done would have left your family with no one to take them out of Russia. Your mother trusts him and will not do anything without him. I do not know what goes on in his head, but I know all that goes on at his orders. I regret that I will not be able to be there when the Russian bank in Paris informs him that the source of his wealth has been confiscated and that he is wanted by the police. I should like to see his reaction to the thought of being without wealth and without power."

From the window of the Hamburg-Paris train, Jonah watched as the driver of a horse drawn hearse on the opposite platform received a coffin from the baggage car of the St. Petersburg-Hamburg train. He watched as four workmen loaded the coffin, bowed to the priest's blessings and left. His train lurched and began to move. The hearse grew smaller and disappeared. He turned to his traveling companions in the compartment and to those who crowded the corridor.

"Well," he began with a broad smile on his face, "It seems I have a story to tell you."